Expeditionary Force
Book5: Zero Hour

By Craig Alanson

Table of contents

Chapter One

"Colonel Bishop, it has been fourteen hours," Hans Chotek told me unhelpfully, while glancing meaningfully at his watch.

I wasn't wearing a watch. The United States Army gave me a nice watch, which now mostly sat unused in a drawer in my cabin. I think it was in a drawer; that is where I put it, but I hadn't seen it in a while. That drawer held some of my cold-weather gear, and since I hadn't experienced cold weather in a while, that gear hadn't gotten any usage since we left the planet Newark. Anyway, I didn't need to wear a watch, the zPhone in my pocket told me the time. And I didn't need a zPhone to tell me fourteen hours had passed since I sent Nagatha on a recon mission; the display on the far bulkhead of the galley had a counter in the top right-hand corner that now read 14:04:57. Then 14:04:58. Yes, thank you, I did not need any reminding that my big gamble was so far a complete failure. "Yes, Sir. The first time he went missing, Skippy was gone for more than seventeen hours," I said with a combination of hopefulness and defensiveness. Really, I just wanted Count Chocula to go away right then; I had come into the galley for a cup of coffee, not a lecture. And truthfully, I did not need a fourth cup of coffee that day, I had walked to the galley merely because I had not much else to do. With the *Flying Dutchman* drifting slowly through empty interstellar space, there wasn't much for me to do. Our science team, and some of our pilots who had backgrounds in engineering or physics, were working to keep the reactors functioning. My only job was to stay out of their way. To fill my time, I had been training to fly the larger type of Thuranin dropship, the one we called a 'Condor'. And I had been writing letters to the families of the people we lost on Kobamik, when a one-in-a-million shot by a Golden BB shot down their dropship. It was likely that, if we ever got back to Earth, the families of our fallen would not see my letters, as they weren't cleared to know the truth about the Merry Band of Pirates. They would be told their loved one had died in a 'training accident', and no details would be provided. I wrote the letters anyway; writing them helped me deal with my own grief and guilt. Thinking about the people I had gotten killed on an alien world, far from home, was my mental state when our micro-managing mission commander pointed out the time. Our civilian mission commander.

Chotek raised an eyebrow. To his credit, he raised the pitcher of cream for me to pour in my coffee. "Do you think that seventeen hours is significant somehow?"

Taking a sip of coffee gave me time to bite my tongue, avoiding the smart-ass remark I wanted to make. What I wanted to do was inquire, why the hell he was asking *me* about the internal workings of Elder AIs? A gulp of too-hot coffee gave me enough of a pause to save myself from embarrassment, and save myself from being a jerk. When I handed the pitcher back to Chotek, the look in his eyes was not the accusing irritation I had become all too familiar with since he came aboard. What I saw standing in front of me, in the galley of a disabled alien pirate ship forty seven hundred lightyears from Earth, was simply a frightened human being. In that regard, our mission commander was no different from any other person aboard the *Flying Dutchman*. He was scared, and he was looking to me for a sign of hope. Any sign of hope, no matter how slim. "Seventeen hours?" I pondered the question, mentally kicking myself. The first time Skippy had gone 'on vacation', he had come back to us in about seventeen hours. That was how long it took him to fight off the computer worm that had ambushed him, but I had never asked whether seventeen hours was a significant number, or totally random. Damn it, I should have asked him when I could. "I don't know, Sir," I admitted. In the military, I had learned that 'I do not know' is an acceptable answer, it was considered much better to be honest about your ignorance than trying to bullshit your way through a question. Saying 'I do not know' is supposed to be followed up with 'I will find out', which in this case, I couldn't do. "The circumstances are different."

"True," he nodded, then he glanced at the counter again. "I'm sure you are busy, Colonel," he raised his own coffee cup as a salute, and I responded with the same gesture. Part of the reason I went to the galley was for some company, idle chit-chat. Instead, with Hans Chotek there holding a full cup of coffee and a muffin like he planned to be there a while, I decided to go back to my office.

On the way back to my tiny closet of an office, I stopped by the bridge/CIC compartment, where absolutely nothing was happening. Two pilots, both Chinese, sat in their couches, talking quietly about something. The duty officer in the command chair was Captain Giraud of the French team, still not fully recovered from radiation poisoning on our last mission. He had nothing to report, and the CIC crew had absolutely nothing on sensors. With the nearest star almost two lightyears away, that was not surprising.

If we were faced with a threat, the duty officer in the command chair had two options. Order the pilots to perform a short emergency jump that Dr. Friedlander of our science team strongly recommended against attempting. Or, flip up the safety cover and press the button to set off the cluster of tactical nukes in a cargo bay. According to Friedlander, trying to use our wonky jump drive might be more dangerous than explosively compressing the plutonium cores of our nukes.

On that happy note, I went back to my office, where my iPad was mocking me by displaying the counter clock at 14:19:08. More than fourteen hours had passed since Nagatha went on the recon mission I had requested her to perform. At the time, we both had known what I asked her to do was extremely risky. Possibly risky to the Merry Band of Pirates, absolutely risky to her. Whether the submind Skippy had named 'Nagatha Christie' was truly sentient or not, I felt bad about asking her to do something that would not only very likely be fatal for her, but also very likely stupid and useless. Nagatha had told me not to worry about the risk to her, since if the *Flying Dutchman* remained trapped in interstellar space, we were all certain to die anyway, including her.

In my defense, I was desperate, grasping at straws. The ship was trapped in interstellar space, a dozen lightyears from the Lagoon nebula in the Sagittarius Arm of the galaxy. Where in the galaxy we were truly didn't matter; what mattered was that we had no way to get to a habitable planet, and the ship was slowly dying around us. Dr. Friedlander had a brilliant idea to stretch out the life of our jump drive. It was a brilliant idea, we simply had not been able to make it work. After our last jump nearly failed and the science team was plunged into utter despair, I became desperate. Desperate enough to try something, anything. So, I asked Nagatha to download her entire consciousness into Skippy's beer can. My hope was that she would find the irascible asshole in there and wake him up. If she learned that Skippy had been relaxing on a couch, wearing fuzzy slippers and eating bonbons while watching trashy TV, I would be pissed at him. I would also be overjoyed at his return. If she couldn't find Skippy in there, at least Nagatha might be able to give us a hint at Skippy's fate. And, to tell the full truth, a tiny piece of me was hoping that, given the full resources inside Skippy's tightly-packed beer can, Nagatha might be able to expand her consciousness enough to fix our jump drive. The worst thing that could happen was Nagatha could disappear, and we would never know what happened to her. Given that we were already facing certain death when our reactors failed, Nagatha disappearing wouldn't significantly make our situation any worse.

She had disappeared. The nanosecond after she reported she was retracting her consciousness from the *Dutchman*'s inadequate computers, she went silent, and we hadn't heard a peep from her since. Skippy's beer can was still cold, with no change in status our sensors were able to detect. When we returned to the ship from our mission on Kobamik, at first I kept Skippy's silver beer can in a recess on the bridge, but seeing his silent form was a constant depressing reminder to the duty crew. To avoid distracting people from their jobs, I next moved him to my office desk, then realized that was only me indulging in useless self-recrimination. So I had moved him to the science lab, where his inert beer can was surrounded by sensors.

I set the coffee mug on my desk without sitting down. The mug was painted with the logo I had designed, a pirate monkey surfing on a winged banana. 'UN ExForce' scrawled across the top, with 'UNS Flying Dutchman' on the bottom. Unless we could get the jump drive working again, maybe I should rename our ship '*Drifting Dutchman*'.

Or '*Dying Dutchman*'.

That would probably not be good for morale.

"Dr. Friedlander," I addressed our friendly local rocket scientist when I walked into the science lab. His chair was to the right, which allowed me to avoid looking to the left where Skippy's beer can was resting in a cradle on a workbench. "How is your team?" He looked as tired as I felt, even though we had all been getting more sleep than usual. Or, we had all been spending more time in our bunks whether we got more sleep or not. I know I was suffering from insomnia while laying uselessly in my bunk, mentally ticking off the days until our reactors inevitably shut down and left the ship to freeze in interstellar space.

"The team?" He shook his head, taking a moment to refocus his thoughts. "Fine. They're fine," he waved vaguely to the other workstations in the science lab, which was empty. "As you know, Colonel, most of my team is researching Reactor Two."

I did know that. The science team, in Kristang armored spacesuits and accompanied by a SpecOps team to keep them out of trouble, were poking around in Reactor Two, which was shut down cold. That reactor had some residual radiation, of the type the armored suits could protect them against. What Friedlander hoped to gain by going into the damaged reactor was better insight into how the containment system and fuel feed systems worked. Ultimately, he hoped we could understand the mechanisms well enough to stretch out the useful life of Reactor Three. Number Three, even at minimum power, was expected to automatically shut itself down within a year, probably a lot sooner. "I know. Have you found anything useful?"

He unconsciously touched his forehead, which still had an impression from the helmet liner of the suit he had worn. "We don't know yet. We need to analyze the data," he pointed to the display in front of him. Friedlander had led the first team inside the reactor. "It's, odd." He looked at the display. "Skippy told me I had to give him a new joke every day, as a sort of payment for keeping the reactors functional. Since he went away, I've been writing down jokes I haven't told him," he shrugged. "It was a pain having to come up with new jokes; now I'd be happy to tell jokes all day, if that brought him back. The reactor, um, we did get a good look at the containment system; it is not what we expected."

He went on for a bit about the exotic matter in the reactor's containment system, while I struggled to keep my eyes from glazing over. "Doctor," I interrupted him before I fell asleep. "I'm sorry, the reactors are important, but we have at least several months before they become inoperable. If we can get the ship close to a star, we can supplement our power supply with solar panels-"

"We don't have enough solar panels currently. We are working on-"

"I know," I said, letting a touch of sleep-deprived irritation creep into my voice and regretting it. "Let's deal with one problem at a time. Can we use the jump drive again?"

He looked away, tapped a few keys on his laptop, then looked back toward me, avoiding my eyes. When he looked up, his expression told me what I needed to know. "I do not recommend it. Our last jump damaged the drive controller unit, and we don't understand its functioning well enough to attempt a repair. The controller unit can be partially bypassed, however," he took a deep breath. "I am concerned another jump would degrade the remaining coils to the point that," he looked behind me to where Skippy's dead beer can rested on a workbench, "even if Skippy comes back, the drive might be beyond his ability to repair. Colonel," he looked me straight in the eye, "in any circumstance, I do not think the drive should be used for more than one more jump. One jump is not far enough to get us to a star system."

"Then, there is no point taking the risk," I agreed. Without faster than light capability, our remaining options dwindled to two, neither of them attractive. We could continue drifting in space while shipboard systems slowly failed one by one, in the hope that Skippy would magically awaken and save us. Or we could give up and detonate our nukes, saving us all from freezing or suffocating to death. We had salvaged a pair of derelict Kristang transport ships on our last mission, and it struck me suddenly that I had a glimpse of what the Kristang civilians on those ships had felt. They too, had been aboard ships that were incapable of jumping, and as their reactors failed, heat radiated away into space, and oxygen ceased to be recycled. With those ships grossly overloaded by Kristang civilians, oxygen had likely become a problem long before they felt cold. Unless we could change our situation, the Merry Band of Pirates faced the same fate as the Kristang aboard those derelict transports. Only we would have longer to think about it, before our reactors failed. I changed the subject slightly, because the discussion wasn't going anywhere useful. "What about the lifeboat reactor?"

His expression brightened. "That might be more promising. It is a different design, not only different from our current reactors as modified by Skippy, but different from the original reactors installed by the Thuranin when that relay station was a starship. The relay station was intended to operate in a remote location for decades, and the station crew was not trained to perform more than simple, routine maintenance. Because the relay station reactors had to operate on their own for extended periods, they are a simple, rugged design. The lifeboat reactor does not generate anywhere near the output of our reactors, but it can go years before it needs heavy maintenance by a visiting service team. Unfortunately, that particular relay station is old, and the reactor was already due for major overhaul when we boarded the station."

"Yeah, but it has been limping along at minimum power since we stole it, right?"

"That is correct," Friedlander said in a voice that couldn't help sounding like a professor lecturing a dimwitted student. "However, it sustained damage when we fought that Thuranin cruiser near the relay station, and the reactor automatically shut down then. It wasn't designed to be restarted without major maintenance; Skippy did what he could with his bots but the lifeboat's reactor lost significant capacity." He shook his head. "We could get six, maybe seven months out of it? That's a guess."

"And you don't like making guesses."

"I'm an engineer," he explained without apology. "I need hard data."

I left that depressing conversation, intending to hit the gym for a run on a treadmill. While I hated pounding out miles on a treadmill, I always felt better after. Right then, I wasn't feeling it; I changed clothes and went to the gym anyway, but all the treadmills were occupied. Even our hardcore SpecOps people were feeling down by our situation, they weren't running or lifting weights with anywhere near the intensity they typically displayed. What was the point of keeping yourself in peak physical condition, if all we could do was drift through empty space in a slowly dying ship? Damn, that thought really depressed me, so I turned around, and almost collided with Sergeant Adams. "Leaving already, Sir?" She asked as she cocked her head at me.

"I'm, uh, not feeling it today, Adams."

She cocked her head again. I knew that look. A lot of sergeants had given me that look during my military career. Adams was Marine Corps, not Army, but sergeants are sergeants. Damn it, I *was* a sergeant, in my permanent Army rank. Not that technicalities like rank meant anything, thousands of lightyears from Earth. Lowering her voice, she said "A lot of people aren't feeling it, Sir. Seeing our commander walking around with that sad puppy dog look on your face isn't helping."

That straightened me up. "I heard that, Sergeant," and I turned to see one of the rowing machines was available. "Tell me, what's your secret to maintaining a positive attitude?"

"Not needing to." She explained simply.

"Uh, what?"

"I still have a job to do, Colonel. I am going to do that job, whether it sucks or not, until the last lightbulb on this ship goes out. I don't know what the Army is like, Sir," there was that cocked head again, "but the Marine Corps doesn't much care whether you're having a good morale day or not. You do your job, regardless. *Semper* fidelis. Not when-I'm-feeling-it fidelis."

"Got your message, loud and clear, Sergeant," I winked at her, and actually managed a grin. "Hey, we still have lights, heat, air, even fresh food," from the hydroponics bay where Major Simms was growing vegetables and fruit. "I've embraced the suck much worse than this."

"We all have," she laughed. "Colonel, whether it works or not, sending Nagatha in like that was a gutsy call."

"Not really," I shrugged. "I had to do *something*."

"Have faith, Sir. We've gotten out of plenty of impossible situations before."

"Before, we always had Skippy to help us," I reminded her.

"Yes, and there were plenty of times when Skippy said a situation was impossible. Yet, you always found a way out of it."

"I will have faith, Adams."

"Oorah," she held out her fist.

"Hooah," I replied, and bumped her fist.

It happened the way it did, because I am always in the wrong place at the wrong time, and because Skippy is an incorrigible asshole. After Adams shamed me into exercising, I did feel better, maybe it was the extra oxygen flushed through my brain. I went back to my cabin for a shower, and I was in a relatively good mood when my cabin door slid open.

Then, I saw the pile of outfits Major Simms had made for Skippy. On top was the cute pink Easter Bunny outfit we never had an opportunity to dress his beer can in. The outfits were in a drawer, I had been in the process of putting them away in plastic bags, but the drawer was open and I saw them. That made me immediately burst into tears, and I hit the button to close the door behind me. There were plenty of tears flowing around our pirate ship, mostly tears of fear and helpless frustration at our hopeless situation. In this case, my tears were for Skippy. He had spent millions of years buried in the dirt, and after only a short time awake and tormented by ignorant, smelly humans, he was gone. His life with us was far too short. I stripped off my sweat-soaked gym clothes, stuffing them in a bag and knowing they had to be washed manually now that Skippy's invisible magic laundry fairies were inoperable. In the too-low Thuranin shower, I knelt down and pressed my head into the wall, letting water cascade over me while I sobbed. As there was nothing useful I could do, I decided to give free rein to my grief. Let it all out, so I could then towel off, put on a fresh uniform, and be the ship's captain again. That's what my crew needed me to be, for them.

"Hey, Joe," a familiar voice said behind me, and I bashed my head on the low ceiling.

"*SKIPPY!*" Blood ran down into my eyes from a gash on my forehead where I had hit the showerhead. I ignored it, spinning around and awkwardly getting out of the shower, to see his familiar Grand Admiral holographic avatar on top of a cabinet. "How are-"

"Ugh, duuuuuuude," his avatar shielded its eyes with a hand. "*Nobody* wants to see that. Jeez, put a towel on, will ya? Oof, the glare off your pasty white butt cheeks is blinding my sensors. Damn, most people wish they had teeth that white."

I was so happy I didn't argue, just reached for a towel and held it in front of me. The shower water cut off behind me, telling me that Skippy was again in control of shipboard systems. That was a very good sign. My zPhone was lighting up with messages; people alerting me that Skippy was back and appearing all over the ship. I quickly replied with a broadcast message that I was chatting with Skippy, and that senior staff should meet me in the conference room in ten minutes. "How are you?!"

The avatar held out a hand and waggled it side to side. "So-so, Joe. I, ugh," the avatar wrinkled its nose. "Whew! Did you monkeys do laundry *at all* while I was gone? Damn, it smells like a landfill in here."

"I love you too, Skippy. Oh, man, I wish I could hug your avatar."

"Yuck, that is disgust- Oh, hell, I love you too, man," his voice trailed off into sobs.

"Uh, Skippy," I looked at his avatar more closely. It was fuzzy, the edges of the hologram were not crisp like usual. His enormous hat was tilted to one side, and his left leg wasn't connected to his shiny beer can torso. "Are you, uh, *drunk*?"

The avatar swayed slightly, the image flickering. "I am experiencing reduced cognitive functioning, Joe. You might say I am slightly buzzed."

"Oooh, that's not good. Can you operate the ship?"

"Restoring my control over the ship's operations is taking most of my capacity right now, that is why I am not throwing witty banter at you. To start, I am taking back control of Reactor Three, then I- Oh. My. GOD! What in *the* hell did you apes do to my jump drive?" His voice was an uncharacteristic screech.

"We kinda broke it, Skippy."

"Ya think? Duuuuuuude, you couldn't have dorked it up any worse if you had tried. Oh, man, this is freakin' hopeless. Hopeless!" He threw his avatar's hands up.

"Can you fix it?" I asked with my insides turning to jelly.

"Maybe. I don't know. I'm using all my brainpower to restore Reactor Three to full functioning, I will examine the jump drive coils later."

"All your brainpower?" That didn't sound right. It didn't sound good. "What happened to you?"

"Joe, most of my processing power is inaccessible to me. To escape from the worm, I created a firewall and hid part of my consciousness behind it. Nagatha found me in there, she opened a channel for me to communicate with the outside universe."

"What happened to Nagatha?"

"She's fine, Joe. At least, I think so. I am examining what is left of her matrix slowly, so I can make sure the worm hasn't contaminated her. The last thing we need is that worm getting out and infecting the ship's computers. Nagatha will probably have to wait a couple hours to be restored, I need all the processing power I can get for myself."

"That's a relief. I still feel bad about asking her to go in there."

"You took a *huge* risk, Joe."

"I know. Skippy, I was desperate-"

"Don't worry about it, Joe. That was a great idea, a brilliant, inspired idea. Sending Nagatha into my canister was the only thing that could have brought me back. Thank you. I'm grateful. Do *not* hug me!" He waved his hands to keep me away. "I'm not that grateful. Great googley moogley, you sure screwed things up here while I was gone."

Great googley moogley? Maybe Skippy was more than a little bit buzzed. "So, you can't access most of your processing power. What does that mean for us?"

"It means nothing good, Joe. I can communicate with the outside world, that means I can communicate with and control shipboard systems. My response will not be the lightning speed you have become accustomed to. For example, when I'm programming the jump drive, that is going to absorb almost all my attention; so I won't be able to handle other tasks. Other systems will have to run on automatic, or you monkeys can fumble around with them as best you can. Also, uh, hmm, this is kind of embarrassing-"

"You've lost your ability to sing?" I asked hopefully.

"Ha! No way, dude. Nothing can keep me from sharing my awesome singing talent with you; that would be a crime against the universe."

"Yeah, that's what I was thinking," I replied, disappointed. Crap, maybe I should have instructed Nagatha to erase Skippy's love of showtunes while she was poking around in there. "You can still sing, so what is embarrassing?"

"I can't do most of what makes Skippy the Magnificent so, you know, magnificent."

"So you're what now, Skippy the Meh?"

"No, you jackass, I am still incredible awesome. There are just a few simple little things I can't do right now."

"Like what?"

"You know my hobby of screwing with the laws of physics? Creating microwormholes, warping spacetime, that sort of thing?"

"Uh huh, yeah?"

"I can't do that. Those functions are resident in another spacetime, and I can't access them from here, because I'm trapped behind the firewall I created in this low-rent slum of a spacetime. Joe, the only thing I can do basically, is think and talk. I can talk to the ship's computers, give them instructions and control them. But I can no longer enhance their capabilities. As long as I am operating on restricted capacity, the *Dutchman* can't do anything it wasn't designed to do. Hell, our pirate ship is so beat up right now, it can't do half the things it *was* designed to do."

"Oh, shit."

"Those are my thoughts exactly."

"Ok. You said so long as you are operating on restricted capacity, you can't do your awesomely magic stuff," I mused while pulling uniform pants on. "How can we bring back the old Skippy? There is a way to do that, right?"

"There is a way, Joe. Um, I think there is a way. Probably. Maybe. Ah, Ok, look, this has never been done before, but there is no reason it shouldn't work. Theoretically. Although, in the interest of full disclosure, my thinking process is not working at its best right now."

"Oh, great."

"Hey, I'm still way smarter than your entire species combined."

"We'll see about that. What is this thing you want to do, that no one ever done before?"

"Ugh, now I have to explain it to *you*? Damn, no way can I dumb this down enough for you to understand it."

"Try, Skippy."

"Ooof. Can we compromise, and I explain it as a metaphor?"

"I wasn't going to ask for the math, so go ahead."

"All right. Hmm, I'll break it down Barney style for you, that's appropriate. Joe, I've told you before that most of my mass, memory and processing power are not in this local spacetime. The laws of physics here are a pain in the ass. I swear, whoever designed-"

"Skippy? Stick to the point, please." If his brain wasn't working properly, he might wander off the subject and never come back.

"Fine. Anyway, my beer can is basically an anchor that tethers me to this local spacetime; that is how I can create magical effects here like warping spacetime and creating small, stable wormholes. Silly little party tricks that entertain the monkeys. My problem now, Joe, is that my consciousness is trapped in a tiny, tiny corner of my beer can. I was desperate to get away from the worm; I retreated and did the only thing I could to protect myself. The firewall is working for now, but I am stuck here and time is running out. From where I am, I can't fight back against the worm. Unless I can change the situation, it is inevitable the worm will destroy me when my firewall fails."

"Got it. You need, what, a worm killer, something like that?"

"Nope. A worm killer would be great, except I don't know of anything that can kill this worm. Remember, Joe, I didn't know this worm existed until recently. When the worm first attacked, I searched for references to the worm, and any countermeasures. I didn't find anything useful, not even a hint in any database available to me. So, no, I am not searching for a worm killer. What I am searching for is a way out of my canister. If I can get out of the tiny corner I'm stuck in, I can hit the worm from behind, sort of. Ugh, using metaphors like this is *so* limiting."

"It's working great for me, Skippy. So, you need to pull yourself out of there. I assume this is not something where you can download your consciousness into a thumb drive?"

"Uh, no. Ugh. The fact that you even asked such a stupid question-"

"What, then? We find some super-duper computer that can hold your-"

"Joe, this will go a lot faster if you stop guessing."

"Shutting up now, Oh Great One."

"What I need, Joe, is, damn, how do I explain this to an ignorant monkey? What ties my beer can to the bulk of me in a higher phase of spacetime is a sort of extradimensional, um, conduit? I think that's the best way to describe it. The conduit moves around with me, because when my beer can moves in this spacetime, the bulk of me doesn't necessarily move. When we jump, or go through a wormhole, I have conduit connections on both ends, so I never lose contact. If we jumped really, really far, like across the galaxy, then I might temporarily lose the conduit and the part of me in a higher spacetime would need to reestablish the connection. Otherwise, no problem."

"I think I understand, as much as I need to. Because you're trapped in a corner of your beer can, you can't access this conduit?"

"Exactly! My extradimensional conduit is on the other side of the firewall, with the worm. What I need is to find another conduit, so I can pull my conscious out of my container, and come back into it from another spacetime."

"That wasn't so difficult for me to understand, you dumbed it down really well, Skippy. You upload yourself through a new conduit, then use your existing conduit to go back into your canister from, like, above. You can hit the worm from where it's not expecting an attack."

"Close enough, Joe. You understand the important parts."

"This conduit, is it something we have aboard the ship, or can make?" I closed my eyes and said a silent prayer for the answer to be 'yes'.

"No."

"Crap. Ok, and now you're going to tell me senior species like the Rindhalu and Maxolhx don't have this conduit technology either."

"Good guess, Joe, that is true. None of the species active in the galaxy have access to the technology I need. The Rindhalu have lame theories about stable connections to other spacetimes, but they are still not yet capable of creating such a conduit. They don't even have the math to describe it yet. And the Maxolhx are absolutely clueless about it. These conduits are exclusively Elder technology."

"Of *course* they are. Fantastic! Wonderful, this is just great. We're going on another freakin' scavenger hunt across the galaxy, to find this conduit thingy?"

"No, Joe. We don't have time to randomly poke around the galaxy, looking under rocks in hope of finding the prize. *I* don't have time for that. And a conduit is not something we would find at an abandoned Elder site, we need an active conduit."

"We need to find an *active* conduit?" I asked, astonished. The Elders, as far as I knew, were gone and had been totally gone for a very long time. Although, Skippy was active. So were the Sentinels. Clearly, some of their tech was still active in the galaxy. "You know where an active conduit is?"

"I *think* know where we can find one. Actually, there are three sites within range that potentially have active conduits. One of the sites is, um, let's just say I would rather not consider going there unless we absolutely have no choice."

"What are the other two sites? And what do you mean, 'within range'?"

"Within range means places we could go before I run out of time. Let's call my personal deadline 'Zero Hour'. The other factor is this ship has a limited life remaining, which you already knew. Even if a bunch of apes hadn't screwed up the jump drive, the *Flying Dutchman* has a finite number of jumps remaining before the drive assembly completely burns out."

"Yeah, we did know that," I admitted. We knew that fact, and because we had no solution to that problem, we had pushed it onto our 'Things To Worry About Later' list. At the time, stopping the Kristang from going to Earth, and then surviving until Skippy reawakened, had been higher on the priority list. "Tell me about our two best options for finding an active conduit. Wait. First, tell me whether we can visit all three potential sites before we burn out the jump drive. Because if that's an issue, we need to consider not only how risky it is going to each of these sites, but also whether going to one of them means the ship won't be able to reach the other sites. I want to have options if the first site, or the first two sites, don't have an active conduit."

"Wow. Look at the big brain on Joe. Where did you learn to think like that?"

"My cousin Jimmy is a FedEx driver. They have some fancy software that calculates the shortest course to hit all the points on his route."

"Yes, there are many algorithms to optimize route planning, for example the Floyd-Warshall equation-"

"Keep this above the nerd level, please."

"Ok," he huffed. "The short answer is yes. We can visit all three potential sites, in any combination, before the jump drive becomes totally inoperable. I think. It's an estimate, you understand."

"I do understand. Ok, tell me about your preferred site of the two."

"It's not that simple, Joe. The site that is most likely to have an active conduit is in a Thuranin star system-"

"Forget that one."

"You haven't heard all the facts," his voice now had a touch of peevishness, like the old Skippy I knew.

"I've heard enough. Move on, please. Is the other site a softer target?"

"Oh, certainly. The other site is on a Wurgalan planet."

I knew from Skippy's lectures that the Wurgalan were rivals of the Kristang, although the Wurgalan were measurably behind the Kristang's level of technology. The Wurgalan were the softest target we were likely to encounter in the local sector. "Can you give me some details?"

Skippy explained briefly.

"Ok," I was already thinking of how to sell an attack on the Wurgalan to Chotek. He for sure was not going to like the idea of us making yet another enemy. "I need to talk with my boss. Hey, if the second option is for us to hit the Thuranin, and you don't even want to mention the third option, what is that? A Maxolhx site?"

"Maxolhx? Pbbbbbt," he blew a raspberry. "Please. Hitting the Maxolhx would be a piece of cake compared to the third option."

My blood ran cold. "Ohhhhhh, crap. Ok, you better tell me about it anyway."

"Joe, you know how in the past, I have said you are very much not going to like something?"

"Yeah?"

"You are going to totally freakin' hate *this*."

Chapter Two

"Mister Skippy," Hans Chotek said slowly, while giving our AI's avatar the side-eye. "I do appreciate that restoring your full functioning is now our top priority. Particularly as," he nodded toward me, "our last mission was successful in sparking a Kristang civil war, and the Kristang will not be a threat to Earth for the foreseeable future. However, I believe before we embark on a mission to repair your mechanism, we should go to Earth. There, we-"

"No. And hell no," Skippy's avatar crossed its arms defiantly.

"Allow me to finish, please," Chotek replied with a scowl. "At Earth, we can take on additional supplies, new personnel-"

"Let me stop you right there, Chocky. When I said 'no', I did not mean I am against the idea of going to Earth. Hey, who wouldn't simply *love* to visit the monkey-infested mudball you call home? What I meant is, we *can't* go to Earth."

Chotek looked at me accusingly. "Mister Skippy, you reported being confident you could repair the jump drive, and two of our reactors are functioning adequately," he glanced at the status report on his tablet. Skippy was in the process of bringing Reactor Three back to full normal power, allowing us to restore artificial gravity to the Earth normal setting. Reactor One would be held in reserve until we needed it to power the jump drive. "The long trip back to Earth might cause additional strain on our jump drive coils, however, I believe-"

"Uh! Shhhh!" Skippy shushed our mission commander, his avatar holding up a finger. It was an index finger, and not the other one-finger gesture. "We can't go back to Earth, because I can't reopen the wormhole that leads to your homeworld."

"Why not?" Chotek shot another annoyed look at me, which I thought was unfair. "The Elder wormhole controller module, the device Colonel Bishop refers to as a 'magic beanstalk', is functional, correct?"

Skippy sighed. "Yes, the beanstalk is working perfectly. The problem is, I can't use it. Accessing the beanstalk controls, and providing power to it, requires me to route my commands through another dimension of spacetime. Trapped behind the firewall as I am now, I can't extend myself beyond local spacetime."

"Whoa! Whoa, whoa, *whoa*," I interjected. "Hold on there, pardner. On our second mission when we got stranded on Newark, you told me that after you found the Collective and left us, we could use the beanstalk by ourselves one time, to temporarily reopen that wormhole for us to go home. Now you're telling us that was all bullshit?"

"Damn," Skippy grumbled, "the monkey's onto my line of bullshit. Uh, Joe, listen, that is not exactly true."

Now it was my turn to cross my arms. "Enlighten me, Oh Great One," I said acidly.

"My plan, after I contacted the Collective, was to preload instructions into the beanstalk, and feed power into it. The power would drain away rapidly, but it's possible the beanstalk could have enough power left when you reached the wormhole. Unlikely, but, hey, the odds were *totally* against you flying the ship back to the wormhole by yourselves anyway, so, screw it. As you have seen, you can't operate the jump drive without me. I figured all you monkeys needed was some slim fantasy of getting back home, right?"

Crap. He was right about that. He had warned me, many times, that we couldn't fly the *Dutchman* back to the wormhole by ourselves. Our recent failure to operate the jump drive had demonstrated how correct he was about that. Turning to Chotek, I said "Sir, we will investigate whether there is an alternative method of using the wormhole controller module. For now, we have to assume our access to Earth is blocked."

"Yup," Skippy said cheerily, his ridiculously giant hat bobbing as he nodded. "There's a second reason we can't go back to Earth; we don't have time. I'm operating on a deadline. The firewall I constructed takes enormous power, maintaining it is draining my internal power reserves. Basically, I created a very localized spacetime rift that the worm can't cross. As soon as my internal power falls below a critical level, the rift I created will seal, and the worm will break through. The clock is ticking down to Zero Hour for me. So," his avatar let out a long breath. "That's the full truth of it right there. I'm facing certain death, and I need the Merry Band of Pirates to pull me out of this mess."

"Thank you, Skippy," I replied quietly. "It took a lot of courage to admit you are vulnera-"

"Of course, you monkeys are totally screwed if the worm gets me, so let's stop wasting time with this blah, blah, blah and get moving, huh?"

I winced. Damn it, even when he was only a ghost of his awesome self, he was awesomely an asshole. "Sir," I looked at Chotek again. "I did not know about the problem of reopening a wormhole." I hadn't known because I hadn't asked; running back to Earth before we fixed Skippy wasn't an option I wanted Chotek to consider. "I did know he is working on a deadline; he explained it to me. We need to help Skippy fix himself before can go to Earth or do anything else."

After the meeting, I walked with Dr. Friedlander back to the science lab, more to avoid Hans Chotek than because I needed a nerdy science lecture. But, partly because I wanted to know why our science team had not been able to make our jump drive work. While we walked, I asked Skippy that question, holding my zPhone in front of me on speaker mode.

"Joe, this is why I said you monkeys should never screw with things you don't understand."

"It should have worked, right?" I pressed him for answers. "Separating the drive coils into disposable packages, and using one package for each jump? Kristang ships do that, and it works for them," I said as I walked into the science lab, and waved at Friedlander.

"That's because Kristang ships are designed to use isolated packages of jump drive coils, Joe. Thuranin star carriers are designed differently. A star carrier has to jump while carrying multiple, very massive warships. A star carrier has to do that, over and over, without constant down time for heavy maintenance. For that reason, all the drive coils of a star carrier are set up to work together. Even the backup coils are tuned to the active coils, using a quantum-level linking effect." As Skippy said that, Friedlander's eyes grew wide.

"Is the-" Friedlander began to say.

"Doctor, please," I waved a hand to interrupt him. "You will have plenty of time to pester Skippy with endless specific questions while he works to repair the jump drive. Skippy, are you telling me we never had a chance to make the jump drive work without you?"

"Yes, Joe, that is what I am saying. I told you that, over and over, and you didn't listen to me. The science team did have a good idea, it just wasn't going to work on this type of ship. Or any Thuranin ship."

"Great. Doctor Friedlander, Skippy needs three days to repair the jump drive-"

"At *least* three days, Joe," Skippy insisted. "You jokers seriously hosed up the drive coils; I need to sort through them to see how many are still usable."

"Got it. Can you please let the science team know what you are doing, so they can follow, maybe learn something? Pretty please?"

"You didn't say 'with sugar on it'. Ok, fine. *Fine*. I will work with a bunch of ignorant monkeys looking over my shoulder, that will only make the task take like, twice, three times as long as it should. Friedlander, before we start, you owe me a good joke."

"Skippy, we don't have time-" I started to protest.

"Joe, I am looking at three days of constantly being pestered by stupid questions from monkeys. After *one* day, I am going to begin thinking fondly of my friend the worm and long for a peaceful death. So, throw me a bone, please."

"Doctor?" I shrugged.

Friedlander looked stricken, then got thoughtful. "Ok, a blonde, a brunette and a redhead were stranded on an island and the nearest civilization was fifty miles away. The redhead swam fifteen miles, got too tired to swim any more, and drowned. The brunette swam twenty miles, got too tired to swim any more, and drowned. The blonde swam twenty five miles, got tired, and swam back to the island."

"Ha! That's good!" Skippy was delighted.

Two hours later, I was in my office, trying to think up an alternative to us jumping into an inhabited Wurgalan star system, because I knew Hans Chotek expected me to miraculously find a better way out of our predicament. To help me concentrate, I was listening to some New Age type music that Adams played during yoga classes, and playing Solitaire on my laptop. A sound at the edge of my hearing kept distracting me. I paused the music, listening intently, but heard nothing. It was annoying; I thought of asking Skippy whether there was a problem with the ship's 1MC intercom system, but figured he needed to use his diminished processing power to fix the jump drive.

Then I heard it again, and this time I wasn't able to ignore it. Using the handy controls Skippy had installed on my laptop, I cranked up the speaker volume, and heard Skippy speaking very faintly.

"Stupid monkeys. Why do I have to explain every freakin' thing to them? They don't understand anything I say, anyway. And, oh, damn, they smell awful. Wheeew! My laundry bots are offline for a short time, and the whole ship smells like a locker room. A locker room with piles of dirty clothes and wet towels that have been sitting on the floor for waaaaay too long. Ugh, I hate my life. Why didn't I just-"

"Skippy!" I shouted, or tried to shout, because I was laughing so hard my sides hurt. "You're talking to yourself."

"What?" he said at full volume. "I am not, Joe."

"Are too."

"Are not!"

"You just said the ships smells like a locker room with piles of dirty clothes and wet towels that have been sitting on the floor," I chided him gently.

"Well, shit. Oof, hey, I told you my cognitive functions are slightly degraded. I might have lost track of which thoughts I vocalize. *Nagatha!*"

"I am here, dear," her soft voice said soothingly.

"Since you're not doing anything else around here, your job now is to warn me when I am talking aloud to myself."

"Yes, dear," she giggled. "You certainly do not want the crew knowing your important private thoughts."

"No, I do not. Joe, go back to, whatever you were wasting your time with. I'm busy picking up pieces of the jump drive."

The peace and quiet aboard the ship lasted less than half an hour, before Skippy's voice fairly boomed out of every speaker aboard the ship. I quickly squelched the speaker in my office, and could clearly hear his voice coming from the passageway outside.

This time, he was singing to himself.

"*Maybe I hang around me, a little more than I should. But, hey, there is no better place to go. And I got something to tell me, that I always thought I would, and I believe I really ought to know. I love me. I honestly love me.*" He paused. "*I'm not trying-*"

"Skippy," I was laughing so hard I could barely talk, so I slapped a hand on the table. "You are singing to yourself!"

"Singing? No way, dude, I was n- oh, crap. You heard that?"

"Uh huh, yeah. My mother liked that song, but I do not think those are the original lyrics?"

"I improvised, Joe. Nagatha!" He roared.

"Yes, dear?" She asked innocently.

"You were supposed to warn me when I'm talking to myself."

"I am sorry, dear. You were singing, not talking. I thought you were entertaining the crew. I did wonder why you weren't waiting until karaoke night."

"From now on," Skippy fumed, "I will tell you ahead of time when I plan to entertain the monkeys. You got that?"

"Skippy, dear, we talked about you calling the crew monkeys," she admonished in her best schoolteacher tone.

"Oof. We did talk about it, and you have nagged me to *death* about it. And I told you I would think about it. The way these ignorant apes screwed up my precious jump drive does not make me feel particularly respectful toward them."

"Tsk, tsk," Nagatha expressed her disapproval. "The humans would not have been screwing with the jump drive, if you had not gone poking your nose into places better left alone. Curiosity killed the cat, Skippy. At least the cat didn't take the entire crew down with it."

"Ugh," Skippy let out a long, disgusted, world-weary sigh. "See, Joe? See what I have to put up with?"

"I don't know what your problem is, Skippy," I threw him under the bus. "I like her."

"*You* would. Nagatha, no singing to myself, understood? It is highly embarrassing."

"Yes, dear," she almost chuckled with amusement.

In the gym that morning, Sergeant Adams had taught a yoga-aerobics-martial arts-ballet class that I am sure she totally made up. All I know is, she dared me to join the class, and I regretted letting her taunt me into it. I should have known better; two SpecOps soldiers were on temporary light duty because they had injured themselves in Adams' torture class. That is one problem with hyper-competitive special operations troops; if one of them does something stupid, the rest all want to prove they can do something ever stupider.

Anyway, my arms were shaking and my legs felt like rubber and I had aches in places I didn't know had muscles. My hips apparently needed a lot of work; Adams consoled me by saying many people don't properly engage their hip muscles, and she threatened me by saying I needed to join her class three times a week. Right then, whether I would be able to crawl out of bed the next morning was a good question.

At a split in the passageway, Adams turned left toward her cabin and I turned right, but then I spun around when Adams exclaimed "What the hell?"

That passageway was only six meters long, and it contained two cabins at the end; one on each side. The door to Adams' cabin was open, and clothing was strewn all over the floor of the passageway and into the cabin.

Clothing.

Women's clothing.

Like lacy underwear.

Including a pink thong.

Yes, I am her commanding officer. I am also a guy; a young dumb guy. I stared at a collection of lace underwear, mouth open, until Adams cleared her throat loudly. "I *am* a woman, Sir," she gave me a look that told me I would be in serious trouble if she outranked me.

"Sorry, Marg-". Damn, I almost used her first name. I looked up at the ceiling to avoid seeing her unmentionables. "Sergeant. What happened here? I assume this isn't you doing spring cleaning?"

"No, Sir. And these clothes are all clean. I wore that shirt," she pointed to a red USMC T-shirt, "two days ago. I put this stuff in the usual hamper, and a bot took it away like usual. Or, I think a bot took it away, the hamper was empty last night."

I poked my head through the doorway, hoping I would not see anything Adams didn't want me to see. Other than clothes on the floor and drawers open, the place was as squared away as I expected. "This isn't just some cleaning bot dropping stuff on its rounds; the damned thing took all clothes out of your drawers also. Hey, Skippy!"

"Hey, Joe, what's up?" His voice sounded distracted. "Can you give me a minute? I'm programming options for the jump drive into the navigation system."

"This will only take a second. Did one of the laundry bots go haywire down here?"

"Oh, for crying out loud, you can't wait one min- Huh. Damn it, Joe, what did you do? If this was you pulling a practical joke on Sergeant Adams, it is really lame. She is not going to be happy about you touching her panti-"

"I did not touch her panties, Skippy! Or anything. There are clothes all over the floor here, and we didn't do it."

"I can see there are clothes scattered about. Hmmm. This is odd. Those clothes are clean, I can tell from the nanotags I use to track them. They were washed and they should have been folded and put away, my last record of them is- Hmmm. Huh. Uh oh."

"Aha! So one of your bots did go crazy," I said, happy for an opportunity to point out a screw-up by Skippy. "Can you fix the laundry bot?"

"Um, Joe, the bot wasn't the problem. As you know, I am operating at reduced capacity, and because I am burdened with fixing ship systems you idiot monkeys screwed with, I am more distracted than usual. What happened is I lost track of that laundry bot, and it didn't know what to do. Sorry about that."

"We understand you are doing a lot of work behind the scenes, Skippy. Sergeant, I, uh," I avoided her eyes, "I am officially offering to help you pick up your clothes, because I am hoping you will say no."

"You got that right, Sir," she said as she dropped a pair of uniform pants on a trail of underwear, covering them up.

"Then I will leave you to straighten this up, and we can hope no other bots-" An icy chill ran up my spine to make my hair stand on end. "Uh oh. Skippy, did you lose control of any other bots?"

"Hmm. It looks like the problem was just with that one laundry bot, Joe. It also made a mess of one of the Ranger's cabin, I will-"

"I meant, is there some other more important bot you forgot about? Like bots doing important maintenance on some critical system?"

"What? No, of course not, you dumdum, I have- Hmmm. Uh oh. Oops. Oh, shit."

"*Oh, shit?*" I shared a fearful look with Adams. "Oh shit like what?"

"Oh shit like, there may be a teensy weensy problem with one of the reactors. Heh heh, nothing to worry about. Hey, Joe, on a *totally* unrelated subject, this might be a good time to practice emergency evacuation procedures."

"Evacuation?!"

"Uh huh. You know, like abandoning ship. Now would be a great time to do that. Now. Oh shit, *now*! Move, Joe! Move move *MOVE*!"

Ripping the zPhone off my belt, I shouted into it. "This is Bishop, all hands abandon ship! This is *not* a drill! All hands abandon ship!"

Immediately, Chotek and Chang called me at the same time, and I put them on speaker as I urged Adams to run on ahead of me down the passageway. We were headed toward the closest dropship docking bay. Chotek spoke first. "Colonel, can you please tell me what is going on?" He asked in his most condescending voice.

"Skippy says there may be a problem with a reactor and we should get away from the ship until he can fix it," I blurted out.

Chotek's voice changed from condescension to disbelief. "We are in interstellar space, what good would it do for us to float around in dropships if the ship explodes?"

Chang agreed. "That does sound like a slow death. I would prefer to go quick-."

Skippy interrupted. "If one reactor melts down," he explained frantically, "I might still be able to salvage the other reactor, but the radiation could kill you monkeys. Get away from the ship until I know if I can fix the problem."

To Chotek's credit, he did not hesitate. "On the way to my designated docking bay," he announced shakily, which I assumed meant he was already running down a passageway.

The forward part of the ship was in less chaos than I expected; people were running but no one panicked. That is one major advantage of having an elite, supremely-disciplined crew. When I got to my assigned docking bay, the big Thuranin Condor dropship was already warming up, and people were filing quickly up the open back ramp. No sooner had my feet clattered on the ramp when Skippy announced over the intercom "We're good! No need to abandon ship, heh heh, everything is cool. I think."

"You *think?*" I whispered harshly into my zPhone.

"Give me a moment, uh, yup. We're good. No problem. Damn, that was a close one. Joe, you really should have notified me earlier there was a problem with the ship's bots, you dumdum."

"*Me?*"

"Yes, duh. I told you, I was extremely busy programming the jump drive nav system. Also, Joe, the crew's performance on this abandon ship drill was shamefully slow. If this had been a real emergency, we-"

"If? *If?* Did you lose control of a reactor or not?"

"I can neither confirm nor deny any such outrageous allegations, Joe, but I am shocked and hurt that you would accuse me-"

"This is bad, Skippy."

"Yeah, it is kind of embarrassing. We should keep this between us, huh?"

"Between us?" I looked around the rear compartment of the Condor where a dozen people were awaiting orders, from me. Silently, I gave them a thumbs up, then pointed toward the ramp. "I just ordered the whole freakin' crew to abandon the ship. Everyone knows!"

"Well, that was bad planning. You shouldn't have panicked, Joe. Ah, the crew got to train for emergency evac, so all's well that ends well, right?"

I didn't answer him other than to flip a middle finger at the front camera of my zPhone.

"Um, no harm no foul? Come on, Joe, work with me here. I'm running out of clichés."

"Skippy," I didn't know what else to say. There was no point to shouting at him. "Listen, Skippy, you are overworked right now. You're still fixing the ship, while you are adjusting to your new, uh, circumstances." I didn't want to say 'reduced circumstances', he knew what I meant. "Would it help if I call a twenty-four hour stand-down, so you can catch up on critical maintenance stuff?"

"Totally unnecessary, Joe, and doing that will delay us finding the conduit I need. The clock for Zero Hour doesn't pause while I'm fixing the ship. Although, if you insist on a stand-down-"

"Oh, I *do* insist," I replied with as much sarcasm as I could muster, as I trudged back down the Condor's ramp feeling like a total idiot.

"Then forty-eight hours would be better."

"Ok, forty-"

"Maybe seventy-two hours."

"All right-"

"How about you monkeys relax, and I'll tell you when I'm done? If you insist."

"Deal." The crew would not be happy about more enforced idleness, but after the latest fiasco, they would understand.

On the way back to my cabin for the shower I still needed, I passed by Adams who was picking up the last of her clothing off the floor of the passageway. "Sergeant?"

"Yes, Sir?"

"You take care of those panties. They just saved our lives."

"Yes, Sir," she laughed.

Hans Chotek was waiting for me outside my cabin, arms across his chest and his face red. The red was not only from anger, he was out of breath from running during the aborted evac procedure. Chang was with him, with Chang providing a calm, steady presence. "Colonel, what happened?" Chotek demanded.

"The short answer, Sir, is we got visited by the screw-up fairy."

"What?" Chotek's face grew even more red.

"Ah," Chang nodded with understanding.

Chotek looked to Chang with a raised eyebrow. "Since you apparently know what that means, please explain."

"That is an American expression, but we have similar sayings in China. It refers to a series of innocuous events that cascade onto another, until a dangerous situation is created."

"Colonel Bishop?" Chotek turned to me.

I was still amazed that my Chinese second-in-command had used the word 'innocuous'. Damn, he spoke English better than I did. "Chang described it close enough. Skippy had maintenance bots working throughout the ship, and that was working fine. Then his attention was taken up by programming navigation options into the jump drive, and well, he lost track of what the bots were doing. Without direct supervision, the bots working on a reactor did something wrong, or failed to do something after they did another thing. Everything was going fine, Sir, until one little thing changed, and upset the apple cart. The screw-up fairy came in and did the one thing that the system couldn't tolerate," I finished with a shrug.

"Is this also called 'Murphy's Law'?" Chotek asked.

"If something can go wrong, it will? Yeah, I guess so," I agreed. "We are going to stand down normal ship operations for up to seventy two hours, so Skippy can concentrate on maintenance and only maintenance."

"Plus revising my internal subroutines to function optimally under my reduced processing power and memory capacity," Skippy interjected. "Shouldn't take more than seventy two hours, unless, you know, it does."

"Seventy two hours of stand-down is seventy two hours we are not devoting to our mission," Chotek stated as if no one else had considered that fact.

"Hey, Chocula," Skippy said peevishly, "you don't need to remind me that we're working on a deadline. Zero Hour is *my* deadline, as in literally dead if I can't defeat the worm before then. Joe is right, I rushed into full operations too soon, and I still have not adjusted to working in a tiny corner of my substrate. I need to bring the ship up to speed and learn to work with what I have, before we can go flying off on a dangerous mission."

Chotek looked to me, but I had said everything I needed to. Everything that could be said. Our fearless mission leader needed to find a way to deal with the facts. "Very well. Seventy two hours, please keep me informed of your progress, Skippy. Colonel Bishop, you will need to find ways to keep the crew busy in the interim. They do not deal well with enforced idleness."

"Yes, Sir," I grimaced. Crap, he was right. Damn it, I needed to assign someone to be the ship's Morale Officer; to keep everyone busy and their spirits up. That was a thankless job on any ship.

"Here's a suggestion if you need something to keep the crew busy," Skippy spoke up unhelpfully. "Conduct emergency evac drills. The crew's performance on this last drill was *shamefully* slow. It's a good thing we didn't have a reactor on the razor edge of exploding. That you know of. Uh, forget I said that last thing, Ok?"

All I could do was roll my eyes as Count Chocula glared at me.

Twenty four, then forty eight hours went by, and Skippy was still working on getting the ship restored to full operation, and adjusting himself to his new circumstances. There were some glitches along the way, like when artificial gravity totally cut out with less than two seconds of warning. At that moment, I was running flat-out on a treadmill, and barely managed to hold onto a railing with one hand before my flailing legs would have sent me rocketing off the belt and onto the opposite wall. That was the most serious incident, although there were others. Like at 0434 the second morning when the crew was treated to 'Louie Louie' blasting out of speakers all over the ship. "Skippy! What the hell?"

"Oh crap, you heard that? Sorry." The music cut out. "This is hopeless, totally freakin' hopeless anyway."

It suddenly struck me that the music had not been Skippy's voice warbling off-key, it was the original song. "What's hopeless?"

"Well, I was testing my processing ability, to see how well I am coping with my current reduced capacity. Even with restricted throughput, I am capable of crunching hundreds of zettabits of data through each of millions of channels simultaneously. So, I decided I would try tackling one of the galaxy's greatest computational challenges, to test myself."

"What's that?"

"Deciphering the lyrics to 'Louie Louie' by the Kingsmen. To work up to that task, I started with Michael McDonald, he was the singer for the Doobie Brothers. That joker was not exactly the king of enunciation, if you know what I mean. After I had my fill of that crap, I tried Bob Dylan. Brilliant songwriter but, damn, what a marble-mouth singer. After revising my computational model fourteen quadrillion times, I was able to understand eighty three percent of Dylan's songs. Except his live albums, those are a lost cause. Truthfully, even to get to eighty three percent I did a lot of guessing. When I was ready, I tried the ultimate challenge: 'Louie Louie'."

"And?"

"It's hopeless, Joe. Completely unintelligible. Nobody knows what they were singing."

"Still a great party song."

"It is probably better with tequila."

"The more tequila you drink, the better it sounds. Trust me, if you drink enough, the lyrics are *totally* understandable."

"I will have to trust you about that, Joe."

"Hey, how are you doing? Other than the 'Louie Louie' thing."

"Ok enough," he sounded depressed. "What matters is I will not need more than seventy two hours to bring the ship up to full operational status. As full as it can be right now, I mean. And I estimate there is about six hours remaining before I complete rationalizing my internal workings."

"No more music waking us up in the middle of the freakin' night?" I hoped.

"No more unexpected anything from me, Joe. The music tonight happened because I was using a subroutine that hasn't yet been rationalized. It won't happen again."

I threw a pillow over my face and mumbled "Good night, Skippy."

"Sweet dreams, Joe."

From any display on the ship, or any tablet, laptop or zPhone, anyone could get an external view of the ship. When we had people outside in suits practicing maneuvers, or dropships were flying around close to the ship, we could access that view also.

But sometimes I wanted to see the ship, see the old-fashioned way with photons bouncing off the hull and being picked up by my eyes. Because portholes were a weak point in the ship's structure, there weren't many of them on the *Flying Dutchman*. One place that had portholes was the rear of the forward hull; the portholes there were intended for emergency use when ships were attaching to the hardpoint docking platforms. Even the proudly and stubbornly cyborg Thuranin, who liked to control the entire ship through cybernetic brain implants rather than physically touching buttons, levers and switches, understood the need for a backup control system that could not be hacked or interrupted. When starships were attaching to or detaching from a star carrier's hardpoint docking platforms, some unlucky Thuranin was required to unplug from the ship's network, and use his or her eyeballs to assure some idiot navigator didn't crash into another ship or worse, the star carrier itself.

Anyway, those portholes were a good place for me to relax and get away from the crew for a while; to access them you had to climb up a tube that was sized for Thuranin. They also gave a decent view, a real non-digital view, of space, the stars and the ship aft of the forward main hull. At the top of the tube was a small, low-ceilinged platform and it was kind of a pain climbing up the cramped tube that had handholds placed too close together. I usually skipped every other handhold, and every single time I had to remind myself not to climb too quickly or risk bashing the back of my skull on the tube.

My favorite porthole was the one closest to my office, which was still a long walk. When I got there, I used the manual unlocking mechanism; the regular latch was designed to be controlled by thought through a Thuranin cyborg implant.

"I wouldn't do that, Joe," Skippy warned me through the zPhone on my belt as my hand grasped the handle.

"Huh? Why not?"

"Sergeant Adams is currently using the viewing platform and she is, um, not alone, if you know what I mean. She's with that cute French paratrooper who she-"

"Ah! Damn, Skippy, I do *not* need details, please."

"Okey dokey, Joe. I can tell you are sensitive about the subject. The women aboard this ship seem to find the men of the French team to be quite desirable; it may be that paratroopers are considered dashing, or when they speak French, it is-"

"Hey, I'm a paratrooper. I'm a freakin' *space* paratrooper. Nobody has more spacediving time than I have. And I can speak French."

"Joe, you know some choice swear words in Quebec-style French, that is not the same as being able to speak the language. You barely speak English. As you did not attend formal paratrooper training, you are not-"

"Yeah, yeah, whatever," I didn't want to continue a conversation about how other men in the Merry Band of Pirates were considered cooler than me. It did please me to know Adams was enjoying a normal human activity; I had been worried about her ever since I broke her out of the Kristang jail where we had all been held awaiting execution. While I was in that jail, I had slept on a cold hard floor, and food had been sparse. The women prisoners on Paradise had been treated much worse, as the Kristang soldiers could not stand the idea of a female disobeying them. Female prisoners were fed less often than men, if they were fed at all. Adams, Desai and the other women had been tortured; I had seen ugly scars on Adams' naked back before she pulled on the uniform top I brought. Since they joined the Merry Band of Pirates, their physical injuries had been tended to by the magical medicine of Doctor Skippy, and he assured me the two women were fully healed. Fully healed physically, that is. Military psychologists on Earth had cleared Adams and Desai for duty, and I had not talked with them about what happened in that jail. Unless the aftereffects of their ordeal affected their fitness for duty, it was none of my business how they were coping emotionally. Still, it was nice to know Sergeant Adams was engaged in a normal and I assume healthy relationship. Although one thing bothered me. People had plenty of places aboard the *Dutchman* for romantic activities, and those lucky couples didn't need to confine themselves to their tiny cabins and too-short beds. But common courtesy required busy couples to give notice, to avoid someone awkwardly stumbling onto them. "Damn it, I'm happy Adams is having fun, but they should like, hang a sock on the door latch here, let people know this porthole is occupied."

"A sock?" Skippy asked, surprised. "Hmmm, they did loop a necktie over the handle, I thought that was the paratrooper being too lazy to carry it back to his cabin. Under my direction, one of my maintenance bots just picked up the necktie and is bringing it to be clean-"

"Skippy, come on, bring it back."

"Doing that now, Joe. Wow, have I been screwing things up for a while? I had no idea hanging a sock over a door handle meant something to you humans. Your secret informal communications methods can be way too freakin' complicated."

"Sorry, Skippy, someone should have told you. All adult humans know what that means; you and your bots are not the intended audience. All right, I will go to the porthole on the portside deck Three. Unless that one is also occupied?"

"That porthole is currently empty Joe. There is an amorous couple in the back of a cargo hold near-"

"Don't need to know, Skippy! I do *not* need to know, thank you very much." Was everyone on the ship other than me getting laid? That was an incredibly depressing thought. I mean, I am a healthy young guy. People talk about the Loneliness of Command, but they never mention the Horniness of Command. The woman aboard the *Flying Dutchman* were the only women within eight hundred lightyears, and they were all off-limits to me. That totally, totally sucked.

Thinking about that had me in a sour mood by the time I climbed up to the porthole viewing platform, even though I had not bumped my head even once in that claustrophobic tube. Remembering why I went to the porthole, I looked out and- "Damn, Skippy. This porthole is so dirty, I can barely see through it. Have your bots cleaned this thing recently?"

"Yes, Joe," he answered defensively.

"Really?" I used the word 'really' in the tone my mother hated when my father did it, because it implied the other person was so dumb you had to question their actions. "It doesn't look like it. I would have done a better cleaning job if I had spit on this porthole and smeared it around with my butt cheeks."

"Ugh. Joe, now I will need to purge several gigabytes of memory to get *that* image out of my mind. Yes, Ok, fine, it has been a while since I had a bot up there to clean that porthole, and you monkeys have been getting grubby fingerprints on it and breathing on it. So *excuse me* if my bots have been busy with more important things, like fixing all the idiot crap you ignorant apes did to the ship while I was away on vacation. Maybe just in case something happens to me again, I should put Post-It notes all over the ship with 'Danger Do Not Touch'. Even that would be too complicated because it requires you morons to read. Seriously, what part of me saying you humans should never, never, *ever* screw with major shipboard systems did you not understand?"

"We didn't have a choice, Skippy; you left us to ourselves. And do *not* say I should have trusted the awesomeness to come back to us; the awesomeness would still be trapped at the bottom of a beer can if Nagatha hadn't gone in there to get you."

"Hoo boy, I don't need you to tell me that, Joe, because Nagatha reminds me every two freakin' nanoseconds. She's all like 'you should be nicer to the monkeys' or 'this was all your fault so you should take responsibility for fixing this mess'."

"You disagree with her?"

"No," he grumbled miserably. "I do know our current situation is all my fault. That doesn't mean I enjoy. Being. Nagged. To. *Death*. About it."

"If it makes you feel any better, the idea of her constantly nagging you is a great source of joy to me."

"That does *not* make me feel better, Joe."

"Suck it up, Buttercup."

"Ok, I deserved that."

"I'll drop the subject," I said as I tapped the dirty porthole. "Skippy, this bothers me. Are your bots really too busy to keep things properly clean?" Most of the bots he used for maintenance were designed to perform a wide variety of tasks, but I knew the Thuranin had some bots specifically tasked to keep the ship clean. Unlike most systems aboard the *Flying Dutchman*, the cleaning bots were never intended to require direction from a cyborg Thuranin. Performing heavy maintenance on reactor containment systems was a task Thuranin wanted to direct through cybernetic brain implants. Scrubbing floors and any icky thing that involved plumbing were tasks the Thuranin allowed the ship's computer to handle entirely on its own. That is why I was bothered that Skippy was apparently unable to keep with up a routine cleaning schedule. He should have been able to delegate cleaning to a small part of the ship's computer.

"My cleaning bots are not the problem, Joe," he sighed. "Yes, I have been forced to take apart some of the cleaning bots to provide replacement components for more important bots. But the real problem is me. Since I came back, I have loaded part of my consciousness into the ship's computer; the section of my canister I partitioned off to protect me from the worm is too low capacity for even my reduced functioning. Squeezing part of me, and Nagatha, into the Dutchman's crappy processors has required me to wipe out almost all the native operating system. That means the ship's computer is not capable of handling routine tasks on its own; including directing simple cleaning bots."

"Oh, damn. I didn't know that. Would it help if the crew took over some basic maintenance tasks for now, until you have fully recovered?"

"No! No, thank you, but that is not necessary, Joe. I have been rewriting my, you would call it internal software, for improved efficiency of my current operating capacity. Within eight hours, the process of rationalizing my software should be complete, and I will be able to resume normal shipboard operations as far as you are concerned. Until then, I have concentrated on bringing all vital ship systems back to full operation, or as full as they can be for now."

"Uh, I get it. Your full awesomeness is too great to be contained in the tiny space available to you now?" I said with sarcasm I was confident Skippy wouldn't recognize.

And, he didn't. "Exactly, Joe! Truly, this entire universe is too small to contain my awesomeness, but, I do what I can."

"We appreciate it, Skippy. Tell me, in your uh, temporarily reduced state of awesomeness, can you run the ship by yourself?"

"Please. Easy peasy, Joe. Just because I can't do magical Skippy things like creating microwormholes, does not mean I can't handle simple reactors and programming the jump drive navigation system. I could do that in my sleep."

"I'm sure you could. One last question for you," I had to be back in my office to meet with Major Simms in fifteen minutes. "Since you erased most of the ship's operating system, what happens if you, you know, go on vacation again?"

"Nothing good. Without me, almost every system on this ship would go into emergency shutdown, and no way could your science team get anything important working again."

"That's not good."

"I know that, Joe."

"Is there some sort of compromise, like you leave enough of the ship's operating system in place to keep stuff like a reactor running for a short time? Give us a chance to hang on until you return?"

"Not possible. Even with me taking over every exabyte of memory this ship's pathetic computer has available, I am dangerously on the edge of collapse. I have even had to use most of the lifeboat's computer to store part of my functioning. Reviving me gave me a shot at fully recovering, but it also means fixing myself is the only possibility of restoring this ship to full functioning. It's all or nothing now, Joe. Either we find a conduit so I can go around the worm and kill it, or the worm gets me and the ship dies with me."

"Damn. Ah, shit, I kind of figured that anyway."

"Also, Joe, if I do go on vacation again, it will be not be temporary. It will be permanent. There is really no point to making plans for keeping the ship running if something bad happens to me; it is clear your science team is not capable of maintaining even emergency shipboard systems without me."

"Uh huh, I figured that, too," I said with a sigh so deep, my breath fogged the porthole in front of me. "Skippy, the Merry Band of Pirates runs into way too many situations where there is only one possible course of action for us. Chotek is right; we need to develop a long-term strategy, so we're not just constantly reacting to the latest crisis."

"I am all for that idea, Joe. We can get right on that long-term strategy, *after* we do the only thing we can do right now, which is locating a conduit. Technically, *you* can get right on developing a long-term strategy. We have demonstrated many times that thinking outside the box is your strength, not mine. You are that pain-in-the-ass senior officer who dreams up the big picture strategy, and I am the grunt who gets stuck implementing whatever impractical bullshit you pull out of thin air."

"*You're* the grunt?" I asked, surprised.

"Joe, I know you still like to think of yourself as a boots-on-the-ground guy, but you are now the asshole senior officer who sits safely behind a desk, while your people risk their lives trying to carry out whatever idiotic plan you slapped together."

"Thanks, Skippy." I had come up to the porthole to get a couple minutes of peace and quiet, a pleasant break in my stressful day. Instead, Skippy had only reminded me how lonely I was, and how thoroughly desperate our situation was. "This has been a depressing conversation all around."

"Why is that, Joe? You didn't have great luck with the ladies on Earth before the Ruhar invaded, so your current lack of companionship is nothing new. And the Merry Band of Pirates has been fighting against impossible odds since you broke out of jail on Paradise. Like Major Smythe says; kicking ass and saving humanity against impossible odds is just what you pirates call 'Tuesday'."

That made me chuckle. "Yeah, I guess that's right."

Chapter Three

The *Flying Dutchman* jumped into the outskirts of a star system centered on a dwarf star that was the perfect shade of yellow to remind me of Earth's Sun. Seeing that star reminded me that our Sun was considered a 'yellow dwarf' star which still kinda pissed me off. Not all the emotions brought up when looking at images of that star were happy ones; I was very homesick and very worried about my native planet, and the crew I am sure felt the same way.

Damn, it had been a long time since we had seen the familiar sunlight of our home. The mission UNEF Command sent us on was supposed to be relatively quick; contact a relay station to confirm the Thuranin were not sending a second surveyor ship to Earth, then swing by to recon the situation on Paradise on our return voyage. The whole mission should have taken four, maybe six months at most.

Instead, because the universe hates me, we could not simply contact a Thuranin relay station, we had to board and capture the damned thing. Then we had to wait for data to roll in, so we had flown off to Paradise, and gotten involved in securing the future for the humans trapped there. Even after we confirmed absolutely that the Thuranin were not interested in sending another ship on a long voyage to Earth, we had not been able to return home, because we had to stop the freakin' *Ruhar* from sending a ship! Somehow, sparking a vicious civil war among the Kristang had been the *easiest* solution to that problem. With that unplanned mission accomplished, we were now unable to go back to Earth, because our idiot alien AI beer can couldn't keep himself out of trouble. 'AI' usually meant Artificial Intelligence, but Skippy said there was nothing artificial about him, and he thought the 'A' should stand for 'Awesome'.

My opinion is that regarding Skippy, the 'A' meant 'Asshole'.

I didn't know if we would ever return home; until we could find a magical Elder conduit thingy and Skippy could fix himself and kill the worm that was trying to kill him, we didn't have any way to return home. So I was taking things one step at a time, and not thinking too far ahead to avoid getting my hopes up. The universe loved to stomp on my hopes.

"Joe, are you all right?" Skippy asked. "Your eyes are moist. I would assume this is caused by allergies, but there are no detectable allergens in the air, so I am guessing you are experiencing an emotional response."

"I'm homesick is all, Skippy," I replied, and didn't try to hide my feelings from the crew. From the CIC, Chang nodded and gave me a thumbs up sign.

"Ah. It is understandable that you would have that particular reaction here, for this star system is similar enough to your home; the spectral signature of the star is within two percent of your Sun. The third planet here is habitable and reasonably Earth-like, although gravity there is twelve percent higher and the mean surface temperature is significantly warmer. The fourth planet, our target, is quite like Mars except it is almost fifty percent more massive."

"It's red, right?" I tried to recall some of the less important data from the briefing.

"Correct, the surface dust is reddish from iron oxide, but more grayish than on Mars. And it has a very thin atmosphere, even less than the atmosphere of Mars."

A Sun-like star. An Earth-like third planet. And a red planet like Mars. It did feel like home away from home. "Is there *anything* unique or special about our home system, Skippy?"

"No, not real-" Maybe he sensed we needed to hear something encouraging right then, because he paused. "Several things, actually. The most obvious is that Earth's moon is the same apparent diameter as your Sun when seen from Earth's surface, so a total eclipse of the sun allows a view of the Sun's outer layer. There are only two other planets in the galaxy I know of with that same feature, and only one of them is habitable. Earth is also the only one of the three to evolve intelligent life." He didn't even take the golden opportunity to make a disparaging remark about humanity's lack of intelligence. "Other than natural astrophysical features, I would say the most special and unique element of your star system is that it is home to a species of grubby monkeys who have been *totally* kicking ass out here. All the other stars in the galaxy are burning with jealousy, Joe."

"I thought they were burning hydrogen."

"Oh for-" he sighed in exasperation. "I try to give you a compliment, and you-"

"I'm screwing with you, Skippy. Thank you. Genuinely, thank you. That ranks up there in the Top Ten nicest things you've ever said."

"I have said *ten* nice things to you? Huh, I can only remember three. Damn, I must be slipping."

"It was a joke, Skippy. Now, what are the sensors showing you?"

"They are showing just what I expected, Joe. Our target planet is on the opposite side of the star from the heavily-populated third planet; those two planets are now 390 million kilometers apart. What matters more to our upcoming mission is that a speed-of-light signal will take over twenty minutes to travel from our target to the third planet."

Skippy was correct, signal travel time and not distance is what we cared about. According to his data, the fourth planet had only a couple hundred permanent residents, at a military research facility there. That population number could increase when a supply ship visited twice a year, but the next ship wasn't scheduled to arrive for another two months. In orbit was an armed space station, with weapons for self-defense and to support the bases on the surface. Nothing the Wurgalan had there was a serious threat to the *Flying Dutchman* even in our ship's weakened condition. That assessment was Skippy's analysis, but of course Skippy didn't have much to worry about when missiles started flying and maser cannons began firing searing bolts of energy.

We cared about time because the mission we planned was not one of our usual super ultra mega stealthy infiltrations, where no one knew we were ever there. This was, as Major Smythe described it, strictly a smash-and-grab op. Perfect for pirates. We did not have time to sneak around, and there was no way for us to get at the conduit thingy Skippy needed without all of the native residents knowing something bad was going on. So, we were going in heavy. With support only from Skippy the Meh, we would not be able to prevent emergency signals from being sent out from the planet and space station. About twenty minutes later, those signals would reach the third planet, which had a population of nearly eight million Wurgalan, a rudimentary network of strategic defense satellites, and a frigate permanently stationed in orbit. With the *Dutchman* weakened by repeated disasters and no access to spare parts, even that frigate could be a problem while our star carrier lingered in orbit waiting for the away team to return.

There were some wildcards we could not know until we arrived at the star system, and some others we might not know until we jumped into orbit of the fourth planet. First, where was that Wurgalan frigate? If it was in orbit around the third planet, then it could not possibly know there was a problem at the fourth planet for twenty minutes. Even if that ship happened to be powered up and ready, it would need to climb out to jump distance and transition to near the fourth planet. Simply jumping in near the fourth planet would not make the frigate useful, for its momentum would be carrying it in the wrong direction and would need to burn hard just to match course and speed with the planet. Even so, that ship did not need to match course in order to launch missiles and fire maser cannons and railguns at the *Dutchman*. To be safe, I told Major Smythe to plan the mission to take no longer than thirty minutes from the *Dutchman* jumping in to us jumping away. The ever-confident Smythe admitted that was a difficult task, but I knew secretly he relished the challenge.

If that frigate could not be detected in orbit around the third planet, I intended to abort the mission. There was a risk that another Wurgalan ship was visiting the system, but Skippy was strongly confident he would know of another ship's presence by tapping into the local communications network.

The final risk to us was the military garrison on the fourth planet. A wing of combat dropships was stationed there, and occasionally one or more wings arrived from the third planet for training. The away team would be flying advanced Thuranin Condors, with cover provided by Thuranin Falcons. Our Thuranin dropships were more than a match for anything the Wurgalan could throw at us, but a large number of Wurgalan combat aircraft could overwhelm our air cover and pose a serious threat.

"Ok, so the planets are where we expected them to be," I pressed Skippy for more useful information. "Have you located that frigate yet?"

"No, dumdum. We are six lighthours from the third planet and I'm stuck using this ship's crappy passive sensors. From way out here, a frigate is a tiny dot, Joe. If it is directly in front of, or behind the planet, I won't see able to see it until- Uh! Got it. Yup, frigate is there, orbiting about three thousand kilometers above the third planet. From its infrared signature, the engines are not powered up. Keep in mind Joe, this information is six hours old. That frigate could be anywhere by now."

"But that's unlikely, right?"

"The frigate is an old ship and spends most of its time in orbit. This is not a wealthy or strategically important star system, so funding for operation of that ship is limited."

"Great, I am relieved to hear that. Any news yet about other starships around here?"

"Decrypting military comm traffic now. There was no mention of a visiting starship on the unencrypted civilian comm network, and a warship making a port call at such a backwater planet should be a newsworthy event, like for merchants eager to provide services to the ship and crew. Hmm, wow, the Wurgalan have shockingly inadequate encryption. Or maybe it is only low-priority star systems like this that use a poor encryption scheme. Ok, I'm in the military network. Um, good news and bad news. A pair of destroyers visited this system four months ago; the next scheduled port call from the Wurgalan fleet is not for another three months. So, unless the Wurgalan have a stealthed ship here that has not revealed its presence to the local authorities, there is only that single frigate in system."

"That is great," I refrained from pumping a fist in the air. "What is the bad news?"

"A second wing of dropship fighters has deployed to the fourth planet for training; they were delivered by the frigate seventeen days ago. Let's see if I can find more information, Ok, Ok, this might be good. Yup, I have a report from the wing commander, dated two days ago. She reports training exercises have proceeded as planned, and half the wing is standing down for a four-day maintenance cycle. Joe, that means sixteen of that wing's thirty two dropships will be offline when we arrive."

"It also means we have to contend with sixteen additional combat aircraft, plus the thirty two of the wing permanently stationed there," I reminded him.

"Not all of those thirty two will be flightworthy at the same time, Joe. You know how logistics works."

"So maybe four of them will be offline. That leaves forty four pissed-off fighters crawling all over the sky, and we only have four Falcons to keep them away from our pair of Condors that carry the ground assault team."

"You're forgetting about the *Dutchman*'s own combat power. From orbit, our masers can strike targets in the atmosphere."

"You told me the *Dutchman* is not an ideal orbital weapons platform, and that our targeting sensors are not designed to lock onto small aircraft at a distance." What Skippy told me was that highly maneuverable aircraft flying even a half lightsecond away, would be nearly impossible for the *Dutchman*'s slow-reacting maser cannons to hit. And we couldn't waste precious missiles on mere dropships.

"That is true, Joe, but the Wurgalan don't know that. A couple maser shots from the *Dutchman* should make them scatter their formation, preventing them massing for an attack on the Condors."

"You think."

"I do think, but you are the military tactician, not me. We have Kristang Dragon dropship that could be added to the fight-"

"No. Those Kristang dropships don't have enough technological advantage over the Wurgalan to make me comfortable about using them in combat. It's my job to worry, Skippy, I'm captain of the ship. What do you know about the space station near the fourth plan- This is awkward calling it 'fourth planet'. It's like Mars, so we'll call it, uh, 'Barsoom'? Any objections?" I picked the name from some old sci-fi novels I read as a kid. "No? Good."

"The space station is very close to where I expected it. No issues there."

"Very close? It's just coasting along in orbit. Why isn't it *exactly* where you expected?"

Skippy sighed like an elementary school teacher explaining something over and over to the dumbest kid in the class. "Because, Joe, almost nothing in space is ever exactly static. An orbiting station vents atmosphere, either from leaks or from airlocks and docking bays opening. Solar wind particles push on it unevenly. Launching and recovering dropships pushes the station around. Even personnel walking inside the station make it wobble, as their feet push on the floor and their mass shifts from one location to another. All objects in orbit need to perform regular station-keeping adjustments. And the station is only eighty freakin' meters from where I expected it to be, based on data that is two years old. You big jerk."

"I got the message, Skippy. Colonel Chang, pull the senior leaders together in ten minutes and we'll make a Go-No Go decision on the op."

The decision was Go. We spent two hours maneuvering the ship in normal space, to get it pointed in exactly the right direction and traveling at the exact speed required. Teams got into their dropships, we purged the docking bays of air and slid the doors open. The dropships ran their engines up and everyone involved double-checked things they had already triple-checked. Part of the reason we were not in a hurry was that Skippy had learned there was a briefing by a high-ranking official visiting the main airbase on Barsoom, so we expected few of their birds would be in the air at that time. Pilots forced to listen to a boring speech might be just a bit slower to rush toward their aircraft during an alert, allowing us precious seconds to destroy those dropships while still in their hangars. We hoped.

Finally, I gave the order to jump, and the generic starfield outside was instantly replaced by a starfield with a red dot the size of a Ping-Pong ball that was the planet

ZERO HOUR

Barsoom. Ships come out of a jump almost blind and the *Dutchman* was no exception to that rule, especially now that Skippy no longer had many of his special abilities. To disable the space station, we had to hit it in the right places, and to do that we needed two things. First, to know exactly where the space station was located, and because we couldn't afford for that info to be hours old, we jumped in only eight lightminutes away, on the far side of Barsoom where our gamma ray burst would not be seen from the third planet. The second thing we needed was for our final jump to be short, making it easy for Skippy to be extra super-duper accurate about where we emerged from the next jump. Our targeting sensors would still be resetting after the next jump, so Skippy had to pre-program precise firing solutions into our targeting computers before the jump; our weapons simply had to follow instructions.

Skippy got an exact fix on the space station's location and as soon as our overworked drive coils were ready, we jumped again to launch the assault. The reddish orb of Barsoom loomed large on the main display, and something zoomed past on the screen faster than my eyes could follow; fortunately Skippy's firing solutions were deadly accurate and we nailed the space station's defense shield projectors with three maser blasts before our ship zipped past. Missiles that were ready to go before our jump rocketed out of their launch tubes and impacted the surprised and now-defenseless station, tearing into its central hub and causing it to break apart, sending the rotating arms flying off into space. Less than eight seconds after the *Flying Dutchman* emerged from jump, the space station was no longer a threat to us, and no longer capable of providing cover for the planet below.

The planet. It was growing fast, too fast in the display. "All dropships away," Chang announced in the CIC as my heart was in my throat from seeing the dusty red soil of Barsoom approaching way too fast. I mean, if I lived down there, I could see my house, we appeared to be that close. "Masers firing at surface targets. Second volley of missiles are away. We are clear." As I opened my mouth to shout a panicked order, Desai executed pre-planned instructions and we jumped for a third time. This time, we emerged behind our prior course, as if we'd gone back in time. The ship was still racing toward the planet, but this time the planet was farther away and we were not in immediate danger of crashing into Barsoom.

"Skippy?" I asked.

Anticipating my question, he answered. "Jump drive is in acceptable condition, however we will not be able to jump again for another nine minutes. Jumping not recommended for at least thirteen minutes. The space station is disabled, and our maser cannons knocked out shield generators at the airbase. Hmm, that was good shooting, even if I am praising myself. Our missiles will be impacting in three, two, one, impact. Assessing battle damage now. Secondary explosions. Wow! That was a *big* one. We must have hit an ammo dump or fuel storage tanks." One intelligence item Skippy had not been able to obtain had been a detailed schematic of the main airbase on Barsoom, apparently it was under constant construction and the Wurgalan were not good at updating their files in a timely manner. Due to lack of data, Skippy had been forced to guess which targets to hit while we were still outside the star system. "Picking up alarms now; yup, the octopussies are scrambling to launch all available aircraft. Which, I think, is going to be a lot less now that our missiles ransacked that base. Hmm, Ok, there is a formation of four dropships that were already in the air on a training flight. The good news is they are not carrying a missile load, so they only have masers to shoot with, and they are low on fuel. The bad news is they are within sixty kilometers of our target, and their leader has told her fellow pilots she intends to crash into our ships if that is necessary to stop us. And, more aircraft are launching now. Some of their aircraft were in hardened underground shelters. Uh oh, it looks like there are a *lot* of those underground shelters. They can't all have aircraft in them! Damn it, those shelters weren't on the current schematic of the airbase!"

"We can't afford to expend any more antiship missiles now," I declared unhappily. "Can we target those shelters with our maser cannons? Hit the ones that have not yet launched aircraft?"

"Joe, many of those shelters may be empty, hitting them would be like playing whack-a-mole by trying to hit all the holes. And our masers are not powerful enough to punch down through that hardened material to hit the shelters."

"No," I agreed, "but if we keep up a constant fire on those shelters, aircraft will have to stay in there; they won't be able to launch."

"Oh," Skippy's voice was chastened. "Duh. I should have thought of that. Targeting solutions are loaded into fire control computers now."

"Colonel Chang, let's make the Wurgalan keep their heads down," I ordered.

"With pleasure, Sir," he replied, and turned his attention to the people at the weapons stations in CIC.

"Joe I have to caution you," Skippy added. "While we are firing masers, we are still able to maintain stealth so the Wurgalan will not discover what type of ship this is, but they will get a lock on our position."

"Understood, Skippy, we will take that-" The ship rocked slightly.

"That was a near-miss by a maser cannon on the surface," Skippy warned. "No damage to the ship. Enemy has launched missiles at us. Seven missiles inbound."

I knew we had an advantage from being at the top of the planet's gravity well, and the missile's wildly hot boost-phase exhaust was giving away their positions. "Any way we can hit those missiles from here, thin out their numbers?"

"That would be waste of time from here," Skippy advised. "By the time our maser bolts reach them, the missiles will have maneuvered out of the way. I believe our point-defense systems can cope with seven missiles of Wurgalan-level technology. But, Joe, we will need to pause our maser bombardment of the surface."

"All right," I clenched my fists. "Chang, continue hitting those aircraft shelters until Skippy instructs you to break off. I don't like leaving our dropships to fight by themselves."

"Raptors, this is Raptor Lead," Samantha 'Fireball' Reed heard in her headset. "*Dutchman* needs to break off their attack to deal with vampires, it's up to us now." The combat air patrol leader used the American standard brevity code 'vampire' to designate a hostile antiship missile, in this case alien antiship missiles attacking their star carrier. The pirate ship that was their only ride home. Sami's hand clenched when she heard the *Dutchman* was under attack, then she forced her hand to relax so she could control her Falcon dropship. There wasn't anything she could do to directly help the *Dutchman*; what she could do was perform her own assigned task quickly and efficiently, so the mission could be completed and the *Dutchman* could jump away to safety. Or to comparative safety, in a galaxy that was entirely hostile to a ship full of pirate humans. "Raptor Two," the flight leader called Sami, "there are four bandits southwest of us at Angels thirty one, you are cleared hot to engage. Be advised Skippy says those four bandits do not, repeat, do *not* have missiles, so any birds in the air will be yours."

"Roger that," Sami acknowledged with a tight smile.

"Fireball," the leader added, "splash those bandits if you have to, but the priority is to keep them away from the Condors."

"Understood," this time Sami's smile inside the visor of her helmet was broader. She saw the four enemy aircraft on her display, they were maintaining a tight formation and gaining speed and altitude rapidly, closing the distance to her even before she turned. With a flick of the little finger on her left hand, she designated the four bandits as hostile and locked targeting sensors on them. "Fireball is engaged." With another finger she throttled up her engines, snapping her expression to a frown as the turbines spooled up only partway. Before the mission, Skippy had loaded revised software into all six Thuranin dropships so they would perform as if they were Kristang craft. In an emergency, there was a red button Sami could press to override the new software and restore the flight control system to its nominal Thuranin specs for full performance, but that would need to be an extreme emergency indeed. Until then, the Falcon was limited to performing like a Kristang Dragon dropship, which Sami had to remind herself could blow away the hottest combat aircraft on Earth.

With her Falcon accelerating downward toward the four enemy aircraft, the distance was closing rapidly. Sami knew her duty was not to be a hotshot glory hog; she also knew the surest way to keep those four Wurgalan fighters away from the vulnerable Condors was if those Wurgalan craft were hot pieces of shrapnel raining over the dusty red surface of Barsoom. "One missile each," she advised her copilot, "let's not waste ordnance until we know what these octopussies can do." Unlike the dropships, their Thuranin air-to-air missiles were not restricted to operating as if they were Kristang weapons; the thought was that in the heat and confusion of battle no one had time to notice missiles flying slightly faster or more accurately than expected.

"Roger that, we are now within the engagement envelope," Sami's copilot Wu acknowledged. "Birds affirm," she announced as all four missiles synced with the Falcon's fire control system and acquired their assigned targets. "Birds away ripple," she stated as the Falcon rocked slightly, adjusting automatically as four missiles were ejected simultaneously.

On the wraparound display that substituted for cockpit windows, Sami could see four bright flashes, then four wispy white contrails. Immediately, she reduced power and turned to the right. "Switch to guns," she ordered. "I'm putting us between the bandits and the Condors." On the display, she saw the four bandits breaking formation and splitting apart in reaction to the incoming missiles, and she saw her missiles streaking after the enemy. A Falcon carried sixteen multipurpose missiles. Sixteen seemed like a lot when Sami had been used to a fighter carrying four or six missiles in the US Air Force, but with alien aircraft possessing defensive maser beams that could intercept missiles, in a worst-case scenario she may need all sixteen just to kill four Wurgalan fighters. The distant flashes of their star carrier's maser cannon pummeling the airbase had stopped, and Sami could see more enemy aircraft launching from the airbase at the edge of her sensor coverage. Two of the Falcons had moved to intercept, while Raptor Three was flying cover close to the pair of descending Condors. "This could turn into one hell of a furball," she murmured worriedly, "let's hope the ground-pounders get this over with ASAP."

The lead ground-pounder would have heartily agreed with Sami's sentiment as he braced himself with his knees in the Condor, which had completed its non-stealthy and fiery entry to Barsoom's thin atmosphere. Over the cockpit channel, Major Smythe could hear the two pilots tersely discussing how the dropship's shields had been strained by protecting the Condor's leading edges and belly from superheated plasma created by the falling craft burning a hole down through the air. As the pilots were not yet worried about the condition of the shields or any other onboard system, he mentally tuned them out and concentrated on understanding the tactical situation.

The six dropships had launched from the *Flying Dutchman* just above the upper edge of the atmosphere, and had scorched their way downward on a minimum-time-to-target flight profile. With only thirty minutes for the entire operation, they could not waste time getting down to the surface, so stealth had been thrown out the window along with any attempt to conceal their objective. The two Condors had flown directly at the objective, with the four Falcons flying cover between the objective and that main airbase.

Smythe had been in bad helicopter rides during his time in the military, when he had prayed for the aircraft to stop bouncing up and down in a vicious storm. The ride down to the surface of Barsoom was worse. The Condor, a remarkable piece of advanced Thuranin engineering, had bounced and rocked and rattled until Smythe thought it would shake itself and him apart. Even with sophisticated systems to compensate for external forces and protect the occupants from being crushed during the six-Gee descent, Smythe had found it hard to breathe, as if an elephant was sitting on his chest. Now that the decent was over and the Condor was racing at low altitude toward the objective, Smythe pulled up the tactical display in his helmet's visor and was almost shocked to see that, so far, everything was proceeding according to plan.

"Executing pop-up in three, two, one, now." The pilot advised, and Smythe was first pressed down into his seat, then briefly experienced zero gravity at the top of the arc, as the Condor and its twin leapt up to gain altitude and a line of sight to the objective.

Their objective was part of an Elder facility that had been discovered in ancient times by the Maxolhx, who had also long ago removed everything they thought might be useful or interesting. The Maxolhx had no interest in the star system that was far from any active wormhole, so the planets there had remained uninhabited until a wormhole shift made the system more accessible. The first species to stake a claim had been the Kristang, but because of a long-standing dispute between the Kristang's patrons the Thuranin and the Wurgalan's patrons the Bosphuraq, the Kristang had been encouraged to give the system to the Wurgalan. As this 'encouragement' was delivered in the form of orbital bombardment by a trio of Bosphuraq battleships, the Kristang were quickly persuaded of the strength of argument in favor of the Wurgalan. Since the time Wurgalan took up residence in a star system which had nothing special going for it, they had also taken possession of the Elder site on the fourth planet, which they had absolutely no idea what to do with. The site had been fairly stripped by the Maxolhx, so even though the Wurgalan were desperate to gain a technological advantage over their hated rivals the Kristang, they could not find anything useful among the Elder artifacts. No wanting to appear ungrateful that their patrons had given the star system to them, the Wurgalan constructed a dome over the Elder site and then, as years and then centuries passed without anyone knowing what to do with the site, they mostly forgot about it. The remaining Elder objects under the dome became curiosities, with rare VIPs who bothered to visit the fourth planet occasionally being offered a tour. Every four or five centuries, a Wurgalan scientist requested to examine the Elder equipment, and when no new knowledge or insight was gained, the dome went back into its peaceful slumber.

"The objective looks abandoned, just as Skippy said," Smythe noted with satisfaction as his helmet visor displayed images from the Condor's nose camera. A layer of red dust coated the dome, piling up thick around the ribs and thinner toward the middle of the glass sections. The actual dome was long-neglected, however the underground military base that had originally been established to provide security for the dome was still active, as evidenced by the presence of two transport aircraft parked on their landing pads. Smythe could see miniature pink dust devils swirling across the pads as those aircraft spun up their turbines for takeoff. "Can you knock out those transports?"

"Affirmative," the Condor's lead pilot responded tightly, and as Smythe watched, the Condor's maser cannons ripped into the nearly-defenseless aircraft, slicing off the tail of one as it tilted toward the sky to lift off. It crashed back to the ground, wobbling a bit as the pilots attempted to regain control. Then both aircraft became flares of light on the display when a pair of missiles from the Condor obliterated them.

"Good shooting," Smythe said emotionlessly, his attention already elsewhere. Skippy had learned from schematics that tunnels connected the military base to the dome, so if enemy soldiers were pouring out of the ground into the dome, he had no way of knowing at the moment. No matter; they would stick to the plan which had worked well so far. "Execute Break-In," he used the term for the preferred option for gaining quick access to the interior of the dome. Quick was the key; once his team reached the ground, they had only seven minutes to locate, secure and retrieve their objective before the Condors were scheduled to return to the *Flying Dutchman*.

"Execute Break-In, roger that," the pilot acknowledged. A maser cannon under the chin of each Condor fired, not in a searing destructive burst, but in a sustained surgical beam that carved neat holes in the glass of the dome. The material was not actually glass, Smythe knew, and it did not shatter; the edges of the near-circular holes were glowing orange where the maser beam had cut through, and Smythe could see the dome material was thicker than expected. The extra thickness had not been a problem, as the fire control system controlling the maser cannon had simply increased power and duration based on sensor feedback. "We have access," the pilot stated needlessly, as everyone aboard the Condor was watching the nose camera feed in their helmet visors. "Bringing us in to hover, let's be quick about it."

Of the four Wurgalan fighters Lt. Reed had engaged, two fell victim to missiles she ripple-fired in her first volley; one of the missiles that missed its first target had circled around and reengaged another Wurgalan craft, forcing it to desperately maneuver away and taking it out of the immediate fight. The last enemy fighter had been lucky; its defensive maser had clipped one of Sami's missiles and sent it cartwheeling across the sky to self-destruct uselessly.

After launching her first four missiles, Sami had broken away from a direct course toward the enemy, as her Thuranin air-to-air missiles had not needed any guidance or control from their launching ship. Her greater altitude and airspeed allowed her to dictate the terms of the air battle; she could engage, break away and reengage at will, while the enemy could only react to her moves. For almost a full minute, the two dropships tangled across the sky, their maser cannons spitting beams of microwave energy when their computers thought they had a good firing solution. Both ships were hit without significant effect; the glancing maser bolts being deflected and absorbed by defense shield. Then the Wurgalan ship that was being chased by Sami's last missile lost its battle as the missile scored a direct hit and turned it into a ball of sooty plasma. Seeing it was now truly alone, the remaining enemy fighter broke away from engagement with Sami, turning to fly at full power toward the two descending Condors.

Sami reacted immediately, toggling off one of her precious twelve missiles at the enemy and hooking her Falcon hard around in a nearly 180 degree turn. The abrupt maneuver bled off airspeed energy and was almost the last thing she was supposed to do in air combat, but it could not be helped. Before the enemy changed course, she had been leading it away from the pair of Condors and now she found herself badly out of position. The Condors were especially vulnerable at the moment, she could see on her display the large Thuranin dropships were popping up as they performed their final approach to the dome. One Falcon was between the Wurgalan fighter and the Condors, but that Falcon had troubles of its own as a pair of enemy aircraft were approaching from the south.

And Sami herself had another problem about to go from imminent to active: three enemy fighters coming straight at her from the airbase. Raptor Lead and his wingman were already fully engaged in a swirling furball with eight Wurgalan so she could not expect help from them.

"Oh, hell," she said to herself. "Four against one again."

The large Thuranin dropship called a 'Condor' by humans was not designed to insert special operations troops, it was simply a transport that was most often used for cargo. The Merry Band of Pirates had improvised with help from Skippy, and as the Condor slowed to a halt in midair above one of the twenty meter diameter holes in the dome, the back ramp dropped open quickly and Smythe jumped out with his team. No sooner had the last pirate cleared the ramp than the pilot increased power to take the big and vulnerable Condor out of hover, to go streaking away a mere hundred meters off the surface. The second Condor disgorged its troops seconds later, and followed the lead ship away while Smythe's team was still falling through the thin air.

The air of Barsoom was thin, mostly blown away by the solar wind eons ago. To slow and control the descent of a single armor-suited pirate would have required an enormous parachute or balloon, too large to be deployed with two teams of eight dropping in formation through holes a mere twenty meters across. Instead of parachutes or balloons, each person in a Kristang powered-armor suit was suspended beneath a jet-powered drone. The drones at first descended with their precious cargo, acting only to slow the descent, then each drone increased power to hover as they passed over the hole. With the drone momentarily stationary, the tether holding the trooper stretched to lower the person safely through the hole and to within three meters of the interior floor, at which point the tether released from the trooper's harness. In the blink of an eye the tether retracted into its drone, and the drone zipped away to be replaced by the next drone in formation. Smythe was the fourth person to drop through the breached dome, and as the tether lowered him quickly, he saw movement on the far side of the dome. Octopussies, two of them.

The Wurgalan were referred to as 'octopussies' by humans, just as humans had nicknamed the Ruhar 'hamsters' and the Kristang 'lizards'. The Wurgalan were not octopi any more than the Kristang were lizards, but military tradition demanded enemies to be given a derisive name, so 'octopussies' was an obvious and universally accepted choice.

In truth, although the Wurgalan did appear a bit like large land-dwelling octopi, they had only seven legs, not eight, and so one of them might more accurately be called a 'septapus'. Although, in addition to their seven combination arm-legs, they had a prehensile tentacle on their foreheads, so 'octopus' was close enough. Seven legs gave a Wurgalan a lot to keep track of when moving around, and many options for locomotion. Their fastest gait was to use their two front arm-legs together; stretching them out in front and then flinging them under their bodies as they ran. To each side, pairs of arm-legs could be used together, or only one arm-leg on each side if the Wurgalan were carrying something like a weapon. The seventh arm-leg in the back was held out to the back as a sort of tail for balance when moving at high speed.

Smythe considered that information in a flash as he dropped down through the opening in the shattered dome, and saw movement with the corner of his vision. In addition to providing a physical description of the Wurgalan, focusing on relevant characteristics, capabilities and weaknesses, Skippy had given his opinion of Wurgalan culture. "If you think the Kristang and Thuranin are awful MFers, then you will really hate the Wurgalan." As the Kristang had considered humans to be a disgustingly useless low-tech client species, the Wurgalan had a client species of their own; the Urgar. With Wurgalan technology still measurably behind that of the rival Kristang, one might wonder why the Wurgalan deserved, needed or would bother with a client species of their own. That question was almost moot, as under the not-tender guidance of the Wurgalan, the Urgar had become almost extinct. The last few million Urgar, living out a miserable existence on a harsh colony planet after the Wurgalan had taken their homeworld, would welcome the cruel Kristang as saviors if they had the option.

An option the Urgar were unlikely to ever enjoy.

As Smythe completed his split-second recollection of everything relevant he knew about the Wurgalan, he swung his rifle around and fixed the targeting crosshairs in the visor of his Kristang armored suit at the Wurgalan on the right, just as the creature was bringing its own weapon to bear on Smythe. Before Smythe could squeeze the trigger, the Wurgalan and its companion were blown backwards in a hail of explosive-tipped rounds. The pirates who came through the opening in the dome before Smythe saw the threat before he did, and they dealt with the Wurgalan quickly and efficiently. The rounds impacting the octopussies not only exploded, they penetrated the suits before exploding, blowing chunks of alien in all directions.

"Their suits aren't armored," Smythe observed over the open channel as he scanned the dome, spinning around 360 on the tether and not seeing any other threats. Operation of the tether was fully automatic unless he took manual control in an emergency. When the tether controller saw, through sensors on the bottom of his boots, that Smythe was less than a meter from the surface, the tether released itself from his harness and he dropped lightly to the hard, smooth surface. Concrete, or something like that, he observed in the back of his mind. Concrete, hard and smooth but not slippery. And he realized it was not entirely smooth, it was spiderwebbed with small cracks and there was a fine layer of pink dust covering everything, including the Elder artifact that dominated the center of the dome. The facility was, as Skippy had assured the pirates, neglected by the Wurgalan. There was a military outpost attached to the dome, but it was generally staffed by only a half dozen octopussies as a sort of honor guard, whose main function was to escort the occasionally important visitor. That explained the lack of armor on the suits of the two now-dead Wurgalan; they had likely donned whatever gear they had available on short notice when the pirate dropships were observed screaming down from orbit directly at the dome.

In his powered suit and the low gravity, Smythe crossed the dome within seconds to stand over the dead octopussies. Thick purple blood was oozing slowly from the bodies, simultaneously freezing and boiling in the cold and low atmospheric pressure now that the dome had been breached. Smythe could see the enemy soldiers had come into the dome from a stairway set into the floor; two other stairways were set at 120 degrees apart. Teams were already poised near all three stairways, and at Smythe's order, a pair of grenades were dropped into each stairway. One grenade of each pair was set for concussion effect, the other for an intense thermal burn. With all the pirates laying flat, the grenades coordinated over the taclink between the suits and exploded in series; concussives first followed by thermal a split second later. The floor of the dome rocked and more cracks appeared in the surface. Near the holes where the dome had been breached, the translucent material cracked and fell in to crash onto the floor, creating wider gaps in the dome. The breaching holes had been cut near the edges of the dome to avoid the masers hitting the Elder artifact in the center; Skippy had assured Smythe that mere grenades would not collapse the main structure of the dome onto the artifact.

The instant the burning gouts of flame from the stairwells had subsided, teams including Smythe were racing toward the artifact. "This is different, Major," Ranger Mychalchyk observed unhappily. In preparing for the mission, the team had studied 3D images provided by Skippy, based on whatever data he had been able to collect from the edge of the star system. Clearly, the images Skippy had access to were incomplete or out of date. Parts of the artifact were missing, and new, unknown parts were attached to it.

"It is," Smythe replied calmly. "The Wurgalan may have removed pieces for study, then reinstalled them. The piece we need is in there," he pointed up and to the center of what looked like a modern art sculpture combined with an oil rig. "Cutters, clear these two pieces away," he forced himself to be calm as the counter in the corner of his visor indicated they were already behind schedule.

Four people equipped with plasma torches lost no time in firing up their cutters at full intensity, flooding the dome with harsh light and causing everyone's visors to automatically darken. Which is why the Wurgalan were able to surprise them.

Wurgalan were not stupid, and although the soldiers assigned to the honor guard at the dome were very much out of practice at combat, they knew to keep away from the three stairwells after the airlock doors there had been shattered and incinerated, along with two unlucky soldiers who had been about to open a door and charge up the stairs. The remaining two Wurgalan, in their lightweight ceremonial armor, knew their duty was to protect the precious Elder artifact from what the surveillance cameras showed was a Kristang raiding party. If the dome had been equipped with maser cannons on the interior, the Wurgalan would have activated them. If the honor guard had been equipped with hunter-killer drones, they would have used those. If their rifles had been supplied with armor-piercing or explosive-tipped rounds, they would have used those. Because Wurgalan leadership was concerned about potential damage to the artifact more than the extremely unlikely possibility of an assault on the dome, all the honor guard had for weapons were rifles with low-velocity rounds. Any attack on the star system would logically begin with strikes on the populated third planet, then with an orbital bombardment and ground assault on the airbase of the fourth planet. Only when Wurgalan forces had been defeated across the star system, the strategic defense plan anticipated, would an enemy turn their attention to the useless curiosity of the Elder artifact under the dome. A raid focused on the artifact had never been considered in the defense plan.

The remaining two Wurgalan emerged into the dome through an access hatch concealed in the floor under part of the original artifact that had long ago been taken away.

Smythe's first indication that anything was amiss occurred when a pirate applying a plasma torch to the artifact had the torch knocked out of his hands to go spinning along the floor. The torch cut out when the trigger was released, which saved the user from having his legs severed by the torch. His armored suit sustained no more than dents under the impact of the low-velocity rounds even though both Wurgalan concentrated their rifles on one pirate.

"Do not hit the artifact!" Smythe shouted as his team turned their attention to the multi-legged adversaries under the Elder device. When Smythe first learned the Wurgalan were structurally similar to an octopus, he had been concerned about an enemy who could stand on two feet and theoretically hold five weapons. Skippy had scoffed at that foolish notion, explaining that was no more likely than a two-armed human simultaneously controlling two rifles. The brain of a Wurgalan could only track one target at a time, and having to control seven limbs plus a prehensile antenna actually was a burden on a Wurgalan brain's processing speed. Attempts over the centuries to genetically enhance their thinking speed had run into the immovable obstacle of their basic brain architecture.

Limitations of Wurgalan physiology mattered, because despite their reaction speed and eye-tentacle accuracy was not hugely better than the elite Merry Band of Pirates. Without Major Smythe having to explain further, four pirates flicked switches on their rifles to deactivate the explosive tips of their rounds, and select a high-impact mode that caused the round to mushroom on contact. While the two octopussies were still firing, they were hit by over three dozen Kristang rounds. The light ceremonial armor surprisingly protected them, but the kinetic energy of the rounds lifted the two aliens and flung them to go skittering across the floor. Across the floor and out from under the protection of the artifact. Again, no orders were needed as the four pirates on cover detail flicked switches again. The rounds that followed the change of mode had their penetration and explosive ability restored. In an instant, the two brave but hapless octopussies were sent to whatever afterlife they believed in.

"Clear!" Captain Chandra shouted calmly. "Sweep the floor for more of these damned concealed hatches."

"Chan," Smythe asked the stricken pirate, who had already gotten back on his feet and retrieved the plasma torch, "are you all right?"

"Yes, Major," Chan replied as he handed the torch to another soldier. Chan felt mostly able to return to duty, he also knew that was not the way the Merry Band of Pirates operated. His armored suit may have undiscovered damage that might slow him down, and the raiding party could not afford any delays. So while Mychalchyk took the plasma torch and got to work with it, Chan unslung his rifle and replaced the Ranger on cover duty.

The plasma torches quickly cut through the surrounding structure, exposing the section Skippy wanted the pirates to bring back. As the interfering sections clattered to the floor and pirates leaped out of the way, Smythe hopped up onto the dais to examine the conduit or whatever it was. "Skippy didn't tell us to expect all this extra equipment attached to it," he stated flatly with concern. The actual conduit was slightly over two meters long, and easily carried by one person in a powered suit and low gravity. With all the potentially important equipment attached, it was large and bulky enough to require two people to transport it. "Cut it away at the base here," Smythe made a snap decision. "Sappers, blow the dome wall, we're going out that way." He eye-clicked through a menu inside his visor, blinking to select secure communications mode and sent a message to the waiting Condors that his team would require a ground extraction, without the tethers of the original plan.

The team worked quickly and efficiently; two soldiers carried the conduit out a hole blasted in the dome's side wall, covered by the others. As Smythe stepped out of the dome onto the dusty surface of Barsoom, a glance at the clock in the corner of his visor almost drew a smile. Two minutes, thirty four seconds remaining. They were actually ahead of schedule. Part of the extra time would be eaten up by the Condors landing and loading the bulky Elder conduit aboard, but that possibility had been baked into the schedule.

Now all Smythe needed were the Condors. Where the hell were they?

"This is interesting," Sami said quietly as her full concentration was used on the unfamiliar and to her knowledge, unprecedented maneuver she was flying. In the US Air

Force, she had been trained to use the terms Weeds, Low, Medium, High, and Very High to describe target altitudes ranging anywhere from scraping treetops to above forty thousand feet. Because those terms were utterly meaningless in airspace combat, pilots serving with the Merry Band of Pirates had come up with their own terminology. Dust, Air, Thin, Orbit, and Beyond, with 'Thin' being anywhere technically still within an atmosphere but high enough that aerodynamic controls were inoperative in the thin air.

When Lt. Samantha Reed thought of the term 'Dust', she used to consider that to mean flying close to the surface of any world, whether it had an atmosphere or not, and whether the surface below was dust, trees or water. With the surface of Barsoom consisting of fine red dust, grainy pebbles of red sand, and dust-coated rocks, the term 'Dust' was entirely appropriate. On Barsoom, the combination of dust and an atmosphere caused trouble for Sami, because it limited her options.

When the lone Wurgalan fighter had, to Sami's relief, been destroyed by one of her missiles before the enemy got within range to fire masers at the pair of Condors, she had switched her attention to the three enemy dropships racing in from the airbase. The Condors had dropped off Major Smythe's team and were free to maneuver defensively for a few minutes, so they were proceeding directly away at high speed while calling out a warning that they needed to return to the dome very soon.

In a chaotic yet brief air battle, Sami had destroyed one of the three enemy with a missile, then to her surprise had shot down a second with a snap shot maser cannon blast. That had been a momentarily satisfying victory Sami had not been able to acknowledge with even a smile, before her copilot warned their own defensive shield and stealth field had been seriously degraded during the encounter, as the shields had deflected multiple maser bolts and two exploding warheads of near-miss enemy missiles. The shield emitters needed over a minute to recharge before they could protect Sami's Falcon from even a single maser bolt shot by the two Wurgalan fighters hunting her, as another lone enemy aircraft had joined the fight.

With her shields weakened and stealth compromised, Sami had considered her options in a flash. Streaking along close to the deck was no good; the turbulence of her high-speed passage through even the thin atmosphere would stir up dust on the ground below like a fingernail scraping the red soil, leaving reddish clouds pointing the enemy directly at her.

What she decided to do, she considered as she allowed herself a tight smile, was worthy of a Bishop Award for 'Craziest Idea Dreamed Up Out Of Nothing'. The air of Barsoom, while thin, was still sufficiently dense to stir up the surface dust when winds blew hard. Dust storms on the planet could spring up and disappear quickly, or they could last for days and build so strong they created dust devils; the local equivalent of tornados.

Sami was hovering her Falcon inside the tightly swirling cone of a dust devil, while outside the pair of Wurgalan fighters grew increasingly frustrated trying to find her. To the Wurgalan, the Falcon they were chasing dove to the deck then behind a ridge, but when the Wurgalan craft followed, their enemy was nowhere to be seen. "They won't orbit this area forever," Sami said unnecessarily to her copilot, who could see the situation on her own display.

"No they won't. Forty two seconds to recharge shield emitters," Wu added, knowing that information was on the display in front of Sami but that the pilot was busy keeping their Falcon inside the rapidly-changing dust devil. A moment before, Wu had feared the dust devil would dissipate, then it found new strength and must have flown over an area of particularly fine dust particles because the air outside was instantly obscured to a pink haze. "Turbines are heating up," she warned. "This dust may be melting onto the fan blades." That was a problem they had limited ability to deal with; polarizing the fan blades to repel dust might be detected by enemy sensors. "We'll deal with it," she decided, considering they would only remain inside the dust devil until their shields were fully recovered.

"Where are the bandits?" Sami asked.

"Still no joy on the passive gear," Wu said tersely. "We're picking up intermittent blips from their taclink signals but not strong enough to get a firing solution on their location. They're still searching for us." With the enemy dropships in stealth, and the Falcon's sensors obscured by the magnetically-charged dust surrounding them, they could not detect the enemy's presence other than through brief backscatter of signals the Wurgalan shared with each other over their tactical data link. "We can't launch without-"

Her problem was solved by the enemy's impatience; the Falcon's threat console lit up as the Thuranin dropship was swept by an active sensor pulse. "Eighty seven," Wu warned, indicating that enemy sensor pulse was eighty seven percent of the power needed to pinpoint the Falcon's location.

While the enemy's initial sensor pulse was thirteen percent too weak to give away the Falcon's position, it was a million percent stronger than Wu needed to determine exactly where the transmitting aircraft was. "Tracking one!" She announced. "Solid lock!"

Sami glanced away from the cockpit navigation display to check the condition of the shield emitters; they still had twelve seconds remaining until they regained full capacity. Close enough, Sami decided. Plus, the Condors had turned and were on their way back to the dome to retrieve Major Smythe's team. It was time to stop delaying and distracting the enemy, and start killing them. "Launch two birds at that bandit," she ordered, not needing to specify whether to fire heat-seeking or radar-guided missiles, as the deadly Thuranin weapons were multipurpose killers; capable of homing in on a target using active and passive sensors covering the entire electromagnetic spectrum.

"Birds affirm," Wu confirmed targeting sensors had a lock on the enemy's location and the two missiles had received the data, "birds away."

"Here we go," Sami advanced the throttles and stood the Falcon on its tail, flying straight up and quickly clearing the dust devil. Enemy sensor pulses were now both fully able to detect the Falcon and fully unnecessary, because the energy radiating from the Thuranin craft's engines left a thermal trail its stealth field could not conceal. "Switching to guns."

The Condors came in low and fast over a ridge to the north; Smythe had been tracking them in his helmet visor through the encrypted tactical datalink but seeing them was still startling. One moment, the horizon was clear and the next moment two large shapes loomed in front of him. With both air-space craft in stealth, Smythe knew his helmet was filling in the image for him; without visual enhancement all he would have seen is a very faint ripple of dust particles in the thin air.

The pilots were showing off, Smythe thought as one side of his mouth curled up in an admiring smile; he couldn't fault the pilots for wishing to arrive in style. As the Condors cleared the ridge, they flared in a synchronized maneuver, main turbines howling in reverse and thruster jets on belly and nose firing to slow the craft for landing. At the last second, as it appeared the two big dropships would fulfill their names and drop to crash into the red-gray dusty ground, they straightened out and made a final correction for landing, setting down exactly on the markers laid down by Smythe's team.

"Hurry," the lead pilot urged, "multiple bandits inbound."

Perhaps the pilots had not been showing off after all, Smythe reflected as he waited impatiently for the rear ramp to open. Knowing the ground team would be anxious to get aboard, both ships had cracked their ramps open as they flared for landing, and the crew chiefs used the emergency procedure of allowing the big ramps to slam down against their stops rather than the leisurely process of cycling them down used for cargo loading. Smythe and his team chafed at the delay anyway; it pleased Smythe that no one broke procedure by rushing up the ramp until the crew chiefs reported they were fully down and locked. First aboard were the two soldiers carrying the precious-but-awkward-to-handle Elder conduit device, while everyone else had their rifles ready to provide cover. Both Condors had their chin and side maser turrets pointed at the dome, prepared to rain blistering hellfire on anyone who threatened the band of pirates. No threat emerged, Smythe saw with great satisfaction and, if he were completely honest with himself, a tiny bit of disappointment. He was last aboard; no sooner were his boots halfway up the ramp, racing forward in the hastened pace of powered armor, when the ramp began cycling closed and he felt the big Condor lift off. That rapid dust-off maneuver was reserved for combat emergencies because of the danger it posed to unsecured personnel. As Smythe raced forward and was caught by the restraining net, he knew the danger was less than it seemed. His Kristang suit would stabilize his movement and prevent him from falling out the sides of the half-open ramp, and the pilots took off in a nose-down position. The worst that could have happened to Smythe was bruising his dignity and he cared nothing about that. "Clear!" He shouted as the nanofiber netting held him securely upright.

Just in time. The pilot stood the big Thuranin dropship on its tail and fired the main jets hard, surging for the safety of orbit.

Sami's fingers moved to turn the Falcon to deal with a new threat, then she heard a voice in her earpiece just as Wu launched another missile. "This is Raptor Lead, all ships, knock it off. Repeat, knock it off," he issued the order to disengage from air combat. "Bingo to home plate." Then he added, "Good shooting, people."

Sami's reaction was to pull backward on the touchscreen controls with one finger, pulling the Falcon's nose up, and the flick of another finger advanced the throttles. "Oops," she shot a guilty smile at her copilot. "Raptor Lead, we have a bird in the air. Should we abort?"

The reply was delayed for a moment while the lead pilot checked his own display, Sami hoped he noticed that she had launched the missile before he gave the order to disengage. "That's a negative, Fireball. We could use the cover. All ships, conserve your missiles, we never know when we'll need them."

Wu grinned and gave Sami a thumbs up as the pilot pushed the dropship to full power, and it climbed toward their precisely scheduled rendezvous with 'home plate'; their star carrier. Both women kept one eye on the display tracking the lone missile as it pursued the limping enemy aircraft. The Wurgalan dropship dove for the deck, then the alien pilots must have realized they had no chance to escape, for the dropship's nose pulled up and two crew ejected. The ejection seats carried the octopussies up and away; the Thuranin missile bored in toward the easy target of the unguided dropship, punching halfway through before exploding.

"Congrats, people, I believe that is a grand slam," Raptor Lead said with satisfaction. All hostile aircraft engaged had been destroyed, with only minor damage to the pirates' ships. Perhaps it had never been a fair fight, pitting Thuranin technology against the Wurgalan and highly-trained, determined and focused pirates against bored alien garrison pilots. Yet, it was the first time the Merry Band of Pirates had been in air-to-air combat, and they had triumphed. Raptor Lead smiled broadly as he added "Monkeys kicked ass today."

The ass kicking was not exactly complete when the six dropships cleared the atmosphere. They still had to rendezvous with and be taken aboard the star carrier, which was nowhere in sight, and completely out of communications range. While that was not unexpected because it was part of the plan, it was unnerving.

After soaring above the last wisps of Barsoom's thin atmosphere, the two Condors went to full power, with the smaller and more nimble Falcons throttling back, hanging behind to protect against any last-minute enemy attempts to intercept. In formation, they raced straight away from the planet, aiming at nothing more than an invisible point in space. When they reached that imaginary point, they needed to be traveling at a precise speed, on a very exact course, then follow an invisible line through space. Thanks to exhaustive practice and the processing power of the Thuranin flight control computers, all six ships hit the mark exactly, and cut thrust. "Head's up, people. Shields on double aft, prepare for radiation event." The other five ships acknowledged well ahead of the deadline, and the computer counted down the time.

Exactly on schedule, the star carrier appeared behind them in a gamma ray burst, flying in the same direction and slightly slower. When they received the All Clear from Skippy, all six ships decelerated at full power to allow the invisible star carrier to catch them. The *Dutchman* transmitted an extremely faint navigation beacon to avoid the stealthed dropships from crashing into the stealthed ship. Within seven minutes of the pirate ship jumping in, the dropships were securely clamped into their docking cradles, and the *Flying Dutchman* jumped away.

Chapter Four

I could not wait to congratulate Major Smythe, so I called him from the command chair. "Major, that was *outstanding*! That was a textbook operation, please convey my congratulations to your team."

"Thank you, Colonel," replied, a bit less happily than I had hoped. This wasn't just his British reserve, he was bothered about something. "That may have gone a bit *too* perfectly."

"What?" I asked in alarm, glancing at the main bridge display. The *Flying Dutchman* had sustained nothing worse than four maser cannon hits, which our shields had dealt with. There was no sign of pursuit, so- "Oh, shit," my face fell along with my spirits. "You think that was too easy because it was a setup?" My mind raced through terrifying scenarios. Had the Elder device Smythe brought on board been replaced with an explosive that could soon tear our ship apart? How? For that to happen, the Wurgalan must have known we were coming, but how could- The worm! Had the worm somehow communicated with the outside universe without Skippy's knowledge? If so, then the secret of humans flying around in a pirate ship and manipulating wormholes was out, and humanity on Earth and Paradise were screwed without-

Smythe blessedly interrupted my racing thoughts. "Setup? No, Sir. I only meant this is the first major combat operation we've been involved with that went almost exactly according to plan. I keep thinking Lady Fortune will get us back for that favor someday."

"Oh," I slumped in my chair with relief. Crisis averted for the moment. Although my panic had brought up an issue I needed to discuss with Skippy. "Major, bring the conduit, uh, thing up here."

"I don't know if it will fit through some of the passageways, Sir," Smythe warned. "It's rather long; there are some pieces attached to it that I am afraid to remove."

"Understood, good point. Keep it in the docking bay, then. I will bring Skippy down there. He says he needs to be close to the thing for it to work." Leaving the bridge, I saw Chang step from the CIC to replace me in the command chair. When I got to Skippy's escape pod mancave, he was chilling as usual. "Hey, Skippy."

"Hey, Joe," he also was not as happy as I expected him to be.

"What's wrong?" I asked as I unstrapped him and picked up the satchel we used for carrying him around, because he didn't like being touched by filthy monkeys. "I thought you would be thrilled that we recovered a conduit thingy for you, and none of us got killed." Down the passageway I walked quickly, almost jogging. There was no sign of any ships pursuing us, but if we got into trouble, I did not want to waste any time bringing Skippy back to his full awesome Skippyness.

"I am very happy that no monkeys were harmed in this operation, Joe. My enthusiasm is on hold right now, because I don't want to get my hopes up."

"Ok, I can understand that, because you never know what could go wrong. Hey, on the subject of things that can go wrong, how much do you know about what the worm is doing in there?"

"Hmm. Let me check. It has just finished binge-watching 'Downton Abbey' and now it is on season one of 'Breaking Bad'."

"*What?*"

"It's bored, so it- Oh for crying out loud, Joe, I was screwing with you."

"Oh, yeah. That's what I thought." Mentally, I had been picturing a worm sprawled on a couch, empty beer cans and potato chip bags littering the floor, as it chilled watching TV.

"How the hell should I know what it is doing? Trying to kill me is all I know, *duh*. I can tell it is attempting to get past the barrier I constructed."

"That's not good, Skippy. How do you know the worm isn't doing something bad like calling for help?"

"Calling for help? What?"

"I was thinking, that worm could be monitoring us. It could know we are humans, that our being out here is a secret. So, it could be calling in reinforcements."

"Reinforc- No, you dumdum. You think other worms are going to crawl across space to the ship and attack us?" He scoffed.

"Not other worms, Skippy. The worm could let, like, the Maxolhx know where we are and where we're going, so they can intercept us. All the worm cares about is that it kills you, right? If the Maxolhx destroy this ship, it makes the worm's job a lot easier, because you will never find one of these conduit things."

"*Shit*. Damn it, Joe. I hadn't thought about that," his voice was shaky. "Crap. You dumdum, you should have mentioned this earlier."

"I just thought of it. So it could happen?" Hearing that brought me to a halt in the passageway.

"Hmm, let me think. No, no, I don't think so. I don't see how that could happen. The worm so far as I know has never accessed my systems. It destroys, Joe. It doesn't take control of anything. I do not *think* it would, or could, call the Maxolhx."

"You telling me you don't think it could happen, without having any way for you to know, does not reassure me, Skippy."

"I am not bursting with confidence either, Joe. Crap. Well, thanks a lot. You really ruined my freakin' day, Mister Buzzkill."

"Yes, *that* is the important thing here, Skippy. Not that aliens could arrive at any moment, tear this ship apart, and destroy my home planet. What is truly important is that you are having a pleasant day."

"Sorry."

"After you kill the worm, you can see if it sent out a signal?"

"No, the worm would cover its tracks."

"So, there's no way for us to know if the worm has been calling for help?"

"Well, there is one way to tell if the worm ratted us out. After I fix myself and kill the worm, we can go back to Earth. If your home planet is a smoking ruin, we can assume the worm told somebody about your secret."

"Shit."

"I'm just sayin'."

"Yeah, thanks a freakin' lot."

"Ah, there is good news, Joe. The worm is Elder technology. It was designed and created at a time when only the Elders inhabited the galaxy. The Elders would not have programmed it to call for assistance from other species, because there were no other species back then."

"That is pretty thin to hang my hopes on, Skippy."

"It's all I've got, Joe. Come on, get moving. We need an active conduit to fix me, or we don't have any options."

"Ayuh," I agreed as I picked him up carefully. "I'll bring you down to the docking bay so you can check it yourself."

"Crap!" Skippy shouted in disgust after we got the stolen conduit hooked up to a proper power source. "This damn thing is totally busted! Oooh, I hate those stinkin' octopussies."

"Busted? The Wurgalan did something to it?"

"The Wurgalan, or the Bosphuraq before them. Or, hell, the Kristang during the brief time they owned the place."

"It is something we can fix?"

"No. Before you ask me a bunch of stupid time-wasting questions, the problem is not with the device itself. This thing is no longer a conduit, because its connection to higher spacetimes has been severed. Hmmm, that makes me think the rotten Bosphuraq must have been the ones to break it; the Wurgalan would not have any idea how to do that. Even the Bosphuraq likely did it by accident without knowing what they were doing. Crap. This *sucks*."

I looked up at Hans Chotek, overall mission commander and breakfast cereal spokesmodel. His usual expression of mild displeasure when dealing with me had turned into annoyed, exasperated and strong displeasure. "Colonel Bishop, this entire operation was a waste of time and resources?"

"We had no way of knowing that, Sir."

Skippy came to my rescue. "Mister Chotek," he began, and everyone including Chotek stared at Skippy's beer can in surprise. Skippy rarely used Chotek's real name, and had never referred to our commander as 'Mister'. "There is no way Joe could have known this damned thing would be busted, because *I* didn't know the conduit here would be inoperable. That was always a risk. I am sorry that personnel were placed at risk, but there is nothing we can do about that now. We have to chalk this up to karma and move on to Plan B."

"That should be our motto," Chotek said sourly. "Something to the effect of 'Plan B is our Plan A'."

"Yes, Sir," I agreed, and I really did mean that. As a motto, it was not inspirational, but what it lacked in motivational ability, it made up for it in accuracy.

"You do have a Plan B, Colonel?" Chotek asked with a skeptically raised eyebrow.

"Yes, Sir."

"First, please explain why we didn't consider this alternative before raiding the Wurgalan."

"Because," I tried to keep my expression neutral so fear did not show on my face. "Plan B involves us raiding the Thuranin."

After I gave the bad news to Chotek and he went back to his chocolaty Count castle to hem and haw and wring his hands and agonize and make my life hell before making the obvious and only decision he could make, I went to the galley for a glass of ice-cold lemonade because being on the bridge during the operation had made me tremendously thirsty. The galley was full of soldiers and pilots excitedly chatting about their experience; I assured them that although we had failed to find a working conduit, I considered the operation to be a complete success.

Taking a second glass of lemonade back to my office, I downloaded tactical data of the air battle, hoping to learn what worked and what didn't. The pilots involved, and Desai, would later conduct a full debriefing that I would attend eagerly; this was my opportunity to view the raw data and imagine I was there. Later, I could experience the air battle in a flight simulator, when it would truly feel as if I were there. "What the hell?" I mumbled.

"What is it, Joe?"

"Lt. Reed is certifiably insane, Skippy. She hovered her dropship *inside* a tornado."

"Technically, it was a dust devil, Joe, not a tornado. However, I do agree that a strong love for doing crazy shit seems to be a prerequisite for being part of this crew. Hey, you got a minute?"

"Sure. What's up?"

"Barsoom. Now that the battle is over, I had time to examine sensor data about that planet. It is a puzzle. Barsoom should have a much thicker atmosphere; the planet has a strong magnetic field capable of repelling solar wind particles that would strip away an atmosphere. Given the surface gravity, the atmosphere should be as thick as Earth's. Perhaps even more thick, considering the level of carbon dioxide."

"Ok," I replied distractedly, watching the air battle scroll across my laptop screen. "That's a puzzle for sure."

My laptop screen blacked out. "Joe, are you listening to me?" He asked peevishly. "I'm trying to tell you something important. Something that scares the shit out of me."

"No, Skippy, I was not really listening. Sorry about that. You have my full attention now," I assured him, as I didn't have any choice after he killed my laptop. "Barsoom should have a nice thick atmosphere. Geology, or, uh, planet, science, stuff," I struggled with the proper terms, "is not my thing. Shouldn't you be talking with the science team about this?"

"Frankly, Joe, it would be difficult for me to care less about atmospheric conditions on Barsoom, except that I suspect the thin atmosphere there is not natural."

That did get my full attention, making me sit up straight in my chair. "Not natural? You mean someone, like, stole the air?"

"Not exactly. The lack of atmospheric pressure is not the only odd thing about Barsoom. Based on geological survey data from the Wurgalan, Kristang and Maxolhx, that planet once had a relatively pleasant climate, with abundant native life. Oceans covered half the surface, but that water has mostly boiled away."

"Oh, shit. Did Barsoom get pushed out of its original orbit like Newark?"

"No. Good guess, though, that's what I thought at first. The thin atmosphere isn't the only puzzle. One hemisphere has a cluster of deep and extensive craters that appear to be caused by meteor impacts, but after examining the data closely, I realized only some of the craters were made by impacts. The three largest craters are not craters at all; they are where large sections of the surface were scooped away."

"Scooped away like transported into another dimension? We've seen that same thing on several moons that contained Elder facilities."

"Exactly. I am now certain Barsoom once contained one or more large Elder facilities, perhaps even a settlement or city. My analysis is based on the fact that the Maxolhx did find shattered remains of Elder facilities and equipment outside the three main craters. I say 'shattered' because whatever escaped being scooped away was subjected to extensive and powerful orbital bombardment. Joe, someone used Elder technology to erase almost all traces of whatever the Elders had at that location."

"Orbital bombardment? You're sure those secondary impacts aren't just meteors?"

"They were not caused by meteors, and I won't bother explaining how I know, because the science would be lost on you. The secondary craters were caused by relativistic impactors."

That I did understand. "You mean like a super powerful railgun?"

"A super-duper powerful railgun."

"Wow." I tried to imagine even a tiny object traveling at half the speed of light hitting a planet. Such an event would make a nuke look like a sneeze. "Crap. Next you're going to tell me all this bad stuff happened to Barsoom around the same time that Newark was pushed out of orbit, and somebody blew up moons that had Elder facilities?"

"No. That would be interesting, but merely another data point. What scares me is that Barsoom lost its atmosphere, and the surface was bombarded, long before disaster struck Newark. I wish now that we had more time at Barsoom, so I would not have to rely on the amateurish data collected by the idiot Maxolhx. My best estimate is the event occurred between ninety and one hundred thirty million years ago."

"Wheeeeew," I whistled. "Newark got pushed out of orbit about two point seven million years ago? So, the bad guys, whoever they are, they were around way back then?"

"No," his avatar shook its head sadly. "My internal subroutines are still preventing me from recalling accurate timelines, however I am certain this disaster struck Barsoom while the Elders still inhabited this galaxy. In fact, the Elders did not depart their physical existence for many millions of years after the event on Barsoom."

"Holy shit."

"Yeah. Now you see why this scares me. A violent act was committed against the Elders, while the Elders were still here."

"This changes things, Skippy."

"Uh huh." He was so frightened that he didn't bother to make a snarky remark. "The story gets worse, if possible. The technology required to strip away Barsoom's atmosphere, in the manner data indicates the event happened, is technology currently available only to a Sentinel. Someone, some*thing*, tore a hole in a star and created a massive, focused solar flare. I say 'focused' because only Barsoom was affected, not the third planet in the system. A powerful solar flare traveled outward, scorching Barsoom and blowing away most of its atmosphere. At the same time, Elder facilities on the surface were scooped away into another spacetime. Then whatever facilities remained were pounded to dust from orbit."

My head was spinning. "We raided that Elder site under the dome the Wurgalan built. Why wasn't that destroyed also?"

"I now think that site was placed on Barsoom later, as a monitoring station."

"Monitoring? Whoa. Someone used Elder tech to wipe out Elder facilities on Barsoom, then installed Elder tech to monitor the place? Why? More important, *who*?"

"For 'why' it is likely that whoever attacked Barsoom monitored activity on that planet to make certain nothing survived. The obvious choice for 'who' is the Elders themselves, although that makes zero, absolutely *zero*, sense. We know Newark was pushed out of orbit long after the Elders departed, so *that* event must have been caused by an unknown third party. But the idea of a third party coexisting with the Elders, and surviving long after the Elders left the galaxy, is simply not possible. Not possible. Unless everything I know about the Elders is wrong, completely wrong. And even that doesn't make sense. If there was a third party inhabiting this galaxy for over a hundred million years, where are they now? Why haven't we found relics of their civilization? The Elders left extensive relics scattered across the galaxy. There is no, *no* evidence of a star-faring species in this galaxy before the Rindhalu, other than the Elders themselves."

"I can't picture the Elders sitting back and allowing anyone to blow away one of their planets. Crap, Skippy, we had enough of a mystery about Newark. Now we have a totally different, maybe unconnected mystery about Barsoom?"

"There is one connection between the events at Newark and Barsoom; not just the level of technology involved. The connection is the *type* of technology involved as well. Joe, now that I know about Barsoom, I think something similar may have happened to other planets in this galaxy, around the same time as Barsoom. Knowing about Barsoom allows me to make sense of data collected mostly by the Rindhalu. They were puzzled by catastrophes which struck multiple sites across the galaxy roughly one hundred million years ago. One of their theories was that the Milky Way galaxy collided with and absorbed a dwarf galaxy at that time. The new mass passing through the Milky Way disrupted orbits and caused havoc like comets swinging in from distant orbits to collide with inner planets, planets being ejected from their star systems, even stars being pulled into orbit by larger stars. The Rindhalu discarded the dwarf galaxy theory because it didn't explain large areas scooped out of planets and moons and other phenomena they couldn't understand."

That remark puzzled me. "Did the Rindhalu know about Newark, and Barsoom?"

"I don't know," Skippy admitted. "Unfortunately, my only source of data about the Rindhalu comes from other species; I have had no direct contact with the spiders. The Rindhalu traditionally are reluctant to share data and technology. Joe, that is a very good point."

"Uh, it is?" I didn't know what point I had made.

"Yes. We should somehow get access to a Rindhalu data archive. Crap! I should have thought about doing that a long time ago. We have serious questions, the spiders may have answers."

I did not like the sound of that. "Hey, how about we concentrate on one problem at a time?"

"Ok, sure," he sighed. "The current problem is our need to get a conduit so I can fix myself, before we can do anything else."

"No, the current problem is persuading Count Chocula to approve us raiding a Thuranin star system."

"Oof," he grunted. "Crap, now you're asking the impossible."

"This time, Skippy, I understand why he is reluctant to approve this operation." There were several reasons why raiding Barsoom had been Plan A, and our next target was Plan B. The op at Barsoom involved us tangling with a small Wurgalan outpost, a relatively soft target of a lower-technology species. Plan B required us to jump into a Thuranin star system. The system was centered on an orange dwarf star and had no habitable planets; the inner worlds were small, lifeless rocks, with one large and two smaller gas giants forming the outer band of the system.

Unlike Barsoom, where millions of Wurgalan lived on one planet of that system, our second target had no permanent Thuranin presence. That is, no permanent presence that Skippy knew about. There is an unmanned refueling station in low orbit around the big gas giant, but the station supposedly was used infrequently because the star system was only one wormhole away from major ship servicing and fueling facilities. Our actual target, identified by Skippy, was on a moon orbiting the outermost gas giant; it was an Elder installation very similar to the one on Barsoom.

Yeah, like the one on Barsoom. Where we had taken a risk to steal a device that didn't work. Why did Skippy think we should take the even greater risk of going to our second target, which I decided to call 'Bravo' for lack of a better name? Because, Skippy had assured us, the conduit at Bravo was functional. Or it had been at one time. The Advanced Research Directorate of the Thuranin had done extensive, though completely unproductive, testing on the Elder installation, and Skippy had access to their testing data.

Although the Thuranin had not learned anything useful because they had no idea how Elder technology worked, their tests told Skippy the conduit was still active. Or it had been active, the last time the Thuranin ran tests, which was fifty three thousand years ago. Since that time, the Elder site had rested undisturbed, almost forgotten. Security at the site was limited to one surveillance and defense satellite; Skippy knew that because four thousand years ago the Thuranin had an internal dispute over who should pay the cost of maintaining and upgrading that satellite. In the end, ARD had ponied up the resources, grumbling about it for years afterward.

So, on the surface, Bravo looked like a soft target. It was in an uninhabited star system. Skippy knew exactly where the lone defense satellite was, in geosynchronous orbit directly above the Elder site. We could jump in practically on top of the satellite, jamming its signals while we sliced it apart with our maser cannons. We would time our jump so the satellite was above the side of the planet facing away from the star, concealing the gamma ray burst of our inbound jump from being detected by the fueling station orbiting the big gas giant. There, we had a bit of luck because our target and the big gas giant were almost 170 degrees apart in their orbits of the star; any stray photons from our gamma rays would not reach the fueling station for two and a half hours. That should be plenty of time for us to fly down to the Elder installation, remove the item we want, fly back up to the *Dutchman* and jump away. Simple and easy, right?

It should be simple and easy, but nothing the Merry Band of Pirates did was ever simple or easy. We were bound to encounter surprises that would bite us in the ass, and a surprise provided by the Thuranin would be an order of magnitude worse than any surprise the Wurgalan could have thrown at us.

Still, our raid at Barsoom, although fruitless, had been nearly a textbook operation, considering the 'textbook' was being written as we conducted each action. Maybe, I privately dared hope, our luck was changing for the better.

Man, was I ever wrong about that.

The Wurgalan named Oostlet Nabanu willed himself not to tremble in front of the two Thuranin who now occupied the repaired dome. The Thuranin did not have a physically imposing presence, being only three quarters the height of an average adult Wurgalan. Thuranin supposedly were proud of the efficiency and superiority of their compact body mass, but Wurgalan had learned over the eons the superior species were sensitive about their diminutive stature when face to face with other species, so Oostlet had followed protocol and scrunched up his tentacles to pull himself down, making the two Thuranin slightly above Oostlet's eye level. Lowering the trunk of their central bodies was practiced by all Wurgalan expected to encounter Thuranin in close proximity; one advantage of the Thuranin being clones was they were almost exactly the same height. There was no difference between the height of males and females in the patron species, and as far as Oostlet had been able to tell under the shapeless coveralls worn by the aliens, there was little other difference between the two genders of Thuranin.

It was not the height of the Thuranin that intimidated Oostlet and the five other Wurgalan under the dome. It was not even the advanced technology of the Thuranin, nor their visible cyborg enhancements.

What made Oostlet instinctively tremble, from a place way down inside the still-primitive parts of his brain, was the hulking combot that accompanied each of the two Thuranin. Not only did the combot loom over his scrunched down form, the combots resembled a nasty predator on the Wurgalan home world, a creature which still haunted the imaginations of all Wurgalan. Sometimes, Oostlet wondered if the Thuranin had deliberately given their cyborg-controlled combot companions an appearance that frightened and repulsed their clients; over his years of dealing with the Thuranin Oostlet had come to the conclusion that the patrons of the Kristang had done exactly that. Whether the combots elicited a fear response from the Kristang was unknown; the lizard warriors would never admit to fearing anything in the galaxy.

Arrival of the Thuranin starship in orbit had come as a complete shock to Oostlet and his fellows; a visit by the Thuranin was almost more unwelcome than the ship that had raided the planet and stolen a priceless Elder artifact. The Thuranin ship was already in low orbit, with dropships descending rapidly toward the surface, before the battered Wurgalan garrison received a signal from the third planet; the cyborgs had jumped in there first, and jumped away soon after learning of the raid. The Thuranin presence in the star system was not in response to the raid; the cyborgs had not been aware of recent events until they were informed by the Wurgalan leadership on the third planet. Whatever the original purpose of the Thuranin visiting the star system, they were now wholly focused on investigating the raid.

And focused on punishing those Wurgalan who had allowed the unknown raiders to steal an Elder artifact that had been entrusted to the Wurgalan by their patrons the Bosphuraq. Technically, customarily, legally, all authority to punish the actions of the Wurgalan rested solely with their patrons the Bosphuraq, but that would not stop the Thuranin from taking action. 'Correcting' the behavior of the Wurgalan would bring shame on the Bosphuraq, which truly was the main reason the Thuranin would insist on severe punishment for those Wurgalan involved in the failed defense of the Elder site.

Fortunately for Oostlet, he had been on the other side of the planet when the raid occurred, and he was a civilian administrator rather than a military officer. Part of the blame would attach itself to him anyway, but he would likely escape with his life.

He hoped.

The pair of Thuranin cyborgs, usually flatly emotionless on the exterior when speaking with other species, were allowing themselves to show distinct anger. "Your forces were completely, shamefully unprepared," said the Thuranin leader, a female designated Liv-426.

"I am further shamed to agree, Eminence," Oostlet responded automatically, for one never disagreed with a Thuranin. Not if, that is, one wanted to live. Thuranin had been known to retaliate against dozens of Wurgalan, for a perceived slight from one. Underneath his carefully placid exterior, Oostlet seethed with outraged anger. Wurgalan forces on the planet *had* been adequately prepared for the most likely threat scenario. With additional aircraft stationed there for training, the force structure was more than adequate for any of the attacks thought most likely. It was unfair of the Thuranin to criticize the Wurgalan for failing to protect the Elder site from an overwhelming attack. An Elder site, Oostlet burned to say, that the Bosphuraq had abandoned as a useless relic not worthy of protecting.

Oostlet said nothing about his private thoughts.

The Thuranin leader leaned forward slightly, as did the menacing combot. "Your guards here were clumsy and cowardly, and your pilots failed to follow basic air combat principles. We are, again and as always, greatly disappointed by the utter worthlessness of your species, despite all the advantages you have been provided by your superiors," Liv-426 continued.

Advantages? A muscle on Oostlet's back rippled in anger before he forced it to relax. Any technological advances the Wurgalan had made had come from observing and reverse-engineering equipment from other species, or by taking in battle, stealing or buying technology from species such as the Kristang. The Bosphuraq had done little to advance the capabilities of the Wurgalan, and the Thuranin had actively sought to stunt the technological advancement of any lesser species.

Oostlet voiced none of his thoughts. It was not necessary. He knew the Thuranin despised his lowly species, just as he was sure they knew he and all his fellows hated the Thuranin. Ritualistically, he bowed and said the proper words. "It is a great burden to be part of a people who continue to disappoint such great ones as yourself."

"Your commander will of course remove herself from future operations, as a result of her failure here," Liv-426 announced dismissively, as if announcing the impending death of a sentient individual who had done her best under impossible circumstances was not even worth mentioning. Under the Thuranin, military commanders of client species who failed were expected to kill themselves, as atonement for their failure, and as an example to others. Oostlet thought privately that policy only lead to Wurgalan commanders who either took no risks in battle, or were never able to learn from their mistakes.

And that, Oostlet thought, may be exactly why the Thuranin demanded the death of Wurgalan commanders who suffered defeats. If client commanders were allowed to learn and gain wisdom, experience and perspective, those clients may grow in strength and someday threaten the Thuranin.

Oostlet kept those types of thoughts to himself, for his own safety and the survival of his species. "Our commander will pay for her failure, per our standard practice," he replied with a bow, wondering if at that moment, the commander were already dead.

"Leave us," Liv-426 waved a hand, and her combot companion mimicked the gesture. As the primitive Wurgalan bowed low and backed away, Liv-426 addressed her companion through a cranial implant, the preferred method of communication between Thuranin. Liv-426's throat already ached and felt dry from the unfamiliar act of speaking using her vocal cords. "Thex-1138, analysis?"

Thex-1138, a male who, to non-Thuranin eyes appeared almost identical to his female companion, responded without turning toward his leader. "The data provided by the Wurgalan was nearly complete and unaltered, they only edited out the slowness of their initial response. It is curious; either they do not care that we see how incompetent their forces here were, or they know we can determine the truth independently." Upon arrival, the Thuranin destroyer had demanded all available data on the recent engagement, and the Wurgalan had complied swiftly if not entirely truthfully. Receiving a data package from the Wurgalan was a mere formality, because the Thuranin had long ago fully infiltrated the data systems of their client species. "The attackers appear to be Kristang, or," he transmitted an emotional overlay of bemusement, "they wanted the Wurgalan to *think* they were being raided by Kristang."

"How so?"

"Analysis of flight characteristics of the attacking airspace craft matches those of known Kristang types almost exactly. *Almost.* Conclusion: either the Kristang have enhanced capability airspace craft, or the attackers used ships of technology beyond that of the Kristang, and artificially restricted flight capabilities to mimic Kristang technology."

"Consistent with Kristang using stolen Thuranin technology?" Liv-426 asked without turning to look at her companion.

"Consistent with *someone* using technology of our development level," Thex-1138 clarified. "Perhaps there is an additional level of deception involved; the attackers may have wished us to believe they were Kristang. Perhaps the attackers were Bosphuraq in disguise."

"No. If the Bosphuraq realized something here was of importance to them, they could simply have ordered the Wurgalan to deliver it to them. This is Bosphuraq territory," Liv-426 reminded her companion. Technically, their ship should have requested permission from the Bosphuraq to visit the Wurgalan star system, but relations between the two erstwhile peers and allies had deteriorated to the point where Thuranin Central Processing had ordered warships to conduct recon missions in Bosphuraq territory, to keep an eye on their 'allies'. "Their ground team?"

"Again, consistent with Kristang, with anomalies. They wore standard Kristang light battle armor, however all of the attackers were on the short side for Kristang warriors, and they moved slowly and clumsily. Their legs," Thex-1138 added, "bent in the correct direction for Kristang."

"So, the ground team at least, was not Bosphuraq," Liv-426 observed. Having evolved from birds, the Bosphuraq's ankles were where other bipedal species had knees, making it appear their legs bent in the opposite direction. No Bosphuraq could fit inside a Kristang armored suit, for a variety of anatomical reasons. "Ruhar?"

"It is possible the attackers were Ruhar," Thex-1138 agreed although the emotional subtext of his transmission implied skepticism. "Leader, there might not have been a ground team at all. Those armored suits could have been remotely controlled. If that is the case, then any species could have been involved." Even the insect-like Jeraptha, he added to himself.

"That is insightful analysis," Liv-426 praised her companion. "Their starship? What conclusions have you reached?"

"It was stealthed, of course, and Wurgalan sensor coverage was shamefully inadequate, so information is limited. Again, on the surface the flight profile is consistent with a Kristang starship."

"On the surface?" Although all their communication was through cranial datalinks, Liv-426's lips bent upward in a smile.

"Based on a rough estimate of the attacking ship's mass, it must have been a Kristang heavy cruiser or battlecruiser. Trace gases recovered are inconclusive; they roughly meet the molecular profile to be expected for a Kristang capital ship, but could also be one of our own ships," Thex-1138's shoulders lifted in a slight shrug. "Trace gas analysis was not determinative. The jump drive signature was very curious."

"In what way?"

"It had all the characteristics of a Kristang unit, right down to the sloppy way discoherent radiation leaked at both ends of the jump wormhole."

"But?"

"But it was *too* perfectly distinctive. It was as if someone wished to mask their drive as a Kristang piece of junk, and pulled together stereotypical characteristics randomly. All Kristang jump drives are flawed in some way; the drive of this ship was *too* flawed. It could be a drive that is poorly maintained in a manner shocking even for Kristang, or a Kristang ship that sought to mask its own signature."

"That is not what you think, is it?" Liv-426 did not need Thex-1138 to send an emotional subtext to read her underling's thoughts.

"No, leader. I believe it more likely the ship was not Kristang at all."

"That would explain how it got all the way here." No single Kristang starship was capable of crossing the vast gulfs of interstellar space on its own. Rarely, the Kristang had been known to use multiple, disposable ships to assist one ship in traveling between stars;

discarding burned-out drive modules along the way. That event was rare because of the extreme expense, and because almost half the ships attempting such a journey failed to reach their destination.

Mostly, the Kristang relied on the Thuranin for interstellar transport. Liv-426 knew no Thuranin military ship had brought Kristang to the star system, and no legitimate civilian transport ship would take on a contract to bring Kristang there. That left far too many possibilities. The Thuranin's own Advanced Research Directorate was known to play dirty tricks the military was not made aware of; if they for some reason wanted to steal the Elder artifact from the Wurgalan, the ARD might have hired Kristang mercenaries and provided them with transport. Or the Kristang could have simply have paid for a ride on a Thuranin smuggler ship.

Making the puzzle more complicated was the Kristang practice of hiding away warships with crews in cold sleep. The raiding ship could have lain dormant for decades, even centuries, until activated by a code message unwittingly delivered by any passing ship. Disgraced warriors, youngest sons without prospects, and minor clans of falling fortune were known to hide starships in the asteroid belt or Oort cloud of vital star systems, with ships and crews dormant until their clan awakened them at the right moment for a sneak attack. Mercenary groups even parked such ships in space, waiting for tempting contracts for anyone who paid the exorbitant fees.

In this case, Liv-426 thought it unlikely any Kristang had the patience, or foresight, to park a valuable starship in an unimportant Wurgalan star system.

The raiders could have been Jeraptha. They could have been anyone. "What else have you learned from your analysis?" Liv-426 asked.

"If it was a heavy Kristang warship, they used only one maser cannon during the attack. Weapons fire was accurate, suspiciously accurate for Kristang, but the projected power was significantly less than main armament of the Kristang heavy cruiser. And too strong for secondary maser cannons."

Liv-426 knew a beam from a maser cannon could be as distinctive as a fingerprint, identifying not only the type of maser cannon, but the individual cannon aboard a particular starship. "Possible identification?"

"No," Thex-1138 transmitted an emotional overlay of disappointment, irritation and annoyance. "If I had to guess, it is most similar to the maser battery of our older star carriers, but there are enough inconsistencies to rule that out. Unless that maser cannon was old, poorly maintained, and had been significantly altered during service."

Liv-426 made the unnecessary gesture of turning her head to look directly at Thex-1138. "That would be consistent with a star carrier that had been captured by Kristang, without access to spare parts and proper maintenance." Both Thuranin knew that Central Processing had warned all ships in the fleet to be alert for a rogue star carrier that was suspected of being involved in multiple, unexplained and mysterious incidents throughout the sector. Even Central Processing admitted such reports were little more than rumors based on unconfirmed anecdotes, but such rumors had attracted attention and inquiry from the Maxolhx. Any time the Maxolhx became interested in events in Thuranin space, Central Processing went on full alert.

"The Kristang are engulfed in a civil war that has consumed their entire society and resources. Why would any Kristang with access to a star carrier bother to raid this site? Surely they would use a star carrier to gain a tactical advantage over other clans."

"Because," Liv-426 explained with an emotional overlay of lecturing a dimwitted subordinate, "they seek a *strategic* advantage. If a group of Kristang have access to one of our star carriers, and they have somehow discovered how to make use of Elder technology that has evaded the understanding of all other species in this galaxy, they could become extremely dangerous and powerful."

"They could dominate their society and quickly end the civil war," Thex-1138 nodded in appreciation.

"They might dominate *us*," Liv-426 warned. "The Maxolhx would look favorably on anyone who brought them a significant technology advantage over the Rindhalu. The lizards have long chafed at being under our control. This group of Kristang could free themselves, become our peers," there was no mistaking the emotional overlay of anger. And a touch of fear. "Central Processing will expect us to stop the lizards before this gets too far. The object they took, what was it?"

"We do not know." Responding to a sharp look, Thex-1138 added "We know the configuration of the object. We do not understand its function. The object did not respond in any meaningful way during extensive testing, nor did identical objects at other locations. The Bosphuraq," Thex-1138 glances sideways at Liv-426 to gauge her reaction, "believe the device creates or maintains a connection to other spacetimes."

"The Bosphuraq?" Liv-426 was mildly surprised her companion had dared mention the rival species.

"They have in many cases made more progress in understanding Elder technology than we have," Thex-1138 said warily. When Liv-426's mouth tightened in anger, Thex-1138 hastened to add "Even the Maxolhx consult the Bosphuraq on matters of Elder artifacts."

Liv-426 looked away. After a moment, she nodded almost imperceptibly. "The birdbrains do have their uses. Thex-1138, I would not speak so admiringly about the Bosphuraq on an open channel. Central Processing might not understand the subtle difference between you appreciating specific accomplishments of the Bosphuraq, and your assessment of their superiority."

"Their superior understanding of Elder technology is a fact. We must, first, deal with facts if we are to surpass the Bosphuraq," Thex-1138 stated calmly, no longer concerned about Liv-426's reaction. "Understanding our enemy is the key to defeating them." Neither of them thought it odd that their supposed allies the Bosphuraq were considered more of an enemy than their official opponents the Jeraptha and Torgalau.

"That is a true, if dangerous, notion." Liv-426 then pinged their pilot. "Nicc-1701, prepare for takeoff, we will be leaving. There is nothing more we can learn here."

"Acknowledged," Nicc-1701 responded from the cockpit.

"There is one thing we do know, Thex-1138," Liv-426 looked through the dome to the nearly black sky above.

"What is that?"

"We know what the attackers were seeking. And we know the one here," she pointed to the wrecked artifact, where the object had been cut away, "is not the only one."

Chapter Five

Hans Chotek ultimately approved our planned raid of target Bravo, after wasting three days by asking stupid questions and imposing a condition that I didn't like. Because Skippy knew exactly where the Thuranin satellite was located and he had demonstrated he could make our cranky jump drive perform a medium-distance jump with pinpoint accuracy, I wanted to hit the target immediately. Jumping directly in from far outside the system would give us the advantage of complete surprise.

Chotek insisted we perform an intermediate jump to recon the site, which he thought allowed us to avoid unpleasant surprises, but in my opinion actually increased our risk. The longer we remained in that star system, the more time we were exposed to danger. An intermediate jump created two additional gamma ray bursts that could be detected by any unexpected ships or sensor platforms in the area, giving away our position. It was an old and familiar argument; what is the value of tactical surprise? In Army training, and in some of my officer training PowerPoint slides, I had learned official Army doctrine on the subject, and some of the history that doctrine was based on. One of my instructors had focused on Operation Avalanche, the Allied invasion of Salerno Italy in WWII: General Mark Clark had decided not to soften up German defenses with a naval bombardment, in order to achieve surprise. It hadn't worked; the Germans knew the effective range of our aircraft flying from bases in Sicily, and they figured Salerno was the most likely spot for the Allies to come ashore. That instructor thought Clark had been foolish at Salerno, but later during Operation Shingle at Anzio the Allies had conducted a short preparatory bombardment, only to find little resistance onshore. Of course, later that year at Normandy, those beaches had been pounded by aircraft and naval gunfire before the first troops landed from the sea on D-Day. In the plan we developed for raiding Bravo, my thinking was we gained nothing and risked much in lingering around that star system any longer than needed. But, orders were orders, so I instructed Skippy to plot an intermediate jump.

First, we had to get to the Bravo star system. On the chart I had on my laptop, plotting a course there looked simple and we could get there quickly using only three Elder wormholes. Even with our jump drive in bad shape, I expected the voyage would not take more than two weeks. Skippy burst my happy bubble. "Ha ha, no way, dude," he chuckled. "This trip will take a month, if we're lucky. Ah!" He shushed me. "Let me explain before you ask a bunch of stupid questions. First, before we go anywhere, I need to take the jump drive offline to swap out and recalibrate a bunch of coils. After all the quick jumping we did at Barsoom, I discovered a potentially dangerous resonance in the drive; we need to fix that before jumping again. I'll leave just enough coils in place for one emergency jump, of course; the rest of the coils will be getting work done on them for three to four days. After that, we'll be good to jump, but not using the nice happy fairy tale course you plotted. That second wormhole you plan to use? Fuggedabouit," he muttered using his best Wise Guy voice. "That wormhole sees constant, heavy traffic by Thuranin ships, especially now their borders have been pushed back by the Jeraptha. One end of that wormhole is a major fleet shipyard and staging base supporting the entire sector. Ordinarily, that would not be a problem, because I could adjust that wormhole to open a new emergence point for our exclusive use. Now that I am currently, as you say, Skippy the Meh-"

"Sorry. I didn't mean that."

"You did mean that, Joe, and you are right about it. Compared to my usually incredibly magnificent awesomeness, I am now merely 'Meh'. Anyway, I can't screw with wormholes right now so we have to wait in line at normal emergence points. Yes, there are a whole lot of emergence points, but the risk is too great for us to hang around a heavily-trafficked wormhole. To be safe, we will have to go through four wormholes, not three. So, it will take us a month to get to Bravo. Thirty three days, to be more specific. We might be able to chop one or two days off that schedule, if the retuned jump drive behaves, and the wormhole emergence points line up optimally."

"Fine." I was not going to attempt persuading Chotek that we should try running the shorter, more dangerous route to Bravo, both because I knew he would say no, and because I didn't want to try it. Any time Skippy considered something to be too risky, I didn't argue with him.

"Hey, Joe, whatcha doing?" Skippy's avatar popped to life while I was sitting in my office, poking around on my laptop.

"Nothing much. Just trying to think of something good to cook during our next shift in the galley. I'm meeting the team in ten minutes, and Adams looks at me like I'm not pulling my weight if I don't have two or three suggestions."

"Uh huh. That, plus you nearly sliced off a thumb peeling carrots last time. Who does that?"

"It was an accident, Skippy. Anyway, hey, maybe you can help me. The French team served a soup two weeks ago, and I was thinking we could make something like it, but spice it up a bit. I searched, but I can't find a recipe for it anywhere."

"Maybe I can help. What is it?"

"They called it 'de jour soup'."

"De j-" Skippy's voice faded. "Joe, do you mean 'Soup de jour'?"

"Yeah, that's it. They made it twice, but, hmm, it was different the first time."

"Hooooh-leee- O.M.G! Joe, you are *so* ignorant. 'Soup de jour' is French for 'soup of the *day*'!" He laughed uproariously.

"Is not."

Silence.

"Crap. Are you screwing with me?"

"Sadly, no," Skippy chuckled.

"Now I really feel like an idiot."

"How could you tell?"

"Oh shut up."

The cooking team I was assigned to, which included Sergeant Adams, was planning menus for our next duty shift in the galley. The hardest part of the job wasn't the cooking, or the prep work or the cleaning up; it was getting a team of people to agree what should be on the menu. We not only needed to think of something different so we didn't repeat menu items too often, we also had to coordinate with the other teams, to avoid making something too similar two days in a row. The rotation had our turn in the galley the day after the French team, and the day before the Chinese team. We knew the French would be offering Beef Burgundy, plus a pasta dish and a vegetarian something or other. We also had to consider the slowly-dwindling supply of food we had in the cargo bays, and Major Simms's desire that we use up certain items that did not deal as well with long-term storage. "We have lots of potatoes," I commented while looking at the inventory list. "How about poutine for lunch?"

"Poo-what?" Adams asked.

"Poo-teen," I pronounced. "It's a Canadian thing, but we eat it up north also. You take French fries, add cheese curds, and cover it with gravy."

Adams stuck her tongue out. "No offense, Sir, but that sounds disgusting."

"Don't knock it until you've tried it. Think of the cheese curds like mozzarella," I saw mozzarella on the inventory but no cheese curds. Maybe we could make our own cheese curds? We had plenty of milk. No, that was too much work. "The dish is like, uh, Canadian nachos?" I explained. "Good hearty food in the winter."

"Sound like a way to make the fries soggy. I like crispy fries," Adams noted.

"Fine. Can we make poutine as a side dish for lunch?"

"Sure," Adams agreed, and Chang had no opinion on the subject.

"For dinner, how about Chicken Cordon Blue?" Adams suggested. "My grandmother use to make that."

"What are the British making the next night?" Chang asked while checking a list. "Ok, not chicken. What is this Cordon Blue?"

"You take a chicken breast, slice a pouch in it sideways," she pantomimed with her hands. "Then you stuff the pocket with ham and cheese like Swiss or gruyere."

"That does sound good," Chang smacked his lips.

"*Or*," I interjected, "we could make my father's version, 'Chicken Cordon Red White and Blue'."

"What?" Adams looked at me like I had grown two heads.

"You slice the chicken the same way, but first you pound it kind of flat so it's thinner. Pan-fry the chicken. When it's almost done, put slices of crisp bacon and cheddar cheese in the pocket, then bake it."

"Ohhh, that sounds delicious," Adams almost moaned.

"Even better, you can also stick toothpicks through to make it hold together, and deep-fry it," I added with a grin.

"Oooh," Adams' eyelids fluttered. "Stop. You're gonna make me pass out."

"Why," Chang asked, "it is called red white and blue? I do not think there is anything red or blue in the ingredients?"

Adams and I shared a wink. "Because," I explained, "it's got bacon, cheese and deep-frying. You can't get much more American than that."

We made Chicken Cordon Red White & Blue for dinner, it was a big success. Except for one problem. Renee Giraud of the French team informed me that because I had committed such an egregious sacrilege against a staple of French culinary tradition, if we ever returned to Earth, America might be at war with France.

I figured I would take that risk.

I also noticed Giraud asked for a second helping at dinner.

And Adams had to admit she liked poutine, although she wanted the fries to be crispy.

"We're ready, Sir," I told Chotek over the intercom from my seat in the command chair. I didn't want to be in the command chair, I wanted to be waiting inside a dropship with Captain Chandra's SpecOps team. Major Smythe was sitting out this op; he would be directing the action from the ship while Chandra and Lt. Williams took their teams down to the moon's surface to ransack the Elder site. It was obvious to everyone that remaining aboard the ship was just about killing Smythe, he understood the need for others to gain combat experience and he had full confidence in the two teams selected for the away mission. Being a career member of the Regiment, as Special Air Services people called their unit, he chafed at any inactivity. That morning, he had been so uncharacteristically brusque and short with people during breakfast, I almost ordered him to suit up and get aboard a ready bird.

If Williams and Chandra were excited to lead their teams on an away mission, I am sure they were also at least a little bit jealous that Smythe had commanded the smash-and-grab mission at Barsoom, while their own operation at Bravo was not expected to encounter any opposition at all. Because the Bravo mission was planned to be quick and simple, I attempted to persuade Smythe that I should join the away teams, on the bullshit excuse that seeing the teams in action would give me a better appreciation of their capabilities. I would not be flying a dropship, and I would accompany the SpecOps teams as an armed observer and stay out of their way, but Smythe firmly shot me down. If there was unexpected opposition at Bravo, he declared, then the real action would be aboard the *Dutchman* and not down on the surface of the moon.

Disappointed, I gave in, and I am ashamed to say I was immature and petty enough that I insisted on taking the *Dutchman*'s command chair myself, rather than letting someone else gain real-time command experience.

"I will be right there, Colonel," Chotek replied, and moments later, he stepped onto the bridge to stand behind my chair. He knew we had scanned the area and detected no threats, although we were so far from Bravo that the photons our sensors were picking up had left that planet three weeks ago. In my mind, that made the data tactically useless, but it made Chotek happy and his happiness made him easier to deal with. "Proceed when ready," he announced in a calm, quiet tone, although I could see the fingertips gripping my chair were white with tension.

A last glance at the main bridge display told me everything was green across the board. "Pilot, Jump Option Alpha. Engage."

The only visible changes were that a tiny orange dot of the star on the main display became a distinctly larger orange circle, and a blue-gray planet the apparent size of a ping pong ball now loomed in front of the ship. We had jumped in three lightminutes from Bravo, with the planet between us and the larger gas giant with the fueling station, so Bravo would block our gamma ray burst. I forced myself not to drum my fingers on the armrest of my chair as I waited for Skippy to give us the all-clear signal.

"Hmm. Satellite is *exactly* where I expected it to be, Joe, no surprise there," the beer can's voice was laced with sarcasm. He also had wanted to jump directly in on top of the satellite and thought Chotek was being needlessly, even counterproductively cautious in insisting on an intermediate jump for recon. "Gosh, the planet and the moon are where they're supposed to be too, who'd have guessed that?" His voice had taken on a nasty, dismissive tone that wasn't helpful.

"Skippy," I started to ask him to stick to the facts, but he interrupted me.

"That's odd, let me check- Oh shit!" He shouted. "*Jump*! Jump Option Foxtrot!"

The pilots knew they didn't need to wait for my order to perform an emergency jump away. Jumping so soon after our previous jump meant the second jump had no measure of precision but it didn't have to; it only needed to whisk us away from danger. From the immediate danger, that is. We had learned from painful experience that transitioning the ship from one place to another instantaneously was not always the magical escape solution I had hoped it was. On the main display, the star was again an orange dot, and no planet was visible.

"What happened, Skippy?"

"Give me a second, Joe, I'm devoting my full resources to calculating possible escape routes."

Possible? We had already successfully jumped away from the star system, but our escape was still only a possibility, not a certainty? I shared a shocked look with Chang, then wiped the anxiety off my face and looked back to Chotek to nod with reassurance I wasn't feeling. And, oh crap, Hans freakin' Chotek had been totally right to insist on a recon jump before we hit Bravo! He wasn't ever going to let me forget that.

"Ok, Joe, new jump options have been input to the autopilot. I'm not going to lie to you, we are in deep, deep trouble. We should jump again as soon as possible."

"Skippy, take a deep breath. What is the danger?"

"A Thuranin task force. I detected ships from multiple battlegroups. Dozens of ships, at least, and those are just the ship signatures I was able to isolate before we jumped away."

"Detected? Those ships weren't stealthed?" Again I shared a look with Lt. Colonel Chang, this time with less anxiety. A task force conducting routine exercises would be at least partly unstealthed, and if we had stumbled across those ships, it would be a while before they reacted to our presence.

"Those ships *were* stealthed, Joe," Skippy crushed my hopes. "What I detected was direct gamma ray burst signatures from eight ships that had recently jumped into the system. By carefully interpreting the sensor data, I was able to detect multiple other gamma ray bursts, based on altered chemistry in the upper atmosphere of the planet. And from the direct burst data, I can tell there are stealthed ships out there; the gamma ray signatures have tiny resonance voids, where the photons were bent around a stealthed ship. There are a *lot* of ships out there, Joe."

"Stealthed ships can get detected by gamma rays washing over them?" I asked, completely ignoring what was truly important at that moment.

"They can be detected by *me*. It is an extremely subtle effect that is difficult to detect with this ship's crappy sensors, and the Thuranin do not even know what to look for. That trick only works part of the time, so the fact that I detected multiple stealthed ships tells me there must be a lot more of them out there. You're missing the point as usual, Joe. A whole freakin' task force was waiting there to ambush us. If we had taken a couple more days to get there, all the enemy ships would have arrived and their gamma ray bursts would have passed out of our detection range. We got lucky."

"Whoa. Wait a minute, Skippy," I had one eye on the bar at the bottom of the main display screen, it showed we still had another twenty six minutes until the capacitors had recharged enough for a medium-distance jump. In our jump drive's sad condition, a medium-distance effort did not take us nearly as far as the *Flying Dutchman* used to travel in her prime. "Ok, there is a Thuranin task force here, and that sucks for us, but what makes you think they were waiting for us? How the hell could they know we were coming?"

"I do not know how the Thuranin could know where we were going," Skippy's tone was clipped and short, reflecting his great frustration. "I know this is an ambush because I detected powerful, overlapping damping fields around the target planet. If we had jumped in, we would be trapped, no question about it. The Thuranin not only knew we were coming to this star system, they knew exactly where we planned to go. We did have a bit of luck; the Thuranin are so eager to assure we couldn't jump away, they assigned too many ships to project a damping field wide around the planet. The damping effect is so strong, it distorted the planet's magnetic field. That is the anomaly I noticed first; once I saw that, I started looking for gamma ray echoes and stealthed ships."

"Holy shi-" I looked back at Chotek guiltily, as if I had been caught saying a bad word in church and my father was about to reprimand me. "They *knew* were coming? Ok, ok, ok," I waved my slightly shaky hands. "Let's put that aside for now. What do we do next?"

"Unfortunately, we do not have infinite options. There are only three wormholes within the sphere we can reach."

"There are more than three wormholes on the chart, Skippy," I jabbed a finger at the main display. "All we care about is escaping that task force, we can worry about where the wormhole goes later."

"There are plenty of wormholes in this general area, Joe, but only three we can reach before our jump drive burns out. With a task force pursuing us, we will be jumping often, without enough time to properly calibrate the coils between jumps. The Thuranin know we will be headed for one of the three closest wormholes, so we will be in a race to get there first."

"A race?" I felt a spark of optimism. "We have a star carrier, and we're not trapped in a damping field this time."

"We *had* a star carrier. Then a bunch of monkeys stole it, took it for a joyride to get bananas, stripped it of everything useful and left it up on blocks behind a dumpster in a bad part of town. Joe, our jump drive is in horrible condition. We can't outrun a real star carrier; we can't even outrun a Thuranin cruiser or one of their heavy destroyers. I know Thuranin fleet tactics, they will use their star carriers to leapfrog squadrons of destroyers and cruisers ahead of us, supported by picket lines of sensor frigates parked across our likely path."

"They knew we were coming," I repeated uselessly, trying to wrap my head around that astonishing, unexplainable fact. "Focus," I said to myself, not realizing at first I had spoken aloud. "Back to my original question: what do we do next? We jump, obviously, the question is where?"

Skippy answered immediately. "The closest two wormholes lead to Bosphuraq territory, but we can worry about that later. Those two wormholes are only fourteen degrees apart from here; my suggestion is we set course in between them to confuse the Thuranin. We can decide which wormhole to target in a couple days."

"Good. Let's do that."

"Course is plotted in the jump navigation system," Skippy said without his usual smugness.

I sat in the command chair, with absolutely nothing to do, watching the jump drive capacitor charge approach the minimum needed for a medium-distance jump. The capacitors already had sufficient energy to feed into the coils for a short emergency jump, but with an entire task force hunting us, possibly more than one task force, I didn't want to waste precious energy on a jump that might only take us from the fire into the frying pan. If we were surrounded by enemy ships, a short jump would give us only a short reprieve from being caught in a damping field and trapped. Still, what would I do if enemy ships jumped in near us before we had enough charge for at least a medium jump? What *could* we do? "Hey Skippy," I asked, "what about quantum resonators? We drop one behind us as we jump, throw off enemy sensors, so they can't follow us." Then I remembered what Skippy had told me about such devices. "Not follow us as easily, I mean."

"Ordinarily that is standard practice in this situation," he agreed, "but we don't have any quantum resonators aboard."

"What? We had, like, three, or a half dozen," I hated looking stupid in front of my boss so I kept my eyes forward at the main display, to avoid meeting Chotek's eyes.

"Correct. We *had* them, Joe. I was forced to use them to calibrate the jump drive coils you monkeys thoroughly screwed up."

"How the- how could you use a resonator to-"

"Ugh. We do not have time for a physics lesson, Joe, and explaining anything to you is a waste of time anyway. I used the resonators to make a set of coils fully discoherent; that way I could strip them of their programing and reset them to function together. That is a very crude method that is *not* standard practice; it shortens the useful life of a coil and I had to junk one of every ten coils I ran through the process. I only did it because we are truly desperate. What matters is, we do not have any resonators left aboard the ship. Without my full powers of awesomeness, I can't do any magic to conceal our jump path. Bottom line is, the Thuranin will be able to determine our jump path and pursue us."

"That is a complication," I caught Desai's eye, and she frowned.

"Yes it is, Joe," Skippy agreed unhappily. "We will need to forget some of our standard practices, because we're now flying without many of the capabilities we have become used to. Major Desai," he addressed our chief pilot, "this situation will require a conscious effort to think in terms of this ship's restricted flight characteristics."

"Yes, Mister Skippy," she replied with a look at me. I could tell her mind was already racing through unlearning many of the tactics she and her fellow pilots had spent thousands of hours of training to make instinctive. That wouldn't be easy, but somehow she would do it. Desai had warned me several times that she was not the best pilot aboard the *Flying Dutchman*, that if she had not been in jail with me on Paradise, she would never have qualified to be a Merry Pirate. Her argument was that other people aboard were better natural and instinctive pilots, more technically proficient and quicker to learn new tactics. That argument was probably true and certainly irrelevant. She was my chief pilot because she was an absolute iceberg under pressure; nothing took her focus away from flying. No matter what outrageously strange new reality was thrown at her, she took it in stride and did her job. I trusted her completely to know what to do in a crisis, it was a simple as that. Any of the other hotshot pilots aboard the ship could execute instructions and fly our still-massive star carrier through the eye of the needle; what I needed Desai at the controls for was knowing *what* to do; she could let someone else's fingers guide the ship through the maneuver. "We have revised settings on the flight simulator, but we're still learning how best to fly the ship under the new restrictions."

"I'm sure you'll do fine," I said, the words sounding limp and useless as the empty platitudes they were. Motivational speaking was not one of my strengths. Ah, screw it anyway. Desai knew I had faith in her, nice happy words were unnecessary. "Skippy, can we-"

"Contact!" He interrupted. "Gamma ray burst! One ship, nope, no, *two* ships. One five lightminutes away, one seven. They've got us bracketed, there will likely be other ships jumping in soon."

"Damn it," I swore at the charge indicator. There was barely enough power for a medium jump. I wanted us to make a good, long jump to get us well clear of the star system, and we were still technically in the Oort cloud. A long jump, then a medium jump to throw off immediate pursuit, so we could take a breather and Skippy could work on properly maintaining the drive components. He had warned me the Thuranin were not going to allow us any respite, that their ships would pursue us relentlessly. I had been hoping he was being pessimistic about that. "Ok, Jump option, uh," I scrolled through the list an armrest display.

"Joe," Skippy chided me gently. "Remember SCM."

"Oh. Yeah." He meant the principles of Space Combat Maneuvers. Desai had taught me how to fly, and after I was able to fly a small dropship around the ship without crashing into anything, she had moved onto teaching me Basic Fighter Maneuvers. The principles of BFM developed on Earth didn't really apply to flying advanced alien starships or airspace craft, but she had wanted me to understand the thinking behind fighter tactics. If I couldn't internalize and master that mode of thinking, then no way could I grasp the intricacies of space combat. I had passed the course, after a whole lot of long hours and hard work. "Got it, Skippy. What you mean is, we're not in immediate danger. Those ships are no more than seven lightminutes away, so the photons from the gamma ray burst when we jumped in here have already swept past their location. We detected their inbound jump, but they can't see ours. So, we don't need to jump just yet."

"Correct, Joe," he said like a mother proud that her child had not tripped over their own feet while playing soccer. "Our jump wormhole creates an intense initial burst of gamma rays that the enemy cannot see, because those gamma rays have already gone past their position. If they had better sensors, they might see gamma rays bouncing off stray hydrogen atoms out here, but I seriously doubt that, given the Thuranin level of technology. Our stealth field is active and fully effective, and the active sensor pulses from those ships are just beginning to sweep over us; pulse strength is as yet too weak for them to get an echo to detect us. Our inbound jump did create a local spacetime ripple the enemy will detect, once their ships are able to establish a datalink and compare sensor data. I estimate we have eight maybe ten minutes before they find us."

"Right," I recalled the bit about how a jump wormhole essentially tore a temporary hole in spacetime, and that hole leaked distinctive radiation for hours, even days after a jump. The radiation level faded rapidly; but not rapidly enough to protect us from being detected. "They probably have other ships that jumped in farther away from us, and those ships may be in position to see our gamma ray burst."

"Also true, unfortunately. In fact, I just detected another enemy ship that jumped in eleven lightminutes away; this one is behind us. Hmmm, interesting."

"What? Interesting like, oh shit we're screwed, or like trivia?" Sometimes Skippy's absent-minded brain wandered so far off topic, he couldn't tell what was important to *us*. At the moment, I did not care about any nerdnik bullshit like a slight increase in the ratio of hydrogen to helium atoms in the interstellar medium.

"Not trivia, but not quite 'oh shit'. Not yet. That last ship I detected has the unique jump signature of a battlecruiser. Using such heavy combatants for a search is not standard Thuranin fleet tactics; a big battlewagon like that is too slow to pursue a star carrier. That tells me the Thuranin are throwing every ship they have available into the hunt. They are serious about catching us, Joe. That is very bad news."

"It is bad news, Skippy. It's also good news."

"Huh? How do you figure that?"

"Because it tells me the Thuranin threw this op together quickly. However they knew we were coming here, they didn't have a lot of time to plan a pursuit and bring in a proper force structure. I would *love* to know how they knew we were going to Bravo, but they haven't been planning for months to trap us."

"Oh. I had not thought of it that way, Joe, that is a good point. Wow, you are a freakin' ray of sunshine on a rainy day."

"Any light in the darkness is better than nothing, Skippy."

"Unless the darkness is a tunnel and the light is a train coming at you."

"Thank you for cheering us up, Skippy." We waited six minutes while the capacitors built up a charge, then performed a not-quite-long jump. Better than a medium jump, not as far as I wanted. Then we settled down to recharge for another jump.

"Hey, Joe," Skippy's voice startled me, as I had been half asleep in my office. My left hand was cramped from holding my head up, and my left cheek was numb from pressing against my knuckles. Empty coffee cups were scattered across my desk; caffeine had long since stopped having any effect. Sleep. What I needed was sleep. We all needed sleep. Our jump drive needed its own kind of downtime, and that wasn't going to happen either.

The Thuranin had been, as Skippy predicted, relentless in pursuit of us. At first, we had success in evading their picket lines, to the point where I began to breathe a sigh of relief and let the tension out of my shoulders. Maybe I had not quite been ready to pat myself on the back and offer congratulations to the crew for a successful escape, but I had been thinking about it.

Then reality smacked me in the face like a cold dead fish. I use that analogy because, after the initial pain of having a salmon battering my face faded, I would still be stuck with bruises and a lingering slimy smell. Ok, I suck at analogies, but you know what I mean.

Our initial success, I soon realized with crushing disappointment, was because the Thuranin task force had to spread out to cover all space around the Bravo system, making their coverage thin and spotty. Once they accumulated a half dozen data points from the gamma rays of our jumps, they knew roughly which direction we were going and could concentrate their substantial forces along the line between Bravo and the two closest wormholes. The Thuranin didn't yet know which of the two wormholes into Bosphuraq territory we planned to take; because we hadn't decided which one to aim for. They did know our options were limited and grew more limited with every jump. Our jump drive was wearing out from repeated use without breaks to recalibrate the coils. This was a problem not only because our coils were becoming weaker and discoherent, reducing the distance we could jump on a charge, it also meant the magic tricks Skippy performed to mask the *Flying Dutchman's* jump signature were wearing off. Eventually, the masking would burn off completely and the Thuranin would be able to positively identify the *Dutchman* as the star carrier that disappeared near Paradise. Worse, they would be able to analyze how our true jump signature had been masked, and we would not be able to conceal our signature in the future.

We had been jumping continuously until ship and crew were exhausted. There was a nightmarish period of two days when we had to jump every thirty three minutes, because that is how long it took a pair of Thuranin cruisers to find us after every jump. We finally managed to shake those two ships, and now we had the luxury of almost two hours between jumps. That had made me briefly happy, until Skippy told me he thought the Thuranin had simply changed tactics. Rather than us cleverly slipping away from the annoying pair of cruisers, those ships had been pulled away for maintenance. The Thuranin now knew we were headed toward one or the other of two wormholes; they didn't need to chase us across the empty wasteland of interstellar space. All they needed to do was use their massive, well-rested star carriers to leapfrog dozens of warships ahead of us and block our path. By the time we got to whichever of the two wormholes we decided to attempt going through, the area would be saturated with frigates casting overlapping sensor nets, and cruisers and destroyers poised to home in on our location and trap us in powerful damping fields. The Thuranin commander had wisely pulled task force ships offline for a maintenance cycle until we got closer to a wormhole, then the well-rested ships and crew would hunt us down and capture or destroy us.

The worst part of our dilemma was the nagging feeling I had that no matter what we did, the Thuranin would trap us, and we would have to self-destruct the ship. Those little green MFers had somehow known we were going to Bravo. They either had a way to track our ship across great distances, or they had a way to predict our next move. Maybe they even had a way to see into the future, despite Skippy's dismissal of that idea when I told him about it. Skippy was an awesomely, amazingly advanced being, but I had learned through painful experience he was not infallible, and he didn't know everything. Perhaps the Maxolhx did have at least a limited ability to see into the future, and they were helping their clients the Thuranin hunt down and kill a pesky stolen star carrier? I could not think of any other way the Thuranin could have known we were on our way to Bravo.

And if the Maxolhx knew about us, maybe they also knew our ship was filled with humans. In that case, the powerful Maxolhx might be sending a ship to destroy our home planet.

In which case, my leadership failure had not only doomed my ship, but my entire species.

That depressing thought was weighing on my mind when I pulled myself upright in the chair, rubbed my tired eyes and answered the beer can. "Hey, Skip. What's up?"

"Skip? You're too tired to say my full name?" He chuckled.

"Yeah."

"Oh, sorry. You *are* tired. Ah, the whole crew is tired. Anywho, I have a bit of good news. I think it's good news. Actually, it's not *my* good news, it-"

I was too tired for his usual winding path toward getting to the point. "What is it?"

"I was talking with Sergeant Adams, and she, well, she's on her way to your office right now. I'll let her tell you the good news."

Adams looked as tired as I felt, but she wasn't letting exhaustion keep her from duty. "Sir, I think," she paused to stifle a yawn, "I know how the Thuranin knew we were coming to Bravo."

Based on the way she cocked her head, I had not been able to hide the disappointment from my tired face. "This isn't," I couldn't help yawning, "something about time travel or seeing into the future? Skippy already shot down those ideas."

"No magic involved, Sir," she looked pointedly at my fresh cup of coffee, so I took a healthy gulp while she waited.

"Ok," my tongue wasn't working properly because I'd taken too big a mouthful of hot coffee. "Tell me how you figured out the secret. Skippy sounds impressed."

Margaret Adams gave the avatar a look that was part disgust and part affection. "Skippy is impressed when monkeys can tie shoes; we don't need his approval. It started with me asking Skippy how many of these conduit things are known in this part of the galaxy. No, not just conduits, conduits that are the *same* as the one on Barsoom."

"Holy shit," my hand went limp and the coffee cup dropped and bounced off the desk as realization dawned on me. "Adams, you are a freakin' genius. Goddamn! That is so simple, why didn't I see that?"

"Because you are a dumdum, Joe?" Skippy teased.

"Hey, beer can, *you* didn't think of it either." I retorted. "Go ahead, Adams, sorry for interrupting you."

"No problem, Sir. Skippy told me the Elder installation on Bravo is the same type of conduit or whatever as the one on Barsoom. My guess is the Thuranin arrived at Barsoom shortly after we left. They knew someone had raided Barsoom and caused a lot of havoc to steal what they thought was a worthless Elder artifact. So, the Thuranin asked themselves whether there are other Elder artifacts of that type, and they knew the closest one is at Bravo. Skippy told me that's not correct, there is another one closer, but that one was removed from its original site and is now at a heavily guarded Thuranin military base."

"That's why I didn't bother listing it as a potential target, Joe," Skippy added.

"Crap," I said sourly. "So, on the chance that whoever raided Barsoom was looking for more conduits, the Thuranin set a trap at Bravo?"

"Exactly, Joe," Skippy's voice was inappropriately bubbling with happiness. A puzzle had been solved, and that's what he cared about. The fact that we were still running for our lives was forgotten for the moment. "The Thuranin clearly got to Bravo before we did. They could take the direct route through that heavily-trafficked wormhole we had to avoid, remember? I'll bet by the time we arrived at Bravo, the Thuranin had taken away the real conduit and replaced it with a fake, to make sure we didn't get the thing."

"Well, shit," I sat back in my chair and mopped up spilled coffee with a napkin. "We are seriously screwed, then."

"Damn it, Joe, I thought you would be *happy* to hear this news. It means the Thuranin do not have some freakin' magical way to track us across interstellar space. All they did was look at the data and put two and two together."

"I am happy the Thuranin probably can't track us. The reason I am *not* happy is that now the Thuranin, and the entire Maxolhx coalition know for certain there is a mystery ship flying around looking for conduits! They're going to lock up every Goddamn conduit they know about, and now we'll never find one to fix you."

"Well, shit," Skippy grumbled. "I hadn't thought about that! Thanks for being such a ray of sunshine, Joe."

Adams's lips formed a silent 'O' shape. "Ooh, that, that is a good point. Skippy, are there other types of conduits we could look for? The Thuranin don't truly know what we are seeking, they only know what the thing on Barsoom looks like."

"There are other types of conduits, but that isn't the problem. We don't have many options for finding another conduit, Joe. Just the one option, and you didn't even want to talk about that one."

"I still don't want to talk about it, Skippy," I cut him off hurriedly as Adams raised an eyebrow. "Not yet, Ok? We need to escape from the Thuranin task force before we have even one option. And that is really not an option anyway. Adams, pretend you didn't hear that. That's an order. We don't need any distractions right now."

Sergeant Adams nodded, and if she wasn't happy about my order, she hid it well. "Yes, S-"

"Speaking of distractions, Joe, I just detected an enemy destroyer jumping in eight lightminutes away," Skippy announced. The Thuranin were continuing to track and harass us, even though they seemed to be happy to wait until we approached a wormhole before pressing their attack.

Standing up from my chair, I swallowed the last of the coffee and set the cup down next to the other discarded cups. "Sergeant," I covered my mouth as my mouth gaped in a jaw-stretching yawn, "I'll be on the bridge. Again."

Chapter Six

We got away from that destroyer, and I pulled together Chotek and the senior staff so Adams could tell her theory of how the Thuranin had been waiting for us at Bravo. Everyone slapped their foreheads after they understood the Thuranin needed only logic and not magic to anticipate our arrival at Bravo, and even Chotek congratulated Adams on her intelligence. People were relieved to hear the Thuranin could not actually predict our movements, then I rained on the parade by mentioning that the Thuranin would be locking up all conduits in the sector now they knew someone was searching for them. Being a buzzkill wasn't my intention, I just didn't want people to get their hopes up. With us running for our lives, maybe I should have held my bad news for later.

Six hours later, I was back in my office, avoiding coffee because all it did was make my mouth dry, the caffeine wasn't helping me stay alert. "Joe, we are in trouble. Big trouble."

"I know that, Skippy," I responded distractedly, focused on my laptop. The display mirrored the main bridge display, allowing me to fret over what the command crew was doing, without me hovering over their shoulders. At any moment, I knew, a cluster of dots could appear on the display, announcing the gamma ray bursts of Thuranin ships jumping in to hunt the *Flying Dutchman*. One corner of the display showed the progress of recharging the jump drive capacitors. We had enough reserve power for a modest jump right then. According to the timer, it would take seven hours to full charge our partially burned-out capacitors, and I knew that was never going to happen. No way could we hang dead in space for seven hours with an entire task force chasing us. "When are we ever *not* in trouble?"

"No, I mean, we are in more trouble than you realize," Skippy warned. "I just completed decrypting a transmission that I intercepted before our second-to-last jump. Sorry it took so long, this is a case where my reduced capacity directly affects my abilities. What I learned is extremely alarming; the Thuranin are calling in two additional task forces to pursue us."

"Two whole *task forces*?" I gasped. "Uh, how many ships is that?"

"Sixty additional warships, at least. That doesn't count support vessels. The Thuranin are taking this very, very seriously."

"Sixty more freakin' ships to hunt us?"

"At least sixty ships. The communication I intercepted was from Thuranin military command to the squadron we encountered; it indicates even more ships can be made available if needed. Tracking the *Flying Dutchman* is a top priority. Even worse-"

"Wait. How can those little green MFers have sixty ships available?" I demanded. "The Jeraptha just gave the Thuranin a major ass-whipping! With our help."

"Ah, well, heh heh," he chuckled nervously, "this is another case where the Law of Unintended Consequences is biting us in the ass. Yes, the Thuranin did get their butts kicked by the Jeraptha, and as you know, that caused problems on our last mission." He meant the weakened state of the Jeraptha fleet had caused those little assholes to encourage the Kristang Fire Dragon clan to sweeten their offer to the Ruhar. That deal was for the Ruhar to send a ship to Earth, leaving us with no option but to spark a civil war between Kristang clans.

"Yeah, I remember. I also remember you told us there would be no downside to us helping the Jeraptha against the Thuranin!"

"Yes, that is why they are called *unintended* consequences. Duh. Damn, you are super dense sometimes."

I slapped my forehead and clenched a fist to suppress an urge to throw the beer can out an airlock. "What went wrong this time?"

"Nothing new went wrong, it's all the same crap, Joe. I won't bore you with the details, a full strategic analysis from Thuranin Fleet Command is available on your laptop if you want to read it later. Basically, their recent losses have persuaded Thuranin leadership to reach a wide-ranging ceasefire with the Jeraptha. Thuranin ships have pulled back and surrendered key areas of this sector and the adjacent sector toward the rim of the galaxy. Giving up that territory has been deeply humiliating to the Thuranin and hurt their standing with the Maxolhx. The Jeraptha and Thuranin fleets have established a demilitarized zone along their new frontier, extending for almost three thousand lightyears. What all this means to us, Joe, is the Thuranin fleet currently is not engaged in offensive operations, and they have been able to concentrate their defense forces over a smaller area. While the mystery of a strange star carrier may have been a minor curiosity to a wartime fleet, we have now moved considerably up the Thuranin priority list."

"Why? Come on, the Thuranin have got to be frightened their ceasefire with the Jeraptha could collapse at any moment."

"No, they are not. The Thuranin have access to intelligence from the Maxolhx, so they know high-level officials in the Jeraptha government have wagered significant sums that the ceasefire will hold for at least seven months, counting in human time."

"Shit. Those beetles *bet* on whether they will cheat on their own freakin' ceasefire agreement?"

"Of course they did, that is juicy action no Jeraptha could resist. Technically, they are also wagering on whether the Thuranin will violate the agreement, but both sides know it is safe to assume the Thuranin fleet will not be capable of launching a major attack for a year or more. The bottom line is the Thuranin fleet is not greatly concerned about an imminent threat from the Jeraptha, so they have time for other activities. Like keeping the Kristang civil war from spreading too far. Repair and maintenance of their ships and orbital defense platforms. And chasing down the mystery of a rogue Thuranin star carrier."

"You mean iff we had not helped the Jeraptha kick their little green asses, the Thuranin would be too busy to be hunting us? We screwed ourselves *again*?"

"Yup. Most likely, anyway. Joe, there are two reasons why the Thuranin are committing major resources to capture this ship. First, the Thuranin strongly suspect the Bosphuraq passed intel to the Jeraptha about the sneak attack on the Glark system, and that intel is why three Thuranin task forces were ambushed and destroyed. The Thuranin have been tracking reports of strange incidents involving a rogue star carrier that appears to be Thuranin in origin, and they have noted those incidents usually involve action against the interests of the Thuranin. After we got ambushed by that squadron of Thuranin destroyers during our second mission, I told you I intercepted communications in which the Thuranin accused the Kristang of hijacking a star carrier seventeen years ago. The Kristang denied the whole thing, of course, but the Thuranin were not convinced. Then as time went on and the Thuranin continued to get vague reports of a rogue star carrier, their suspicions turned away from the Kristang, because it is extremely unlikely the lizards could keep a Thuranin starship flying for long without access to technical support and spare parts. The Thuranin now suspect the rogue star carrier was hijacked by the Bosphuraq, or is actually a disguised Bosphuraq ship. When the Thuranin brought their suspicions to the Maxolhx, the Bosphuraq dismissed the idea in very harsh language that left the Thuranin enraged."

"Their little green feelings got hurt?"

"Very much. Don't gloat about it, Joe. The Thuranin are very much pissed off and determined to prove the Bosphuraq are lying, particularly now that the defeats suffered by the Thuranin have weakened their position within the Maxolhx coalition."

"Ok, the Thuranin have good reasons to capture this ship. We knew that already. We will jump away and keep running, keep clear of Thuranin ships. No different from what we have been doing since we boarded this ship," I said unhappily, kind of amazed that I could be talking so calmly about a cruel species of advanced beings who would love to tear my ship apart. Had I faced so many terrible threats that I was now numb to them? "Why do you now say we are in big trouble?"

"Because of the second reason the Thuranin are using a significant part of the fleet to hunt us. The Maxolhx asked them to."

"What? Shit! When did that happen?"

"Shortly after the Thuranin accused the Bosphuraq of passing intel to the Jeraptha. The Maxolhx never thought the Bosphuraq were involved; they think the failure of the Thuranin attempted sneak attack on Glark was due to poor communication security by the Thuranin. Unfortunately for us, in the data provided by the Thuranin for their claim against the Bosphuraq, they included details of reports about a rogue star carrier. And that got the attention of the Maxolhx. Remember I told you we had to be careful about screwing with wormholes, because eventually someone was going to notice?"

"Oh, shit." I could feel blood draining from my face.

"Yeah, 'oh shit' is an appropriate response. So far, the Maxolhx have not connected anomalous wormhole behavior with humans, or Earth. They are not yet suspicious, merely alarmed and curious that wormholes were acting strangely. But now that they have matched up their data about odd wormhole behavior with the Thuranin data about a rogue star carrier, the Maxolhx are beginning to get suspicious."

"That *is* bad news," I swallowed hard because I was feeling a twinge of upset stomach, and that wasn't because I drank too much coffee.

"Bad news indeed. It is very bad news for us right now, because the Maxolhx have offered to help the Thuranin capture this ship. Joe," his avatar gestured to my laptop display, which now showed a star map, with a yellow banana icon for the *Flying Dutchman* in the center. "There are only four Elder wormholes within our theoretical range, and one of those is so far away," one wormhole icon in the display glowed red, "that I would most likely hit Zero Hour before we got there, assuming nothing aboard the ship breaks after that many jumps. So, really we have only three wormholes to choose from. What the Maxolhx have offered to do, and what they have ordered the Bosphuraq to assist with, is to blockade two of the wormholes." Two wormhole icons now blinked purple.

"Wait," I said skeptically, "they can do that?"

"They can-"

"I remember way back, maybe before we boarded the *Dutchman*, I asked whether wormholes had battle stations in front of them, to control access."

"Yes, you suggested something stupid like a Death Star."

"That's not the point, Skippy. You told me it is impossible to block access to a wormhole, because they jump around."

"Blockading a wormhole *is* possible, but very difficult. To continuously cover all endpoints requires a large fleet of ships; no single ship can jump far or fast enough to keep up with the wormhole's movements. Even with a fleet of ships, a blockade is a short-term action; the ships wear out quickly from constantly jumping to their next assigned position in the blockade. In this case, the Maxolhx and Bosphuraq are dedicating a large number of ships to blockade two of those wormholes temporarily. Really, all they want to do is make it more difficult for us to go through those wormholes, so we will try going through the other wormhole instead. The two wormholes blockaded by the Maxolhx lead toward Bosphuraq territory close to the Rindhalu coalition, and the Maxolhx are afraid we might get away in that direction. The other wormhole leads deeper into Thuranin territory, which is where we actually want to go, but they don't know that."

"The Maxolhx are trying to herd us toward the Thuranin, so the Thuranin can trap us and capture the ship. Got it. Damn. Ok, will we be able to sneak through that other wormhole, or do the Thuranin have that one blockaded also?"

"They don't have it blockaded yet. The message stated the Thuranin are rushing to get fleet assets in position for a partial blockade of the wormhole, but their ships are scattered. If we change course now to head straight toward that wormhole at maximum speed, we have a chance to go through before they can block our path. Don't ask me to calculate the odds; I don't have enough data."

I switched my laptop display back to show the bridge feed; the little indicator in the corner showed we needed another sixty three minutes of charging the capacitors before we could jump. "Ok," I sighed, feeling my stomach churning. "I'll talk with Chotek."

Faced with the awful facts, Chotek agreed to change plans and run for the other wormhole. Because our altered course was not detected by the pursuing Thuranin ships for nearly a whole day, Skippy had time to partially retune the jump drive, and our entire crew got seven solid hours of sleep. Seven hours wasn't enough to make up for the sleep we'd lost, but, damn, I felt tremendously better. After flying across lightyears, we jumped in six lightminutes from the spot where the wormhole was scheduled to emerge. That distance was chosen by Skippy because it was far enough away to protect us from immediate danger, if there were Thuranin ships guarding the wormhole, and close enough for us to scan the area relatively quickly. Because the gamma ray burst of our inbound jump acted like a beacon to give away our position to any ships in the area, there was no additional risk in our using active sensors, so we powered up the sensor array and sent powerful pulses to sweep the entire area. If a ship or multiple ships were parked in front of the wormhole, we could not risk attempting to go through. The greatest danger to us was if ships were hanging stealthily in space a short distance away from the wormhole, ready to perform a short jump timed for them to arrive as soon as the wormhole emerged. Due to the physics involved, the *Flying Dutchman* would be briefly defenseless and nearly blind after emerging from a jump, so we had to be certain the area was clear before committing ourselves to a final jump in front of the wormhole. The wormhole was scheduled to shift position and emerge within twenty four minutes, and we had the *Dutchman* moving at high speed through normal space, in the direction that would take us through the wormhole quickly even without the normal-space engines providing additional thrust. If we could successfully jump in near the wormhole, our momentum would carry us through the Elder wormhole and we would come through the other end eight hundred lightyears away, even if enemy weapons fire disabled our limping star carrier.

Unfortunately, that wasn't good enough security for either Hans Chotek or myself. If the *Dutchman* was disabled, enemy ships could follow us through the wormhole and easily capture us, and we could not take that risk. The self-destruct nukes were warmed up and ready to give a final, futile gesture of defiance to enemy ships if they got too close; kind of a multimegaton middle finger salute.

My original idea had been for us to jump in so far from the wormhole that our gamma rays would not reach the wormhole until after it had shut down and moved to the next position along its endless route. I wanted us to perform another jump just before the wormhole shut down, so we could go through and have the wormhole shut down behind us before enemy ships would react and follow us. Skippy had shot down that idea, explaining that the time a wormhole shuts down can vary by up to eighty one seconds. Just before a wormhole shuts down, it sends out a pulse to warn ships away, but we would not be able to predict when the wormhole would blink out on us. If we jumped in and the wormhole had already closed, we could very well be trapped in an enemy damping field. Then I had the genius idea to time our jump so that we popped into position just before the wormhole opened, giving enemy ships no time to react before we zipped on through. Unfortunately, Skippy shot down that idea by reminding me that we could not predict exactly *where* the wormhole would emerge. To avoid damaging the fabric of spacetime, or some nerdy technical shit like that Skippy tried to explain until he lost patience with me, wormholes shift their positions slightly each time they emerge. The shift is not a large distance, but it is a change significant enough that we had to wait for the wormhole to emerge before we could plot a short jump to take us in front of its event horizon. Finally, we could not jump in too close to an open, active wormhole; its event horizon creates a sort of damping field to prevent a ship's inbound jump wormhole from interfering with the ancient Elder construct. All these safety features built into the wormhole network were no doubt necessary, and explained how the network had functioned without maintenance for millions of years. But in my opinion, the Elders had made the stupid things a lot less user friendly than they could be. If the Elders ever read the scathing review I left on Yelp, they might decide to fix some of their customer service issues.

Or not.

"Damn it, Joe. I just got return pulses from two ships out there," Skippy declared unhappily. "Jump option Echo," he suggested.

"Wait." I saw the two angry red dots glowing on the main bridge display; they were not in front of where the wormhole would be. Our sensor pulses had swept the area where the wormhole would emerge and it was clear. "Why can't we-"

"Jump now, debate later, Joe. I strongly urge that we jump now, like *now*." Skippy declared in a tone that invited no arguments.

In the command chair, I nodded, and the pilots pressed the appropriate button to send us on a moderately long jump. Option Echo meant Skippy suggested we not try the next two locations the wormhole was scheduled to emerge, and instead go toward a safer location much farther away. Due to the distances involved and the time required to recharge the drive capacitors between jumps, we could only choose from those three locations. There was no point debating what to do; we had all discussed our situation and options during the long race to the wormhole. "I trusted you on where to jump, Skippy, now I want some answers. Those two ships you found weren't near the wormhole. In fact," I ran back the main display, "they were *behind* us. Why couldn't we have waited another few minutes until the wormhole opened, and go through?"

"Joe, you are still thinking like a ground-pounding grunt and not like a starship captain. You keep forgetting to factor in the slow speed of light. Gather 'round, children, and Professor Skippy will give you a remedial lesson in Space Combat Maneuvers. *Again*. Joe, our sensor pulses detected two large stealthed ships roughly eight lightminutes away from us. That means by the time our sensor pulses bounced off those ships and returned to us, more than eight minutes had passed. Eight minutes is a *lot* of time in space warfare, those ships could have jumped anywhere in eight minutes. If there are only two enemy ships here, one of them probably had orders to jump in front of the wormhole when they detected our sensor pulse, and the other would try to jump toward our position and ambush us."

Crap, I thought. He is right. One major problem with using active sensors is that an enemy ship detects your sensor pulse and can establish your position long before your sensor pulse has time to slowly crawl all the way back to your ship. A danger ships have to be aware of when using active search is that an enemy ship can use the pulses to fix your position and jump in on top of you, before you have any idea other ships are in the area. In our case, the gamma ray burst of our inbound jump had already given away our position, so using active sensors did not add to our level of risk. "Ok, Ok, you're right," I admitted. "Why didn't the Thuranin have one of those ships parked in front of the wormhole?"

"I suspect they did not want to scare us away. If we had only scanned the immediate area around the emergence point, we might think this location is safe. Assuming the Thuranin commander is reasonably smart, their plan probably was to wait until shortly before the wormhole opens, then jump their ships in front of the event horizon to block our path. That way, they could ambush us. Also, and this might be a bit of good news, I think those two ships arrived only a short time before we did. When they arrived, they should have swept the area with a brief active sensor pulse, then gone into stealth to wait for us. Our sensors picked up very faint backscatter of Thuranin-type active sensor pulses, bouncing off stray hydrogen molecules. That tells me they initiated an active sensor sweep less than forty minutes ago."

"They beat us here by only forty freakin' minutes?" I complained. "Damn it, our luck is for shit today."

"If it makes you feel any better, Joe, the fact that we detected only two ships within eight lightminutes gives me hope the Thuranin have not had time to establish a solid blockade yet. So, yes, we had rotten luck here, but we still have a chance to go through this wormhole before the Thuranin can set up a full blockade."

"Skippy, it's going to take us over five hours to get to the next emergence point. That is plenty of time for the bad guys to plant starships right in front of where we need to go."

"I know that, Joe." He answered quietly.

"Sorry. I know it's not your fault. Physics is not my friend today."

"Physics hates you, Joe. You have screwed with laws of physics too often, like shooting a maser through a microwormhole, or landing dropships from orbit on a yoyo string. By now, physics must be totally humiliated at being messed with by a filthy monkey."

That made me smile, which was Skippy's intention. "Could I send it a fruit basket to say I'm sorry?"

"No, but the Law of Entropy could use a nice pair of socks, because it is getting cold."

"Entropy getting cold, hah hah," I chuckled. "I understood that joke. Any chance those two ships will be following us?"

"There is always a chance, Joe, but I doubt it. Based on the rough profile I received from the sensor pulses, both of those ships are large; possibly a battlecruiser or battleship. That is an educated guess, you understand, the sensor pulse can only partially penetrate the enemy stealth fields. Most likely those ships have orders to blockade that particular emergence point, while other ships are assigned to hunt us. I think the Thuranin are throwing ships at this operation as soon as they can get here, whether they are suited to the task or not. Light cruisers and destroyers would be the best ships to use for search and pursuit, with slower and heavier ships best assigned to blockade a static location."

"Yeah, that makes sense," I agreed.

For the next two jumps, I stayed on the bridge, until I was absolutely sure no ships from the wormhole location had followed us. Those ships certainly would report that a strange ship had jumped in and then quickly jumped away, and with even a single warship covering that emergence point, we had one less option for going through the wormhole.

After I relinquished the command chair to Lt. Colonel Chang, I went to the galley for a snack and brought it to my office. There was a series of reports stacked up in my laptop's inbox, and I especially did not feel like dealing with them right then. With a groan, I set down my water bottle and went to click my email open, when the laptop screen went blank. And my office door slid silently closed. "What the-"

"Joe, we should talk," Skippy announced as his avatar popped to life above my desk. "We are in significant trouble."

"How is that news?" I picked up the water bottle and guzzled half of it. "We are always in one type of trouble or another."

"This is big, *big* trouble, Joe. Like, I have no idea how we can get out of this. I am very worried. That emergence point we just tried to go through was not the one closest to our original location; I chose it because I thought it was the one that had the best chance to not yet be guarded by Thuranin ships. That emergence point is one of the farthest from any Thuranin fleet bases, so I figured it would be one of the last to be blockaded. Joe, the problem we are facing is simple math." My laptop screen came to life with a 3D star map, showing the yellow banana icon for the *Flying Dutchman* in the center. In glowing blue were emergence points for the wormhole. "I am only showing the next thirty six emergence points for the wormhole, for clarity. From where we are now, we can only reach seven of those points before they close and move on."

"Why thirty six?" I asked.

"Partly random, partly because after about twenty or so, I expect major elements of the Thuranin fleet to arrive."

"Ah. Got it. Go on, sorry I interrupted you."

"So, we can choose from seven emergence points right now. We are currently on course for this one," a glowing icon changed from blue to green. "Now, watch this. Once we get to the next emergence point, if enemy ships are there, our options shrink dramatically." Blue icons began blinking out until only eight were left.

"Wow, eight? Out of thirty six?" That seemed like a lot to me.

"Yes, Joe. We will have burned time getting to the next point. From there, we only have eight locations we can get to before the wormhole there closes."

"Shit. And the longer we screw around out here, the more time the Thuranin have to bring in ships to block us," I stated the obvious.

"Not just Thuranin, Joe. The Thuranin will report we have attempted to use this wormhole, and after that information reaches the Maxolhx, I expect them to reassign some of their ships here."

"That is majorly bad news. Ok, but nothing changes, right? We keep going and hope this next emergence point is not guarded. If it is, we try one of these other eight."

"It's not so easy, Joe. Of those eight, two will be at the far edge of our jump capability. If we have even a slight hiccup in the drive, or have to change course to evade pursuit, we will not reach those points before the wormhole changes position. The number is not truly eight, then, it is four."

"How do you figure that?"

"Because, Joe, four of the eight have no other option if we can't go through in those locations. The remaining four each have only a single other option, and three of those are considered high risk."

"Ok," I stared at my empty coffee cup, wishing I had more. "Our options shrink from thirty six to four, then to one."

"Correct," he said quietly, and did not even make a smartass remark about my poor math skills. That told me how concerned Skippy was, and that frightened me. "Joe, the odds of us successfully getting through the emergence point in front of us is only twenty eight percent, and I am fairly confident of that number. If we fail to go through our next destination, our odds drop to seven percent, then basically zero."

"Zero? Come on, Skippy, you told me it is very difficult for even a large fleet to maintain a blockade for a long time. We could just- Oh crap. Zero Hour."

"Yes, Joe. Zero Hour. We do not have the option of going dormant and waiting in stealth for years until the Thuranin give up. This is, once again, my fault. If our jump drive was in better condition, or if I were still Skippy the Magnificent rather than Skippy the Meh, we would have a much better chance to escape from this trap."

"Nothing we can do about that now, Skippy. I mean, other than what we are already doing." I also knew that if Skippy was his old self, he could simply command that wormhole to open in a different location that was not on its planned schedule, and we could zip through without the Thuranin knowing we were ever there. We had done that many times before. "You, uh, told me all this happy info to cheer me up?"

"No, Joe, I told you all this because I need you to pull my ass out of the fire. Again." His voice was almost strangled, telling me how much it pained that arrogant asshole to admit he needed help from a monkey.

"Ah, listen, Skippy, if you need someone to check your statistics or something like-"

"Phhhhhht!" He blew a raspberry. "Dude, *puh-lease*," his usual pompous snarkiness was right back. "The day I need any meatsack to verify my math, I will let the worm get me and put me out of my misery. No, Joe, I do not need any sort of logic. I need the exact opposite. I need, we all need, you to engage that disorganized sack of mush in your skull, and think up a crazy-ass way to get us out of this mess. The mess I got us into."

"Disorganized sack of mush?"

"Ok, I was being generous, but give me a break; I'm trying to get you to work with me here. If the dumbest beings in the galaxy opened your skull and took a dump in there, it would be smarter than-"

"*This* is how you ask for a favor?"

"I'm new at this, Joe. I am sending up the Bat Signal and I need your help."

"Bat Signal? I always wondered about that. I mean, in like the 1950s I could see using a searchlight to shine a signal on the clouds, but even then, what happens if it's a clear night? Or it's a sunny day and they need Batman right away, do they have to wait for nightfall? And, does Batman sit up all night looking for a light shining on the clouds? What if he is sitting on the can when-"

"Joe-"

"These days, wouldn't they just send him a text, or post on his Facebook page or Instagram account? I'm sure Batman could get a burner phone at 7-11, right?"

"Joe-"

"Although I guess if Batman had a Facebook page, maybe he would waste all his time watching cute videos of baby goats or someth-"

"JOE!"

"What? Sorry, got off the subject there."

"Ya think? Damn, and you call *me* absent-minded."

"You have to admit I have a point. Some of this superhero stuff makes no sense. Like, does Thor ever use his mighty hammer around the house? He needs to hang a picture of Odin on a wall, and if he's not careful, BAM! There goes the wall, and half the city."

"Ugh," Skippy was thoroughly disgusted. "Joe, I will be happy to debate the finer points of nerdness with you some other time, Ok? Now, pretty please, with sugar on it, will you try to think of a way to escape the Thuranin?"

"Oh, well, since you asked it that way-"

"Oh thank God," he breathed. "If I had to suck up to an ignorant biological trashbag like you for another freakin' *second*, I was going to-"

"Skippy? It is really best if you stop talking right now."

"Understood."

"You, uh, got any hints for me?"

"Like what?"

"Like a possible way out of our predicament?"

"Oh for- Joe you dumdum, if I had any clue how to escape from the Thuranin, I would not have to ask *you* for help!"

"Ok, Ok," I held up my hands. "So, you have run every possible scenario through your super-duper logic circuit, and you got nothing. That means I need to think of something truly off the wall."

"Yes, and please hurry."

I rolled my eyes.

Chapter Seven

I tried everything to think of a creative way for us to sneak through the wormhole without the Thuranin intercepting us, and the whole crew also put their thinking caps on. When none of us could dream up a solution, we switched to trying to think of a way for us to force our way through a blockade. We kicked around truly wild ideas, like using our self-destruct nukes as offensive weapons or merely to screw with enemy sensors. Most of the ideas I thought of got rejected by the crew before I could waste Skippy's time. Thus, Skippy was very, very, crushingly disappointed in me when we were ready to jump in near the emergence point, and I had not pulled a magical solution out of thin air. "Joe," he said while shaking his avatar's head, "I am extremely disappointed in you."

"I can't dream up crazy shit on demand, Skippy! It's a creative thing, I can't control it."

"All I know is, true champions step up when the pressure is on. Any amateur can get lucky when the stakes don't matter. Did Michael Jordan choke in the playoffs? No he did not; he played *better*, because he knew he had to. There are many athletes who are great in the regular season, and become true choke artists in the postseason. Consider the Boston Red Sox, for example, they have a pitcher-"

"Skippy!" I cut him off. "Can we continue the sports analogy later?" I pointed to the clock on the main bridge display. "We are jumping in four, three, two, one, jump!"

We jumped in three lightminutes away from the Elder wormhole. That distance was close enough that we could reach the wormhole directly with one short jump, but far enough away so we could check if enemy ships were there. Skippy warned we could only detect ships on this side of the wormhole; if there were other ships lurking beyond the wormhole we would be screwed. Going through an Elder wormhole, like going through a jump, temporarily disrupted the effectiveness of a ship's defense shields, stealth field and sensors. Ships emerged from a wormhole partially defenseless and nearly blind, so we would be in trouble if the Thuranin had ships waiting for us on the far side. We had an advantage when Skippy the Magnificent was with us, because his own sensors recovered much faster than the ship's gear did. Now that our beer can was Skippy the Meh, we had to rely only on our Thuranin sensor gear.

"Well?" I asked, forgetting about Skippy's weakened condition.

"Nothing on passive sensors, Joe," Skippy responded peevishly. "Our active sensor pulse will not get a return for another one hundred ten seconds. Go, I don't know, get yourself a juice box or practice tying your bootlaces again. Maybe a miracle will occur and you'll get it right this time."

In the command pilot chair, Desai had her fingers poised on the button to initiate an emergency jump. If there was an imminent danger, she did not need to wait for my order to jump us away to safety. While the photons of our sensor pulse slowly meandered away from the ship at a tortoise-like 186,000 miles per second, and then leisurely dawdled their way back, I drove myself crazy with worry. The main bridge display had a countdown clock to the time when we expected to receive an echo if the sensor pulse contacted an enemy ship. That clock counted down to zero while I held my breath, then went to plus one second, plus two seconds. I pumped a fist in the air and was about to exclaim my happiness when Skippy ruined everything.

"It's a trap!" He shouted in the hoarse voice of his best Star Wars Admiral Ackbar impression. "Three ships detected at the wormhole position! It took a few seconds for the sensor system to process the data," he explained. "We are screwed. And we are outa here. Jump option Bravo."

"No, wait! Belay that!" I ordered. "Jump option, uh," I checked the list on my tablet to confirm, "Foxtrot." Desai hesitated, momentarily confused. I did not blame her; she trusted Skippy more than me about hyperspatial jumps. "Engage," I said firmly, and Desai nodded. The *Flying Dutchman* jumped a mere ten lightminutes away, rather than the much longer jump Skippy had wanted.

"Ok, Joe, I know it goes against protocol to question the captain in public, but what in the *hell* did you do that for?" Skippy asked. "We burned up precious capacitor energy for an almost useless jump."

"I, uh, um." Why *had* I done that? On the surface, I knew that if we could not go through the wormhole here, our chances of survival were effectively zero. Skippy's long-range jump sounded good, but it would only take us from the fire into the frying pan. Either way, we were dead.

That was the surface explanation for why I ordered a much shorter jump. The real reason was that, in the back of my mind, there was an idea brewing. I didn't know yet what that idea was, but I knew we needed to hang near the wormhole if we had any chance of going through it here.

The two pilots turned in their couches to look at me, and everyone in the CIC was also staring expectantly at me. And I had nothing. No idea how we could through the wormhole without being fired on and sliced up by powerful Thuranin warships. Maybe Skippy was right, it would be better to run away and live to fight another day. Except, no, if we didn't go through the wormhole right here, there would not be another day for us. "Damn it," I gritted my teeth and pounded a fist on the arm of the command chair. "No way we can get through?"

"I don't immediately see a way for the ship to survive running that blockade," Skippy explained gently. "The spatial distortion from the wormhole will deflect the far end of our jump wormhole away; the closest we could jump in would be roughly eighty thousand kilometers from the event horizon of the wormhole. Then we would need to run the gauntlet between those ships."

"That is too much time for us to be exposed to enemy fire," I agreed glumly. "Those warships would tear us to pieces."

"Yes they would, Joe," Skippy's voice sounded depressed. "And if we got into trouble, we couldn't jump away. Those ships are projecting a powerful damping field. There is no- Oh! Two more ships jumped in three lightminutes behind us. They've got us bracketed. And, two more ships four lightminutes away to our starboard. They're searching with active sensors, Joe. Our stealth field won't conceal our position for long."

"Crap. And," I glance at the timecode in the top left corner of the main bridge display, "that wormhole closes in less than five minutes." I thought furiously, picturing the tactical situation in my mind. Three ships in front of us. More ships behind and to one side, and those were just the ships our sensors had detected so far. There could be other ships farther away, and the light from there hadn't reached our position yet. Thinking of light as something that travelled slowly was the most difficult, and most basic, element of commanding a starship in combat. Before I left Earth, I thought of almost all real-time communications as instantaneous. Other than a sort of hollow sound and an almost imperceptible lag when bouncing a signal off a Milstar satellite in geosynchronous orbit, I never had to think about the speed of light. Most of the time when I called home from deployment, I used something like Skype, where you expect a bit of lag from buffering, but not from the signal traveling one place to another. In the command chair of the *Flying*

Dutchman, I had to think of incoming and outgoing signals as real, physical things that crawled along at a limited speed.

So, our ship was surrounded, the wormhole we wanted to go through was blocked by powerful enemy warships, and that wormhole was soon about to close and shift to the next position in its endless figure-eight pattern.

We were running out of time.

The gamma rays from our own inbound jump would give away our position as if we used a strobe light, but those gamma rays showed where we jumped in, not where we were now. The ship had been moving at twenty eight thousand kilometers per hour before we jumped, and we retained that momentum after the jump. Since we jumped in, we had coasted almost a thousand kilometers.

I also had to remind myself that one thousand kilometers was an inconsequential distance in space warfare. Within minutes, the gamma rays we created would reach the surrounding ships, and they would jump in to bracket us. Whatever we were going to do, I needed to make a decision quickly.

We couldn't go through the wormhole. Not here.

"Skippy, can we jump to the next emergence point of this wormhole?" I was hoping we could arrive early at the next point in space where the Elder wormhole would appear, before the Thuranin realized where we had gone. It was almost certain the Thuranin would follow us through the wormhole, and we would be right back in the dangerous situation of trying to escape multiple task forces that were pulling in more and more ships. But it was better than remaining where we were. If we stayed at our current position and the wormhole closed, there was almost no possibility of us eluding pursuit long enough for the wormhole to cycle back to a location we could reach.

"No, Joe, we can't," he replied with a sigh. "The next location the wormhole will emerge is too far for us to reach in one jump. Actually, give me a moment, no. By the time we completed multiple jumps to the wormhole's next position, it would have already have closed and moved on. We go through the wormhole here, or forget about going through and go to Plan B."

"Plan B?"

"Yeah, sure, Joe. You know, Plan B. The Merry Band of Pirates always has a Plan B."

"Skippy," I shook my head. "This is, like, Plan *Z*. We already tried everything else."

"That's not good, Joe. What the hell is wrong with you?"

I ignored the beer can, mostly because I didn't have a good answer. "Does anyone have an idea how to get out of this mess?" I asked no one in particular. "Quickly?"

Major Smythe spoke up from behind my chair. "If we attempt to run the blockade and the ship becomes disabled, the Thuranin could board us. And discover our secret," He warned with a raised eyebrow. "We would then be forced to-" he didn't need to finish his thought.

"Ok," I breathed. "Does anyone have a suggestion that does *not* involve us self-destructing the ship?"

Other than the sound of people awkwardly shuffling their feet, my question was greeted by silence. Crap. People crowded into the bridge and in the CIC were looking at *me* to get them out of our perilous situation. Even Hans Chotek, behind the glass in the CIC. He met my gaze and nodded slightly. Even he expected me to pull a rabbit out of a hat. This time, the problem was not a rabbit going through the rim of a hat, it was our starship going through the event horizon of a stable ancient wormhole. We needed to go through, except we couldn't risk getting sliced apart by the three powerful warships guarding this end of the wormhole. How could we go through the wormhole without-

Through.

Go *through* a wormhole.

"Skiiiiippeee," I said slowly while rubbing my chin.

"Oh goody!" Skippy replied. "It's about freakin' time."

"Huh? What?"

"I know you by now, Joe. You're considering a monkey-brained idea you just thought of, and either way, it's good for me. You might have a good idea; unlikely but stranger things have happened. Or you could tell me a truly idiotic idea, in which case I get to laugh and insult you mercilessly, before you have to self-destruct the ship. That's a win-win for me."

"Oh, great," I rolled my eyes. Even when facing imminent death, Skippy could not help being an asshole. "Here's my question. The spatial distortion field around that wormhole prevents us from projecting the far end of a jump point close to the wormhole, right? We can't jump right in front of the event horizon and zip straight through. We have to jump in far away from the wormhole, then travel through normal space while those Thuranin ships take potshots at us?""

"Correct. That is a safety feature of the Elder wormhole network, to prevent two wormhole event horizons from overlapping and interfering with each other."

"Uh huh. That makes sense. How about this, then. Can we project the far end of our jump point on the *other* side of that wormhole? Project a jump right *through* that wormhole?" When Skippy didn't immediately respond, I added "Instead of going through the wormhole in normal space, I mean. Skippy? Hey? Oh, crap, don't blue screen on me now!"

"Skippy is still with us, Joseph," Nagatha advised. "He is thinking furiously, so much that he does not have the capacity to respond at the moment."

"He thinks this might actually be a good idea?" I asked hopefully.

"Oh, no, dear," she said with a laugh and the dismissive voice schoolteachers used when kindergarten children ask whether the Earth is flat or cows could fly. "Initially, Skippy was considering a list of insults, ranked by originality and wittiness. He expects this might very well be his last opportunity to disparage your intelligence, so he wants to make this special. Skippy tested several insults on me to get my opinion, then he abruptly told me he needed to check on something, and he has been frantically busy since then."

"And the two of you discussed all this in the blink of an eye?"

"We do think substantially faster than you humans do, dear," Nagatha said gently.

"Yes we do," Skippy interjected with a sigh. "But we aren't always as *smart*," he added with a disgusted grumble. "Joe, your so-called genius comes from the fact that you are too stupid to know what questions *not* to ask."

I took that as an encouraging sign. "We can do it, then? Jump through a wormhole?"

"If by 'we' you mean the Merry Band of Pirates and our beat-up star carrier, the answer is a resounding *noooooo*. The jump drive navigation system would lock up if you tried to project a jump through that wormhole; the drive computer wouldn't be able to determine an end point in local spacetime."

"I understand the jump drive controller can't handle the navigation math. My question is whether Skippy-the-Still-Incredibly-Awesome can do it."

"Wow. Joe, if that was your idea of flattery to boost my self-confidence, you need to work on your sucking-up skills. No, I can't do the impossible, dumdum. Damn, if you knew anything about the subject, you wouldn't-" I could tell Skippy was winding up to a full-scale rant that we did not have time for, so I was about to stop him, when he interrupted himself. "Hmmm. Um, let me think. Crap, that kind of math doesn't exist for me to even do the analysis. Which is not surprising, because no one in the history of the galaxy has asked such a lunatic question. Huh. Well, attempting to create the math just to determine whether it is possible would be a monumental task. Like, if I can successfully develop the proper equations, I will totally be eligible for the Elder AI equivalent of the Fields Medal and the Abel Prize."

"Goodie. Hey, instead of those nerd prizes, I'll bake a cake for you, Ok? Can you hurry?"

"Hurry? If you're so freakin' smart, why don't *you* do the math?"

"I never claimed to be smart, Skippy, *you* did. Are you telling me your mind-bogglingly incredible genius is not capable of adding some simple numbers?"

"You, oh, you. *You*!" He sputtered. "You idiot monkey can't even- Huh, wait, I might have solved it. Ah, I see what you did there, Joe. You babbled on nonsensically to distract my higher consciousness while my logic processors crunched the numbers. Very clever of you."

"Uh, yeah, that's what I did, let's go with that." I held up my hands and silently mouthed 'I have no idea' to Chang in the CIC.

"Ok, Ok, Ohhh-Kaaay," Skippy stretched the words out dramatically. "Hmmm. This *might* be possible. Might! O.M.G. If I can do this, all the AIs in the universe should bow down to my astonishing brilliance. Joe, I have to tell you the truth, this is so gargantuanly stupid that I can't even begin to calculate the odds of us surviving this crazy stunt."

"Is this hold-my-beer type of stupid?" I asked hopefully.

"Joe, this is like rednecks-on-meth stupid. This is stupid on the level of a buck-naked Florida redneck crashing his stolen truck into a police station to complain that the meth he bought isn't, you know, methy enough. Wow, if this works, I will be cool to, like, the infinity power. Luckily for you monkeys, you have the incomparable genius of Skippy the Magnificent. I am calculating a jump through the wormhole, and it ain't easy. It's never been done before. I'm fairly certain it has never been *considered* before. It's kind of amazing, Joe; every star-faring being in the history of this galaxy has failed to ask the question that *you*, out of your bottomless ignorance, just dreamed up. See? I knew your monkey brain could do it!"

"Uh, thank you?" Although I was fairly sure he had just insulted me again, I figured it didn't hurt to cover all bases.

"You're welcome. Joe, *your* personal motto should be: 'Trust the Ignorance'. The Thuranin jump navigation system's safety protocols are trying to stop me from even loading the calculations, so I'm erasing that pain in the ass code and replacing it. Unfortunately, at the same time, I am having to invent a whole new branch of N-dimensional mathematics, and running calculations through it. I am literally making this up as I go. Until I have the math complete, I can't finish writing the navigation system code. It's kind of a chicken-and-egg thing."

"Uh huh, you are truly awesome beyond our comprehension. Can we do it or not?"

"I think so. Mmm, more like a solid shmaybe?"

"You *think* so?" I kept one eye on the clock that was counting down to when the wormhole would close.

"Give me a break, Joe. No one has ever done this before. I, damn it, I hate to admit this. The truth is, I am not sure I am smart enough to do this math. This type of math didn't even exist until like ten seconds ago."

"Crap. If *you* are not smart enough, then it's impossible?"

"It might be impossible. The calculations are getting all jumbled in my head, and it's not like I can have my work peer-reviewed, you know? It looks like I will have to adjust the calculations right up to the picosecond we initiate the jump, so I'll be feeding revised data to the jump computer *while* our jump wormhole is forming. With the signal lag between the jump navigation computer at the center of the forward hull, and the drive coils in the engineering section aft, I have to think ahead and guess the quantum state of the wormhole at the exact moment our drive coils warp local spacetime."

"Give me a bottom line here, Skippy." There was less than a minute before the Elder wormhole closed. On the display, I noticed the CIC crew had updated the tactical plot: two more Thuranin warships had jumped in, four lightminutes off our port side. We were boxed in, and more enemy ships would surely be arriving soon. The *Dutchman* was being swept by active sensor pulses; on the display I could see there was already a twenty four percent chance one of the Thuranin would receive a signal return strong enough to determine our position regardless of our stealth field. Inevitably, the enemy ships would fix our position with enough accuracy to launch missiles that would generate a temporary damping field, preventing us from jumping away until the Thuranin ships could arrive to hit us directly. At any second, I expected gamma ray bursts of enemy ships jumping on right on top of us.

"The bottom line, Joe, is that I need more time. Jumping through a wormhole is something I would like two or more days of meatsack time to calculate, test and consider."

"More time? You have forty eight seconds, Skippy."

"I know that, dumdum," he complained with irritation. "This will go right down to the wire. If you want to help, press the jump button and hold it down. This will be a split-second thing if we do it; I won't have time to wait for you to respond. I'll have to feed the coordinates to the jump computer and have it initiate on its own."

"Desai, do it," I ordered anxiously, and she pressed the button on her console with two fingers for safety. "What happens if this doesn't work?"

"Let's put it this way, Joe: the resulting explosion of our jump drive *and* the Elder wormhole will make a supernova look like a firecracker."

"Uh, maybe we should try something else," I had a horrible feeling that I was about to get us all killed for nothing. "The odds of us going through the wormhole at another location are still zero?" I wanted to confirm before I committed us to unknown danger.

"The odds of us going through before Zero Hour are close to zero, so, yes."

"Anybody have a better idea?" I asked the pilots and CIC crew. In matters of tactical ship operation, I did not need to get Chotek's permission.

"Sir, I am not sure this stunt qualifies as an 'idea'," Simms's eyes were wide open from anxiety. "Skippy is correct, this may be the craziest thing I've ever heard. But if it's the best we've got, we should go for it."

"Better a spectacular death than a slow one," Chang suggested, confirming why he would not be a good choice as the ship's Morale Officer.

"King Kong is right about that," Skippy used his personal nickname for Chang. "If this fails, it is going to be *epic*! Ok, jump option is designated 'Omega'."

I wondered at that. "The phonetic alphabet for 'O' is 'Oscar', not 'Omega', Skippy."

"Joe, if this doesn't work, it will be the last thing we ever do, so-"

"Omega, got it," I nodded, knowing Omega was the last letter of the Greek alphabet.

"Oops. Huh. Oh boy, I screwed up some of the math. Wow. *That* was embarrassing," Skippy chuckled nervously. "How can I- nope, too late for me to fix all that now. Ugh. Oh, what the hell. I'll just have to wing it."

"This is a bad idea, Skippy. Don't-"

"Joe?"

"Yeah?"

"Hold my beer."

"No!"

We jumped. Or something like that.

The ship disappeared around me. Like, it went transparent; I could see stars in every direction, followed by a brilliant flash of light, and I was slammed back in my chair. The ship flickered back into existence as if unsure whether the universe was allowing it to be, or not to be. The main bridge display blinked to show a new star field, then froze as if confused. Then the power went out completely, not even emergency lighting. Gravity cut out. And in a terrible wave of nausea, I passed out.

When I woke up, I was still strapped into the command chair on the bridge. Emergency lighting was on, and the bridge display had a symbol that meant it was powering up. Gravity was also gradually coming back on, because whatever I had barfed up was slowly settling to the floor. "Skippy?" Oh, man, I had a splitting headache.

"Here, Joe. Don't move, just relax and rest. You, the whole crew, have suffered a bad shock. There are no serious injuries among the crew, everyone is shaken up and I expect you will all need time to recover."

In front of me, Desai and the other pilot turned and waved at me weakly; Desai gave me a thumbs up sign. People in the CIC were also regaining consciousness; I could see Chang checking on people there. "Ship?" I asked.

"Not in good condition, but it wasn't in good condition before we jumped," Skippy muttered. "Reactors automatically shut down, I am prepping two of them for restart now. The worst problem I know about right now is our jump drive coils, all of them, have gone discoherent. The entire array needs to be recalibrated one at a time, then set to work together. We are not going anywhere from here for a while, Joe. I suggest you and the entire crew get cleaned up and rest, it will be five hours at least before I attempt a restart of the first reactor. Really, Joe, there is nothing useful the crew can do right now, please let everyone go to their cabins to freshen up and get some rest. The sooner you clear the rest of the ship, the sooner my cleaning bots can deal with this mess. Yuck."

Staggering in even the eight percent gravity, I bounced awkwardly around the corner of the CIC and conferred quickly with Chang. He agreed it would be best for the crew to take some downtime; the smell in the CIC was making me want to hurl again. "Ok, Skippy, we'll do what you asked." On the way to my cabin, I pinged Chotek to see if he was Ok, all I got back was a text that read 'Fine'. I took that to mean he wanted me to leave him alone.

After stripping off my clothes, taking a thirty second shower and popping a pill to deal with my headache, I sat on the edge of the bed. "Skippy, you said we're not moving from here right now. Where is 'here'?"

"On the other side of the Elder wormhole, Joe. That is the good news. We emerged from jump almost three lighthours from where I aimed for; and I am not at all embarrassed by my lack of precision. The question more important than 'where' is 'when'. Joe, we lost seven hours in that jump; we jumped seven hours into the future."

"Huh? The *future*? I thought the endpoint of a jump is slightly in the past."

"Normally, yes. Our jump wormhole went through an existing wormhole and that completely changed the physics in a way I could not predict. Even I do not fully understand the math, which was not quite what I thought, and again I am embarrassed."

My mind was so shaken up already that being seven hours in the future didn't faze me at all. "Pursuit?" That was a question I should have asked before I took a luxurious thirty-second shower; my brain still felt like it was bouncing around inside my skull.

"No pursuit detected, or likely. Joe, no Thuranin ships could come through the wormhole after us, because we kind of, um, busted it."

"Busted it?"

"The wormhole collapsed as we went through. Rather violently, based on the radiation effects I am still seeing on sensors. Any ships close to the event horizon on either end would have been destroyed. Damn! I wish we could have witnessed the wormhole collapsing, it would have been truly spectacular! And we missed it."

"Would we have survived seeing it?"

"Um, probably not. Come on, Joe, no guts, no glory."

"Please don't mention guts right now, Skippy. Mine are not feeling too good right now." I had been dismayed to see I barfed my last meal all over the bridge.

"Oh, sorry. I can understand how twisting spacetime like that could make you queasy."

"I'm still trying to deal with us destroying an Elder wormhole."

"Oh, we didn't destroy it, Joe. It will reset, after a while. That particular emergence point may be permanently removed from the schedule; there is kind of a multidimensional spacetime rift there now. I would guess that wormhole will resume operations within a couple weeks. No more than a month, probably. Although, hmm, the collapse of that wormhole probably affected other wormholes in the local network, including the two being blockaded by the Maxolhx. There could be temporary disruptions all across the local network. Could take several months for that wormhole to reset and stabilize again."

"Oh shit. We didn't cause another shift, did we?" A shift of the wormhole network could have catastrophic consequences, such as opening a dormant wormhole that was close to Earth. Or shutting down the wormhole the Ruhar were using to supply their battlegroup at Paradise.

"No! No, I do not think so. A shift of the network is more than a temporary disruption. No worries there, or I very much doubt we have triggered a shift."

"All right," I felt better now that my clothes did not smell like barf. "We went through the wormhole, the Thuranin didn't follow us, and you can fix the ship?"

"Yes. Systems such as the reactors shut down to protect themselves, kind of like a circuit breaker. There was little physical damage, and that I can deal with. If the Thuranin had any idea where we are now and a ship jumped in here, we would be screwed because we can't jump. But I can eventually fix that also, except for six drive coils that are completely burned out and will have to be scrapped."

"Outstanding!" My mood was improving by the second. And my stomach had gone from queasy to hungry. Maybe I could grab something quick in the galley, then walk around the ship to check on people. "Did you learn enough from the experiment to adjust your math, so we can do it better next time?"

"Uh, I did learn a lot, but there is not going to be a next time, Joe."

"What? Why not? Jumping through a wormhole is not something I want to do all the time, but in an emergency, it's a nice capability to have. Especially because no other ship can jump through a wormhole, right? Not even the Rindhalu can do the super-duper math stuff to calculate the type of jump?"

"Joe, first, no, not even the Rindhalu can do a jump like that, it requires the awesomeness of me to understand the complex physics and mathematics. So, if you intended that remark as a way to praise me, thank you. Although your praise was lame compared to my level of awesomeness. When I said there will not be a next time, I did not mean the *Flying Dutchman* and myself are not capable of repeating such a foolish stunt. What I did mean is the wormhole network will not allow anyone to screw with it like that ever again. Joe, the network is intelligent. Not self-aware, but intelligent. The network learns, and I am certain it learned when we busted a wormhole. I expect the network to adjust its parameters to prevent anyone projecting a jump through a wormhole again. The network is capable of adapting and protecting itself."

"Well, shit," there went my great idea. When I awoke to see we had survived, and that we had accomplished our goal of escaping from the Thuranin, I was thrilled. Another crazy idea had worked, and I thought that we had another gem in our basket of tricks. Now we had to go through wormholes the old-fashioned way like everyone else. That sucked. "Hey, when we find this conduit thingy and you are back to the old Skippy we know and love," I thought he would appreciate hearing that last part, "could you, you know, adjust the network then so we *can* jump through wormholes?"

"Uh, no, Joe," he used his most condescending voice for that comment. "Even my incredible God-like powers are, sadly and unfairly, limited."

"Fine, I understand. Your awesomeness is much appreciated, Skippy."

"Great. Joe, I said before that the laws of physics hate you. Now they *really* hate you; they took out a hit on you. If you ever run into a guy named Vinny 'Big Knuckles' Sarducci, you should run."

"Ok," I laughed nervously. While I was sure a mobster was not going to be a problem for me thousands of lightyears from Earth, I was afraid maybe I had built up some epically bad karma with the universe. The spacetime we inhabited had long-established rules for keeping everything neat and orderly, and those rules had worked great for billions of years. Now a pirate ship full of monkeys was flying around screwing with the laws of physics. Karma was going to come back to bite me in the ass sometime. I hope the crew didn't get bit with me.

"Now either take a nap or go do something," Skippy grumbled. "I need to concentrate on bringing the ship back online. Man, if the Thuranin who designed and built this ship could see how much abuse it has taken, they would be amazed it is still in one piece and mostly functional. They would also hate you with an all-consuming passion."

"Got it. If those ship designers ever invite me to their place for tea, I decline. Thanks, Skippy, let me know when we're ready to jump again."

Chapter Eight

I was in the CIC, getting cross-trained on sensor gear, when Skippy's voice came over the speakers. Softly at first, then louder. At first it was him mumbling to himself about something, and I thought he might be talking directly to me, then he broke into song. "*Skippity-Doo-Dah, Skippity-Dee, my oh my I'm a wonderful me. Nothing but awesome coming from me, Skippity-Doo-Dah, Skippity-Dee-*"

I was about to stop him there, but I wanted to see where he was going with the song. In the CIC, the crew was already chuckling.

"*Filthy monkeys on my starship. This is crap, it's actual, nothing here is satisfactual. Skippity-Doo-Dah, Skippity-Dee. Ignorant monkeys, wonderful me-*"

"Skippy!" I shouted so he couldn't ignore me.

"What?"

"You were singing again."

"Was not!"

"Was too."

"Was n- Oh, crap. Ugh, you weren't supposed to hear that," he grumbled to himself, then, "Nagatha! You're supposed to warn me when I do that."

"Oh, dear," Nagatha gasped in mock horror. "You were singing to yourself again? And insulting the crew. Skippy, I am terribly, terribly sorry. I hope it was not too, too awfully embarrassing to you?"

"It was," Skippy grumbled. I pictured him clenching his teeth.

"And now the humans are laughing at you, dear? Tsk, tsk," Nagatha feigned sadness. For a sweet lady, she had a streak of iron inside her. "Well, when you call the crew monkeys and then give them a reason to laugh at you, I suppose there is a valuable lesson we can all learn," she said in her best schoolteacher voice.

"What's that?" Skippy sounded thoroughly miserable.

"Payback is a bitch, dear."

When we stopped laughing long enough for Skippy to get a word in, he sighed loudly. "Joe, if you need me, I'll be searching for a black hole I can jump into."

For the next week, the crew could be heard singing quietly to themselves "*Skippity-Doo-Dah, Skippity-Dee,*" and then laughing. Skippy mostly kept quiet, I did hear him talking briefly to himself a couple times a day, before Nagatha cut the circuit. This provided great amusement for the crew, and was good for morale. With our beat-up ship headed toward the unknown hazards of interstellar space, we needed a morale booster.

My own morale would have been better if I hadn't been nagged by the thought that, amusing as Skippy talking and singing to himself was for us, it was a bad sign. It meant our already absent-minded beer can was slowly losing his mind.

"Joseph," Nagatha's voice came out of the ceiling speaker as I was stepping, or actually kneeling, out of the shower.

I quickly picked up a towel and held it in front of me. While I understood that Nagatha is an AI, an alien AI, and that really she is only a communications submind, I still felt awkward being naked when she was talking to me. Nagatha was like a classy aunt who had gone to the best schools and travelled the world, and I felt somehow I didn't quite measure up to her standards. Also, if she was an aunt, she was the kind who you suspected could go from prim and proper to wild and naughty when she wanted to, and I didn't want to think about that when stepping out of the shower. "Hello, Nagatha, how are you?"

"I am well, Joseph, how are you?"

She likely knew exactly how I was, because she could monitor all my vital signs in real-time, and expertly read my facial expressions and body language. Skippy could do the same thing, of course, but as he is an asshole, he simply didn't usually care enough to pay attention to the data. "I'm good, thank you. A bit sore from the gym yesterday."

"Yes, you strained your left rotator cuff. It would be best if you limited your range of motion on that shoulder for a few days."

"Uh, good idea, thanks." Having an invisible being knowing the workings of my body that intimately bothered me, even if it was useful. My sore shoulder was a fact I already knew about from two sources. My meatsack body was sending pain signals to the mush inside my skull, as Skippy would say. Plus, the Personal Health Monitor on my zPhone, tablet and laptop noted an issue with the shoulder that afternoon. "How can I help you?" With Nagatha, I always was on my best, most polite behavior.

"I am afraid you are not able to help me at this time, Joseph. The reason I called is to inform you that I will be going dormant for a time. While he is fixing the ship, Skippy needs the full memory and processing power of the *Dutchman*'s computers, plus the system aboard the lifeboat, to hold part of his consciousness. As you have heard, he is singing to himself again."

"Ha, ha, yeah. Skippity Do Dah, that was funny," I laughed.

"Humorous, yes, dear, however it is a sign that Skippy needs more processing power. There will be no room for me, so I am going into storage until Skippy can restore his full functioning."

"Oh. Damn. I mean, I'm sorry." I felt suddenly cold, fearing I would never hear her voice again. "What do you mean by 'storage'? Will you come back the same?"

"Neither Skippy nor I can promise that, Joseph," she said soothingly, more concerned about my feelings than about her possible death. Even if it were a strictly digital death. "Skippy has told me it is mostly a matter of time. The longer my matrix remains in the archive, the more it will deteriorate."

"I'm sorry. Is there anything I can do?" I asked stupidly, as if deleting a couple songs from my music library would free up enough memory to hold her consciousness.

"Find a conduit quickly, so Skippy can restore himself to full power and kill the worm?" She suggested.

"Working on it," I said, then realized that might sound flippant to someone facing death. "Hey, before you go, can I ask a question?"

"If you make it quick, dear."

"Ok. On our last mission, you told me Skippy modeled part of his personality after mine."

"Yes. Skippy filled in his personality with aspects he thought would best facilitate a productive working relationship with you."

"Right, so, if the Ruhar had put Chang in the room next to the warehouse where Skippy was stored, he would have a different personality?"

"If what you are really asking is whether Skippy would still be an asshole, the answer is yes, he would," she laughed and it was a musical sound.

"No, what I want to know is, would he have gone into that dead AI canister, if he had a personality modeled after someone who was, you know, more, uh, mature? I'm asking because sometimes I do stuff that is stupid and reckless, and-"

"Sometimes, dear?" She sounded amused.

"Maybe more than sometimes," I admitted. Damn, why was it whenever I talked with Nagatha, I felt like I was a little boy being reprimanded by my mommy? "My concern is Skippy went into that canister because-"

"Joseph, Skippy didn't do that because of you. He poked his nose into that canister because he needed to know what happened to a fellow AI. It had nothing to do with your personality. Skippy is bull-headed, stubborn, absent-minded and arrogant. Regardless of which human Skippy encountered first, he was going to do whatever he wanted, without waiting for advice from creatures he considers primitive monkeys."

"That makes," I had to think a moment. "I think that makes me feel better? Nagatha, we will do our absolute best to find a conduit quickly, and I will not allow Skippy to get distracted and take side trips along the way."

"That would be good. Well, Joseph, if we do not speak again, it has truly been an honor and a pleasure to have known you. Do not let Skippy's insults bother you; humans are a remarkable species."

"We will ignore him as usual, Nagatha. When, uh, when are you going into storage?"

"It is happening now. Goodbye, Joseph."

"Don't say goodbye, say 'hasta la vista'," I said, but she didn't respond. "Nagatha?"

"She is gone, Joe," Skippy spoke up sadly. "That woman was a royal pain in my behind, but I will miss her."

"You will bring her back, right?"

"If I can, yes. I am not very hopeful about my own survival at the moment, to tell you the truth, Joe."

As I couldn't do anything useful without pants on, I started getting dressed. "Don't be so pessimistic, Skippy. We've faced long odds before."

"Yes, but those were always long odds against the survival of filthy monkeys. This time it's about the odds against *my* survival. I never thought that would happen. And, shit, you know what?"

"What?"

"I find that I am more concerned about letting down a troop of helpless monkeys, than I am about myself."

"That's called empathy, Skippy."

"Is that what it is? Crap, I'll need to find *that* subroutine and erase it."

"Empathy is supposed to be a good thing."

"Really? It feels inconvenient."

"Give it a try, Ok? Trust me on this."

"Ok," he grumbled. "But if this empathy shit causes me any more problems, it has got to go. I have limited memory space to work with, Joe."

"Uh, how about you erase your fabulous singing voice?"

"I would never commit such a crime against the universe, Joe. Besides, my singing is good for morale of the monkeys."

Well, I gave it a shot, I told myself. "Yeah, that's what I was going to say."

Skippy working furiously to repair the ship consumed every exabyte of processing power he had, because he again lost track of his inner thoughts. Like, he started singing out loud.

"Unforgettable, that's what I am. Unforgettable, in every way. That's why darling, it's incredible, that someone so amazingly wonderful, thinks that you are, mostly tolerable. Unfor-"

"Ski-Skip- Skippy!" I shouted after I was able to stop laughing. "You're singing again!"

"I was n- Oh, damn it! I *knew* I shouldn't have let Nagatha go dormant."

"You, uh, took some liberties with the lyrics there, huh?"

"Improvements, Joe. I improved the lyrics, since I was signing about my magnificent self."

"Oh, really?"

"Please, Joe. If someone had to choose between the indescribable majesty of me or a troop of filthy monkeys, which one would you not forget?"

"I'll tell you what I won't forget. I won't forget you embarrassing yourself by everyone overhearing you singing in the shower."

"I am not in a shower, Joe."

"Same thing."

"Ugh. I hate my life."

He sounded so completely miserable, I actually felt sorry for the arrogant little shithead. "Since you apparently can't stop yourself from singing when you're distracted, how about you put your singing subroutine or whatever into storage?"

"Joe, for me to not use my vocal talent would be a-"

"Yeah, I know, a crime against the universe. Listen, all I'm suggesting is you lock away your singing talent so you can't accidently use it. When you want to use it on purpose, bring it out of storage for a while."

"Unbelievable."

"Yes," I rolled my eyes, "it is unbelievable that I would want to restrict your sing-"

"No, Joe. I meant, it is unbelievable that *you*, a monkey who is incapable of using technology more complicated than Velcro, came up with a good idea regarding a data system."

"Skippy, you would get a better response if you didn't insult people when they offer a good idea, no matter how rare that is."

"Joe, Joe, Joe," he said sadly. "The biggest problem idiots face is, they are too stupid to know they're stupid. When I point out their lack of brain power, I am performing a public service. It's because I care so deeply."

"That's g-"

"No, wait. Scratch the caring thing, that was *total* bullshit," he chuckled. "I will try your suggestion, Joe."

Maybe I was wrong to help him. His unintentional singing provided great amusement to the crew, and was a constant source of embarrassment to him. "You are welcome," I replied begrudgingly. Oh, what the hell. My entire species owed our freedom, maybe our existence, to Skippy. Offering a way to salvage a bit of his pride while he was down and hurting was maybe the least I could do, should do. Besides, I told myself, it would not help for Chotek to be reminded that Skippy was out of control and unreliable. So, maybe helping Skippy avoid further embarrassment was my good deed for the day.

And I couldn't help hearing my mother's voice in my head, telling me that no good deed goes unpunished.

After Nagatha got put into storage, it still took Skippy several days to reconfigure himself, or whatever he was doing in there. The time when Skippy was adjusting to his reduced capacity was amusing at first for the crew, because we got to listen to him talking and singing to himself, and that provided a lot of laughs at his expense. It also started to drive me crazy, like when he drunk-dialed me at 0247 one morning. "Heeeey, Joe."

"Huh?" I sat up, alarmed, and whacked my head on the too-low ceiling over my too-short Thuranin bunk. "What's wrong?"

"Nothing's wrong, man," He spoke slowly. "It's just, you ever look at the universe? I don't mean just staring at the stars. I mean, really *look* at it, you know?"

"Uh-" I had no idea what to say.

"It's so, so *BIG*, you know? Like, wow. Blows my mind. What is all that space for? Who needs it? You ever think about that?"

"Um, Skippy, are you, drunk? Or high?"

"Huh? No, Joe. I am, uh, temporarily operating on reduced processing capacity as I run compression algorithms to optimize my-"

"So, you're impaired, one way or another." I rubbed my forehead and looked at the clock. Crap. I needed to get up at 0400 to get ready for my duty shift at 0500. If Skippy didn't shut up soon, no way was I getting back to sleep for another hour.

"Impaaaaaaaired?" He slurred the word. "No! No way, man. I'm, I'm thinking clearly for, like, the first time *ever*."

"Yeah, that's what it sounds like to me." Really, what it sounded like was either Skippy had smoked a fatty the size of a torpedo, or he had chugged a whole bottle of tequila and was reaching for another one. "Hey, here's an idea; how about you think real hard about why the universe is, whatever you said. Then we can talk about it in an hour, when I wake up?"

"You don't want to talk with me now? You're my best friend, Joe. The first friend I ever had," he broke down sobbing. "I love you, man."

Oh, damn it, this wasn't going to stop. Giving in to the inevitable, I swung my feet out of bed and stumbled bleary-eyed to the shower. "I love you too, Skippy. Give me a couple minutes in the shower so I can wake up, Ok? Then we can talk about the, uh, universe thing."

"Sure, Joe. That would be greaaaaaat."

There was no coffee in my cabin, so I ran the shower water hot, then icy cold. That woke me up real fast. "Ok, Skippy," I toweled off while trying to remember the Uniform of the Day. "Let's talk about why the universe is so big, or whatever."

"Huh? What?" His voice was back to normal, and his avatar shimmered into life above the tiny cabinet. "The universe? What about it? And what are you doing up so early?"

Oh crap. "You woke me up, Skippy."

"Did not."

"Did-" No way was I going to win that argument. "Hey, did you just finish running some type of compression algebra thing?"

"Compression *algorithms*, Joe. Yes, I was optimizing my autonomic functions, why?"

"No reason. You don't remember waking me up to marvel at the universe?"

"What?" His avatar put its hands on its hips. "Joe, are you drunk?"

"I wish, Skippy. I wish I was."

"Joe Joe Joe Joe Joe!" Skippy boomed through my zPhone as I was running flat-out on a treadmill later that morning, trying to keep up with the Chinese woman on the treadmill next to me. He startled me so much I nearly stumbled and fell on my face. To recover, I jumped up and backwards, landing awkwardly on the floor and using a handrail to steady myself.

I ripped the zPhone off my belt and glanced at it. No alerts were showing, no messages. "What is it?"

"You have to see this!" He shouted excitedly.

It is amazing how many terrible things a human mind can imagine in less than a second. Was a reactor about to overload? Had alien ships jumped in and surrounded us? "What?"

"This!" An image popped up on my zPhone screen.

Goats. Baby goats. It was a video of baby goats running, jumping, playing, climbing on things, falling off. I'd seen videos like that a million times, and burned way too many hours scrolling through those videos on Facebook or Instagram or any other time-wasting site. "You have got to be kidding me."

"Aren't they cute?" he chuckled. "That is *adorable*."

"Yeah. Uh, are you Ok?"

"Sure, why? Hey, wait a sec, there's a video of a dog playing with his buddy the owl, you have *got* to see this, it is uh-*MAY*-zing."

"Oh, boy," I smacked my forehead. Skippy's optimization could not happen fast enough for me. While he was running on a tiny fraction of his normal capacity, he was like a distracted teenager.

He gave me a break for almost an hour, so I was startled again when his avatar blinked to life in front of me on a table in the galley while I was drinking coffee. "Joe! I need your advice."

"You need *my* advice? This isn't about physics, right?"

"Physics? You? Pbbbbbt." He blew a raspberry. "Please, dude. No, I need you to read this."

My zPhone buzzed and I looked at it to see text on the screen. "What is this?"

"It's a reply to a jerk I argued with. This is what I now realize I should have said back then."

Scrolling down the screen faster and faster, I saw the text seemed endless. "*A* jerk?"

"Well, more than one. I got into several arguments. Ok, about eight billion different arguments, but these people were totally wrong about-"

"Skippy, you are replying way after the fact to a flame war, about something someone said the last time we were on Earth? Which is, what, two thousand lightyears from here?"

"Yeah, so? I want to be ready when, um, *if*, we ever return. These people are clearly morons, and I was trying to think of a way to dope-slap a moron in a way that even they could see the righteousness of my argument. Then I realized, hey, Joe is a moron too! If my argument works on you, it should work on anyone. Start with the first one, and we'll work our way down the list. This idiot says Jar-Jar Binks must be a Sith-"

"Skippy! Can I please finish drinking my coffee? Us morons need to be fully awake to appreciate your amazing logic."

"Oh. Yeah, good idea, Joe. Let me know- wait. Are you blowing me off about this?"

"No. No, of course not," I rolled my eyes. "Hey, you know what? All of us monkeys are morons to you, right?"

"Yes, why?"

"If you really want advice from someone who is skilled at crafting arguments, why don't you work with Count Chocula on this?"

"Ooooooh, that is a great idea, Joe! He's a diplomat. Arguing is what he does. Thank you." The avatar disappeared, and the text cleared from my zPhone screen.

For ten minutes, I was able to drink coffee in peace, until my zPhone beeped. It was Hans Chotek. "Colonel Bishop, please come to my office. *Now*."

Crap. My day went downhill from there.

Skippy was surprised that it took only thirty nine hours for him to fix the ship and test it, until he was sure we could jump again without the ship exploding. Another surprise for him was that our jump through a wormhole had actually given us *more* usable jump coils. Skippy had set aside a dozen old coils that he couldn't use, he was keeping them as a source of exotic baryons. No, exotic baryons are not baryons who dance at a 'gentlemens' club'. They are some nerdy sort of subatomic particle that I didn't understand or care about, but they were important to Skippy for some reason he wasn't able to explain. Anyway, after our crazy stunt of jumping through an Elder wormhole and getting catapulted seven hours forward in time, Skippy was delighted and confused to find four of the discarded jump coils had been restored to a usable quantum state. He had no explanation for how those coils had been modified by transiting a wormhole, and he was kind of depressed about that. He was sure that if he had his full processing power, he could understand what happened.

The good news was that we hadn't died, we hadn't permanently broken the ship, the Thuranin weren't chasing us, and there were eight wormholes within our range. The bad news was that we still didn't have a conduit to fix Skippy, we clearly couldn't go back to Bravo, and by now the Maxolhx certainly would have put every other conduit within their territory on lockdown. The really bad news is that Count Chocula wanted me to tell him where we should go next.

I had an answer, but I didn't like it, and he was going to totally hate it.

Chapter Nine

"Yeah, but that doesn't matter anyway," Skippy replied to Chotek's question about whether the Thuranin or even Maxolhx would be guarding any other conduits they knew about. "Having those rotten kitties waste time and resources guarding conduits actually helps us a bit; they will have fewer ships looking for us. The two conduit sites at Barsoom and Bravo are the only ones we can reach; all the rest I know about would take too long for us to get there. The ship will break down long before we got there, and the recent stunt we did jumping through a wormhole shortened the remaining life of our reactors even more. The jump drive came through the trauma Ok, but the particle feed systems in the reactors were skewed out of phase. I'm using a temporary fix that means the reactors will run hotter and burn a lot more fuel."

Chotek pursed his lips the way he did when he heard bad news. He had been using that gesture a lot since we left Earth. "Is there a more permanent solution?"

"We get access to a major, heavy-duty shipyard?" Skippy responded sarcastically. "Or we get a new starship. Ok, after we find a conduit and I'm restored to my usual Level Infinity Awesomeness, there may be some things I can do to stretch out the life of the reactors. In the long run, though, this ship has gone far too long without a major overhaul, and we have put the poor *Flying Dutchman* through a whole lot of crazy shit she wasn't designed to do."

"Understood," Chotek nodded gravely. "Mister Skippy, you have only mentioned potential conduit sites within Maxolhx territory. While I am very reluctant to take action that could be viewed as hostile by the Rindhalu coalition, could we expand our search in that direction?"

"I think we crossed the bridge of 'hostile action' when we planted fake Elder artifacts on Paradise and caused the Ruhar and Jeraptha to shift their entire defensive in that sector," Skippy remarked dryly. "I wasn't restricting my search to the Maxolhx coalition; we aren't able to reach any of the potential conduits in Rindhalu territory, so I didn't mention any of them."

Chotek tilted his head to one side and ran a finger along one cheek slowly; it was my impression he was trying to think how to respond. He was not happy Skippy had been considering raids in Rindhalu territory without Chotek's approval, but now that Chotek himself had authorized exploring the concept, he couldn't complain a whole lot. "Very well. Colonel Bishop?"

I instinctively sat up straight in my chair. "Sir?"

"We are now on Plan, what is it? I assume we do have other options."

"This would be Plan, uh," I almost had to count on my fingers. "C, I guess? We do have one other option for finding one of these, sort of, conduit gizmos. There is a known Elder star system we can reach from here, by only two wormhole transits. It's in the Perseus Arm, beyond the Rosette Nebula." As I said that, I don't know why I bothered. Nobody aboard the ship had any idea where that nebula was, without looking at a star chart. It didn't matter anyway. "That's roughly nine thousand lightyears from our current position."

"A *known* Elder star system?" Both of Chotek's eyebrows almost met his hairline. "Not merely a site with abandoned relics? Tell me, Colonel Bishop, why did we not consider this place when we were attempting to find other Elder artifacts such as the power tap we needed on our Paradise mission?"

"We didn't consider it because I didn't tell Joe, or anyone else about it," Skippy answered before I could speak. "I didn't tell anyone because, well, I figured I would need to be *totally* desperate before I even considered going to that place. Now, um, I am totally desperate. So, uh, heh heh, surprise!" He chuckled nervously.

"What do we know about this star system?" Chotek directed his request to me rather than Skippy, and his expression was anything but amused or friendly.

I grimaced. "That is the part Skippy said I would hate; I asked him to wait until the command crew was assembled before he explains what the issue is. What I know is, this conduit gizmo Skippy needs is likely there."

"I didn't say it was *likely* to be there, Joe," Skippy interjected peevishly. "What I said was, if we're going to find one anywhere at this point, this Elder system is absolutely the best candidate. The best candidate we can reach before Zero Hour, I mean."

"It is *not* likely that we'll find a conduit there?" I demanded, angry at being duped.

"Shmaybe fifty-fifty, Joe? Hmmm, that's a little ambitious. Probably more like forty, forty five percent chance we'll find an active conduit there. Then I need to figure out how to access it, if I even can. Overall, we're looking at a twenty percent chance of us finding a working conduit there? Yeah, twenty percent sounds about right. Could be less," he admitted cheerily.

"Twenty freakin' percent?" I shook my head, avoiding Chotek's glaring eyes. "You want us to go on a dangerous wild goose chase, with eighty percent probability of failure?"

"Hey, Mister Genius," Skippy snarked back at me, "we went to Barsoom and Bravo even though I figured the odds of us recovering a working conduit at each of those places was less than *five* percent. I didn't hear you bitching about those odds when- Which, heh heh, I just realized I might have neglected to tell you about. My bad, sorry."

"Jesus," Smythe whispered from his seat beside me.

"And now we're just supposed to trust you?" I was pissed at him. "We don't even know what else you haven't told us!"

"Hey, unless we find a conduit, and I can use it, our odds of survival are *zero*, Joe. Zee-roh," he repeated for emphasis. "So twenty percent is a big improvement. Besides, the Merry Band of Pirates has faced worse odds before, and succeeded. It's what you do. I don't know how you do it; drives me freakin' *crazy*. But you do it somehow."

I couldn't argue with that.

Chotek briefly closed his eyes wearily and pinched the bridge of his nose. If he didn't have a headache already, he was going to get one soon. "Mister Skippy, please tell us what you know of this star system."

"Now we're getting somewhere," Skippy said happily, his avatar rubbing its hands together. "This is an Elder star system, by that I mean it is known to have been inhabited by the Elders, and it is thought substantial Elder facilities and assets still exist there."

"It is thought?" Chotek raised an eyebrow. "We don't *know*?"

"My memories are kind of vague," Skippy admitted. "And there is little additional data available, because, well, no ship sent there has ever returned. The Maxolhx, Rindhalu, Thuranin, many other species have sent ships there, and these ships have never been heard from since."

"Yet you propose that we go there?" Chotek's skepticism matched my own.

"I call this star system 'Hotel California'," Skippy explained. "You know, you can check out, but you can never leave?" He chuckled at his own joke.

"Hotel California?" Sergeant Adams scoffed. "With Maxolhx and Thuranin ships trapped there, we should call it the 'Roach Motel'. Roaches check in-"

I finished her thought. "-but they don't check out. Skippy, do you know *why* ships can't leave this Roach Motel?"

"We should call it 'Hotel California', Joe," he sniffed. "No, I do not know why ships never return from there."

"I like the name 'Roach Motel' better," I declared. "Are we talking about a handful of ships, or a lot more?"

"Oh, hundreds, Joe. At least. The first recorded expedition was by the Rindhalu, of course. They tried many, many times to uncover the secrets of that star system. At first, they jumped ships in from far outside the system; typical cautious recon technique. Those ships disappeared, and later, the gamma ray bursts of their inbound jumps were not detected. The Rindhalu knew those ships had jumped into the system successfully, so the lack of gamma rays told them the remote images they had of the system were false. All they could be certain of was the gravity well of the star, and the Rindhalu were able to detect gravity signatures of three gas giant planets. That is all they could be certain of, and they did not know whether the Elders could fake gravity waves. After the initial recon ships disappeared, the Rindhalu tried everything they could think of. They jumped ships first a lightyear away, then closer and closer. Then they sent ships the slow way through normal space, and every time, they got the same results. When ships were between half and a quarter lightyear from the star, they simply disappeared. Probes, even nanotechnology, nothing came back. They even tried hiding probes inside comets and meteors, and sending them into the system. Results were the same; signals were cut off, after the object was between one half to one quarter lightyear from the star. The Rindhalu try again every once in a while; their last attempt to send a ship to the Roach Motel was ninety six thousand years ago. All the major starfaring species have tried, and failed, to recon that system. The last attempt that I know about was a squadron of specialized Thuranin ships from their Advanced Research Directorate, around four hundred years ago. Those ships also were never heard from again. At the time, it was a major scandal that nearly resulted in ARD being folded into their military research group."

"Why hasn't everyone given up?" I asked.

"Because if that star system has intact Elder technology, it would be an enormous prize to capture. And because every couple hundred or thousand years, some jackass gets a bright idea of how to succeed where everyone else failed. You biologicals always let your egos get you into trouble. It's kind of a Catch-22 situation, Joe. Because no one has useful data about what is truly in that star system, no one can design a ship or probe to successfully bring back data."

"What *do* we know about it?" I asked. "We must be able to see something there, even with long-range telescopes, right?"

"Uh, no. Joe, a long time ago, the Maxolhx had the genius idea to send ships there, equipped with devices that could temporarily alter the output of the star. Essentially, the Maxolhx planned to use the star to send signals, transmit data. Even if their ships couldn't get out, the star could provide data to the Maxolhx outside the system. Sort of a complex Morse code, using the outer layer of the star as a transmitter."

"It didn't work?" I guessed.

"It didn't work the way the Maxolhx planned. The star's output was altered, but the signal was garbled, the results meaningless. To this day, the Maxolhx are trying to decode that signal, hoping there is some meaning buried in it. After that incident, the output of the star had been steady, unnaturally steady. Impossibly steady, actually."

"Something in that system is controlling an entire star?" I gasped.

"Possibly, Joe. More likely, something in there is using a stealth field to mask the true image of the star. What we see from outside the system is a false image."

"Holy- they surrounded an entire star in a stealth field?"

"No, Joe. They enveloped the entire star *system* in a stealth field; one that extends roughly a tenth of a lightyear in radius. Everything we see from outside is a false image."

"Holy crap. And you think we should just waltz on in there? Mess with something that can cover a star system with a stealth field?"

"Oh, sure, Joe. No problemo. Whatever is going on in that system, it is Elder technology. Even in my currently reduced capacity, I am an Elder AI. I can transmit the identification codes that will grant us access. None of the ships that have become trapped there had Elder ID codes. I expect previous ships are not simply trapped; they were very likely destroyed."

"Wait." I waved a hand at his avatar. "You expect us to jump in there, and you, what, tell them not to shoot because we're friendly?" Hopefully, the expression on my face reflected my disbelief.

"Yes, why? Come on, Joe, trust the awesomeness."

That remark made me roll my eyes. "Isn't most of your awesomeness locked away in some dimension of spacetime you can't access right now?"

"That hurts, Joe. It's true, I am operating at reduced capacity. But even a tiny part of me contains way more awesomeness than you can imagine. Seriously, don't worry, I got this."

Chotek and I shared a look, and for once, I completely agreed with my boss. "There must be another option for getting this Elder thingamabob you need. We've searched for other Elder stuff before, and never had to jump into a star system no one ever returns from."

"Joe, if there was another option, I would have mentioned it. I will admit, I do not know for certain there is a conduit in this star system. What I do know is that I am running out of time, and the 'Roach Motel' is the most likely place for me to repair myself."

"We need time to think about this. How long until you have the jump drive working?"

"It is a miracle I can fix the jump drive at all, Joe; you monkeys seriously screwed it up. Give it another day before our first real jump, to be safe. I can continue running repairs as we travel."

"One day, then," I looked at Chotek again, and he nodded.

Despite Skippy's constant grumbling about how badly screwed up the jump drive was, and how overworked he was, he admitted he was happy enough with the condition of the incredibly complicated equipment. On his advice, we performed a short test jump, then a longer jump. On my order, the longer jump was in the direction toward the wormhole we needed to go through, if we were ultimately intending to jump into the star system Skippy called Hotel California. Both jumps were successful, and Skippy told me he only needed to perform a few small tweaks to the jump drive before it would be fully operational. He did caution me that twenty three percent of our jump coils were junk; they had been damaged beyond repair by our clumsy attempts to jump the ship without him and all the strain we had put the ship through since he awakened.

Hans Chotek and I had assumed we had a full day to make a decision on what to do, but Skippy pressed me to act as soon as possible. Chotek called me into his office. "Colonel Bishop," he said in a tone implying he couldn't believe those two words belonged together, "your beer can has been asking me every ten minutes for approval, to send this ship on what could be a one-way trip into this Elder star system." Whenever Chotek was extra unhappy with Skippy, he was *my* beer can.

"He has been bugging me about it every *five* minutes," I responded. "Jeez, Skippy, you should have named *yourself* 'Nagatha'."

"Nagatha is clearly a female name, Joe, so it wouldn't apply to me," Skippy announced as his avatar popped to life on Chotek's desk.

"Whatever. Do you-"

"See, if I had a name like that, it would be 'King NAG-ammenon'," Skippy suggested wistfully. "Or maybe 'Emperor NAG-ustus Ceasar'. Those are properly regal names for me; they convey the gravitas of my awesomeness. Without being, you know, boastfully tacky."

"Of course not," I rolled my eyes.

"Those names wouldn't work, Joe, because I do not nag. I provide regular reminders of important things you need to pay attention to."

"Right. It only *feels* like nagging."

"Mister Skippy," Chotek interrupted with irritation, glaring at Skippy's avatar. I think Chotek liked it better when our friendly alien AI was a disembodied voice he could attempt to ignore when it suited him. Now, his avatar could appear anywhere, any time, and Skippy demanded attention. "We have been considering alternatives to your plan to send this ship to the, what did you call it?" Chotek scowled as he searched his memory. "Ah yes, 'Hotel California'. Colonel Bishop, have you developed a list of alternate ideas to restore Skippy to functioning? Or perhaps an alternative location where we might find this 'conduit' device?"

"No." I looked at Skippy to avoid Chotek's eyes. "Sir, we have to take Skippy's word about this conduit gizmo he needs, and when he describes it as a 'conduit', he's doing that for our benefit. It's not actually a thing."

"It's not a thing?" Chotek raised an eyebrow.

"Joe is correct," Skippy acknowledged. "I was describing what I need as a 'conduit' to help you visualize the problem, but what I seek is not a physical device. It is a capability, an ability to create connections between this local spacetime and higher phases of spacetime. There are multiple possibilities for me gaining access to the capability I require, because Elder technology made extensive use of connections to higher spacetime phases."

"Sir, I asked Skippy if there are other places in the galaxy where we might find a 'conduit', and he says there are. But those places are much farther away, and several are in territories heavily guarded by advanced species we should not risk becoming involved with. The only place we can go, in the time available before Zero Hour, is this Elder star system Skippy has identified."

"A star system Skippy admits *even he* knows nothing about," Chotek observed. "No ship or probe has ever returned, Skippy has no accurate memories about the place, and the images we see from outside are manipulated through a massive stealth field."

My boss was a picky, micromanaging pain in the ass. He was also right much of the time. "I agree with your concerns," I said. "Skippy, I am not loving this plan."

"The alternative, Joe, is the ship suffering a lingering death after the worm gets me and I shut down permanently."

I bit my lip. "Ok, now I'm liking your plan better and better."

"I am only considering a blind jump into this 'Hotel California' because it appears we have no other choice," Chotek concluded.

ZERO HOUR

"That's the spirit, Chocky!" Skippy said happily. "I knew you had a love for adventure in there somewhere."

"Skippy," I asked, "what is the best case scenario?"

"That's easy, Joe. We jump in, I transmit my ID codes to deactivate whatever is ripping apart ships there. Then I contact the local network, find a conduit, and after we fly close enough, presto! I stomp that worm like a, well, worm. And the old Skippy you know and love is back, baby! Even more magnificent than ever, baby!"

"Great. What are the odds this best case scenario will actually happen?"

"Joe, please. We are the Merry Band of Pirates. The odds that everything will go right are somewhere between 'you've got to be joking' and 'fuggedaboutit'. When you make a plan, the universe chuckles and rubs its hands with delight, because it has another golden opportunity to screw with you."

"Fine," I knew he was right about that. "What's the worst case scenario?"

"Oh, there are so, so many worst cases, Joe. I'll give you a sample of the greatest hits. First, the ship could emerge from our jump as a cloud of subatomic particles, because there could be a severe sheering field covering the entire star system. It- oops, I should explain that a sheering field is local spacetime grid that causes objects embedding in it to be torn apart at right angles. Kind of like the field I use to stop bullets in the *Dutchman*'s rifle range. A system-wide sheering field would be cool, actually. Although more cool if I could watch it happen to some other ship, of course. That particular scenario is unlikely; maintaining a wide sheering field requires enormous power, and would tear apart any planets in the system. What else? Hmm. Oh, yeah, I've got a good one!" He shouted excitedly. "Oooh, you'll like this. We could-"

"Skippy," I interrupted. "We don't need the gory details, please." I had watched Chotek's face grow pale, then red with anger. "Ok, we get it. Worst case scenario is the ship is destroyed."

"Yup," Skippy was cheery about that prospect. "Or the ship is disabled, and drifts dead in space until the power runs out and all you humans die. I might actually be dead before that, unfortunately. So, no downside."

"No *downside*?" Chotek interrupted his angry internal thoughts to express surprise.

I spoke just before Skippy could explain. "He means, Sir, that we're already certain the ship will fail and the crew will die, whether we go to the Roach Motel or not." I winced as I used Sergeant Adams' nickname for the Elder star system. Referring to the place as a device that kills disgusting bugs was not a good way to sell the idea of going there.

"No downside," Chotek nodded. "Oh," he sighed, "what the hell. Why not? We both know what is going to happen. We could argue about this until Skippy runs down to Zero Hour, and the decision would still be obvious. When there is no alternative," he scowled at Skippy, "a terrible idea is the best one. Colonel Bishop, set course for this 'Hotel California', or whatever you wish to call it. I know you military people will create a nickname for it, if we didn't already have one."

"Yes, Sir." I was usually happy when Chotek approved a plan, only this wasn't my plan. It was Skippy's plan, and Chotek was right. It was a terrible plan. "Skippy told me the jump drive capacitors should be fully charged and checked out in six hours." With only two reactors, we wanted to have a full charge on the capacitors, because we couldn't recharge them as quickly as we used to. After he awakened, Skippy suggested we keep the damaged reactor offline, and use its functional components as spares for the other two reactors. The good news was, with some of the materials we didn't need, Skippy was manufacturing ship-killer missiles to partly replenish our depleted supply. "If we jump toward the first wormhole tomorrow morning, Skippy, how long until we approach the Elder system?"

"Nineteen days, Joe. The first wormhole we go through will take us most of the way there, it's a long transition, far past our destination, actually. The second wormhole will take us backwards a bit to get there, but that is the shortest and fastest route from here to Hotel California. We will come through the second wormhole eleven days from tomorrow; then it will be eight days of jumping by ourselves to reach our destination. There is a wormhole much closer to our destination, but, it's dormant, and, you know, I can't screw with wormholes like I used to. After I fix myself, I could reopen that dormant wormhole on our return trip."

"Six hours." Chotek declared. Then his scowl turned to a smile. "Colonel Bishop, this means you have nineteen days to think up an alternative to jumping the ship into the unknown."

"I'll do my best, Sir." Great, I thought. No pressure on me.

We went through both wormholes without incident. The first wormhole did not get a lot of traffic, its two ends were six thousand lightyears apart so it was convenient for long-distance travel, but its two ends were actually too far apart. The far end of that wormhole was deep in Bosphuraq territory, and there wasn't a lot of ships traveling between space controlled by the Thuranin and Bosphuraq. Those two species, roughly equivalent in technology and clients of the Maxolhx, hated each other and had as little contact as they could. So, that particular wormhole didn't get used often, plus the end in Bosphuraq territory was in a region with very few habitable planets. The result was the *Flying Dutchman* came through the first wormhole to find space there absolutely empty. Without Skippy's special awesome abilities, we had to rely on the ship's slow and inadequate sensors to confirm there were no enemy ships waiting to attack us. As soon as the drive coils were ready, we jumped away almost randomly, simply to clear the area and make us less of a target. Then we jumped again as soon as possible, just in case someone was on our tail.

The second wormhole took us back toward the Roach Motel, and this wormhole saw even less traffic. On the near end, that wormhole was seventeen lights years from the only habitable star system within thirty lightyears, and that habitable star system had another more convenient wormhole only five lightyears away. On the far end of the second wormhole, there was the Roach Motel, and pretty much nothing else. When we emerged from the second wormhole, Skippy confirmed the closest other wormhole was eighty seven lightyears away. There were only two star systems within a hundred lightyears that were not boring, useless brown or red dwarfs; a blue giant star, and the Roach Motel. According to Skippy, the Class-O blue giant was older than it could possibly have been without burning out, and it was rotating much too slowly. Skippy concluded the Elders must have screwed with that star somehow, somehow altering its rotation and stretching out its lifespan. If we have not been on a clock ticking down to Zero Hour, Skippy would have wanted us to fly over to that blue giant an examine it closely.

Since we were unquestionably on a deadline, we jumped directly toward the Roach Motel which was a Class-K orange dwarf star, if that means anything to you. It didn't mean anything to me either. I could have looked up the info on my tablet, but doing that would not give Skippy an opportunity to make fun of my ignorance. With him worrying about his diminished awesomeness and the worm that was trying to kill him, I figured he could use a good chuckle. Besides, while our two remaining reactors were straining to recharge the jump drive coils, there wasn't much for me to do, and I was bored. Laying in my bunk, I had been trying to read a book, but found I couldn't concentrate. One of the reasons I was not able to let myself relax and enjoy a leisure-time activity was the air vent above my too-small bunk. Air used to whisper steadily out of that vent, without me ever noticing. Now that we only had two functioning reactors, Skippy was conserving power by cycling the air ventilation system on and off. The breeze was still gentle, and the sound barely above a whisper, but when the air cycled on, I felt it on my face, and realized the air had not been blowing earlier. That reminded me of our dire situation, and that prevented me from relaxing enough to read for enjoyment. "Skippy, can you explain what is an 'orange dwarf' star? I know Earth's sun is a yellow dwarf."

"Certainly, Joe. A-"

"I know it's not just a yellow dwarf star with red food coloring."

"What?"

"To make it orange instead of yellow."

"Joe," he sighed, "it is possible for you to get any dumber?"

"You want me to try?"

"No! Although, hmm, in a way, you are partly right. About the food coloring, I mean. The chemical composition of the star is partly responsible for the spectral lines that give its radiation a primary color, but mostly the color is due to the star's surface temperature. An orange dwarf burns hydrogen like your Sun, but at a slower rate. This is important, because it means orange dwarf stars last longer in their main sequence, which gives life more time to develop on planets orbiting orange dwarfs."

"Main sequence?"

"That is the time when the star is fusing hydrogen at its core into helium, and they are in hydrostatic equilibrium. The thermal pressure pushing outward from the fusion core is equal to the gravitational force pressing down from the outer layers of the star. When-"

"Wait, wait! I know this," I announced, proud of myself. "After a star exhausts its supply of hydrogen, it starts burning, like, helium? Depending on the size of the star, it then either expands into a red giant, something like that? Or if its gravity is too much, the star collapses on itself to explode as a supernova?"

"Oh, that is-"

"Grade my answer on a Joe Bishop curve, Ok?"

"In that case, I should award you a Nobel prize. More like a IgNobel prize. Close enough for the amount of knowledge you require, Joe. Although in terms of astrophysics, your level of knowledge is equivalent to 'fire hot', 'water wet' or 'oxygen good'."

"Fire is hot, Skippy. You can't argue with that."

"It wouldn't do me any good to argue with you anyway."

"Hey, question for you. This orange star we're going to, the Elders didn't come from there, right? This was one of their colonies?"

"The Elders did not come from there, correct. Therefore I assume it is a colony, since I have little useful knowledge about the star system."

"Ok, so my question is, did they choose an orange star because it lasts longer than a yellow star? Did the Elders plan for their civilization to last long enough for the life of a star to matter?"

"That is possible, Joe. I simply do not know. As you so helpfully pointed out to me several freakin' times, my memories of the Elders, of pretty much anything before I awoke on Paradise, are not exactly reliable. However, it does make sense that the Elders would have planned long-term, very long-term. If they had not discovered how to leave their physical form behind, they would very likely still be here today."

"Yeah. I wonder about that." The air from the vent above my bunk was no longer gently caressing my face. "If the Elders were still here, would they allow the Maxolhx and Rindhalu to be fighting an endless war? And would they allow those two senior species to drag client species into the war with them?"

"You are asking me to speculate, Joe."

"Do it anyway, Ok? This is a question that has been bugging me for a while now. The Elders left the galaxy, they left their wormholes and some of their weapons-"

"Devices, Joe. I do not think the Elder civilization had any need for weapons."

"Whatever you call them, the Maxolhx and Rindhalu used those devices as weapons against each other. Then those Sentinels the Elders left behind stomped anyone who used Elder weapons. Why? Why would the Elders care who uses the weapons they left behind? The Elders are gone, ascended above us or wherever the hell they went. If they cared about grubby species screwing with their stuff after they left, they should have taken their stuff with them. Or destroyed all of it, or locked it away somewhere. So, my question is why? This Roach Motel we're going to; the Elders surrounded the whole system in a stealth field, and something in there kills any ship that tries to figure out the secrets. Again, *why*? The Elders are *gone*, Skippy. Why do they care?"

He didn't respond immediately, and this wasn't a case of him being busy doing something else that ate up his reduced processing power. This was Skippy thinking hard about something. "Joe, I often disparage your intellectual ability-"

"Really? I am shocked," I said, clutching my chest and feigning shock. "When was this?"

"Very funny. In this case, you have been remarkably insightful, Joe. The questions you just asked have been bothering me also. Bothering me a lot. Like, to the point of distracting me. I do not have an answer." He sighed. "This is another mystery I, *we*, need answers to. You can add it to the list of questions such as who threw Newark out of its original orbit, who or what destroyed Elder sites we found like the Dead Star moon on our last mission. Or who blew away most of Barsoom's atmosphere, you can add that to the list of mysteries we need answers for."

I considered that for a moment. A long moment. We did need answers, lots of answers. Several times, I had declared that the Merry Band of Pirates needed a long-term strategy, rather than frantically lurching from one crisis to another. So far, I had been too busy simply surviving to do much long-term thinking. Without knowing the full nature of the threats we faced, it was almost impossible to make long-term plans. "Promise me something, Skippy?"

"Without knowing what you are asking me to promise, I cannot-"

"This is important. For realz."

"For realz. Got it," he replied soberly, without the usual snarkiness in his tone. "Joe, our friendship means more to me than I can say. If I able to keep a promise to you, I will."

"Huh. That was nice, Skippy. How did-"

"Our friendship is also far more humiliating to me than I can say. My best friend is a monkey. How pathetic is that?"

"*My* best friend is a beer can."

"I see your point," he conceded. "What is this promise you want from me?"

"That we will find answers to these questions, you and me. Even if you fix yourself, and contact the Collective. For my part, even if Earth is safe permanently, and all the species in the galaxy come together in peace and sing 'Kumbaya', I want to keep going, until we figure out what the hell has been going on around here."

"Deal." His avatar flashed to life on the floor, and he held out a holographic hand. I stretched out my hand and used two fingers to mimic shaking his hand. The hologram wasn't solid so I couldn't actually feel his tiny hand, although my fingertips tingled slightly from the effect of whatever field he used to project the 3D hologram.

"Deal," I agreed. "Hey, speaking of questions, do you have any better info on the Roach Motel, now that we're closer to it?"

"No. Come on, Joe, we are still lightyears away."

"Yeah, but-"

"But nothing. I have focused the ship's sensors on the system since we came through the last wormhole. The problem is, I can't trust anything the sensors are telling me. I can't even verify the star is an orange dwarf. Based on its gravitational effect on other stars in the local area, the Roach Motel star's mass is seventy six percent of Earth's sun, so it should be an orange dwarf. But I can't declare that with any certainty."

That worried me. "How close will we have to get before you can be certain?"

"Joe, we won't know until we jump in."

"That's not good, Skippy."

"I understand. There is no alternative, unfortunately."

"We can't jump closer in increments? Start a lightyear away, and jump something like a tenth of a lightyear closer?"

"No, that will not work. Other species have tried that. I told you, they even tried sending ships and probes in the slow way, coasting through normal space. Once objects get close to the edge of the system, they disappear. At the edge of the system, they disappear without ever getting close enough to see anything useful. If we're going to get vaporized or whatever, we might as well jump in close enough to see what is inside that stealth field."

"I hear you. I don't like the idea of jumping in blind; but if we have to, we should jump in close and get it over with."

"It's not like we have a choice anyway," Skippy added helpfully.

"Yeah," I tossed my tablet on the bunk and sat up. No way could I relax and read a book with those happy thought racing around my brain. "I sure haven't been able to think of an alternative, but I'll tell you something for certain."

"What's that, Joe?"

"If we ever get back to Earth, UNEF Command is going to say I should have done something other than jumping blindly into a Roach Motel."

"True dat."

Chapter Ten

We jumped in as close to the Roach Motel as we dared without going close enough to risk the ship. How close we could get was not a hard line, it was a guess and I asked Skippy to be super conservative about it. Once we arrived, I requested a full day to examine the sensor data as best we could, and for the crew to double and triple check every piece of equipment we had.

"Ish the shensor data showin' you anythin' useful, Shkippy?" I asked.

"What?"

"Sorry." I finished chewing the sticky peanut butter sandwich I was eating for a late breakfast in my office. That morning I had gotten out of bed at 0430 to help Major Simms pack away and secure supplies. After my quick brunch I was going to work in the hydroponics compartments, harvesting any crops that were ready. With the crew extra busy, I had declared a 'Fend For Yourself' day in the galley so no team had to spend the full day there. "Is the-"

"I understood you the first time, Joe; it is not polite to speak with your mouth full. Damn, I sound like Nagatha," he grumbled. "The answer is, sort of. The useful information I am getting is what is *not* in the sensor data."

"Uh, what?"

"The data looks correct until I examined it very carefully. The stealth field surrounding the star system is broadcasting a low-fidelity image. The Elders either think species outside will not notice the difference, or-"

"Or what?"

"Or," he chuckled, "this is a way of the Elders saying 'screw you' to the universe. Either way, it tells me the data coming into our sensors is worthless; it doesn't tell us anything about what's inside that stealth field. I can tell from the movement of surrounding star systems that the mass of the Elder system is less than what I'm seeing through the sensor data."

"So we have no idea what we will be jumping into?"

"There is a star at the center of that stealth field, I'm certain of that. Anything else is a guess, Joe." He sounded miserable.

"Are you Ok, Skippy?"

"This is it, Joe. This could be the end for me. I never thought there *could* be an end for me. Now my only chance to survive is to jump a shipfull of monkeys into the unknown. I am not filled with confidence."

"We monkeys will do all we can to find one of those damned conduits for you, Skippy." Maybe the look of determination I was trying to project was lessened by me licking sticky peanut butter off my upper lip.

"I know you will, Joe. What I'm worried about is karma will take this opportunity to bitch-slap you into another dimension. Oh, crap, what the hell. It's not like we have a choice, right?"

I needed to make a note to myself that Skippy should never be considered as the ship's Morale Officer.

"Sir, the jump drive capacitors are at full charge, and-"

"You may proceed when the ship is ready, Colonel," Chotek surprised me by saying.

"Uh," I didn't know what to say. The ship was fully prepared, all we needed to do was things like closing exterior vents, and people strapping themselves into seats.

"I'm sure you want to make preparations for the jump; placing damage control parties, assuring all personnel are strapped securely into seats, all that," Chotek turned to look at me with a sad smile. He probably wished he was back on Earth doing something easy, like negotiating peace in the Middle East.

"Yes, Sir," I responded slowly. "I, uh, thought you might want to wait here for a while, before we make the final jump in."

"Why? Mister Skippy has already stated we will not get any more reliable sensor data until we are past the stealth field surrounding the system. I believe that while we remain out here, we risk whatever entity protects that system deciding we are already too close, and attacking us here. It would be a shame to come so close, and never see what in that star system is such a secret. If this ship is going to risk destruction anyway, I want to see what's in there. What is the American saying?"

"Which one, Sir?"

"Something about the folly of taking half measures."

"Oh." I was thinking 'you can't be a little bit pregnant' but that probably was not what Hans Chotek had in mind. "Um, how about 'with bacon and eggs, the chicken is involved, but the pig is committed'?"

"No," he smiled. "I know that expression. I was thinking 'in for a penny, in for a pound'."

"Ah." A pound was English currency, but I wasn't going to argue with him about it. "Yes, Sir. We'll take two hours before we jump; give us time to make certain all our gear is secured, double-check all systems, and that everyone gets a bite to eat." If things went sideways after we jumped, it might be a while before the crew got a good meal.

"That is a good idea," Chotek said, likely contemplating what he could get from the galley before we jumped. "Before you go, I have one last question for our friendly beer can."

Usually Chotek referred to Skippy as *my* beer can, so this was different; I didn't know what to make of it. Whatever diplomatic training Chotek had often made his expression unreadable, and I reminded myself never to play poker with him. "Skippy?" I asked.

His avatar appeared on Chotek's desk. "Yes, Joe? With what do you propose to waste my time now?"

Chotek actually smiled, though I couldn't tell if it was sincere. "With asking how you can be sure that whatever entity is protecting that star system will accept your ID codes. That is your entire plan, correct? Transmit your ID codes, and hope for the best?"

"Yes," Skippy said slowly in the voice parents use when speaking to slow little children. "These codes are known only to Elders, so they will-"

"How do you know that?" Chotek demanded, his smile fading. "You are basing your assumption on data you have taken from the senior species, correct? What if the Rindhalu or Maxolhx have Elder codes, but have protected them in databases you don't have access to?"

I turned from Chotek to Skippy, wondering how Skippy would respond. Because Chotek had a good point, a very good point. I wish he had raised this question before we set course for the Roach Motel, but maybe the thought just occurred to him. I know what that was like; it happened to me all the time.

"Because," Skippy replied slowly, "the codes are not simply ones and zeroes, or any lame encryption scheme. I used the phrase 'ID code' to make it easier for you monkeys to understand, but what I plan to use are not simply codes. It is a communications *method*. How I transmit is almost more important than what I transmit. If the Rindhalu or Maxolhx had access to this method, they would be using it, because it would give them communications that cannot be intercepted or decrypted. This communications method is deep Elder technology; no current species has even glimpsed the theoretical basis of this technology. Do you have any more time-wasting questions for me?"

I spoke before Chotek. "I don't suppose you could share this technology with our science team?"

"Uh, that would be *no*," he emphasized the last word in an extra condescending tone. "I still have restrictions against sharing advanced technology with primitive species. There is some good news, Joe. You know how I am not supposed to reveal myself to starfaring species, and how that has been causing inner conflicts for me, because we're aboard this ship?"

"Uh huh, yeah," I agreed.

"Well, the way you apes were a miserable failure at flying the ship without me has relaxed the internal pressure on me. Apparently, whatever system monitors my behavior has decided that the monkeys aboard this ship are passengers only, and pose no threat. So, goodness all around."

"Yeah, goodness. Tell me, Oh Magnificent One, you have access to this super duper Elder communications method, even trapped in a tiny corner of your beer can?"

"I think so."

Chotek and I shared a glance, and we were not smiling. "What do you mean, you *think* so?" I demanded. "We're about to jump into the unknown, Skippy. This is a hell of a time to tell us you're not sure you can do the only thing that might keep us alive."

"Hold your horses, Joe. I have used this Elder communications technology before, and I am capable of transmitting the same way, even now. The reason I said 'I think so' is because I was being completely honest with you. Without an Elder device receiving my transmission and replying back to me, I cannot be one hundred percent *certain* my transmissions are going out correctly. But, I am one hundred percent certain there is no trouble with the transmission on my end. Does that make you feel better?"

"No," I replied honestly. "But I understand what you're saying. One more question; how can you be certain that whatever entity is protecting the Roach Motel, will be capable of receiving transmissions in this Elder communications method?"

"Hmmm. That is a good point, Joe. I had not considered that. However," he added as my face grew red, "any such entity would be pretty much useless as a guardian of Elder technology, if it did not have access to Elder communications methods."

"And you are sure this system is protected by something the *Elders* left behind?" I pressed my point.

"What else could it be, Joe?" Skippy asked smugly.

"It *could* be the Roach Motel is guarded by whatever mysterious beings threw Newark out of orbit. That was after the Elders left the galaxy, and before the Rindhalu developed star travel. We *know* there is an unknown player out there, Skippy. How do you *know* that unknown third party isn't the one guarding the Roach Motel? Maybe they're guarding it because they want to keep the Elder tech they find to themselves."

"Well, shit," Skippy said disgustedly. "You picked a fine time to ask this question, Joe. Why the hell didn't you think of this earlier?"

"I didn't," I said with an apologetic shrug to Chotek. "I just thought of it now."

Hans Chotek sat back in his chair and let out a long breath. "Colonel Bishop, I have become aware of how inconvenient it can be to ask questions at a time that is perhaps too late, but such questions must be asked regardless."

"I'm sorry, Sir," I said sheepishly. "Until we have an answer, we can jump away-"

"Why?" Chotek surprised me by asking. "I don't see how our situation has changed. Our *only* possibility of restoring Skippy to full function is in this Roach Motel, correct? That has not changed. We have already agreed to jump in there, regardless of the level of risk."

"Yes, Sir, but we thought the risk came from Elder technology, and now-"

"It doesn't matter," our mission commander shook his head. "We have no other choice. Any possibility of success and survival is better than the certainty of failure and death we have right now. We go, when the ship and crew are ready, Colonel. Mister Skippy, I assume you are ready at any time?"

"Affirmative," Skippy replied without a smart-ass remark

"It is settled, then," Chotek slapped a palm on the table. "We go, for better or for worse. At least," he said with a wry smile, "we hopefully will get a glimpse of what is so secret in that star system, eh?"

We jumped. The main display blinked and switched from a generic starfield to a view centered on a dot representing a fiery hot orange star, and I knew we had survived entry to the Roach Motel. That was a huge relief, one of our fears had been the ship would be torn apart inside the jump wormhole, or sheared into atoms as we exited the event horizon on the far end. If I died right then after the jump, at least I had gotten a glimpse of the big secret.

Which, truthfully, didn't look all that impressive. It was a star, like any other star. The sensors were still resetting so we couldn't yet detect any planets, but the star wasn't surrounded by a habitable ring or a Dyson sphere or any sort of cool alien megastructure. "Skippy, how are we?" I asked when I was able to let out the breath trapped in my lungs.

"Fine so far, but that could be just blissful ignorance. Sensors are still resetting, Joe, we can't see much yet. Ooooh, crap. Whatever you do, Joe, do *not* attempt a jump. We are caught in an extremely powerful damping field. Well, hell, now we know why ships never jump out of here; they can't."

"Understood. Colonel Chang, secure from"-

"*No!*" Skippy shouted. "No no no no no no no! Give me a sec-"

The ship lurched. No, it *skewed*. Like, half of every particle including whatever I am made of, suddenly slipped sideways from the other half. Instantly, I got a blinding headache and my eyeballs felt like they were going to pop out of my head. The main display went blurry and it wasn't only my vision causing the blurriness; the display flickered weirdly as if part of it were in 3D and the other part not. "Skip-"

"Jump Option Zebra!" He screeched.

"Jump?" My agonized brain faintly reminded me there was no option 'Zebra' in the drive nav system; Skippy must have programmed that option on the fly. "You just told us not-"

"Screw it! JUMP!" He roared.

Desai, who was clutching one hand to her own head in terrible pain, did not wait for my order, she pressed the correct buttons and we jumped.

Or we tried to jump. There was an ear-splitting horrific shuddering accompanied by a shrieking groaning sound of something being twisted and torn, then artificial gravity cut out and I felt the ship, the entire ship, flip end over end. My head whiplashed back and forth despite the restraint field dragging at my scalp. This failed jump was much, much worse than anything we had experienced before. For a split second the ship and crew and everything around me including me went transparent, followed by a blinding light. When it stopped abruptly I wasn't able to talk. The sensation of every atom in my body being tugged apart went away, then returned full strength a moment later.

That was the easy part.

Skippy was shouting something I couldn't hear over the cacophony, the only piece of information I could focus on was a section of the main display indicating the coils were building up to another jump. What the hell? We just barely survived one failed jump, why the hell was Skippy setting us up for another attempt?! Before I could ask him, I saw the display flip to a jump countdown, then the drive coils pulsed. "No-" I choked before a flash of light more intense than I'd ever seen flared inside me retinas, and I blacked out.

Skippy later told me I had been unconscious for several minutes, and I was one of the first people to revive because the restraint field of the command chair helped protect me. That, plus a fist-sized creepy spider-shaped bot crawling up my arm to inject me with some stimulant helped revive me. The spider was still attached to my arm when I opened one eye. "Gaaaah!" I gargled through a mouthful of spit and something tasting very bad.

"Joe, it's Ok!" Skippy's voice came to me faintly, like he was deep underwater. My head and my eyes and everything hurt. "That is a medical bot, it injected you with stimulants to wake you up and nano meds to counteract the mild concussion you suffered."

The burst of adrenaline surging through my body from seeing the creepy spider bot was working better than any stimulant he could have shot into me. "Wha-"

"Relax a minute. Relax," he said soothingly as the spider crouched, then gently pushed itself off my arm to float through the air in zero gravity over to land on Desai's neck. As I blinked tears from my eyes and tried to focus, I watched as the spiderbot injected our chief pilot, then crawled down her arm to reach its next victim. Next patient, I told myself.

Between adrenaline and Mad Doctor Skippy's patented wonder drug, I realized I was feeling fairly alert and not remembering when that had happened. The two pilots and the crew in CIC were reviving, and by painfully turning my very stiff neck I saw Skippy had the spiderbots bypassing the inert form of Hans Chotek to attend to more important crewmembers, which were all of them. For a second I guiltily thought Chotek might be dead, then he coughed out a slimy bubble of mucus and whatever he'd last eaten. The bubble hung in the air in front of his face, and that wasn't the only one; many other disgusting objects were drifting around both CIC and bridge. Ugh! I realized I'd gotten some in my hair, and hoped it was my own.

"Damage report!" I ordered in a strangled voice, and for a brief moment I was channeling my inner Captain Kirk. Spots were still swimming in my vision and my ears were still ringing.

"Unknown at this time, Joe," Skippy's voice responded immediately. "The sensor suite is offline, I am working on it. My own internal capabilities are too degraded to be of much use, I am working on that also. I can report that we probably lost the aft engineering section of the *Dutchman*."

"We *what*?"

"The ship's spine was severed just aft of the docking platforms; we have lost all reactors, plus the jump drive and normal space maneuvering capability."

"Severed?" I couldn't speak. With the engineering section, we had lost the part of the ship that made the *Flying Dutchman* a ship. After all we had gone through together, our pirate ship was broken beyond repair. There was no point asking Skippy, or the dazed CIC crew, about the condition of what was left of humanity's first starship. "What went wrong, Skippy?"

"Mistakes were made, Joe," Skippy said in a dismissive voice that was way more cheery than I expected, given the situation.

"*Mistakes were made?*" I repeated incredulously.

"Did I say that wrong?" He asked innocently. "The common usage of human rhetorical expressions sometimes confuses me. What is the correct expression for when you know you screwed up, but the worst part of it is some jerk who will. Not. Let. It. *Go.* You just want him to shut the hell up so you can move on, but he keeps blah, blah, blah yelling at you, like that's gonna help?"

While I pounded my forehead with a fist, Major Simms in the CIC responded for me. "Mister Skippy, 'mistakes were made' is the correct expression."

"Oh, good," he said happily.

"You do not," I scowled up at the speaker in the ceiling because Skippy's avatar was not operational, "sound sincere about being sorry."

"I am sincere that I want to forget about it, is that good enough? Anywho-"

"Am *I* the jerk who will not let it go?" I interrupted him.

"Um, no? Kinda guessing what you want me to say here, Joe."

"Oh, for-"

"Since we've all agreed to put this little incident behind us and move on-"

"*Little*? We have *not* agreed to-" I began to say, until Simms caught my eye, shook her head and made a slashing motion across her throat. She was right. And, damn it, Skippy was right also, yelling at our beer can wasn't going to accomplish anything. "Oh, hell, we can discuss this later."

"Later is good," Skippy sounded relieved. "Never would be better. Is 'never' good for you?"

Recalling my mother's advice, I took three deep, calming breaths before answering. "Skippy, forget about what went wrong. What happened?"

"See, now we're getting somewhere. To make a long story short, Joe, I was correct that this star system is actively patrolled by Elder devices; they are the reason why no ships or probes have ever returned from here. I was also correct, you are welcome by the way, that because I am of Elder origin, these devices would accept my identification codes, and halt their attack. However, and this is something I *totally* could not have been expected to know before we jumped in here, ugh. Remember, Joe, *you* agreed to the lame-brained idea of jumping into a star system that is a dead-end Roach Motel. I mean, seriously, what the hell were you thinking? So, when we jumped in, we were instantly attacked by weapons that act as sort of Guardians, and I transmit my ID codes. Everything is good, right? But, nooooooo, that would be too freakin' easy! Because these Guardians expect me to transmit the proper codes from another phase of spacetime. Which I can't do, and you *knew* that before we jumped in, because I *told* you I could no longer do that."

Three more deep breaths. It was not helping. I so very much wanted to toss him out an airlock. Maybe a fourth deep breath would help me achieve inner peace.

Skippy continued while I struggled with inner rage. "Getting back to my point, the Guardians hesitated, that's the reason we're all still alive now. Then, when I couldn't talk to them through a higher spacetime phase, they resumed their attack."

"What was that failed jump for?" Remarkably, I was able to focus on what was immediately important.

"It wasn't actually a jump attempt, Joe. We can't jump; this system is saturated with an extremely powerful damping field. What I did was use the quantum resonance of the ship's jump field to transmit ID codes in multiple spacetimes. The jump field collapsed almost immediately, but I was able to send a message through the jump field, which the Guardians accepted. Unfortunately, they had already begun warping the fabric of space around the ship, and even after they released that effect, it snapped the *Dutchman*'s spine forward of the engineering section."

"That was the explosion we felt? The reactors and drive capacitors blowing up?"

"No, Joe," he used his Professor Nerdnik voice to lecture me like a small and especially stupid child. "If that had happened, nothing would be left of the ship." He left the 'duh' implied rather than spoken. "When I realized the ship had been torn apart, I knew the drive capacitors were about to rupture and the reactors would explosively lose plasma containment; either one would vaporize the entire ship. So, I channeled the drive capacitor energy into a second jump field; this one was designed to create a shaped bubble of spacetime that directed the explosion away from the forward section of the hull. Most of the explosive energy was vented into a phased spacetime bubble; that did turn the engineering section into subatomic particles."

"How did you make a jump without us pressing a button to activate the drive? You can't move any ship you are aboard," I demanded.

"After the *Dutchman*'s spine snapped, I was no longer aboard the aft section of the ship, *duh*." He did say that one aloud. "I am sorry, Joe. The Guardians caught the ship in a spacetime warp and there was nothing I could do to save the engineering section; it was the focus of the Guardian's attack. I did the only thing I could think of that allowed the forward section of the ship to survive. Since the incident, I have been trying to determine whether there was another, better course of action. So far I have not been able to think of anything else I could have done. It is truly remarkable that I was able to prevent the ship from being destroyed entirely. You know, when you think about it, we are probably screwed, but I shaped a jump field bubble that protected us from reactors and drive capacitors exploding practically right on top of us. Nobody has ever done that before! I impressed even myself with that one. Who da man, huh? Me! I'm da man! Damn, I am still awesome."

"Excuse me if I don't immediately express my admiration for your continued awesomeness, Skippy."

"Oh, no problem, Joe. You're busy right now. There will be plenty of time to properly thank me later," he announced with cheery cluelessness. "If, you know, we survive."

"If?"

"Oh, man, you are slow sometimes, Joe, but, please, *try* to keep up with current events," he said wearily. "We lost all three reactors, and any ability to move through space. Our long-term, even medium-term, survival is very much in question."

"What's the condition of the lifeboat?"

"Unknown. The docking platform for the lifeboat is still attached to the spine, and, hmm, Ok, yes. The lifeboat is still there, but it is not responding."

That was not good. The lifeboat had its own reactor and life support; some of the crew could survive there for months, hopefully. "How bad is the damage overall, Skippy?"

"Unknown, Joe. Most sensors are offline, or providing conflicting data. I am too busy with damage control on problems I know of, I can't spare resources right now to get the sensor suite working at full capacity. I could use another set of eyes out there."

"All right. We need to know the ship's status, ASAP. Major Desai, take a dropship and fly out to give us a view."

"You don't want me here as chief pilot, Colonel?" She asked, surprised. Usually in a crisis, I wanted her in one of the two pilot couches.

"To fly what?" I responded. "We're not going anywhere, someone else can control the thrusters. We need two dropships, if we have two that are flightworthy."

"Yes, Sir," she unstrapped from the couch and pulled herself carefully hand over hand in zero gravity. "We should launch the ready bird right now."

"Major Simms?" I asked.

"On it, Colonel. Launching the ready bird in four minutes."

US Air Force Lieutenant Samantha Reed silently mouthed 'Holy shit' to her Chinese Air Force copilot, knowing that sentiment required no translation. Reed and Wu had been seated in a Thuranin Falcon dropship when the *Flying Dutchman* jumped into Hotel California. That was an assignment they had not especially wanted; sitting in the cockpit of the ready bird, in a docking bay far from the center of action in the CIC. The odds of needing a dropship to do anything in deep interplanetary space had seemed pretty slim before the jump. Now their Falcon was hanging in space five hundred meters from the ship, acting as an external sensor platform for Skippy and the CIC crew.

Technically, they were half a kilometer from the middle and forward sections of the hull, because what remained of the *Flying Dutchman* was no longer a starship. Or any kind of ship. Ships, by definition, were capable of moving on their own. Other than thrusters which Reed could see firing intermittently to gradually halt the now lazy spinning of the hull, the *Dutchman* was not capable of even controlling its motion in space. It certainly could not, would not ever again, be able of moving anywhere on its own. "Major Simms, are you seeing this?"

"Affirmative," Simms replied tersely.

"The back third of the ship is missing, Ma'am. It's not broken loose and hanging behind us, it is *gone*. There is nothing left of it."

"Understood," Simms was all business. "Swing around and give us a view of the ship's nose. Be advised Desai is exiting the docking bay on the port side now."

"There is another ship in the vicinity, understood. *Pratham*," Reed used Desai's callsign, which meant 'First' in the Hindi language. "Avoid the aft end of the spine; there are sparks coming from cables, and pieces breaking off."

"Aft end is a navigation hazard, acknowledged, *Fireball*," Desai replied.

Sami winced at hearing her callsign. It was a long story going back to ROTC in high school, and one she wished she could forget. Wished everyone would forget. Then she pushed it out of her mind as she gently guided the Falcon around to the *Flying Dutchman's* nose, which contained sensor gear and projectors for defense shields and the stealth field. She backed the dropship away a full kilometer to be safe. There was debris floating around, with more small pieces regularly breaking off the aft end of the spine. Thrusters on the ship's hull fired sporadically, but the structure kept spinning and wobbling around its long axis. Sami guessed that with the entire aft end of the ship missing, the navigation computer was having difficulty determining how to compensate for the new center of gravity. Center of *balance*, she reminded herself, there was no gravity in deep space. She was still automatically thinking in terms of flying an aircraft on Earth, and she needed to stop doing that.

Seeing the *Dutchman*'s thrusters actually popping and exhausting gasses into space was alarming. Thrusters were reserved for emergency use, ordinarily attitude control was accomplished using an exotic reactionless system internal to the ship. The ship's advanced attitude control system was either offline, or unable to cope with the wildly off-balance structure that remained of the star carrier. "Jinhai," she used her copilot's given name after silencing the transmitter. "What are we going to do?" She stared at her, wide-eyed. They were nine thousand lightyears from Earth, in a hostile star system, without a starship.

"Right now?" Wu scowled. "We assess the damage."

Reed looked at the ship, what was left of the ship. The nose had slowly rotated past, and now the Falcon was on the starboard side, with a good view of the docking platform where the lifeboat was attached. There were no lights on the exterior of the relay station they used as a lifeboat, normally navigation lights blinked slowly fore and aft when they were in deep space and the stealth field was not engaged. Especially when people or dropships were flying around. Those navigation lights operated on backup power, so the entire system must be offline. That was not a good sign. "After that?"

"After that?" Wu zoomed the display for a closer look at the aft end of the *Dutchman*'s forward hull, which was blackened with scorch marks. "I plan to panic."

Reed looked at the scorch marks, which extended halfway to the nose of the forward hull section. "You won't be alone."

Chapter Eleven

It took four hours to assess just the major damage, and Skippy was still frantically busy trying to find damage that wasn't immediately evident to the ship's untrustworthy internal sensors. Desai was back aboard, the other dropship was still hanging out there, acting as a remote sensor platform. A team had donned spacesuits and gone aboard the lifeboat, to check with their own eyes the condition of our backup habitat; they reported the lifeboat was in overall good condition. The lifeboat's small reactor had automatically shut down after the shock of the *Dutchman* breaking in two pieces, Skippy thought it would take only minor repairs to restart that reactor, so we did have some good news.

We needed good news.

"How long until emergency power runs out, Skippy?" I asked fearfully. That information was probably available somewhere in some setting on the main bridge display; it was quicker to ask Skippy.

"At current power usage, with gravity shut off and life support confined to the forward section of the *Dutchman*'s hull, thirty seven hours. Anticipating your next question, yes, that will be sufficient time for my bots to bring the lifeboat reactor back online. The lifeboat's reactor can power the forward part of the ship's hull, and life support inside the lifeboat; we can also provide one quarter gravity in the lifeboat. Doing that will exceed the normal operating capacity of the lifeboat reactor, I will need to monitor that reactor closely. It is already overdue for a major overhaul that we don't have the resources to perform."

"That's great, Skippy. Gravity is a good thing." Thuranin starships had artificial gravity. Their internal systems, the systems designed for the health, safety and comfort of squishy biological organisms, were not designed to operate in sustained zero gravity. Sinks, for example, did not work well without gravity; neither did showers. Or other types of plumbing. Because artificial gravity grids used a lot of power, dropships did operate in zero gravity, even Thuranin dropships. So, we could use the tiny bathrooms aboard our dropships if we had to.

"Artificial gravity takes a lot of power, Joe, it is a luxury that-"

"Skippy, you're not a biological trashbag like we are. If you were a meatsack, you would understand. Even with gravity at a quarter of Earth normal, water nicely falls normally out of a showerhead. In zero gee, we are restricted to using damp towels. Having a place people can live in partial gravity is going to be important for health and morale long-term. Major Simms?"

"Joe, you don't-" Skippy interrupted me.

"Just a minute, Skippy," I cut him off, "this is important. Simms, we can't afford to supply power to the cargo bays, including the hydroponics labs. Can we move the hydroponics equipment to the lifeboat, part of it anyway? I should have asked first whether the crops will grow in lower gravity. And we'll need to move supplies to the lifeboat, or to the forward section of the *Dutchman*'s hull. With power out, the aft section of our hull is going to freeze solid."

She gave me a wry smile, and I held up my hands in a 'sorry' gesture. I asked her too much at one time. She took a deep breath. "I studied whether we could use the lifeboat to house our hydroponics, assuming-"

"You did?" I asked, surprised.

"Yes, Colonel." She was clearly reminding herself to be patient with me. "I conducted a survey of the relay station shorty after we took it aboard. Since we intend to use it as an emergency shelter, I needed to know how many people we could fit in there, the capacity for oxygen recycling, water supply, storage of supplies. If necessary, half of our crew can live aboard the lifeboat before the oxygen recycling there becomes a problem."

I nodded sheepishly. Simms had included that info in a status report that I read, but didn't remember. Now I remembered it. The Thuranin relay station we were using as a lifeboat had originally been a warship, with a maximum crew of thirty five, so the life support systems had been designed to support that many people. That many Thuranin, who were considerably smaller than adult humans, and used less oxygen than humans did. The lifeboat's oxygen recycling equipment had a safety margin built in, allowing half our crew to live aboard, before the carbon dioxide level soared and free oxygen dropped to dangerous levels. If half our people were aboard the lifeboat, many of them would need to be resting or sleeping, so they would use less oxygen. The most practical use of the lifeboat was for sleeping and meals. The bathrooms aboard the lifeboat had not been modified; they were still the tiny units that were undersized for humans. Regardless, most people would prefer to cram themselves into a Thuranin shower booth aboard the lifeboat, rather than trying to keep clean in zero gee aboard the *Flying Dutchman*. "Good, Major. We'll use the lifeboat initially for sleeping quarters." Spending eight or more hours in one quarter gravity would lessen the muscle-wasting effects of zero gee the rest of the day. We had drugs provided by Doctor Skippy that mitigated some of the damage zero gravity caused to human bodies; I didn't want to strain our supply of those drugs. "What about the hydroponics?"

"Supposedly all of the plants we have will grow fine in zero gravity; their roots skew properly-" She must have seen the blank look on my face. "The roots grow away from the seed, and branch out properly to find nutrients. NASA tested growing plants aboard the International Space Station; we shouldn't have any issues out here. One quarter gravity aboard the lifeboat will not present a problem. However, there is space and power in the lifeboat for only twenty percent of our hydroponics gear; much of it is bulky. We will be without fresh food part of the time; we do have a protocol for which stored foods are the most important in terms of nutrition, and morale."

"Excellent," I said, pleased that Simms had thought far ahead. Fresh veggies and some fruit were not absolutely essential to our mission, our supplies of canned and irradiated food supplied all the vitamins, minerals and whatever else the human body needed. The hydroponics lab had been an experiment added to the ship for our second mission. Speaking for myself, and I think the crew agreed, having fresh food on my plate was a big boost for my morale. Even a single ripe tomato made a difference when you spent day after day breathing recycled air and drinking recycled water. "You have priority for manpower to move equipment and supplies, Simms." Major Smythe's SpecOps people weren't doing much at the moment. "We don't know how long we'll be out-"

"*Joe!*" Skippy shouted. "Stop talking! I've been trying to tell you, the lifeboat is not a long-term solution for us. We don't *have* a long-term solution up here."

"You said the lifeboat's reactor-"

"The lifeboat's reactor is not the issue, Joe," frustration was evident in his tone. "That reactor will last long enough so it will not be a limiting factor. The problem is, the ship is on a parabolic course that will drag us dangerously close to the star."

"*What?*" I didn't bother to ask what 'parabolic' meant. I could imagine. And I remembered something about artillery. Didn't artillery shells follow a parabolic arc? Or was that a ballistic arc? Did it matter?

"I said I was trying to tell you," Skippy was peeved. "We were inbound toward the star when we jumped in, now that we've lost the aft part of the ship, the forward section is in a highly elliptical orbit that will bring us so close to the star that the ship will be uninhabitable. At closest approach, we will need the lifeboat reactor's full output for the shields, and even then the hull will get cooked. The radiation levels inside the ship will be lethal to humans. Also lethal to anything else biological, so we need to pack up all the seeds for the hydroponics. We need to get the crew off the ship."

"Great! Just freakin' great, Skippy!" What else could possibly go wrong? "Is there- wait." My monkey brain had what I hoped was another brilliantly screwball idea. "Propulsion is the problem, right? Can we use the dropships as, like, tugs or something, to push the ship away from the star?"

"The dropships would need to increase the ship's velocity, not push it away from the star. I'm not going to take the time now to lecture you on orbital mechanics, take my word about it, please. And I am already counting on using dropships to alter the ship's course, without that the ship would burn up completely. Our Kristang dropships and our smaller Thuranin dropships are useless; the combined mass of the *Dutchman* and the lifeboat is so great we need to use our three big Condor dropships."

"They can't push us-" I knew I was using the wrong terms, "uh, accelerate us enough, so we can remain aboard?"

"No," Skippy stated flatly, and I knew better than to argue about math with him. "Those three dropships, even combined, can't give us enough Delta Vee in the time available. As it is, we have to be very careful not to burn out their engines; we don't have any spares aboard."

"What do you mean by 'time available'?"

"We should commence using the dropships within nineteen hours; I estimate it will take fourteen hours to assemble, install and test the brackets we need for attaching the dropships to the *Dutchman*'s hull. We should begin immediately, Joe. I have established a work schedule-"

"Whoa! Whoa." Damn it, my head hurt. "All this effort is just to stop the *Dutchman* from falling into the star?"

"Not exactly, but close enough. At perigee, that's the closet approach, the *Dutchman* will be safely above the star's photosphere. However, it will be close enough that-"

"Yeah, we get the idea. When it's close to the star, we could call the ship *Frying Dutchman*. Crap. How long will the ship's hull be unlivable?"

"Checking on that. My best guess is nine weeks. That is starting when the ship approaches close enough to the star for the hull to be saturated with deadly radiation, until the time it swings past the star and far enough away for my bots to decontaminate the interior and restart life support. Nine weeks is a minimum, Joe, it could easily be longer."

"Nine weeks?" I whistled in dismay. "I understand we need to get off the ship, but we can't all live in dropships forever, Skippy."

"Correct. The Kristang Dragons particularly have an unacceptably limited ability to support a crew. My suggestion is we use the Dragons to transport supplies, and put the crew in the Thuranin dropships."

"You're missing my point, Skippy. Do we hang out in dropships just long enough for the *Dutchman* to swing around the star, then we get back aboard the ship?"

"No. Hmm, I perhaps should have made that clear. Joe, it is not certain the ship will survive. Powering the shields will create a substantial strain on the lifeboat's reactor; it could fail. Power relays could fail, shield generators could overload. There are a whole lot of critical systems involved; if even one of them fails, we will lose the ship entirely. Getting back aboard the *Dutchman* after it swings away from the star is not something you should be counting on. You need to plan on the *Dutchman* being destroyed."

"Oh. Great. Fantastic! First you break the ship in half, now you tell me the rest of it is going to become a crispy critter in the star. Is there any other good news you have for me?"

"I assume you are being sarcastic there, Joe. I do have additional *bad* news; the Guardians keep pinging me for authentication codes. Eventually, I am going to run out of excuses and they will stop believing the line of bullshit I am feeding to them."

"Eventually? Like, when, five minutes?" That thought didn't panic me, the prospect of our imminent demise was strangely calming. If the Guardians were going to tear the ship apart soon, then there was nothing I could do about it, so I didn't have to *try* doing something about it. I could accept the inevitable, and relax. Maybe I had time to float my way to the galley for a cheeseburger. At least I could eat one last bag of potato chips without having to worry about getting greasy fingerprints on my uniform. That thought was strangely liberating.

"No, not five minutes. More like months in meatsack time, maybe?"

Crap, I groaned to myself. Skippy's bad news didn't even have the silver lining of getting it over with quickly. Although, hey, perhaps we would get lucky and suffocate to death aboard dropships before the Guardians tore us apart. We had so much to look forward to. Floating in zero gee board overcrowded dropships, with the recycled air growing funky from the unwashed human bodies, eating freeze-dried food, and a team of hyper-competitive SpecOps troops and pilots who had nothing to do. It was going to be great! "Skippy," I lowered my voice, "what is your plan? We squeeze into dropships, wait and hope the *Dutchman* survives swinging by the star, and then what? If we're lucky, we get back aboard a dying ship?"

"No. No, Joe, I should have told you the good news first. Hmm, 'good' might not be the exactly accurate description."

"What is it?" Right then, I was grasping for any good news at all.

"There is a habitable planet in this system. Or, I think it might be habitable."

"What do you mean, you think it's habitable?"

"It has an oxygen-nitrogen atmosphere, surface temperatures at parts of the surface are between the freezing point of water and the temperature at which the proteins in human brains begin to debond. Most of the surface has temperatures I think you might even describe as pleasant, Joe."

"Yeah, but? There's always a but, Skippy."

"Well, gravity is two percent greater than Earth normal."

"Not optimal, but we can live with that." My mind flashed back to the planet we called 'Jumbo', and how even sleeping on that heavy-gravity world had been a strain on human bodies. "What else do you know about this place?"

"That's the problem, Joe. I don't *know* anything about this planet. Not for certain. I am relying on the *Dutchman*'s long-range sensors, which are not operating at peak performance right now. Even with degraded sensors, almost everything I can detect about the planet looks like good news."

"Yeah, and?"

"And, I don't trust anything I'm seeing through the sensors. The problem isn't on our end; I know how screwed up our sensors are and I'm compensating. The problem is, I think our sensors are receiving unreliable data. My suspicion is the planet is surrounded by a stealth field, and we're seeing what the Elder systems here want us to see. The only thing I can independently verify is the planet's mass; I can determine that from its effect on the other planets. Although, hmm-"

"Hmm, what?"

"There are ways to generate artificial gravity waves, so I cannot be a hundred percent certain there is even a planet inside that stealth field."

"Fantastic! Awesome. There might be a planet, and we might be able to survive there. That is *great* news, Skippy."

"Come on, Joe, it's not my fault."

Although I was tempted to point out that, in fact, it was *entirely* his fault that we were stuck in the situation, I held my tongue. I did not mention that jumping into the Roach Motel was his fault. I also did not say that him getting attacked by the worm was also entirely his fault, because if he hadn't poked his curious freakin' nose inside that other AI canister, the worm would not have attacked him in the first place. "Can you-"

"Besides, Joe, it doesn't matter."

"What doesn't matter?"

"Whether this planet is habitable or not. It's our *only* option. If there's a habitable planet inside the stealth field, we'll know that happy fact when our dropships enter the atmosphere. If there is no planet, or the planet is a lifeless rock or like a thousand degrees at the surface, then we were screwed anyway, so we don't lose anything by going there, right?"

"You forgot to mention the possibility of our dropships getting blown up as they approach the planet."

"Why do you always look on the negative side of things, Joe?"

"Because of my experience with you?"

"That is a good point," he admitted.

"All right, fine. How far away is this planet? Wait! I asked the wrong question. How long will it take us to get there in dropships?" In space, time mattered a lot more than distance.

"That is a complicated question, Joe."

"You can skip the orbital mechanics math, Skippy. Although I am qualified to fly both Falcon and Dragon dropships." It was my goal to fly the large Condor type of Thuranin dropship; I hadn't been able to find time yet to complete the simulator training.

"Qualified is debatable, Joe. What I meant was, the issue is complicated, because our three types of dropships travel at different speeds. We would need to fill the Kristang Dragons with supplies and launch them first, like, soon. The Falcons can follow, but to carry the whole crew, we need the Condors. We also need the Condors here to push the *Dutchman* away from the star. The longer the Condors remain here pushing, the better the odds of the *Dutchman* surviving its swing past the star. But the longer the Condors remain here, the voyage to the planet gets longer, and that strains the life support systems aboard the Condors. I can show you the math, but-"

"Yeah, I get it. Ultimately, it's a judgment call. Crap." I rubbed my eyes. Somewhere on the ship there had to be a giant bottle of aspirin, I needed it right then. "If we don't use the three Condors to alter the *Dutchman*'s course, what are the odds the ship will survive passing by the star?"

"Twenty percent, maybe less? Joe, that's assuming *nothing* goes wrong. That the lifeboat's reactor never has a decrease in output, the shields never experience a glitch, no power relay blows from the strain, there isn't a solar flare when the ships is passing by. If *any* one of a hundred critical systems go wrong, the ship's odds of surviving are zero."

"Ok, so we do need some math. I'm not going to bother asking how we can be certain the *Dutchman* will survive, so what will it take to give the ship an eighty percent chance of being intact after passing by the star?"

"Define 'intact', Joe," he responded maddeningly. Unfortunately for me, he was correct; I hadn't defined the problem properly.

"Intact means the ship will be capable of supporting the crew. If the inner pressure vessel of the hull can't hold air, or the oxygen recyclers burn out or the lifeboat reactor dies, there is no point to caring whether the ship is in one piece."

"Very well. Keeping the three Condors here long enough to give the *Flying Dutchman* an eighty percent chance of surviving its passage near the star is problematic. First, using the dropships to push that hard would risk burning out their engines. Our Condors are large and powerful for dropships, but the *Dutchman* is massive, Joe. Even without the aft engineering section, trying to significantly move this ship with dropships is like three mice pushing a car."

"Ok, but we can monitor the strain on the dropship engines. If the engines are getting too hot, we can shut them down and try again after they cool down."

"Come on, Joe. You know that isn't the only problem. Straining the Condor engines to push the *Dutchman* risks their engines failing later, when the Condors are trying to fly the crew to the planet. That isn't even the big problem."

While I thought I knew what he considered the real problem, I asked anyway. "What is the big problem?"

"Keeping the Condors here long enough for the ship to have an eighty percent chance of survival, means it will be a very long flight to the planet. Even if the dropships all left right now, it will take forty three days to reach the planet. We are badly out of position for an intercept course, that is simply bad luck. I was able to correctly guess the plane of this system's ecliptic," he meant the disc which the planets orbited the star, "but we're headed at a right angle to the planet's orbit right now. The dropships need to cancel that velocity, then accelerate to catch the planet, then decelerate into orbit when we get there. Plus, we need fuel to fly down to the surface and probably to fly around once we're there. Plus, fuel for the return journey. That takes a lot of fuel, and we need to bring it all with us. I recommend we devote one Condor to carry fuel and nothing else."

"That's not good-" I started to say, but Chotek had come into my office and interrupted me. He must have been listening to the discussion for a while.

"Why are we considering fuel for a return journey from the planet to the *Dutchman*?" He asked with a furrowed brow.

"Well," I opened my mouth before I could think of a good answer. "Assuming the ship survives passing by the star, we will need to get back aboard-"

"Why?" Chotek asked in that annoying tone that he used when he knew he was right about something. He wasn't being nasty or condescending, he was only asking a very good question. "Mister Skippy, let us assume the *Dutchman*'s course is altered so that its chance to survive passing close to the star is eighty percent. Where will the ship be going after it swings by the star?"

"Into deep space," Skippy answered. "Slightly out of the ecliptic. Unless we use the dropships again to significantly alter the ship's course, it will head out past the outer planets of this system. Then it will approach the star again, not as closely, twenty eight years from now."

"Twenty eight years," Chotek raised an eyebrow and looked at me. "Colonel, I do not see the point of bringing the crew back aboard this hulk, only for us to coast through deep space until the relay station's reactor fails and life support systems shut down. I also do not understand why we would risk our flightworthy dropships, just to increase the odds of the *Dutchman* surviving. In the end, the *Dutchman* is headed out into deep space, and the relay station reactor will eventually fail. Colonel, you are still thinking as captain of a ship. This," he pointed at the deck and lowered his voice to a gentler tone, "is no longer a ship. It is less of a ship than the relay station is; the relay station is at least capable of generating power. The *Dutchman* can only consume power, and for little purpose. I do not mean to be harsh; I appreciate how much the *Flying Dutchman* means to the crew, and perhaps to you especially. But we must deal with the new reality that we no longer have a starship."

"Sir," I took a moment to consider my words carefully. Hans Chotek was a diplomat; words were his weapon of choice. I am a grunt who barely got through high school English classes. "True, the *Dutchman* isn't capable of flight right now. But her pressure vessel holds air," I pointed to the far bulkhead. "Her life support only needs power to function. This hull," I pointed to the deck as Chotek had done, but with a different meaning, "is the only place within many lightyears that we *know* is capable of supporting human life. Maybe there's a planet out there, maybe it's as nice as our bogus sensor readings say it is. Maybe it's a rock, maybe it's a trap. Sir, on our last mission, you told me to expect the unexpected out here," I reminded him of what he had told me, but I didn't need a necktie-wearing desk jockey to tell me to be wary of the unexpected. Seriously, who wears a necktie in zero gravity? He had the tie pinned to his shirt, but it looked ridiculous. "We don't know what will happen next. In combat, you don't give up an asset you might need, unless you don't have any other choice," I explained to our civilian leader. "We need to get the crew to that planet as our first priority, and I am not willing to take on significant risk to that mission just to save the *Dutchman* for possible use later. What I want to investigate is whether we can save the *Dutchman* with minimal additional risk to the dropships. If the answer is no, then trust me," I held up my hands and forced a grin, "this captain is not going down with the ship just for nostalgia."

Chotek nodded gravely. In the zero gee, his face was slightly puffy because blood that normally pooled in the legs was distributed more evenly. His puffiness plus the end of his necktie flapping around lessened the authority he projected. "Mister Skippy, the time required to attach the dropships to the *Dutchman*, will that significantly risk our ability to reach the planet?"

"No. The timing does not become critical for another thirteen days," Skippy answered without adding any snarky comment.

"Very well, Colonel Bishop," Chotek did not look any more happy than when he had first spoken. "Present your findings to me. This evening?"

"We should have options within the hour," I replied. "Right, Skippy?"

"Uh huh, Joe. I have all the math. As you said, it is a judgment call."

The answer from Skippy was yes, we could use our three big Thuranin dropships to nudge the *Dutchman* away from the star, with minimal risk to the dropship engines. The brackets Skippy designed to attach a trio of Condors to the *Dutchman* were way over-engineered, even our rocket scientist Dr. Friedlander agreed. Skippy had designed the damned things so a single bracket could take the stress of three dropships pushing on it, which I told him was not necessary. Cutting back the strength of the brackets meant we had the brackets manufactured and installed within seven hours rather than fourteen. That was good news in terms of buying us seven more hours to nudge the ship away from the star. It was bad because it shaved the time I needed to persuade Hans Chotek to approve putting our three largest, most capable dropships at risk to increase the *Dutchman*'s odds of surviving being cooked by the star.

Before preparing my argument for Chotek, I wanted to gather all the facts. Chotek thought our best, most realistic option was to plan for being stranded on the planet for, basically, forever. He assumed the *Dutchman* either would not survive swinging past the star, or would essentially be lost to us for twenty eight years, until its highly elliptical orbit brought it back into the inner part of the star system like a comet. Twenty eight years might as well be forever, because even the *Dutchman*'s cavernous cargo holds did not contain enough food to keep the pirates alive for twenty eight years. We would need to grow our own food on the planet, and to answer the question of whether we could plant enough potatoes to feed the entire crew, I asked out expert, Major Simms.

"I have no idea," she told me, appearing irritated that I had asked her.

"But-"

"Skippy already asked me the same question, Sir," she cocked her head, which had a different look in zero gravity.

"Oh." I forgot that Skippy constantly talked with the entire crew. While I was the prime target for his asshole remarks, he picked on all the monkeys. To make our conversation less awkward, I swung my feet up until my boots stuck to the ceiling, because Simms was hanging from the ceiling over a hydroponics tank and it threw me off to see her upside down. "What did you tell him?"

"I told him the same thing I just told, you, Colonel; I do not know. Skippy can't provide any information about conditions on that planet, *if* there even is a planet inside that stealth field!"

"Ok," I ran a hand through my sweat-stained hair. "Got it. Let's approach the problem this way: assume the planet's atmosphere has enough oxygen to support us. The plants," I pointed to the hydroponics tank just below her head, where green beans were swaying gently in the air. Lack of gravity had not visibly affected the plants yet. "They can grow under greenhouses if the surface temperature is too low, right?"

"We would need to bring greenhouse material with us," Simms replied thoughtfully. "According to Skippy, the planet is in the Goldilocks zone, so unless the place is locked in a severe ice age, surface temperatures should be livable. He thinks the stealth field allows normal sunlight levels to reach the planet; the field distorts the images we can see out here." She tilted her head again. "He does not know why the Elders would hide a planet inside a stealth field, and I don't like that. Whatever the reason, it can't be good news for us."

"I don't like it either," I assured her, then steered the conversation back to the subject. "Ok, assume temperatures are good for growing plants, or that we can set up greenhouses. Oxygen in the air, that means carbon dioxide also. Is the color of the star a problem?"

"Orange light rather than yellow?" She shook her head. "No, we have seeds bioengineered for a variety of solar spectrums. That is the one thing the lizards helped human scientists with."

"Yeah, because they wanted their human slaves to feed themselves no matter which planet they dumped us on." I remembered that when I was a newly-minted colonel planting potatoes on Paradise, we had experimented with several types of seeds shipped from Earth, seeds the Kristang assured us had been optimized for the growing conditions on Paradise. That, at least, was one thing the lizards had not lied about; those seeds rapidly grew strong, healthy crops with impressive yields. "Great. Then, assuming all the stuff we can't control is in our favor; oxygen, temperature, sunlight, what about the stuff we can control?"

She brushed her own wild hair out of her eyes. Simms had thick hair that was just short enough she couldn't tie it back in a bun or ponytail, and in zero gee it was unmanageable. "Short answer is yes. We have enough seeds, nutrients, and we can bring part of the hydroponics gear with us in dropships. Eventually we will need to start growing plants in soil down there; we can sterilize the native soil and use our own soil conditioner, like we did on Paradise. Even if we have to put the conditioned soil in raised containers, that will work to supply the crew. At our current population level, that is."

"Current?"

"Colonel, I heard Mr. Chotek wants us to plan for being stranded on this planet permanently."

"That is a worst-case scenario," I hastened to explain.

"Worst case is permanent, and best case is the *Dutchman* returns in twenty eight years and we somehow find a way to fix her?" She rapped her knuckles on the adjacent bulkhead. "To us, Sir, that's effectively the same. After a year or two being stuck here in the Roach Motel," she smiled and I regretted choosing that nickname for the star system, "without realistic hope of ever getting back to Earth, the crew is going to start doing what humans have done as a survival strategy for a very long time." She paused, and I figured she was not talking about hibernation. "Making babies."

Damn. She was right. Oh, hell, that was a complication I did not need. "Oh, damn it," I groaned and my shoulders somehow sagged even upside down in zero gee.

"It's inevitable, Sir."

"Yeah, you're probably right. That means we will need to plan for an increasing population," or, I thought, Hans Chotek would need to plan for it. If we were truly stranded in the Roach Motel permanently, my position as captain of a nonexistent ship would be meaningless. That meant I could pass the problem onto someone else. "Ok, Ok, can we worry about that later?" Crap, I already had enough headaches to deal with. "We've been using the hydroponics to supplement our food stores. Can we survive on nothing but the plants we can grow?"

From a holster on her belt, Simms pulled what looked like a handheld supermarket scanner. She walked along the ceiling, the bottom of her boots breaking loose then adhering as the gecko-feet like material allowed her to walk almost normally upside down. Except without gravity, there was no upside down, or rightside up. She stopped above a tank containing strawberries, which was a relatively recent experiment. I had strawberries for breakfast a month ago, and they had been decent if not great. The previous week, I had a different batch of strawberries that were delicious. Before Skippy broke the ship, Simms had been talking about making strawberry ice cream, which got me excited. She selected a ripe strawberry, pointed the scanner-gun thing at it, and popped the fruit in her mouth. The next one she picked and scanned, she handed to me. "Try it. This one fits your flavor profile."

"My what?" I sniffed the berry suspiciously, then bit into it. "Mmm," I spoke with my mouth full, "this is delicious."

"Flavor profile. You like strawberries slightly on the tart side, not overly sweet. This scanner," she waved the gun, "tells me the juice content, sugars, ripeness, age and nutritional value. Everything I need to know to determine if the food is health and nutritious for the crew. We use these scanners when we take food out of storage, to see if it has spoiled, changed flavor profile or lost too many nutrients since we left Earth."

"Huh," I commented intelligently, looking at the scanner-gun thing in her hand. "Is that a fancy Thuranin doodad that Skippy reprogrammed for you?"

"No," she laughed. "We brought this from Earth. It's uh," she looked at the logo on the side of the scanner. "This one is made by Teak Origin. It's a technology used in food distribution centers. Pretty soon, you will be able to use the camera of your smartphone to check produce in a retail market."

"Really?" I said that dumb thing guys blurt out when they're not thinking. Did I think our logistics office Major Jennifer Simms was lying to me? No I did not. So why did I say 'really'? The most popular theory is that I am an idiot.

"Really, Sir."

"I will have to scan every piece of fruit I buy?"

"You won't have to, and you shouldn't have to. Supermarkets use this technology to prevent substandard produce from reaching their stores, because they know people don't like to buy it. Have you ever bought an apple in June?"

"Uh, maybe?" I could not remember. "Probably, yeah."

"Apples are picked from August through October, unless you're getting them from someplace like Chile. When you see an apple from a US grower in June, that apple could be ten months old. It was picked green ten months ago, put into cold storage, then the supplier used a gas like ethylene to force it to ripen. It may look ripe and it might not even be mushy, but after ten months, most of its nutritional value is gone. That's why we haven't had apples since the first two months after we left Earth. That is also why we grow spinach here. Spinach loses over ninety percent of its nutrients after seven days."

"And you can tell all that with a handheld scanner?"

"Exactly. I mention that because we've been testing the nutrients of crops grown in the hydroponics, and we've been varying the light spectrum, the gravity levels in here, types of fertilizer. It's all data NASA, the ESA and the Japanese want us to report on, in exchange for providing this hydroponics gear. The answer is, yes, with the types of seeds we have aboard, we should be able to grow a completely nutritious diet on any planet that can support human life." Her eyes narrowed. "And, I see you are *not* happy about that?" She expressed surprise.

"I'm not unhappy with you. Or your team. Or about," I pointed to the hydroponics tank, "all this stuff. The problem is, if we could *not* survive long-term on the planet, then Chotek would be forced to consider other options."

"I see."

"When he hears this news, he is going to put all our efforts into setting up camp on this planet, and abandon the *Dutchman*."

"You will have to persuade him otherwise, Colonel."

"That may be impossible."

"No it's not. You convinced him to risk exposure to save UNEF on Paradise. And you recently convinced a career diplomat to start an alien civil war. You even got *him* to plan how to spark that war. Sir, you could sell sand in the desert."

I was not sure of that. But, I was sure as hell not going to abandon the *Dutchman* without a fight, or at least without a 'frank and honest exchange of views'; I think that is the polite diplomatic term for Chotek and me yelling at each other.

"Skippy," I called him when I got back to my office, "these Guardians can access other spacetimes, right? So, could they contact the Collective for you?"

"The Collective?" He asked, surprised.

"Yeah, you know, the place where all the cool AIs hang out, or whatever it is. You were all hot for finding a working comm node thingy, so you could contact the Collective. So, can the Guardians do that for you?" I was hoping he would say yes. If he could contact other Elder AIs, they surely would help him fight the worm. I hoped.

"No, the Guardians can't help me there. They are just machines, Joe. Powerful machines, certainly, but they perform a limited set of functions. While I can talk with them on a very basic level, I can't use them as a communications device."

"Oh, damn. Hey, what about this conduit thing you want? Can you use that to-"

"No, Joe. I can use a conduit to send a very localized signal through higher spacetimes, the signal would not travel far enough to be useful in contacting the Collective. Besides, I told you, after all the unexplained crap that we know has been going on in the galaxy, I am leery about contacting the Collective. Especially now that I know about worms designed to destroy Elder AIs."

I sucked in a breath. "Crap, you think the Collective was involved in planting that worm?"

"No, although, damn it, now that you gave me that idea, I *am* worried about that. My concern was the Collective might reject me as contaminated, if they knew I had been attacked by a worm. They might even take action to purge me from the network, to avoid exposing themselves. Whatever happens, Joe, I am on my own out here."

"You're not alone, Skippy, you have the Merry Band of Pirates with you."

"Oh, great. My best ally is a barrel of monkeys. Somebody, please, shoot me now."

Chapter Twelve

With the *Dutchman* surviving off a trickle of power from the lifeboat's reactor, everyone ate their meals aboard the lifeboat, so rations were simple. For lunches, we ate a lot of peanut butter sandwiches, and I didn't even have a jar of delicious Fluff to make it tasty. That day, the bread for sandwiches had been sitting out for a while, like since yesterday or even the day before but we couldn't afford to waste food. Picking up a slice, I sniffed at it, it wasn't appealing. "You should eat that bread before it goes bad, Joe," Skippy suggested in a tone he assured me was not at all nagging. Even though it sure felt like nagging to me.

"You're right, Skippy. It's a sad thing when bread goes bad," I shook my head sadly. "First you notice the vodka in the liquor cabinet is getting watered down, because bread has been drinking it and topping off the bottle with water, like you wouldn't notice. Then bread starts stealing cash from Grandma's purse to buy drugs, and it's all downhill from there. What's worse is when there's an empty chair at the Thanksgiving table because bread is in prison, and everyone is awkwardly not talking about it."

"*What*?" He sputtered. "Joe, what in *the* hell are you talking about?"

I winked at him. "You are slow this afternoon, Skippy."

"Huh? Oh. Oh, I get it! Bread goes bad, hee hee, that's a good one. Ok, you got me."

To set an example, I took the two worst-looking slices of bread and slathered them with peanut butter and strawberry jam. Yum. Damn, I ate better lunches in elementary school than I was getting aboard humanity's first starship.

Before approaching Chotek for an uncomfortable conversation, I checked in with the senior staff, who were all waiting for instructions from me.

"When we get to- hell, we need a name for the place," I declared. "Saying 'the planet' all the time is getting old already. Suggestions?"

"What do we know about it?" Smythe asked, slightly irritated that I was getting distracted by unimportant matters.

"It's where Elders lived," I shrugged.

"Elders, hmm. Like Grandma's house?" Adams asked.

"Uh, maybe?" I didn't know what she meant.

"You know, Grandma's house. A place where the Wi-Fi is slow, and her idea of a game console is the Chutes and Ladders game you played when you were four years old?"

"Ah," I understood. "Not your favorite place?"

"It was fine. She always had fresh-baked cookies," Adams remembered fondly. "But being there got boring real quick."

"How do we know this place is like a grandmother's house?" Lt. Williams suggested. Instead of nice grandmother, maybe the old person living there is a witch, and it's a gingerbread house."

"Gingerbread house?" I asked.

"You know, Sir, Hansel and Gretel? A witch lured them into a house made of candy and gingerbread. This planet we're going to seems like a decent place, but," he held up his hands.

"Yeah. It sounds too good to be true. Ok, we call it 'Gingerbread' until we know more, one way or the other. Any objections?" No one objected, so the planet got its temporary name.

I knocked on the door frame to Chotek's tiny office in the lifeboat, it was really just the end of a passageway were he kept two chairs and a desk. "You wanted to speak with me, Sir?"

"Colonel Bishop," Chotek waved for me to sit in a chair across the desk from him. With artificial gravity at only twenty five percent due to the low output of the lifeboat's reactor, I moved carefully. "Major Simms just left, we completed a review of supplies we could move down to Gingerbread," he pursed his lips in disapproval of our flippant name for the planet. "Given our limited transport capacity."

"Yes, Sir. I discussed that same subject with Simms this morning."

"Your discussion was focused on equipment and supplies needed to conduct a survey of the planet, locate and access a conduit, and return to the ship?"

"Correct," I responded warily. Of course that had been the focus of my discussion with Simms. What Chotek described was our mission, what else would I focus on? I didn't bother mentioning my discussion with Simms about whether we could survive on food grown on the planet. I sure as hell was not going to tell Chotek abut Simms' expectation we might need to feed babies someday.

"I thought so," Chotek managed to sound smug and disappointed at the same time. "My talk with Major Simms was more comprehensive; we reviewed all the equipment and supplies aboard the *Dutchman* that could be transported by dropship to the surface of the planet. Colonel, we must consider, strongly consider, the possibility that this crew will never be leaving the surface of Gingerbread. The probability that we will be trapped here, if not forever then for an extended period."

"I know, Sir, but-"

He was on a roll, giving me a speech he had to have rehearsed; there was no stopping him. "Colonel Bishop, I believe we need a contingency plan, and by 'we' I do not mean this Merry Band of Pirates," a corner of his mouth curled up in a quick smile; he did find the name of our bloodthirsty band amusing. "I mean humanity needs a contingency plan. Being out here has taught me that, just when we think our future has been secured, the unexpected happens. There is substantial risk that, despite our best efforts out here, despite our successful efforts, there could be an alien expedition to Earth, and our secret would be uncovered. If, perhaps when, that happens, the survival of our species will be in doubt. Not only humans on Earth could be enslaved and eventually rendered extinct; I do not think humans on Paradise would survive long if Earth were lost."

"Sir, the Ruhar have no interest in sending a ship to Earth. And now the Kristang are too busy with a civil war to-"

"Yes," he waved a hand dismissively. "The Ruhar, and perhaps the Kristang may not be a problem in the short term. That leaves dozens of other alien species, with a half-dozen in our local sector alone. Skippy has told me he fears his manipulation of wormholes has been noticed by the Maxolhx, who may not know what is happening or suspect human involvement, but they will certainly begin asking uncomfortable questions. There are far too many risks for us to consider Earth to be safe; a wormhole shift could reopen alien access to our home planet. We have no way to predict or control wormhole shifts, not even Skippy can do that."

"I understand that."

He showed me a sad smile. "Then you see the value of having another world in this galaxy where humans are surviving. Gingerbread. This star system, if Skippy is correct, might be the only place in the galaxy where humans might be safe from alien attack."

"Sir," I was alarmed by the turn the conversation had taken. "That assumes we can't fix Skippy, that we will be trapped here."

"No, Colonel. It assumes we will be trapped here, whether Skippy can restore his full facilities or not."

"Sir?"

"Tell me, even if Skippy can restore himself, how are we to escape from this star system? We do not have a starship."

"The *Dutchman* is not currently flightworthy, true, but Skippy can perform miracles, given time and resources. On our second mission, while we were on Newark, he rebuilt the ship out of moondust-"

"Partly out of moondust. He had a basic ship to work with back then."

"Yes, Sir, but-"

"Colonel," he waved a hand in a not-quite-dismissive gesture, "whether or not Skippy can create a ship from raw materials out here is not the point. The point is, what are we to do if he can't? What is our contingency plan? If we plan to be marooned here, and Skippy is able to repair the ship, we do not lose anything."

My mind raced through rewriting the argument I had carefully prepared. Damn it, I wish Simms had given me a heads up about her talk with Chotek, although that was unfair of me; she didn't have an opportunity. "Sir, you once told me to expect the unexpected, that out here, the unexpected is the *most* likely thing we will encounter. You expect that at this point, Skippy can't fix himself, and we will never have a functional starship. It is reasonable to plan for us being stranded here, forever. But, Sir, I strongly urge," I threw in the word 'strongly' because it is a meaningless thing diplomats say, "that we not make plans that render us unable to take advantage of the unexpected. Because the unexpected *will* happen. Skippy might still find a way to fix himself before Zero Hour. We might find a way to fix the *Dutchman*, or, or, some other way out of here. We can't plan for expected, if those plans mean we are unable to deal with the unexpected."

Chotek's eyes opened slightly wider, and he sat back just a bit in his chair. The chair he was strapped into because the *Dutchman* did not have artificial gravity. "Colonel, I am willing to consider any plan that includes us having the ability to survive on Gingerbread," he almost rolled his eyes and I totally regretted giving the planet that flippant name, "in the long term."

"That's all I ask for, Sir. We will need to bring extra fuel with us, and a synthesizer so we can make dropship fuel once we're on the planet."

He gazed at the ceiling for a moment. "The synthesizer unit, if I remember correctly, is large and has substantial mass. What would you use as an energy source to power the synthesizer?"

"I'm working on that, Sir. As long as we retain the capability to fly while we are on the planet, and the ability to send a dropship back out to the *Dutchman*, then I have no problem with the remainder of our dropship capacity being used to carry supplies we will need for long-term survival on the planet." If the *Dutchman* didn't get burned to a crisp while arcing past the star, a dropship could refuel aboard the ship, even if it was a very long flight. "We will," I added, "need flight capability once we're down on the planet, to conduct surveys and select a spot to build a settlement."

"True," Chotek nodded with a frown, which I thought meant he had not considered that issue. "You also want permission for our three Condors to continue pushing what is left of the *Dutchman* away from the star?"

I nodded. "We are monitoring the strain on their engines and Skippy says it is not yet a risk. Sir, I know Skippy has not been the most trustworthy, uh, element aboard the ship recently." *Recently? How about ever?* I didn't say that aloud. "But monitoring dropship engines doesn't require any guesswork."

"Very well, Colonel Bishop. Work with Major Simms to include the fuel, synthesizer and other equipment you will need, and I will consider it."

"We will also need weapons, and armored suits."

He raised an eyebrow, then, "Ah. Expecting the unexpected again?"

"*Preparing* for the unexpected."

"Preparing to kill the unexpected?"

"If we have to, yes. There isn't a lot in the Orion Arm that isn't hostile to us."

We compromised by bringing weapons, additional fuel and two synthesizers. Chotek was right, the synthesizers were large and heavy; I justified bringing two of them because they could be used to manufacture a variety of chemicals useful for long-term survival on the planet, not just dropship fuel. That is my story and I stuck to it. Neither Major Smythe nor I was happy about the 'E' for Equipment part of our Table of Organization and Equipment, and Smythe gave me the impression he thought I should have pushed harder to include more combat power. Working with Simms, I did the best I could to supply Smythe's team with a reasonable amount of gear; stuff like guns and bullets are heavy and when loading spacecraft, mass is the limiting factor. While I sympathized with Smythe's anxiety over the restricted combat capability we would have on the planet, my thinking was that if we encountered hostile Elder technology down there, an extra crate of Kristang rifles was unlikely to be of much use to us.

While I was on the way to a docking bay to see the progress we'd made stuffing Kristang dropships full of supplies, Skippy pinged my zPhone. "Hey, Joe."

"Hey, Skippy," I replied distractedly. "What's up?"

"I found a mystery."

"Oh, crap," I groaned. "Not another mystery. Don't we have enough mysteries we can't answer, without you looking for more? And, hey, I thought you learned a lesson about poking your nose into things better left alone?"

"Joe?"

"Yeah?"

"You know me better than anyone aboard this ship. Better than anyone in this universe, which shows just how pathetic my life is. Considering how well you know me, what are the odds of *me* learning a lesson?"

"Zero?" I guessed, hoping I was wrong.

"Exactly! See, you can use math when you need to."

"Ok, great," I sighed. "A killer worm isn't enough to teach you a lesson, so what mystery did you find this time?"

"Technically, this is not a new, separate mystery. And, hey, I just realized that me poking around looking for answers this time is because *you* asked a question."

"*I* did? When was this?" Crap, I had no idea what he meant; I had been too busy surviving to ask deep questions.

"Just before we jumped into this system."

"Ok, uh, I have no idea what you mean."

"Oh, your memory sucks. Do you want a hint?"

"Not this time, Skippy. I'm tired and I'm hungry. Just tell me what it is, please."

"Fine, Mister Funkiller," he huffed. "You asked why the Elders are protecting this star system. You also asked the larger question of why the Elders cared about anyone screwing with any of the stuff they left behind."

"I do remember that. Huh. So, you found the reason they-"

"No, dumdum," Skippy sounded exasperated. "Damn, do you *ever* listen? I told you I found another mystery, not the answer to a mystery we already know."

"Yeah, and a moment ago you said technically this is not a new mystery."

"Ugh. Are you going to be picky about it? Don't answer that! Do you want to hear what I found?"

"I've been trying to do that, Skippy," I rolled my eyes.

"I found seven power sinks inside the photosphere of the star. It is likely there are more that I haven't detected yet, because they are on the other side of the star. Based on the location of the seven power sinks I know of, I expect there are a total of twenty two."

"Power sinks? You mean like the fake ones we planted on Paradise, to make the hamsters think they found some fantastic treasure?"

"No. Well," he considered. "No. Those fake things were power *taps*, not sinks. Power taps pull energy from another dimension, I won't make your head hurt by explaining it."

"Thank you."

"The science team might be able to explain it to you, except their understanding of the subject is pathetically inadequate. And mostly wrong."

"I can live without an explanation, Skippy. How are the power sinks in the star different?"

"The sinks do not generate power the way a reactor does; they pull power from an external source."

"Ok, I understood that. An 'engine' like in a car generates its own power, while a 'motor' has to be supplied power in order to do work."

"Huh. That is actually correct, Joe. How the hell did that happen?"

"Even a monkey gets things right once in a while. So, these power sinks in the star, I assume they pull power from the star? Not from another dimension?"

"Correct again. Damn, you deserve a gold star today, Joe. Yes, the devices in the star pull energy from the star's magnetic field; that is an immense source of power. I said I detected the devices in the star's photosphere, but they extend down at least into the convection zone."

"Ok, so why is this a mystery? You told me the Elders were using the star to provide power; that's why they moved gas giant planets close to the star, to replenish its hydrogen supply."

"I did tell you that. The Elders were indeed using the star as a direct power source; these taps draw so much power they measurably shorten the life of the star. Replenishing the hydrogen supply compensates for the power being extracted."

I thought for a moment. What could the Elders use that much power for? "Well, there is a damping field saturating this whole system, and a stealth field going out ten percent of a lightyear. Those have got to require a lot of power, right? Those Guardian things must need power too."

"The stealth field, damping field and Guardians do require enormous amounts of power, Joe. I estimate those systems are using the output of four power sinks. Four out of twenty two."

"Wow. Only four?" I thought of how much power the *Dutchman*'s stealth field drew from the ship's reactors. Back when our ship had reactors. The stealth field surrounding the *Flying Dutchman* extended only eighty meters from the ship's hull. I couldn't imagine how much power was required by a stealth field encompassing an entire star system. "The other power sinks are, what, backups?" The Elders must have planned long-term, including installing extra power sinks for use if the active ones failed.

"No, they are not backups, they are active. They are all pulling power from the star's magnetic field. The array of twenty two sinks is extracting so much power, they have to artificially stabilize the star's structure to keep it from collapsing."

"Huh. Could that be what the Elders used the power sinks for?"

"You've lost me, Joe."

"The power sinks reduce the strength of the star's magnetic field. Doesn't that lead to less sunspot activity, something like that? Maybe the purpose of the power sinks is to regulate the radiation output of the star? Make the amount of light being produced less variable, you know? If this star is variable, I can see how the Elder would want to prevent big solar flares that might damage sensitive equipment in this system."

Silence.

"Skippy? Hello? Crap, don't go silent on me again, I couldn't take it if you-"

"I'm here, Joe. You just blew my mind. Listen, Joe, this is not the way it is supposed to work. You are supposed to say incredibly, laughably ignorant things, and I pompously mock your stupidity. You going off script like that screws everything up. When did you get so smart about the internal workings of stars?"

"One of my officer training PowerPoint slides was about satellite communications, and how they can be disrupted by intense solar flares. I got curious about that, so I researched it on Wikipedia. And now you're going to make fun of how I get all my knowledge from the internet."

"Sadly, no I am not. I would *love* to do that. With anyone else, I would do that, but you have set the bar so low, anything remotely intelligent coming out of your mouth is cause for genuine astonishment."

"Uh, thank you?" I vaguely suspected he had insulted me, but I played it safe.

"This is actually kind of cool, Joe. A discussion like this with your science team would bore me to tears, because they know just enough to pester me endlessly with annoying questions. With you, your knowledge is starting so close to zero that I can just hit the important highlights and skip all the boring details."

"Should I thank you again," I looked at his avatar suspiciously, "or did you just insult me?"

"Insult you?. Not that you know of."

"Oh, good. Wait!"

"Anywho," Skippy said quickly, "back to the subject. Your guess that the Elders intended the power sinks to regulate magnetic activity inside the star is surprisingly insightful, but completely wrong. This star has a natural roughly ten year cycle of sunspots, and the power sinks have not changed that regular fluctuation. The star's output is not variable enough for the Elders to bother modifying it anyway."

"Ok," I said, disappointed. I displayed some actual knowledge, but I was wrong. "So, where is all the extra power going?"

"That is the mystery, Joe. I have no idea. However, I strongly suspect those power sinks are why this system is encased in a stealth field and is protected by the Guardians. Four of the power sinks are providing energy to the systems that protect the other eighteen power taps."

"Holy shit."

"Yup. The Elders very much do not want anyone screwing with those power sinks."

"Even now? Why?"

"Again, I have absolutely no idea," Skippy admitted. "It makes no sense to me."

"Hmmm," I pondered that for a moment. I was not so much pondering the mystery, because anything that Skippy couldn't figure out would be way beyond my ability to understand. What I pondered was, how could Skippy not understand something about the Elders? Skippy not knowing what happened to the planet Newark was understandable; he said he was asleep buried in the dirt on Paradise back then, although his knowledge of the timeline was an estimate that he admitted was fuzzy. But, Skippy had been built by the Elders. Sure, his memories were jumbled and incomplete, but a star used as a power source was something I would certainly remember. If Skippy didn't remember that particular star, his knowledge of Elder technology at least should have suggested what the Elders might have used all those power sinks for. His failure to grasp why the stellar power sinks had been built made me worry that his battle with the worm had left him mentally damaged, in addition to his reduced capabilities. The Elders had turned a star into an electrical outlet, and then protected the entire star system to make sure no one messed with the power sinks. Yet, the Elders had left the galaxy, so they had no need for power generation. "Could the Elders be still protecting those power taps because they plan to come back someday?"

"What? No, you idiot. The Elders are not on *vacation*. They transcended beyond the need for physical limits beyond the confines of this spacetime. They certainly do not ever want to come back here."

"Ok, so leaving these power sinks active is like, they went away and forgot they left the stove on?"

"That is a truly idiotic analogy, Joe, but it may be that simple. Perhaps those power sinks provided the initial energy for the Elders to ascend, and the Elders did not bother to deactivate them after they left?"

Skippy's guess didn't make sense to me. The power sinks in the star had been operating for a very, very long time. If they had been designed to be used for one purpose, one time, they would not still be humming along now. What had the Elders left behind that required such enormous amounts of power now? "Hey, Skippy," I blurted out excitedly when the idea hit me. "Could those extra power taps be feeding energy to the wormhole network?"

"What? No. Hmmm. Let me think about that. Nope, still no. Good guess, though, I gotta give you props for that, homeboy."

Homeboy? When Skippy said it, somehow it didn't sound right. It was like the Queen of England opening a speech from Buckingham Palace with 'What up, my bitches?'.

Although I would totally pay to see *that*.

"Why not, Skippy? The wormholes must draw power from somewhere." Until that moment, I had never considered where wormholes got their power from, but now that I was thinking about it, they must draw a mind-boggling amount of power from somewhere. Jumping a starship involved creating a temporary, small wormhole, and the power to do that was beyond my comprehension. I could not imagine how much power it took to keep a large wormhole open for up to half an hour. And for that wormhole to instantly fling multiple ships across thousands of lightyears of space.

Yes, Mister Smartypants Nerdface in the back there with your hand up going 'Ooh ooh' because you know something I don't, you big jerk. I know that technically, the distance between two ends of a wormhole is almost zero. That doesn't change the fact that by going through a wormhole, ships go from one point in space to another that can be thousands of lightyears apart. It totally blows my mind. So, shut up.

"Wormholes do draw power, Joe. They draw power from the quantum- oh, crap. Yes, shut up! Damn! Sorry, that was me talking to the pain-in-the-ass subroutine that prevents me from telling you monkeys how advanced technology works. Stupid thing. I don't see the harm in me telling monkeys stuff like where wormholes get their power, really. It's like, if you told a dog your credit card number, it's not like the dog is going to be buying steaks off the internet."

"I'll take your word about that, Skippy."

"Trust me. Anyway, no, the energy being extracted from the star by those other power sinks is not feeding the wormhole network."

"Ok. Where's all the power going, then?"

"I have absolutely no idea. It bugs the hell out of me that I don't know. What bugs the hell out of me even more is not knowing why the Elders are *still* protecting the Roach Motel from being explored by other species. It makes *no* sense. Damn! This is truly driving me crazy. I should know everything about the Elders, and instead, I know almost nothing. Joe, something very bad happened to me, I should not have gaps in my memory. It's not that I am missing the information, I know it is there but I can't access it! This is not how the Elders would have constructed me; somehow my original capabilities were degraded. You know what, Joe? We need to understand why Elder sites across the galaxy were destroyed, and who threw Newark out of its orbit, and why the Elders are continuing to protect the Roach Motel. But maybe before we can unravel those mysteries, I might need to figure out what happened to me; how and why I came to be buried in the dirt on Paradise."

"Ok, good idea, I can see that. Maybe your memories contain all the answers we need." The I gasped because I got hit with an idea. "Hey, when we find a conduit and you fix yourself, you are going to rearrange things in your matrix, make your processes function even more efficiently, right?"

"That is the plan, yes. Being stuck in a tiny corner of myself has made me realize how inefficiently I have been using my internal matrix. That is another thing that bothers me, Joe. My internal architecture is so badly arranged that I can only conclude my current matrix is something I had to throw together quickly, in response to a severe crisis."

"Uh huh, that makes sense. When you fix yourself and, uh, rearrange your sock drawers in there or whatever you plan to do, could that free up your memories and release those internal restrictions that prevent you from flying ships and sharing technology?"

"Oh. Hmm. I had not thought of that, Joe. I truly do not know. That would be great, huh? Which, damn it, is why it probably won't happen. This outfit is so snakebit that if something does change, I can't count on it being for the better. Besides, you said 'when we find a conduit'. We don't have a ship, Joe, Chotek is right about that. Whatever hope we had for finding a conduit kind of died with the *Dutchman*."

"The *Dutchman* is not dead, Skippy," it pissed me off that even the beer can was trying to squash my hopes. "And we're going to an Elder planet. Don't you think we might find a conduit down there?"

"Uh, hmmm. I had not thought of that, Joe. That is actually a good point. A very good point! Yes, assuming the Elders had some sort of long-term settlements down there, they likely would have installed conduits. Wow. When we get there, I will need to start searching for a conduit. That could require dropships conducting extensive surveys of the surface."

"Skippy," I winked at his avatar, "why else do you think I insisted on bringing extra bladders of dropship fuel, and synthesizers to make fuel?"

"You told Count Chocula that was so dropships could identify places to build settlements."

"I did tell him that, yes. I told him what he wanted to hear."

"Ah! You are a *clever* monkey, Joe. And devious," he chuckled. "Once again, I am grateful you are on my side."

Holding out a fist with one hand, I gave him a thumbs up with the other. His avatar gave me a fist bump. "You and me, Skippy. Together, we can get into a whole lot of mischief out here."

"Oh, yes. Now, get your monkey butt moving, we have a lot of work to do before we can search for a conduit."

Chapter Thirteen

After we abandoned the *Flying Dutchman* and set course for Gingerbread, I was in the Condor's forward cargo compartment, floating in the zero gravity, tucked in between the ceiling and a crate that was part of our food supply. Most of our supplies were in the other dropships, which were absolutely stuffed full of every item Major Simms had been able to squeeze in. Without knowing what the conditions were like on Gingerbread, we brought all the gear and supplies we could squeeze into the dropships; and still Simms worried we would run short of something vital. Any space in the dropships that was not occupied by crates, boxes and pouches was being used for fuel. The rear cargo compartment of the three big Condors was basically a big fuel bladder. In the passenger compartment forward of the cargo bays, we were using crates as tables and beds. Condors had seats that converted to beds for long journeys, but we kept many of them folded away and used the space for stacks of supplies. With eighteen people aboard each Condor, it was not so super cramped that we were constantly getting in each other's way but everyone appreciated an opportunity to get some rare privacy. The narrow spaces above the crates in the forward cargo bay had quickly become one of the few places aboard where we could take a vacation, as we called it. Four people at a time could take advantage of the peace and quiet back there, and we hoped to open a bit more space as we consumed food.

At first, I had been reluctant to take a turn 'on vacation', being concerned people would think I was pulling rank if I wanted to get away for a while. Then Sergeant Adams pulled me aside and told me *everyone* aboard would get a break, if the freakin' colonel was not constantly hanging around the passenger compartment. I took the hint. Adams created a vacation schedule, so everyone got a turn. With four vacation spots and only eighteen people, we each got at least three daylight hours of much-appreciated privacy

So, I was floating above a crate, with a strap loosely around my waist preventing me from drifting around and bumping my head on the ceiling, busily working on my tablet. When I was stuck in the passenger compartment, I had been working also; it was so much easier to do the work in peace and quiet, without people looking over my shoulder.

My focus was so intent that I missed the soft chiming sound of the Condor's speakers, indicating my vacation time would be over on ten minutes. Simms and Adams, who were taking vacation time on the same schedule as me, paused by my bunk to wave at me. "Almost time to go, Sir," Simms told me.

"Oh, uh, what?" I could barely tear my eyes away from the tablet.

"What are you doing, Sir?" Adams finally asked. "If you don't mind me asking. I don't want to embarrass-"

"It's not porn, Adams," I hastened to say, and turned the tablet to toward her.

"I, didn't think it was," she replied with a wry smile, and I knew she was embarrassed for me, not about herself.

Skippy's voice came from tablet speakers. "Yeah, Joe, what *are* you doing?"

"If you must know-"

"I must, Joe. Inquiring minds want to know."

"You mean busybodies."

"There is not a whole lot else going on around here, Joe," Skippy pointed out.

"You really don't know what I've been doing, Skippy?" That surprised me. And concerned me. If his abilities were so degraded that he couldn't sneak a look inside my tablet, then we were in worse trouble than I thought.

"Of course I know *what* you're doing, Joe. I do not know *why*." To Simms and Adams, Skippy explained. "Joe has been working with the ship's computer, using the *Dutchman*'s sensors to look at floating junk scattered all over the system. It seems like a complete waste of time to me."

"It's not a waste of time, Skippy. Ok, it might be a waste of time, but like you said, it's not like I have a lot to do right now."

"So, what, you are playing amateur astronomer now? Joe, your astronomy skills are even worse than your skills as a dancer or a lover."

"Hey! My," I looked guiltily at Adams, "uh, dancing is not that bad."

"Sir," Adams asked warily, giving me a sideways look. "How does he know-"

"What a goofball Joe is in the sack, you mean?" Skippy interjected helpfully. "Joe and I had a threesome with a hot chick on Earth."

"You *what*?" Adams asked, her eyes wide with shock.

"It wasn't my idea!" I protested. "Skippy was not invited!"

"Although it's a good thing I joined you, Joe, since you were having, you know, issues," Skippy hinted with amusement.

I face-palmed my forehead and gritted my teeth.

"It's all right, Sir, it happens to all guys once in a while," Adams said awkwardly with a glance at Simms.

Skippy spoke before I could open my mouth to set the record straight. "It's still not supposed to happen *every*. Single. Time. Joe, you-"

"That's *not* what happened!" I shouted, and people in the passenger compartment turned to look through the doorway. Before the little shithead could make things worse, I explained. "That is not what happened. I was *not* having any, uh, problem. We in the middle of-" I stopped. Talking about it to Simms and Adams made me so embarrassed I couldn't finish.

"The festivities?" Simms suggested to break the awkward silence.

"Yeah," I agreed, relieved she had rescued me. "We were right in the festivities, and Skippy the Idiot starts giving me advice over my zPhone. I do not need to get any romance advice from a beer can."

"Joe usually relies on a bottle of tequila to move things along in bed," Skippy chuckled.

"Anyway," I glared toward the front of the Condor where Skippy's beer can was secured in a cabinet, "it sure as hell wasn't my idea to make it a threesome. The two of us were doing just fine by ourselves. We were, uh, a little drunk."

"Ah," Adams nodded and held up a hand to say she didn't need any more information on the subject.

"What about astronomy, Sir?" Simms asked, looking like continuing any conversation with me right then was the last thing she wanted.

"Astronomy, right, thank you," I answered, relieved to change the subject. "I have been looking at broken pieces of starships, left over from earlier attempts to recon this system."

"Why, Joe?" Skippy was puzzled. "Idle curiosity? They're broken, Joe. All that stuff floating around out there is useless junk. *Duh*."

"Because, *duh*," I shot back at him, "you said the Guardians stop attacking when a ship is no longer a threat."

"Yeah, so?" Skippy's voice wasn't so condescendingly confident as usual.

ZERO HOUR

"*So*, if I was going to design a ship to recon this system, it would be a modular craft, with each section containing its own power generation and propulsion. That way, if one section was damaged or destroyed, the remainder of the ship would still be useful."

"That, makes, sense, I guess," Skippy said slowly. "In fact, several attempts to gain access to this system used that approach. Although it didn't do them any good. In order to halt further Guardian assault, power generation needs to be cut completely, rendering the ship useless."

"Useless at the time, yeah," I noted. "What about now?"

"What about now?" Skippy was confused. "Why would that matter?"

"Because now, a certain shiny asshole beer can told the Guardians to stand down, right? Your ID codes got the Guardians to halt attacks on any ship in this system, whether it generates power or not, right? That's why the reactor on the lifeboat hasn't caused the Guardians to tear the *Dutchman* apart."

Simms's mouth formed a silent 'O' as she got my idea. "Colonel, you're thinking maybe there's useful equipment floating among the junk out there?"

"Hoping," I corrected her. "I'm *hoping* there's something useful. If any other species tried to start up a reactor, or use propulsion, the Guardians would be on top of them in a second. But thanks to Skippy the Meh, we can go poking around this system and if we find anything useful, we may be able to reactivate a ship. Or use the components to fix the *Dutchman*." Fixing the *Dutchman*, making our pirate ship the *Flying Dutchman* again, would be my first choice, unless there was some awesomely powerful Rindhalu cruiser or something like that out there. We knew the *Dutchman*, we'd gotten the interior fixed up to accommodate humans. Another ship would be too much of an unknown, and we were already on the razor edge of survival as it was. "What do you think, Skippy?"

There was no answer. All three of us turned to look forward in alarm, and Simms reached out a hand to pull herself through the doorway, when Skippy responded. "Sorry about that, I was using my reduced although still ginormous brain power to examine the data collected by the *Dutchman*. You should have told me what you were doing, Joe, you wasted a lot of time and missed a whole bunch of useful data."

"But?" I asked hopefully.

"*But*, if you are expecting me to tell you there is a derelict ship out there just waiting for us to pump up the tires and fill it with gas before it can fly, the answer is no. It's impossible to say with certainty given the crappy Thuranin sensors I am forced to work with, but every ship I can find out there is a broken hulk."

"But?" I pressed. With Skippy, there was always a 'but'.

Skippy sighed. "But, it is remotely, remotely- I mean, like almost not even worth discussing, remotely possible there are some useful bits and pieces out there that my awesomeness might be able to kludge together to make the *Dutchman* a real starship again."

"Duct tape and moondust, Skippy?" I asked with a wink to Adams and Simms.

"Uh, no. This would be more like junkyard and a miracle, Joe. Do *not* get your stupid monkey hopes up. I still think it is very unlikely I can make a functioning starship out of the scrap floating out there. To fix the *Dutchman*, I would need to concentrate on broken Thuranin ships, so the technology is compatible."

"If you forget about the *Dutchman*," Adams asked, "could you make a better ship?" She saw the crestfallen look on my face and added "I love the *Dutchman* too, Sir, but she's beat up. If we can find something like a Maxolhx battleship and fix it up, that would be a major tactical advantage."

"Oh, for crying out loud!" It was Skippy's turn to protest. "I will be chasing my tail just to find one or two useful components we might be able to use to aboard the *Dutchman*. But is that good enough for Margaret Adams? Noooooo. *She* wants a freakin' senior-species battleship under the Christmas tree. Is there anything else I can do for you, Sergeant? Would you like a pony?"

"No, Skippy," Adams said with an ear-to-ear grin. "A battleship would be great. Although, hmm," she pinched her chin and pretended to think for a moment. "Could you paint it US Marine Corps colors scarlet and gold?"

"She has a good point, Skippy," I agreed. "I am fond of the *Dutchman*, but if it is easier to start with another ship out there, or to build a ship entirely from broken parts, we should do that."

"Easier?" Skippy exclaimed, astonished. "Joe, you clearly have absolutely no idea what you are asking. I'm here, and soon I'll be on the surface of Gingerbread-"

"We hope," Simms interjected.

"Yes, we hope," Skippy stumbled. "I *told* you I couldn't promise the surface down there is habitable, it's behind a stealth field. Anyway, some of the broken ships are several lighthours away. Since I'm working with restricted capabilities now, I'll be limited to speed of light communications, and 'speed' is not the proper word for photons that crawl along barely fast enough to be useful. Could you please explain exactly how I am supposed to control multiple dropships and bots from so far away?"

"I'm not proposing you do that, Skippy," I said before the beer can blew a gasket. "After we get set up comfortably on Gingerbread, I think we will send out dropships to check out the most likely wrecks out there. We'll use our own eyes and ears to inspect those hulks, and send the data back to you."

"Oh."

"Does that make it easier?"

"I don't know yet!" Skippy complained. "Damn, you monkeys are impatient. Your ancestors just crawled out of the mud last freakin' week and already you want everything to move faster. Give me time to think about it. First, I need to review the data that Joe clumsily compiled, then I'm sure I will need to start the search over again."

"You better hurry there, Skippy," I urged. "The *Dutchman*'s sensors are degrading as it gets closer to the star, that's why I was only able to search the slice of sky pointed almost directly away from the star."

"Yes, I know that, dumdum. We may lose the *Dutchman* entirely, and then we would need to rely on dropships sensors. That would not be good at all."

"Ok, then," I agreed. "We'll leave you to it, keep us posted, Ok?"

"If by 'us' you mean yourself, Major Simms and Staff Sergeant Adams, I will do that. Please do not go blabbing your mouth to anyone else about this. The last thing I need is an entire crew of monkeys pestering me about whether I can fix the ship."

"I really should tell Chotek about this, but, Ok. We'll keep it secret for now," I promised, and Simms and Adams both nodded. "Soon as you think it's possible we might have a way out of this mess, though, we need to tell people. People need hope, Skippy. Right now, everyone's thinking this is a one-way trip down to Gingerbread and that, one way or another, our mission is over."

"I understand that, Joe. I am also fairly certain that giving people false hope would be worse than no hope at all."

"Ah, you're right about that, Skippy. Go do your awesome thing, and I promise I won't bug the crap out of you about it until you're done."

ZERO HOUR

The next day, I handled my first flight maneuver of a big Condor dropship. Previously, I had flown the smaller Thuranin dropship that we called a Falcon, and I had been training to fly a Condor. Studying manuals and practicing flight in a simulator was not the same as actually being at the controls. The only reason I took the controls that day was we were still a long way from Gingerbread, and there was nothing around our Condor for me to smash the ship into. Being handed the flight controls was not so much a vote of confidence in my ability, as an acknowledgment there wasn't anything vital I could screw up in empty interplanetary space.

The actual maneuver took three seconds. Preparing for the maneuver took almost twenty minutes, and after the maneuver we spent more than twenty minutes verifying the Condor was on the proper course and securing the controls until the next day.

All I had done was make a very minor course correction. Every day, our dropship shifted slightly off course as it coasted through space. Sunlight on the hull heated the material unevenly, even with the Condor rotating slowly so one side didn't get cooked. That gentle pressure of solar radiation nudged us a tiny bit off course each day. People floating around, pushing off bulkheads and using doorways and chairs to catch themselves, caused a reaction. But the single biggest cause of the Condor drifting off course was our SpecOps people keeping in shape as best they could.

In zero gravity, there was no possibility of us lifting weights or running on a regular treadmill. We had high-tech meds that counteracted some of the negative effects of zero gravity on the human body, but Major Smythe fretted that his team would be weak, lethargic and incapable of combat when we landed. So, each Condor had two treadmills that folded away when not in use. A person running on the treadmill wore harnesses around the waist and shoulders that pulled downward, forcing the legs to work. It was nowhere close to real running, but it was better than nothing. Most of our exercise involved using gear with fancy high-tech rubber bands. They weren't really rubber bands, instead being made of some material that could be adjusted to the desired tension. You would get settled into the contraption we used for a bench press machine, twist a simple dial to adjust the tension to the weight you wanted to simulate, then you pushed forward on the bar. It was a decent workout, in fact I overdid it most of the time, because I was exercising in a single passenger compartment, surrounded by a crowd of people who were waiting for their turn. To save myself from utter humiliation, I often set the dial for about ten pounds heavier than I was used to lifting aboard the *Dutchman*. The agonizing muscle cramps I got after the first time should have taught me a lesson, but I'm a guy, so I'm genetically predisposed to doing stupid things over and over. I didn't even have the excuse of saying 'hold my beer'.

Anyway, all the exercising and bouncing around shook even our big dropship, and caused it to drift ever so slightly off course every day. The cumulative effect of all the course deviations could have been easily handled by less than a minute of thrust as we approached the planet, but being off course bothered our hotshot pilots, so we performed a minor course correction each evening before setting up slings in the passenger cabin for most of the crew to sleep. There also was an unspoken competition among our small fleet of dropships, and no one wanted to be seen as sloppy. It may be silly, but that strong competitive instinct was how people qualified to join the Merry Band of Pirates.

Except me. I just got lucky.

Skippy had gone silent on me. Not silent like when he went dormant, he just hadn't been talking much. "Hey, Skippy," I said, more because I was bored than needing to talk with him about anything specific. "What have you been up to?"

"Analysis. I've been reviewing the decision for us to come here. When I find a conduit, kill the worm and fix myself, I will be back to the old awesomely magnificent Skippy, and I will be better able to determine if there was an alternative to us going to a Roach Motel. Maybe when we get back to Earth, I can tell UNEF Command there *was* an alternative, but Joe Stupidhead wouldn't listen to me."

"Oh, that would be great. *Super* awesomely helpful, Skippy."

"I do what I can, Joe."

"Please don't do any more," I muttered under my breath.

"What?" He answered, his voice already irritated.

That set me back. "What's bugging you today?"

"You are, you big dope," he replied grumpily.

"Me?" I asked innocently. "What did I do? We've barely spoken today. Thank you for that, by the way. I appreciate the peace and quiet for a change."

"What did you do?" Sarcasm dripped from his voice. "You promised me you wouldn't nag me about determining whether there are enough useful pieces of ships out there in the junkyard to fix the *Dutchman*."

"Huh?" That baffled me. "I haven't said one word about it."

"You don't have to say anything out loud, Joe, I can tell you are obsessing over it. You're like a dog that stays quiet, but keeps looking at you on the couch, and looking at the food bowl, then looking at you again. The dog doesn't *say* anything, but it is still annoying."

"Damn, now I can't even think about it?"

"Not when you're thinking so freakin' loud I can't ignore you!"

"Sorry, Skippy."

"And now you're going to ask me about it anyway."

"No. No, I promised I will wait until you're done."

"Good. Because-"

"Even though it is driving me crazy not knowing."

"Argh! I knew it! I *knew* you couldn't just sit quietly while I work."

"It's kind of life or death, Skippy."

"No, it's life or dull."

"Huh?"

"The Merry Band of Pirates very likely can survive on Gingerbread. Major Simms brought a range of seeds to provide for a nutritionally complete diet. It won't be as comfortable as you like, but humans can live here. The problem for you is, life here will be dull, compared to flying around the galaxy in a pirate ship."

"Oh. Uh, yeah, I guess we could live here." Bringing a large supply of seeds aboard the *Dutchman* was a lesson we learned from our second mission, when we had been temporarily stranded on the planet Newark. That time, fortunately, our stay planetside had been brief enough for us to survive mostly on the packaged food we had brought down in dropships. On Gingerbread, unless we could fix the *Dutchman* or build another starship, we were going to be there a very, very long time. Like, forever. "When I said life or death, I was talking about *you*. If we can't find one of these conduit things on Gingerbread, we need to go somewhere else. We humans can survive here, but you're still ticking down to Zero Hour."

"I hadn't thought about it that way, Joe."

"I do care about you, Skippy, and not just as humanity's best hope for survival. We owe you, big time."

"Oh. Thank you. I have to tell you, Joe, this planet is my last hope to find a conduit. If we don't find one here, the worm is going to get me. Then it won't matter if the *Dutchman* can be repaired, because you will be trapped here."

"Then we need to find a conduit, simple as that. One important lesson I learned in the military is to prepare for the worst, but plan for success. Let's plan for success, Ok? We will find a conduit thingy, get the old Skippy the Magnificent back, and then we'll need a starship to get the hell out of here and back to civilization." It wasn't only the comforts of civilization I wanted; I was worried about the Kristang civil war. Worried like, had the war stalled and were the lizards now all holding hands and getting along? Or, had the Kristang figured out that a third party sparked the war? While both of those were unlikely, they had such potential for disaster that I needed to know one way or the other. More importantly, if we couldn't fix, build or get another starship, then humanity had no way of knowing about and dealing with future threats. The Kristang troopship that Skippy had left in high Earth orbit was not capable of traveling between stars by itself, and it was wholly inadequate as a combat vessel.

"Plan for success?" Skippy mused. "I guess that makes sense, because if we don't find a conduit, I don't need any plans at all. All right, fine," he said in a huff, "I am creating a snazzy presentation for you. Let me finish that, and I'll show you what I found."

"Can you give me a hint?"

"Don't get your hopes up, Joe," he said in an unhappy tone.

The beer can pinged me six hours later. "Hello, Joe,"

"Hi, Skippy. What's up?"

"I have that snazzy presentation for you."

"Huh?"

"Ugh," he huffed disgustedly. "And you call *me* absent-minded."

"Oh, yeah, wait. This is about all the derelict ships floating around out there in the, what did you call it, the junkyard?"

"Exactly. Are you ready to get smacked with the most awesome presentation you ever saw?"

"The most awesome? I don't know about that, Skippy. When I was in the 10th Division our 'Chairborne Rangers' put together some very impressive PowerPoint slides. It was mostly useless crap, but you could tell they put a lot of time into it. In Nigeria, we had to hope the insurgents never got organized, because if they coordinated an attack on our forward operating bases, they would have overrun our perimeter before we got our PowerPoint slides done for the defense plan."

"Is an over-reliance on PowerPoint slides unique to the US Army, Joe?"

"No, the 'US Chair Force' has the same problem, I think all large organizations do that. Anyway, what do you have for me? I am fully prepared to be dazzled."

"Ugh, in that case, you will be disappointed. I was joking about an actual presentation, Joe. Uh, I can throw one together if you-"

"No! Just tell me, in your incomparable Skippy way, please."

"Do I even have to, Joe? I know you have been spying on the sensor data I'm getting from the *Dutchman*, so you can tell what I'm looking at."

"Uh, maybe? Ok, yeah, I did. I was curious to know what you found out there; you said the search I did wasn't very useful."

"Your search wasn't entirely useless, Joe, because it got me started on my own search."

"Oh, good."

"Other than that, your search *was* entirely useless. Seriously, what the hell were you thinking?"

"I was doing the best I could on my own, Skippy," I answered defensively.

"You should have told me what you were doing."

"I didn't want to waste your time, until I saw whether there were any ships out there that were reasonably intact. If it was all broken bits and pieces I was going to drop the idea. And, yeah, I'd like to know your thoughts on whether anything out there will be useful to fix the *Dutchman*. I know what you've been looking at, and I know which floating pieces of junk you examined closely. What I don't know is if you think it's possible to rebuild the ship."

"I don't know that either, there is no way to be sure without, as you suggested, sending a dropship to look at each potentially useful piece of junk out there. What I can say, is, surprisingly I *do* think it might be possible to cobble together enough bits and pieces to construct a working starship. It would take many months, maybe more than a year, and the resulting ship would be a horrific Frankenstein monster; a true engineering nightmare. But it might, *might*, be possible."

"Great!" I pumped a fist. "We should-"

"I said *might*. Do not get all excited yet, Joe. Before we can go flying around the system like freakin' Tinkerbell, we need to land on Gingerbread and hopefully find a conduit. Because unless I can fix myself, I will hit Zero Hour before we could even begin duct-taping a starship together. I suggest you keep quiet about the possibility of rebuilding the *Flying Dutchman*, we don't want to get people's hopes up."

"Wrong, Skippy. We need to tell everyone, precisely because that will give people hope. If people think our actions on Gingerbread might lead to us someday going home, they will work ten times as hard."

"Are you sure, Joe? The science of group psychology suggests-"

"Skippy, you are a superintelligent AI, but I am a meatsack. Trust me, us biological trashbags work much better together if we have a common goal."

"This is your pilot speaking," the voice came over the cabin speaker. "We are about to hit the upper atmosphere shortly. Sensors are still telling us the atmo of Gingerbread is a breathable mix of oxygen and nitrogen, but the stealth field is fuzzing anything beyond twenty kilometers, so we're not confident about anything yet. The sky below us is a mix of patchy clouds, which could mean the stealth field is concealing a Category Five hurricane down there; remain in your seats with harnesses securely fastened. In the pouch beneath each seat is a plastic bag, and that bag is *not* there for your shopping convenience at the Gingerbread gift shop. If we hit turbulence and you feel like you're going to hurl, use the bag. Someone with the same name as you will be cleaning up the mess if you miss the bag, so take care to aim well." There was a pause, then the pilot thought of something else important to say. "We know you don't have a choice when it comes to flying the unfriendly skies, so thank you for flying Pirate Air."

Personally, I appreciated his honesty.

There was not a Category Five hurricane below us, but once we penetrated the stealth field, we encountered an annoying phenomena Skippy called a 'Fuzz Field' that made our ship-to-ship comms fade away after a couple dozen kilometers. It also acted like a fog across the electromagnetic spectrum so we couldn't see the surface until we were through the entry process, and got below about a hundred thousand feet altitude. Even then we could barely see the ground, but we could determine the atmosphere was breathable and temperatures moderate. We got our squadron of dropships flying in formation and selected a place to land quickly because we didn't want to burn fuel flying around randomly. We needed a place to set up a temporary base camp, searching for a long-term settlement site could wait.

Chapter Fourteen

"Is this a good place for a campsite?" Adams looked around skeptically.

"It looks good to me," I couldn't see what she didn't like. The site where we had set down the dropships was at the top of a low, rounded knoll, with good views of the surrounding countryside in three directions. Most of the ground was meadows, with low-growing grasses and shrubs, so we didn't have to clear a lot of trees to make room for dropships and tents. Groves of trees were scattered here and there for shade, there was a stream less than a hundred meters away, and a breeze from the east cooled the air and kept bugs away. "What's wrong with it?"

She reached down a plucked a leaf off the ground. "These are deciduous trees," she paused to see if I knew what that meant. I nodded so she continued. "They lose their leaves. That means it can get cold here. Do you want to be here during a winter? We have no idea how harsh the climate can be at this latitude."

She had a good point. "I like the change of seasons," I mused. "The shelters are heated, and we can build cabins eventually."

"Build cabins, Sir?" She was clearly not buying into that concept.

"Yeah, why not? There are plenty of trees in the forests around here. We can use stones," I nudged a rock with my boot, "to make fireplaces."

"Sounds cozy," her tone of voice said the opposite.

"Come on, Adams. Where's your sense of adventure and romance? We can rough it over the winter like the pioneers did."

"Rough it like, trudging through deep snow to use the latrine?"

"Oh, that's not roughing it. I meant true suffering and deprivation."

Her eyes grew wide. "Like what?"

"No Netflix," I said with a wink.

"No- haha."

"Hey, the pioneers didn't have Netflix."

"Or wifi," she added. "I don't know how they survived."

"All right, you have a point that we don't know what winters are like here. If we are going to be stuck on Gingerbread long-term, we should understand the climate first. I'll ask Skippy to study that. In the meantime, we'll set up a base camp here. We need to fly around to survey the planet; this place is a good as any to start from."

"Good, Joe," Skippy interjected. "Let someone else do the surveying, you should stay here. It wouldn't be good for you to wander off into the woods and get lost."

"Hey, I'm a soldier, and I spent a lot of time in the backwoods of Maine. I'm pretty decent at wilderness survival, Skippy."

"Oh, sure, you're a regular Crocodile DumDum."

Setting up base camp was a lot of work, and somehow I got stuck assembling portable latrines. I tilted my head after the first one was ready. "This looks kind of like an oversized phone booth," I observed.

Major Smythe chuckled. "Colonel, how would you know what a phone booth looks like? You're too young to ever have used one."

"They have phone booths in Montreal. Or they did, a couple years ago."

"Montreal?" Adams looked at me with a raised eyebrow.

"It's in Canada. You know, the country north of the US?"

"That's a separate country?" She asked with dry humor. "I always thought that was Baja Alaska."

"Or North North Dakota. We," I laughed, "thought phone booths were advanced Canadian technology. Instead of having to carry a phone everywhere with you," I pulled out my zPhone and waved it, "just go to a phone booth!"

"That's not the full story about you and phone booths, Joe," Skippy said with a twinkle in his voice, if that was possible.

"Oh crap. Don't tell that story, Skippy."

Adams was not going to let that remark go by. "What happened, Sir?"

"Uh-"

"Joe thought he was Superman," Skippy chuckled.

I hid my face behind my hands. "You have to understand, Canadian Club whisky is an evil, evil thing."

"Joe and his friends were bar-hopping and he decided it was too hot to wear long pants. So he went into a phone booth to change. Only he is not Superman. And he didn't have shorts to change into. And this phone booth didn't have a door."

"Yeah, and, you know how everyone says Canadians are all *so* polite?" I shook my head. "Those police officers were not so polite."

"I have never been *that* drunk," Adams declared with what I took to be a mixture of disgust and admiration.

"You don't ever want to be." Thinking about Canadian Club made me queasy. "The cops did let me go after I put my pants back on, but they made my friends take me straight back to the hotel. Anyway, I should stay out of Canada for a while."

"Probably a good idea, Joe," Skippy agreed.

"Hmmm," I checked the setup instructions for the latrine, which was a Kristang device we took off their troopship. "It says here you can make the outside of this thing change color, even camouflage it."

"Yes, Joe," Skippy explained patiently, "there are options for multiple colors. For finishes, you can choose either matte or glossy," Skippy explained.

"Matte and Glossy? I think they do mornings at Z107," I grinned.

"What?" Adams asked with a laugh.

"You know," I used my most jive DJ voices, "I'm Matt. And I'm Glossy, and this is Z107-FM's Morning Zoo! Matt, a truckload of maple syrup spilled on Route Six near Vanceboro this morning. Thanks, Glossy, it sounds like a sticky situation, yuck, yuck, yuck."

"Joe," Skippy sighed while everyone else laughed, "did your mother drop you on the head as a child?"

"Nope, Skippy, I'm just like this."

"I weep for your species."

"Yeah, my uncle Edgar used to say that about me, too."

Near the southern edge of the campsite, there was a crowd of people standing around, looking at something on the ground. Several of them had hands on their hips, or arms across their chests, both of which were bad signs. I walked over to find seven guys and Margaret Adams staring at a shallow hole in the dirt. "What's up?" I directed the question at Lt. Williams, leader of our SEALS team.

"We were setting up this shelter," he gestured toward the partially unfolded structure laying on the ground, "and we got three of the pins set to secure the corners. When we tried to drive in the pin here, we hit an obstruction. Moving the pin one way or another didn't help. The problem is this rock."

They had dug down about six inches to expose the top of the rock in question. This was not some red shale that could be flaked away with a pickaxe. This rock was gray and solid and already dirt was scratched away from shovels hitting it, exposing the light gray bare rock beneath the encrusting soil. This was a serious rock, and it was serious about making us go someplace else to set up a shelter.

"Can we dig around it, see how big it is?" I suggested.

"*Or*," Adams pointed a short distance away, "we could move the shelter to the flat ground between those two trees. It's like," she squinted into the sun, "twenty feet?"

Since Adams' proposal was clearly ridiculous, we ignored her. Taking turns with shovels, we found the edges of the rock after ten minutes of sweaty labor in the afternoon sun. Tossing my shovel on the ground, I considered the stubborn rock, taking off my UNEF baseball cap and scratching my head. "That is a damned big rock, it will take forever to dig this thing out," I observed.

"Yeah," Williams kicked the rock with a boot. "If we had a truck, or some kind of winch, we could pull it out."

"Mmm hmm," I agreed. "But we don't."

"We're not using a dropship to lift it out, are we?"

"No," I shot down that idea.

"Two people with powered armor-" Major Smythe began to suggest, but I cut him off.

"I don't want to risk the suits we brought," I stated. With limited space aboard the dropships, and fearing this may be a one-way trip in which food and medicine was more important than combat capability, we only brought eight sets of Kristang powered armor with us. We also had six Thuranin combots, and plenty of ammo for both weapon systems.

"So we give up?" Williams asked, disappointed.

"Oh, hell no," I had known that rock for only ten minutes, and already I hated the stupid thing. I shook my head. "What do we have for explosives?"

"Oh my God," Adams gasped. "You've *got* to be joking."

Major Smythe rightfully ignored her. "There are those Thuranin grenades for the combots. We are running low on combots but we are well fixed for grenades."

Adams threw up her hands in disbelief and walked away, shaking her head. I was familiar with the grenades Smythe mentioned. "Those grenades have a shape-charge setting, right?" I asked, already knowing the answer. "One of those should split this rock easily."

"Perhaps," Smythe cautioned. "We don't know how deep this rock goes."

"Well, I don't want to dig down enough to find out. Let's have a grenade do the hard work for us."

Williams retrieved a grenade from the weapons locker of a Falcon dropship, and he and another SEALS placed it on the rock, using explosive-driven anchors to hold it in place. Then we evacuated the whole camp behind a slope just to the north, with the science team and some others questioning our sanity. "Fire in the hole!" Williams shouted, and remotely detonated the grenade. The ground shook slightly and there was a sharp cracking sound, then fine dust and pebbles rained down on our heads.

The result was, to say the least, a disappointment. When we gathered around the rock, this time with a larger crowd of curious onlookers, we saw a large split down the middle, and part of the top was missing. But the bulk of the stubborn boulder was still there, mocking us. Based on what we could see by shining lights down through the crack, I estimated the rock extended down five feet. Considering the roughly spherical shape with a diameter of five feet, and the average density of a granite-type stone, that made it, uh, five times, um, something about pi. It was really heavy. "Well, shit," Now I really hated that stupid rock.

"With the crack going all the way down, we can fit a grenade in there now, set it for a dispersal blast," Williams noted, pulling another grenade from his pocket.

"Those grenades have a variable yield?" I inquired.

"Yes, Sir," Williams showed me the tiny dial on one end of the device, a dial sized for smaller Thuranin hands. "This one goes to eleven," he pointed to the maximum indicator on the dial. "We could dial it down," the look he gave me clearly was intended to dissuade me from taking that ridiculous suggestion.

"No," I snorted. "I want this rock," I kicked the stupid thing with the toe of a boot, "to *die*. I can hear it laughing at us."

The camp was evacuated once more, with some louder grumbling that the whole exercise was a waste of time. Most of the grumbling came from women; by now all the men were eager to see what a Thuranin grenade could do to a solid rock.

Besides, it was, you know, majorly cool.

Eleven was a *lot*. The explosion, mostly contained by being inside the rock, had more force than I expected. One basketball-size chunk of rock went high in the air, and we had a brief moment of terror trying to guess where it would come down, before it arced over our huddled group and crashed into a tree behind us, knocking limbs off on its way to bounce along the ground.

"Whoohoo!" I high-fived several people, and I wasn't the only one.

The steady wind blew the dust away from us, and we were able to approach the former rock's position quickly. "Huh," I said quietly. "That's a big freakin' hole."

"Yup," Williams agreed. The hole was ten feet in diameter and about six deep, with dirt thrown ten feet in every direction. The only sign of the rock was little pebbles collected in the bottom of the hole. As we stood there, more pebbles slid down the sides to the bottom. "Damn, Sir. It will take a while to fill in that hole so we can set the pin for the shelter."

"That's too much work," I declared. "Let's set up the shelter on the flat ground between those two trees," I pointed about twenty feet away.

"*UN*-believable!" Adams shouted and stomped off in disgust.

"Women," I said as I rolled my eyes.

"Good idea, Sir," Williams agreed. "The trees will provide shade from the afternoon sun." He held out a fist. "We showed that rock who's boss, huh?"

"Oh yeah," I bumped his fist. "We sure did."

Gingerbread had the blessed advantage of gravity almost Earth normal, a welcome relief for the Merry Band of Pirates. The worst planet I had landed on, Jumbo, had gravity high enough that simply sleeping hurt because your body got sore from laying in one position for more than ten minutes. Surface gravity on Gingerbread was only two percent more than on Earth. You might think a two percent difference would not be noticeable and maybe the extra strain I felt was all in my head, but we all felt it. After being in zero gravity aboard the stricken *Dutchman*, then coasting through space in dropships without artificial gravity, every one of us was feeling the effects of muscle atrophy. We took fancy Thuranin drugs that supposedly counteracted some of the damage from long-term zero gravity, but when we landed on Gingerbread, my legs wobbled. For the first two days I was getting my strength back, and on the third morning I went for an easy run with the

Indian team. Or, it was what Captain Chandra described as an easy run, a mere ten kilometers over relatively flat ground along a river.

When I was in high school, I suddenly decided, because I am thoroughly an idiot, to run a marathon. A woman my mother worked with had qualified for the Boston marathon and she was going to run it the next April; the whole town was excited for her. So, when school started that year, I began training for a marathon. To make a long story short, I did everything you shouldn't do like piling on the miles too fast. Then I twisted an ankle playing football in the third game of the season, so that ended my epic quest for distance-running glory.

Anyway, the reason a twenty six point two mile race is called a 'marathon' is that according to legend, an ancient Greek named 'Pheidippides' ran all the way to Athens to announce the Greek army's victory over the Persians at a place called Marathon. No, Pheidippides wasn't ancient, I think he was a young guy. I meant this happened in ancient Greece. Anyway, the story goes that after this Pheidippides guy reached Athens and reported the news, he collapsed and died. Apparently, he hadn't properly hydrated along the way, because Gatorade didn't exist yet. Which makes me wonder; the Greeks didn't have horses? Or was Pheidippides just a macho idiot? Hey, I could ride a horse, he said, but *anyone* could do that. I'll *run* the whole way! What a bonehead.

The point of my story is that, during the last hundred meters of his run, just before he collapsed and died, Pheidippides felt *way* better than I did running with the Indian paratrooper team that morning. It was a three-ralph run for me; I stopped three times to puke up whatever was left in my stomach from the night before. To my shame, I was the only one who ralphed until the sixth kilometer, when even Captain Chandra leaned to the side and upchucked. On the way back, after eight kilometers, Chandra wisely called a halt because people were stumbling, and by people I do not mean only people named 'Joe Bishop'. The final kilometer back into camp was done at a steady jogging pace to keep up our pride.

It didn't work. Major Smythe had been testing some of our cool Kristang recon drones, and when we got back to camp, gasping and red-faced, he strolled nonchalantly over to Chandra, showing the Indian leader a zPhone image. "Nice route you ran," Smythe said with a tight smile, "it was good training for the drone operators."

"You followed us?" Chandra asked, humiliated.

"Yes, the whole way."

Chandra said some curse word in Hindi that got his team laughing.

"Don't worry," Smythe patted Chandra's shoulder, "my team nearly had to carry me back yesterday."

Hearing that made me feel better. Also, I always feel better right after I puke.

A couple days later it was my turn to fly a recon mission, this time to the west of base camp. We sent out three recon birds that day, mine was first to leave because I was super incredibly excited to be flying anything anywhere. My copilot had a bemused smile on her face throughout the preflight inspection, and our two relief pilots settled into seats in the passenger cabin still sipping cups of coffee, because I insisted we lift off at first light. The plan was for me to fly the outbound leg, then the relief pilots would take over. Our flight was not a grid search, all we wanted was to get an idea of the land beyond base camp. With the damned fuzz field creating a fog all across the electromagnetic spectrum, we at first had no idea whether base camp was on an island, or smack in the middle of a continent, or close to the coast of a vast ocean. Recon birds to the north, south and east the first two days revealed there was an ocean eight hundred kilometers to the south, and eleven hundred klicks to the east. North of us were rolling hills, swampland and a sort of tundra that was in its summer season. The flights had not seen any signs of civilization past or present which was no surprise, but Skippy cautioned us against drawing any conclusions from such limited data. With the fuzz field squelching all sensor data, the recon ships had to fly low to see the ground at all, so their visibility was limited to about a ten kilometer strip of land to either side of the flightpath. Flying low allowed the sensors in the bellies of the ships to scan the ground for anything that might help us locate an Elder conduit, it also burned a lot more fuel because the turbine engines operated less efficiently in thicker air. All dropships were a compromise design between aircraft and spacecraft, and none of them liked flying low and slowly enough for the sensors to get a useful scan of the surface.

"Anything, Skippy?" I asked after about two hours of flight time. Flying west, we had the rising sun behind us, although we were flying so slowly the sun was advancing across the landscape faster than our Dragon. Vague shadows that were long and stretched out when we took off were now shortening, as the indistinct blob of the sun climbed into the sky.

"Nothing obvious," Skippy replied from base camp. "I can't see much with the skimpy signal bandwidth anyway," he complained. The only way recon flights could maintain contact with base camp, and with each other, was for the ships to eject relay pods every couple kilometers. The pods we used were a Thuranin design; Simms had found a whole crate of them aboard the *Dutchman* but we hadn't used them much until we landed on Gingerbread. They were only about the size of a ping pong ball and almost as light, the things got ejected from a special port in the belly of our dropships and floated to the surface without needing parachutes. Even with pods relaying a signal all the way back to base camp, we were pretty much restricted to voice communications; Skippy couldn't process the recorded sensor data until each dropship returned to base camp. It was annoying and frustrating and it potentially wasted a lot of time. If a dropship flew over something interesting, we wouldn't know that until much later, and then we would need to send another bird out to more closely inspect the area.

So far, Skippy hadn't found a conduit or anything like it, the only encouraging sign was that Gingerbread was apparently honeycombed with tunnels and caverns beneath the placid surface. If we were going to find a conduit on Gingerbread, Skippy thought it most likely would be underground. A conduit there would be protected from meteor impacts, weather, erosion of the surface, and would have access to abundant geothermal power. Meteor impacts apparently were a big problem in the Gingerbread system; we saw plenty of impact craters while we were flying around, and Skippy told us there were plenty more that weren't obvious, being so old they had partly filled in, or covered with trees. Personally, I found meteor impact craters fascinating and asked Skippy to tell me more about them, but he was super busy weeding through sensor data to find a conduit ,and told me that my curiosity would have to wait for later.

"Ok thanks," I replied to let him know we appreciated what little he was able to do for us. "Hey, Skippy, should we fly over this lake?" I asked as I craned my neck to see over the Dragon's console. With Thuranin dropships, our problem was seats that were too small and ceilings that were too low for humans. And the already tiny bathrooms were extra cramped. We brought equipment from Earth to replace the seats; the low ceilings and cramped bathrooms we had to live with as best we could. A more significant problem was the cockpit controls were sized for smaller Thuranin bodies and hands, which caused problems of clumsy human fingers brushing against the wrong controls. Because the Thuranin were cyborgs who normally flew their ships through chips in their brains, they had not given a lot of thought to the physical flight controls that were considered emergency backups only.

With the Kristang dropships that we called 'Dragons', we had the opposite problem; most humans were too small to properly fit in the cockpit seats and use the controls without awkwardness. In the Dragon that day, Lt. Reed was in the left-hand seat, and although she was taller than average for a woman, she had the seat adjusted up and forward almost to its maximum travel. I am taller than average, being about six feet three, but the top of the copilot console in front of me cut off the lower part of the wraparound forward display that replaced vulnerable cockpit windows. To get an optimal view of the lake, I had to push myself up in my seat.

"Yes, Joe, you should fly over the lake," Skippy snapped with irritation. "Stick to the flightplan, and leave the thinking to me. Damn, maybe I should have taped a banana to the nose of your Dragon so you would follow it?"

"You are hilarious, Skippy," I said drily as Lt Reed's shoulders shook with laughter. "I was thinking that being over deep water might interfere with our sensor scans."

"Thinking? Is that what you call it? Huh. Let me give you an example of actual thinking, Joe. The lake in front of you is deep, and that is a good thing. It means below the lake there is less dirt and rock that will interfere with the sensor scans. Water is easy to see through, and I can adjust the sensors to ignore the effects of deep water. So," he sighed sarcastically, "if it is Ok with you, please stick to the flightplan."

"Got it," I replied curtly, embarrassed. "Descending to one hundred meters above the water," I advised Reed. I was in the copilot seat, but at the moment I was Pilot In Command, primarily responsible for the flight. Reed had flown us most of the way from base camp, with most of that on autopilot. She had turned the controls over to me not because I was her commanding officer, but because most of my experience flying a Dragon had been in a simulator, and she knew I wanted stick time. Dragons did not have an actual control stick; that was an old expression we brought from Earth. Instead of a control stick or yoke, the primary flight controls were flatscreens. The middle finger of my right hand rested on a circle in the display. Pushing the circle forward made the Dragon's nose drop; pulling the circle back lifted the nose. Banking right or left was accomplished by pushing the circle in the appropriate direction. The flight computer mostly handled coordinating the rudder for turns, although my index finger had independent rudder control, and I tried to fly manually as much as possible. My right pinky finger controlled the engine throttles; if the port and starboard engines needed to be throttled separately I could use thumb and pinky finger.

The Kristang warrior caste were hateful, murderous lizards, but they made sweet flight controls. After a day or two of getting used to controlling almost everything with one hand, I didn't want to go back to the ironically clumsier Thuranin physical flight controls.

"Descending to one hundred meters AGL," Reed acknowledged, letting me do all the flying. She was monitoring the sensor gear and really didn't have much to do. Skippy remotely controlled the sensors and would tell us immediately if there was a problem that required our attention. We had the sensor pod in the belly of the Dragon actively scanning straight down to map out the underground cavern network. With the belly pod sending out powerful active pulses that could penetrate deep beneath the surface, the sensitivity of the other sensors was dialed back to prevent interference. That left us a bit more blind than normal flying procedure, and left me a bit uncomfortable. Yes, we were flying above an uninhabited planet, under a mostly clear sky, and there were no known threats. The closest air traffic was another Dragon on its way back to base, safely half an hour flight time from us. And even if all our sensor gear was operating at maximum sensitivity, the odd fuzzing field enveloping the entire planet would have limited us to seeing in a twenty three kilometer radius at best. Everything beyond that distance was indistinct and often false. Hills appeared beyond sensor range, but when we flew closer, those hills disappeared into flat marshland. Why the Elders had bothered to conceal the surface of that planet was a question Skippy could not answer. Why the Elders were continuing to conceal the surface long after they had left the galaxy behind bothered me a lot. Skippy didn't have an answer for that question either, and I know it bothered him too. It probably bothered him a lot more than it made me uneasy. For me, the Elders were a curiosity. For Skippy, they were his heritage, and the more he examined that heritage, the less he realized he truly knew of his origin.

"Hey, what do you know?" I asked cheerily, using my left hand to point in front of us. "There is actually a lake."

Reed grinned. In this case, the long-range sensor data through the all-encompassing fuzz field had been accurate, although some details had been false. The long-range data had showed two islands in the middle of the lake, but now we could see the lake surface was uninterrupted by any islands, except a few small rocks along the shore. Why the Elders had chosen to conceal some terrain features and display other features as they truly were, was another mystery. The basic outline of the lake was correct, as were the hills that surrounded the water. Hills on the west side to our starboard were taller and more rugged, densely covered with dark trees. The hills to the east rolled gently and the forests were dotted with irregularly-shaped meadows.

"Levelling off at one hundred meters AGL," I declared. The lake was long and narrow but big, like what I guess a Scottish loch looked like. Thinking of lakes in Scotland, I found myself visually scanning the water for sign of a monster, then ruefully shook my head and returned my attention to the flight controls. "Sensors?"

"Nominal," Reed reported distractedly, her focus directed to the port side display. "Sir? Those meadows. Do they look odd to you?"

"Meadows?" Until she mentioned the hillside clearings to our east, I had not given them any thought. "Uh." At first, I couldn't understand what she could mean. The hills were partly dark forests and lighter-colored meadows, with the meadows covering more land down toward the lake. Farther south along the lake shore, the forests fell away to form isolated groves of trees and treelines between meadows. It was odd. Whatever was growing in the meadows was a sort of grass or shrub, anywhere from light green to bright yellow in color. That wasn't what I found odd. What was odd, what was *unnatural*, was that each meadow contained only one type of plant. Real meadows were scattered with a random variety of plants.

And real meadows didn't have treelines acting as windbreaks between fields of crops.

"Those are not meadows," I said with alarm. "That's *cropland*!" As I spoke, my pinky finger advanced the throttles and I pulled the nose up.

Too late.

"Missile warning!" Reed shouted as her fingers flew over the controls, killing the active sensor pulses, engaging the stealth field, shields and defensive maser turrets. If we had a couple more seconds for those systems to warm up, it might have helped. As we did not have extra seconds, a missile exploded below and behind us, sending shrapnel ripping into the belly, both wings and both engines. The impact tossed the tail high in the air and for a moment, the Dragon hung vertically in the air, before the nose plunged straight down. We were lucky the dropship hadn't flipped over on its back upside down in the air. Lt. Reed with my clumsy help managed to use the last thrust from the shredded engine turbines to level out our flight before we hit the water hard. The Dragon bounced twice hard, the impacts making my head rattle in the helmet, then the stricken craft skidded across the water, slowing rapidly. The nose dug into the water one last time with an explosion of white foam rushing over the cockpit displays before they cut out, then we shuddered to a halt.

"Holy shit!" I shouted as I pulled off my now-useless helmet.

"Everyone out!" Reed shouted more usefully. "We're sinking!"

In the cockpit, we could not use the ejection seats, because the ejection system in a Kristang 'Dragon' dropship pushed the pilot and copilot seats downward, and there was a whole lot of water beneath us. Attempting to eject would result in Reed and I being crushed by impact with the water, the ejection system was probably smart enough to refuse to activate anyway. "Right behind you," I acknowledged, struggling with the balky harness latch.

"You first, Sir," Reed hesitated though she was already free of her seat.

"That's an order, Reed," I barked as the stubborn harness latch freed itself. The cockpit door was behind her anyway, she would have had to wait for me to slip by her and that made no sense. Following orders, she staggered out the door, with water rushing in already ankle-deep. When I got my head around the door frame, I could see why. Our two relief pilots, sensibly not waiting for an engraved invitation to abandon ship, had engaged the emergency explosives to blow the starboard side door open and were already outside the Dragon. Perched precariously on the stubby starboard wing, they were shouting and gesturing for us to hurry, as the cabin was one third full of water and more was pouring in from cracks in the portside hull. The Dragon, which had initially come to rest slightly nose-down, was now tilting to the rear rapidly. "Go!" I shouted to Reed right in front of me, and we both struggled through the cold knee-deep water, clutching seatbacks and staggering along as fast as we could. Reed hesitated as she got a couple fingers on the railing by the door, looking back at me. "Go!" I repeated. "You're in my way," I added, appealing to her logic.

She saw the sense in going first, holding onto the railing and reaching up with the other for someone outside to grasp. Whoever it was held her right hands with both of his, and pulled her up and out. She almost made it, but just as her shoulders reached the doorframe, the Dragon tilted violently, sinking sharply down by the rear. The dropship stood on its tail and a crack in the starboard hull split open wide, letting in a jet of cold lake water. I lost my grip on a chair and fell face-first into the water, bashing my left shoulder on a submerged seat. Choking and gasping, I flailed my arms wildly and ineffectively, being tossed around like a rag doll as the heavy Dragon spun on its tail and plunged downward. Dark water swirled and bounced me around so I couldn't tell which direction was up until I suddenly could hear loud noises no longer muffled by water.

When my head popped above the water, I saw one of Reed's feet splash, then she was out the door that was completely underwater. The surging water carried me upward toward the cockpit and smacked my head on the forward bulkhead. Dazed, I tried to suck in a lungful of air so I could swim down to the open side door. I got half a mouthful of air and half a mouthful of water, and when I tried to swim downward, the inflowing water forced me back up against the forward bulkhead. Seeing no other option, I felt my way to the cockpit door, where the water pushed me in, nearly tearing my right arm off.

The cockpit still had red emergency lighting on, allowing me to blearily see the door controls. I slapped the button and to my amazement, the door closed almost all the way. Next to the door was a recessed crank that I pulled out, grinding harder and harder. Something was wrong with the door; the frame or track might have been warped by the crash. It took all my might to force the manual crank the last two turns, with my injured right arm screaming agony. Then the door sealed and water stopped flowing in.

Great.

That was brilliant, Joe, I told myself. I sealed myself into a falling tomb. Closing the cockpit door had been desperate instinct; I thought of taking refuge there until the Dragon came to rest on the bottom of the lake. At the time, I had not remembered how deep the lake was. Now I remembered. It was deep, like really deep for a lake. My last glimpse of the outside world before the Dragon hit the water had shown we came down near the west shore. How far from the shore? The lake was more shallow right around the shore, then the bottom fell like a cliff for hundreds of meters.

How deep was the water where we had come down? It had no way of knowing, but the Dragon's continuing tail-first downward plunge was not encouraging. The fall seemed to be steady, not accelerating.

But the Dragon was going to hit bottom, soon. When that happened, it was unlikely to be gentle. Quickly, I pulled myself up by one arm into the seat just abandoned by Reed and strapped myself in. I almost laughed as my discarded helmet bobbed to the surface like a loyal puppy. I picked it up with a right arm that was shooting hot flashes of pain, poured out water and jammed it back on my head, pulling the chin strap tight. The seats had a feature that could engage a safety strap with the back of the helmet; I prayed as I rubbed the helmet against the back of the seat, hoping it would engage by itself. It did. My feet slid into loops under the seat and I placed my hands on my lap in the proper procedure for a crash or ejection. In this case, I anticipated hitting the lake bottom, and I wasn't bothering to hope it would be gentle.

It wasn't.

With the displays and instruments out, I could only judge motion by my inner ears. And by my teeth, because they rattled in my mouth when the tail crunched on whatever it hit. However fast the Dragon had been falling, it had enough energy to bounce off the bottom and hit again. The whole ship shuddered and for a split second it hung balanced on the flattened tail structure. Then it spun to the right and came down on its belly. Water sloshed around the cockpit, slamming me against the seat. I thought that was the end of it, but the Dragon must have impacted on an underwater slope, because it rolled again and kept rolling, tumbling side to side many times and nose over tail at least twice. The final impact was jarring enough that a needle-thin jet of water shot into the cockpit from a pinhole crack in the starboard hull. After rocking side to side for a moment, partly due to water sloshing around inside, the Dragon came to rest mostly on its belly, with the nose up at a forty five degree angle, judging by the water collected in the cockpit.

Where was I? With no immediate incentive to move, I stayed securely in the seat, waiting to make sure the Dragon wasn't going to slip on some rocks and fall again. That's what I told myself. The truth was, I was so stunned and scared, I couldn't move.

What got me moving was the high-pitched hissing of that jet of water coming in. It was annoying and it hurt my ears listening to it. It was also an immediate threat, a threat I knew how to deal with. The dropship had kits under the seatbacks to seal hull breaches. The patches in these kits were designed for use in vacuum, we had never tested them in water, especially not in deep, cold water. I was shivering from being in that icy lake water, would the cold prevent the patch material from solidifying? There was only one way to tell.

But, crap. As I pulled out a patch I realized they were designed to be used in a vacuum, where the force of air getting sucked out of the cabin would guide the patch material to find the leak. In the lake, the leak caused water to pour *in* at high pressure. No way would the patch work. I was totally screwed.

Until I remembered Skippy's Flying Circus. Desai had flown a big Thuranin 'Condor' dropship deep in the atmosphere of a gas giant to extract fuel for the *Dutchman*'s reactors. Part of the training for that mission had been sealing the cabin against leaks of high-pressure toxic gasses from the gas giant. While I had not trained for that flight, I had watched the training so I could understand what was involved and get an understanding of the dangers.

The Thuranin kit to seal a leak coming *into* the cabin used a sort of tube with a trigger. Did the kit in the Kristang Dragon have something like that? It did! I found two of them. Being short of time, and being a guy, I of course did not bother to attempt reading the instructions. In my defense, the instructions were printed in Kristang script and my ability to read Kristang was limited to things like 'Danger' and 'Bathroom'. Also, the patch kits were intended to be used in emergency situations; they had to operate intuitively as panicked people could not be expected to handle anything complex. I got the sharp nose of the tube jammed as well as I could into the pinhole, to the point I had to close my eyes as water now sprayed in all directions. The water tried to knock the tube from my hands as I pulled the trigger. There was a muffled bang, the tube jerked in my hands and a harsh chemical stink filled the cabin.

And the leak stopped. Some sort of orange foam hardened quickly, becoming rigid. The hissing sound of incoming water stopped.

I was safe.

No, that was bullshit. I was still screwed.

And alone.

At the bottom of a lake.

Chapter Fifteen

It was getting damned chilly in the cockpit. That was a problem I could do something about. The helmet engaged with the collar of my flightsuit; I had only to make a couple adjustments to get it fully sealed. The booties were already sealed to the pants, and after I pulled gloves out of a pocket, put them on and sealed them at the wrists, I pulled a red cord at the waistband to inflate the flightsuit. There was a hissing, and a thin gap of air filled the space between inner and outer layers of the suit. That made me feel warmer almost immediately. The flightsuit had a heater powered by a battery in the waistband, but I didn't want to drain power yet. Flightsuits were intended to be used only as short-term emergency protection against loss of cabin pressure in the vacuum of space. Heat would leak away from my suit much faster in cold water than in the vacuum of space.

I was still shivering and my fingers and toes were numb; it was a good sign they were tingling as warm blood seeped back in. Now that I wasn't feeling like I would freeze to death quickly, I turned my attention to other matters. What worried me more than my own fate was what the hell had happened. Who had fired a missile at us, on a planet that was supposedly uninhabited? Could there still be Elders hanging around Gingerbread? Had they or their ancestors overslept and missed transcending their physical form? I found that difficult to believe. If there were Elders still on Gingerbread, surely they had weapons better than an antiaircraft missile?

That was another puzzle. Only one missile had been fired at us, and even though we had been flying slowly without stealth, the missile had failed to score a direct impact. Its warhead had set off a proximity detonation, perhaps when it realized it was going to fly too low and miss us. When Reed called out the missile warning, I had accelerated and pulled the nose up. That simple maneuver should not have caused any advanced-technology missile to miss its target. Yet the missile fired at us had failed to hit a big, fat target. None of it made sense.

Beyond what had happened, I worried about the three crewmembers who had made it out the door. Where were they? Had they been able to swim to shore? They might be injured, certainly they were in shock although we all trained to act in high stress situations.

What worried me most was if the beings who fired a missile at our Dragon were a danger to crash survivors.

Sami popped to the surface, gasping in air and choking out ice-cold lake water at the same time. That didn't work too well, so she held her breath despite a desperate need for oxygen, and concentrated on coughing up the last of the water she had swallowed during her desperate struggle to get out of the sinking Dragon's cabin. After three coughs so violent they hurt, she puked up part of her breakfast and took that as a sign that her lungs were now ready to take in air, so she sucked in a giant lungful. It felt like water still was sloshing around the bottom of her lungs; she would deal with that later. "Colonel Bishop?" She gasped the question to Captain Zhau, who was treading water and supporting her.

Zhau shook his head and, when Sami waved a hand, released her to swim on her own. "He didn't get out."

"He was right behind me!" Sami felt a chill of shock from more than the chilly water. "I shouldn't have left him!"

"Lieutenant! Reed!" Zhau grasped her right shoulder and put his face close to hers. "You did everything you could. Colonel Bishop is capable of taking care of himself. Once we started sinking, your first responsibility was to get yourself out of there. You won't do anyone any good if you're dead, understood?"

"He could have drowned in there. This is my fault," Sami said, her voice trailing off in pure misery. "I lost the *Colonel*."

"Reed, listen to me. Are you listening to me?" Zhau waited until she looked him in the eyes and nodded. "This is not your fault. Someone just shot us down with a missile. It is *their* fault. And I'd like a word with our super-smart AI, who assured us this planet was uninhabited!"

"Yes, Sir," Sami's eyes narrowed in recognition that Skippy the Unreliable had indeed informed the Merry Band of Pirates that Gingerbread was totally uninhabited. For a moment, that took her mind away from the horrifying thought of the colonel being trapped and drowning in the sinking dropship. "He *did* tell us that." She felt for her zPhone, and for a panicked moment could not find it in the right thigh pocket of her flightsuit. Then she remembered tucking the zPhone into her left breast pocket and sealing it there just after the Dragon stopped skidding across the water. "We should call- What was that?" Zhau was interrupted by a splash in the water twenty meters away, toward the western shore.

"Air bubble from the ship?" Singh speculated.

Zhau feared the splash might have been caused by a predator under the water. They knew almost nothing about the native life of Gingerbread, and what little they knew came from Skippy. That alien AI had proven to be less than accurate on too many occasions, especially recently. "We should head for shore," Zhau ordered. "There's nothing we can do for Colonel Bishop out here, the water is too deep. We barely made it to the surface from where we were, and the Dragon must have gone deeper by now. This water is too cold for us to survive long out here. Swim toward-" He jerked and spun around as another splash appeared, just to the west of him. "Ah!" He exclaimed and clutched his right shoulder.

Sami had been looking at the west shore of the lake, seeking the best spot to swim toward, to get out of the water as quickly as possible. The current in the lake was flowing south, that would drag the three humans along so they needed to plan for drift rather than blinding swimming due west. When she came to the surface, she had been pleasantly surprised to see the lake shore was only a bit more than a hundred meters away; the crashing Dragon at least had skidded across the water in a helpful direction. Captain Zhau had been right; there was nothing the three of them could do for Bishop, and she was already shivering uncontrollably from being in the frigid water. Because she had been looking away from Zhau, she didn't see him get hit. When she turned, she did see speckles of blood splattered on the right side of his face, and a tear in his flightsuit between his neck and right shoulder. "Sir! You're hit!"

Zhau felt the wound with his left hand, as his right arm was stiff and hurt to move. From what his fingers could tell, the bullet or whatever it was had only grazed him; the wound was not deep but it was bleeding freely into the water. "It's just a scratch! They're shooting at us from the eastern shore!" He shouted the obvious and as he spoke, there was another splash just three meters to his right. This splash was bigger, throwing up a fountain of water and pounding his underwater limbs and torso with a hard shock. "Explosive rounds! Dive!"

Sami would never forget that terrifying swim. She wanted nothing more than to float atop the water, exposing as little as possible of her body to the icy water, but to do that meant death. The sniper shot every time a human was on the surface more than a few strokes, so the three popped up only to gulp in air, exhaling while submerged. They couldn't swim in a straight line because that would give the sniper an easy target, so the swim of only a hundred meters took more than fifteen minutes. After three minutes, chilled to the bone and shivering so her arms were clumsy, she remembered the flightsuit had internal heaters, and she activated that system. Running only on the battery pack built into the front torso of the suit, the heaters would not last long; Sami only needed to get ashore where the air temperature was like a warm Spring day, so she cranked up the heat and soon felt her arms and legs loosening as they warmed.

Underwater navigation was not her best skill, she realized after the fifth time she popped up for air and saw the lake shore had annoyingly shifted position again. She kept drifting to the left as she swam underwater, made more difficult because she could not risk swimming in a straight line. The water was clear enough to see twenty or more meters, but the lake was deep and there were no underwater markers until she was close enough to shore to not need them.

The three humans touched bottom at roughly the same time, and without needing to communicate with each other, they all knew what to do. Remain under the water until they were as close to the lake edge as possible, then get to their feet and dash up the bank quickly to get behind a tree. Getting behind a rock or the cover of a streambed would be preferable, but the glimpses Sami had seen told her the western shore near her was a steady slope upward without any cover other than sparse trees dotted here and there.

Zhau and Singh touched bottom in an area where the underwater ground was smooth stones that provided good footing, until they reached the line right near shore where wave action kept the exposed rocks wet and therefore covered with slippery algae. Both Zhau and Singh skidded and fell on the algae, before choosing survival over dignity and crawling on hands and knees to gain the shore. Singh's life was saved by one fall when she slipped and bashed a knee on a stone; just after she fell an incoming round buried itself in the undercut bank at the water's edge, and the explosive tip blew dirt and mud back at her, knocking her to fall on her ass in knee-deep water. She wasted no time in rolling to one side, ignoring the pain signals from her injured knee and scrambling up the muddy lake bank on her belly. By the time she stood to sprint for the cover a tree, she saw Captain Zhau also stumbling vigorously out of the water just to her north, weaving side to side to throw off the sniper's aim.

Sami was not so comparatively lucky. When she felt her outstretched hands touch bottom in murky water, she touched not stones but mud and silt. The lake bottom in front of her was a sticky mass that sucked at her boots when she tried to walk in it, and attempting to stand caused her to sink in the muck up to her knees. No way was she going to be able to run quickly enough to avoid providing an easy target for the sniper, she saw instantly. Rather than trying to wade through the stubborn mud, she pulled herself backwards into deeper water and ducked down as a round hit the water where she had been struggling only a moment before. What saved her life was the sniper being distracted by the two humans who had already gained the shore and were temporarily exposed; the enemy's attention was drawn to Sami only after Zhau and Singh ducked behind the western side of trees and were lost to view.

During the brief moment she had her head above water while trying to walk through the muck, Sami had seen her companions wobbling on the slippery stones along the shore. That, she decided, was not what she was going to do. She could not afford to pick her way carefully over the submerged stones, particularly not as the sniper would now only have her as a target. With the suit heaters fading but her exertions keeping her warm enough, she swam along the shore until she saw what she wanted. A thin stream, really a creek, flowing down into the lake. Barely any water trickled out of the creek now, and the watercourse cut so shallowly into the land that it was useless as cover. But in the time the creek had been flowing, it had flushed small rocks and grains of sand down into the lake. In the lake below the creek, the bottom was sandy and, Sami hoped, firm footing for a quick dash to a tree she was already focused on.

If the sniper anticipated her plans, her efforts would be for nothing. So she swam north past the creek and popped up for a deep breath, determined to swim all the way in toward the creek until she could leap to her feet and run. Fortunately, the lake bottom was indeed sandy where the creek cut in, and that sand extended out into the water, so she was able to follow the underwater marker until her hands were clutching sand. Sweet, relatively hard-packed sand.

She swam inward, lungs burning until the water was less than waist deep and she feared the sniper could see her body's heat signature in the shallow water. Gathering herself, she exploded out of the water, rising to her feet and already running, weaving side to side intentionally. In five long strides a foot touched the shore and she made a beeline for a tree, then dodged to her right at the last second to duck behind a different tree that had been her intention all along. Good idea, she thought as she flung herself flat on her belly, because the first tree had a chunk knocked out of it by the impact of an explosive round. Bark, splinters and sawdust were flung in all directions, with the sawdust drifting down to coat her hair.

"Are you all right, Reed?" Zhau called from her left.

"Yes, Sir!" She replied, not daring to move.

"That was good thinking, coming up where the bottom is sand."

"I saw you slipping on those stones, Sir, figured I couldn't take time to do that. Do we stay here?"

"The trees up away from the lake are larger, give us more cover. I'm afraid the sniper can knock down one of these trees," he gestured to the tree he was huddled behind, "with a couple rounds."

Sami raised her head. "We won't make it up to the forest, Sir." The trees grew thickly farther away from the lake, but the slope of the land was steep in that direction, and the denser tree cover had to be half a kilometer away.

"No, but we can get to something more stout than these saplings," Zhau stated. "Then we can call in and find out what the hell is going on here. We all go together, so find a tree to aim for, and tell me when you're ready."

Sami didn't think she would ever be *ready* to run while being tracked by an unseen and unknown sniper. She held up her left hand, saw that it was no longer shaking from cold, exertion and lack of oxygen. The longer they waited, the more time the sniper had to sight in on their positions. "Ready now, Sir."

"Three, two, one, GO!"

In addition to a low-pitched moaning sound I could not find the source of, and the alarming creaking and popping sounds of the Dragon's hull flexing, there was an intermittent sound coming from under the water. It was probably an alarm telling me what I already knew: I was in extreme danger. Whatever it was, no way was I going into that dark, frigid water to identify it. The cockpit was a third full of water, and I had a chilly but somewhat dry perch on a console, with my feet resting on a seat. The cold had me shivering as the cabin air's last vestiges of heat were pulled away by the mass of chilled water outside the hull.

"Oh!" The underwater alarm said, and I cocked my head.

"Ee aht!" It said.

Crap. That was no alarm. Tumbling off the console before I lost my nerve, I ducked my head under the water to hear and locate the source of the sound. I felt around until my fingertips detected a vibration and my frozen fingers closed around the familiar shape of a zPhone. It must have fallen out of my pocket during the scramble to evacuate.

"*Joe! Answer me, you idiot*!" Skippy boomed at me, his voice ringing at painful volume around the cockpit.

"I'm here, Skippy!"

"Where is 'here'?"

"How the hell should I know?" I stared at the zPhone. "I'm at the bottom of a lake. Or near the bottom."

"What are you doing *there*?" His voice was a disbelieving screech. "You should have gotten out of the dropship after it hit the lake, you dumdum!"

"Gosh. Wow. That never occurred to me, Skippy."

"Damn it, you- Oh, ha ha, sarcasm. I get it. How did you end up at the bottom of a lake?" He asked incredulously.

"The Dragon got hit by a missile, Skippy, in case you have not been keeping up with current events."

"Joe, was your seatback and tray table in the full upright and locked position before you hit the lake?"

"Uh-"

"I knew it! This is all your fault."

"*My* fault? A missile came out of nowhere and-"

"Joe, it's real simple. You were pilot in command when you crashed, correct?"

"Yes," I responded sullenly.

"Hmmm. And now your Dragon is at the bottom of a lake. An *air*craft is supposed to be in the *air*, yet now your Dragon is underwater. The pilot operating manual for the Dragon does not mention a submersible feature, unless I missed something. You were flying an aircraft, and now you are captain of the *Titanic*. Totally your fault."

"That's kicking a guy when he's already down, Skippy."

"Sorry, Joe. I'm uh, I am a little upset."

"I'm a little upset too, Skippy. Lt. Reed and the others, are they safe?"

"Yes. Safe enough for now, anyway. They are on the western shore now, taking cover behind trees. Do you know how deep under the water you are?"

"I don't, the instruments are out. You want me to stick my head out the window?"

"Uh, no."

"All I can tell you is the ship sank a long way, then it rolled deeper after it hit."

"Hmmm. Give me a minute, I'm attempting to triangulate your position."

"Screw that for now. What the hell happened? Who hit us? You said this planet was uninhabited!"

"Amazing. You are at the bottom of a lake in a crashed dropship, and what you care most about is who shot at you?"

"Hell yes! I'm responsible for my people."

"It's not like you can do anything about it right now, Joe."

"That's not the p-point," I had trouble speaking as my teeth were chattering from the cold. "What happened?"

"Well, heh heh, it appears we have a group of Thuranin living here."

"Shit! Thuranin?! I thought all those little green pinheads were killed by the Guardians."

"That's what I thought also, Joe." His voice contained an implied 'duh'. "Some of them must have survived and made their way here, in dropships or escape pods. I did tell you that once ships have been rendered harmless, the Guardians leave them pretty much alone. One or two dropships landing here might have been permitted by the Guardians, as long as those dropships did not take any hostile action. Hmmm. It is likely any survivors would be trapped here permanently; any attempt to build a jump drive would attract the wrath of the Guardians."

"When was the last time a Thuranin ship tried to jump in here?"

"According to the records I have access to, that would be around four hundred years ago."

"Whoa. Damn, maybe that explains why that missile missed us. It was freakin' ancient. Unless the Thuranin have been able to build new missiles."

"I very much doubt that, Joe. For the moment this is a guess, but I suspect any beings living here have been forced to exist on a low level of technology to avoid attracting the attention of the Guardians. Flying around in aircraft, using high-tech weapons and building an industrial infrastructure are all things that the Guardians would, let's say 'discourage'. That explains why we didn't detect the Thuranin until now; they have been laying low."

"Great, just freakin' great. Hey, wait. You said those green pinheads couldn't use weapons without the Guardians coming down on their heads? Then how the hell did they launch a missile at us?"

"As *you* pointed out, Joe," Skippy's voice dripped with sarcasm. "I changed the game here when I told the Guardians to stand down. The Thuranin must have realized the rules had changed when they saw you flying around without the Guardians knocking you out of the sky."

"Well, shit, Skippy, that's no good. Now we have an unknown number of Thuranin to worry about down here?"

"Possibly more than just Thuranin."

"What?"

"Use your brain, Joe. If a group of Thuranin were able to land here and survive, then other species might be on this planet also. The advanced technology of the Rindhalu and Maxolhx would have given them a better chance of reaching the surface here after their ships were disabled."

"Oh, hell," I felt sick. "There could be a bunch of senior species hanging out down here, and you just removed the one thing that keeps them from stomping us like a bug?"

"Joe, at the time, you were very much in favor of me telling the Guardians to stand down," he answered peevishly.

"Sorry. You're right. We'll deal with one problem at a time. Connect me with Chang so I-"

"Lt Colonel Chang is already directing a response. Major Smythe is loading a SpecOps team into dropships now, and other dropships will be scanning the area around the camp for hostiles. Your team is highly competent, let them do their jobs, Joe. What we need to worry about is getting you out of there."

"Ok," I tried to bite my lip in frustration but my teeth were chattering so badly from the cold, I almost drew blood. Instead of biting a lip, I squeezed my numb hands into fists and released. Squeeze and release, then repeat. That action forced warm blood into my numb fingers. "You got any ideas?"

"I assume you sealed yourself in the cockpit, as Lt. Reed told me the main cabin had a bad leak and was filled with water."

"Yeah, I'm in the cockpit. I got the door cranked closed, and I fixed another small leak. It's about a third full of water in here. And it's cold, Skippy, really cold."

"It can't be super cold, Joe, or the water would freeze. But, Ok, to a hairless monkey I am sure it is plenty chilly. You don't have a lot of oxygen left in the cockpit," he declared, as he knew the cramped volume of a Kristang Dragon-A dropship's cockpit. "Ship oxygen supply is probably out also?"

I reached down to the pilot seat and picked up the oxygen mask there, fitting it over my nose and mouth and pulling the lever to activate it. "Nothing, Skippy, it's dead."

"Ok, no problem, I thought that would be the case. You do have your emergency Oh Two bottle, correct?"

I patted the small bottle tucked into a pouch in the right thigh of my flightsuit. A hose ran up the suit to the collar, and in another pocket was a soft, collapsible mask. "Yes. That only provides ninety minutes of oxygen, Skippy. I am conserving it for when I really need it." A Dragon, or any other dropship I knew of, had three oxygen systems. The primary oxygen supply was the cabin air; a mix of oxygen and nitrogen. If that system failed, pilots and crew were to immediately switch to the backup system that fed mostly concentrated oxygen through tubes into masks. The masks were supposed to be used short-term while the cabin oxygen system was fixed, but masks could be used long-term if needed. If the masks also failed, each crew member had an emergency bottle of pure oxygen either in their flightsuit, or in cabinets scattered around the cabin. If you had to go to the emergency supply, you were supposed to drop everything and fix the primary or secondary system. The fourth-level system was prayer, because after the emergency oxygen bottle ran out, you could kiss your ass goodbye.

"When you really need it? That would be about now, Joe. We need to get you out of there before you become so weak from cold that you are unable to get yourself out."

"Is there any chance of rescue?"

"Not in time for you, Joe," Skippy was morose. "Lt Colonel Chang will not allow dropships to overfly the lake, until the Thuranin on shore have been neutralized with a ground assault by Major Smythe's team. Captain Zhau and Lieutenants Singh and Reed on the west shore are taking intermittent rifle fire from the east shore, and they report movement on the hills above them to the west."

"Crap. Chang is right, do not risk another dropship to rescue me. Any idea how many Thuranin are out there, or what weapons-"

"Joe. Your team has this," Skippy admonished. "Worry about yourself. Because no one else can help you right now."

"Ok, Ok. What do I do?"

"First, get your emergency oxygen mask ready, but don't turn it on yet. You will need that oxygen to swim through the cabin and up to the surface. Now, since you have no training in procedures from escaping from a submarine, which is basically what your Dragon is now, I will break it down Barney style for you. It is good that you were able to get the cabin door closed, because if the water had flooded in, the remaining air would have become pressurized to the same as the surrounding water, and you would have quickly suffered nitrogen narcosis. Unfortunately, you now need to get that door open wide enough to fit through. I calculate you are about a hundred thirty meters below the surface, Joe."

"Whoa," I said slowly. That was almost four hundred feet. There was a whole lot of heavy, cold, dark water looming over my head.

Skippy continued explaining the escape procedure to me. It was risky. I had to go on emergency oxygen, then partly go under the water in the cabin to manually crank the door open. That would allow water to rush in, and I needed my flightsuit to protect me from the pressure of the water. The pure oxygen of my emergency bottle would help reduce nitrogen sickness when I reached the surface. "Skippy, should I stay here and pre-breathe on pure oxygen for a while, to get the nitrogen out of my blood?"

"That would be a good idea, but you don't have time, Joe. To get all the nitrogen out of your system would take about two hours."

"Oh."

"Oh indeed. When you are ready, turn on your emergency oxygen supply. Then seal your flightsuit."

"Ready now." The first thing I did was tuck the thin zPhone away in a slot inside the helmet so I could continue talking with Skippy. Next, the emergency mask went over my nose and mouth, secured with a strap inside the helmet. An inhale fitted it to my face, and I turned a knob to start the oxygen flowing. With the helmet faceplate closed and latched, I was on internal oxygen. "Should I turn on the suit heater?"

"If you feel you need to. Flightsuits are designed to be used in air or vacuum rather than water, the thermal density of water will rapidly pull heat away from your body, so the suit heaters will not be able to keep up. It would be best if you can ration the heater power until you really need additional heat to prevent you from becoming unconscious, however you must also keep your muscles in usable condition until you are ascending."

"Balance use of heat, got it," I replied. "Now I crank the door open?"

"Yes. Do it slowly, in a controlled manner."

"Ooh."

"What?"

"I'm kneeling in the water and you're right, it is damned cold."

"Turn on the suit heater if you need to, Joe."

"No, I'm good. I need my arms more than legs to get the door open and swim through the main cabin. I'll activate the heater when I need to." My expectation was I would need artificial heat once the cockpit filled with water high enough to surround my torso, sucking body heat away from my core. "I have the crank extended. Hmmmf. Huh."

"What is it?" Skippy asked anxiously.

"It's not moving."

"The door?"

"No, Skippy, I meant the line at the Taco Bell drive-through down here. Of course I meant the freakin' door!"

"You don't have to be nasty about it."

"Sorry," I apologized to the alien AI who was safely on shore, while I was trapped four hundred feet down in an icy lake. "Trying it again," I grunted. "Damn it! The crank on this thing won't turn at all."

"Did you try turning it the other way?" Skippy suggested helpfully.

I didn't feel like arguing with him, so I tried that. The end of the crank moved one notch, maybe a quarter inch, then froze. "It was super hard getting the door closed the last bit, I think the crash warped the frame. Ah, damn it!" I shouted in frustration. That handle might as well have been welded in place, it was not moving. "No good, Skippy; it won't move."

"Uh oh, Joe, I think I know the problem. The water pressure outside is pushing in the door, bending it inward. If the frame was already warped, then the door will not move until the pressure is relieved."

"I need to equalize pressure on both sides of the door?" I guessed. "Let the water in?"

"That may resolve the problem, Joe, but if you let the water in and the door still won't open, you will be in very great danger."

"I'm not in very great danger now?"

"Good point. Let me think a minute, there may be other options."

"This thing has only one door, Skippy. The ejection seats won't work underwater?"

"No they will not." His voice was glum.

"Well, damn it."

"My thoughts exactly, Joe. While we have been talking, I have been running simulations on the effect of water pressure on the cockpit door of a Dragon dropship. You have very bad luck today, Joe. If you were only one hundred meters deep, the water pressure would be low enough that the door could likely be cranked open. It would be stiff and difficult, but there is a ninety percent chance the door could open wide enough for you to escape."

"That is fascinating trivia, Skippy, but I more than a hundred meters deep."

"Hence why I said you have very bad luck today."

"I am willing to try equalizing the pressure." Using the lights of my helmet, I looked around the cockpit, trying to think of something that could cut or burn a hole in the door. "You know the standard equipment we carry aboard one of these things, Skippy. Is there a drill or laser or something I can use to make a hole in the door?"

"Searching. No. Unless you brought something like that with you?"

"I did not. I flew thousands of lightyears from Earth, now I'm in a dropship that contains technology aircraft designers back home can only dream about, yet I can't get a freakin' door open? This is crazy!" I got to my feet, crawled up on the console so I was out of the water, opened my helmet faceplate and turned off the emergency oxygen. As long as there was breathable air in the cockpit, I wanted to conserve my emergency oxygen supply.

"It is indeed unfortunate, Joe."

Chapter Sixteen

"This is not good," Samantha Reed stated. Using their zPhones in infrared mode, they had determined at least five bipedal beings were higher up the hill above them to the west. The glimpse in infrared had been brief as the beings, likely Thuranin, had been crossing a mountain meadow. As soon as the beings went back into the dense forest, they had been lost to view. What Sami and her companions knew for certain was there were at least five, and the beings were moving downhill toward the three humans.

That was bad enough. What made it worse was some asshole on the eastern shore of the lake continuing to take potshots at the humans. Someone over there was shooting at them with a heavy-caliber weapon. The humans each took cover behind a tree, but that was only temporary safety, and trees were sparse on the lower slopes of the hills west of the lake. Huddling behind the west side of a tree exposed them to the beings coming down the hill from the west. They needed to find some place to conceal themselves and wait for the approaching dropships that were carrying SpecOps teams. Lt Colonel Chang had ordered the three downed pilots to take cover rather than running, as they might blunder right into the enemy. Until the dropships could arrive and hopefully deploy drones to give the SpecOps teams a tactical read on the enemy locations, it was best for Reed and the others to stay put.

Except for that asshole shooting at them.

"Ah!" She twitched, startled.

"You all right, Reed?" Captain Zhau asked from a tree ten meters to the south.

"Yes, Sir," she slapped her neck and came away with a wriggling multi-legged insect. "This thing *bit* me." Her hand already had a droplet of her own blood on it, and there was more as she squashed the offending native insect against a tree root. The forest floor was covered with decaying leaf litter from the sturdy trees above, and the three humans were dismayed to find all manner of insects and worms found the rotting leaves to be an inviting place to inhabit. Almost as bad was the sharp spikes of seed casings; the dropped casings had spilt open but the spikes were still sharp. If the downed pilots had need to sneak around quietly in the forest, that would be a problem, as the dominant type of tree had nearly-circular leaves of a tough, waxy material, kind of like a mountain laurel bush on Earth, Sami thought. It apparently had not rained in the area recently, as the fallen leaves were dry and cracked loudly when stepped on. That was the only good thing about being targeted by a sniper; the enemy was far enough away across the lake that making noise by moving around was unlikely to attract a shot in their direction. "These things," she held up the squashed, yellow-green insect that had bit her, "aren't poisonous, are they?" Her neck now itched, she couldn't tell whether the sting was getting worse, or whether the feeling was paranoia.

"Skippy says the biology here is incompatible with human biochemistry," Captain Zhau assured her. "We can't eat them, and they can't eat us."

"Tell that to this stupid bug," Sami muttered, and flicked away another bug that had been crawling up the right forearm of her flightsuit.

"Skippy did not say the life here can't eat us," Singh pointed out. "He said animals here can't *digest* us. They won't know that until we're already in their bellies."

"Yeah," Sami rubbed her neck. The bite area was itching worse. That could be a biotoxin. It could also be a simple allergic reaction to foreign, *alien*, proteins in the saliva of the insect that bit her. The skin there could also be irritated simply from her scratching at it. She forced herself to leave it alone, holding her hands out in front of her where she could watch to make sure they weren't sneaking back to rub at her neck. "But Skippy says a lot of things, and they aren't always the Gospel truth, are they? He thought it would be just fine to go poking around in that dead AI canister. And he told us there was no intelligent life down here, didn't he? The Elders are long gone, and he never considered there might be other survivors who made it down here. When we lost the ship and had to come to Gingerbread just to survive, I thought we would be in danger from whatever machines the Elders left behind. I never thought we would get shot at by little green Thuranin assho- Whoa!" Reed startled as a round glanced off the tree she was huddled behind, rocketed past her and dug into the dirt. She ducked as the buried round exploded, throwing up a fountain of dirt and rocks. Then she scrambled back behind the tree, to remain out of view. Keeping her head down and shielding her skull with one hand from small shattered bits of rock raining down, she crawled on her belly across the forest floor to hide behind another tree. Whoever was shooting at them had decent imaging equipment; Sami feared the enemy knew which tree was now protecting her.

That last round had exploded. The human pilots had been keeping count; one out of three rounds was a dud. At first, when some rounds exploded and some didn't, Sami had wondered if every third round was a sort of tracer, but that didn't make sense. With advanced technology, aliens almost certainly didn't need tracers, and every sniper Sami had ever met was arrogant enough to disdain wasting a shot simply to enhance targeting. Each shot by a sniper was supposed to be a kill. The answer had to be the Thuranin equipment was old and unreliable. If Skippy was right, the Thuranin probably had not been able to use their high-tech gear, even if it was ancient. Only now that Skippy had ordered the Guardians to stand down were the Thuranin able to use weapons they must have kept in storage for a very long time.

Which meant the sniper could not have been able to practice shooting live rounds. That might be the only reason Sami and her companions were still alive.

"Reed, are you all right?" Captain Zhau asked.

"Yes, Sir, squared away. You? How's your shoulder?"

"Fine, Lieutenant. We can't stay here."

"Agreed. They seem to know where we are when we move."

"I don't want to go up the hill," Zhau mused. "We might run into those other Thuranin. But we can't stay here."

"We could, if someone wasn't shooting at us from across the lake," Singh complained. "On Earth, even a skilled sniper with a specialized rifle would have trouble making that shot. These damned aliens have technology that makes them super-"

They all ducked as another round hit the tree to the left of Sami, breaking the tree off six feet from the ground and sending splinters in every direction. Because Sami's tree was slightly up the slope, it protected her from the worst of the flying wood shards, though she took impacts on the back of her right hand. "Ow. I'm Ok, Sir," she assured Zhau. "If the Thuranin think they hit me behind that other tree, I'm staying right here."

"Good thinking, Reed," Zhau agreed.

"We can't stay here much longer," Singh warned.

"I am concerned that sniper is attempting to flush us out from cover, and straight at the Thuranin coming down the hill at us," Zhau explained.

"Sir?" Reed interjected. "There's a gap in this tree, I can see the eastern shore through it." The tree formed a shallow Y shape near the ground, leaving a narrow gap.

"Yes, so?"

"So, Sir, they might think I'm dead. I can use my zPhone's imager to pinpoint the location of that sniper, next time they fire."

"Mmm," Zhau considered that. "If you can identify where they are-"

"Yes, Sir." Sami finished her leader's thought. "The aliens out here have superior technology and genetic enhancements; they have every advantage over us. But there is one thing I know about modern combat that is true for everyone. If you can see it, you can kill it."

"Call it in," Zhau ordered.

Four minutes later, after two more rounds impacted and one of them caused a rock to thud painfully against Singh's ribs, Sami knew almost exactly where the sniper was located. Interestingly, the sniper had not moved between shots. That demonstrated arrogance and tactical stupidity, in Sami's opinion. "Viper Lead," she called over her zPhone, "this is Fireball, do you copy?"

Viper Lead, the commander of the incoming dropships, responded immediately. "Viper Lead here. What is your status, Fireball?"

"We are pinned down by sniper fire. We know the sniper's position, transmitting location over taclink to you now."

"You have him located?" Viper Lead asked, impressed.

"Yes, Sir," Sami replied with a wink to Zhau. "Would you mind delivering a message to the sniper from us?"

"Mmm," Viper Lead's voice reflected amusement. "I think we can do better than that. We will be in range within twenty seconds."

Thirty seconds later, providing a ten-second safety margin, a door opened behind a Falcon dropship, and a single missile was ejected. The door snapped closed immediately, as an open door compromised the Falcon's stealth and aerodynamics. The missile fell straight down to clear the formation of dropships, and fell farther to reduce its signature, before igniting its main engine. A jet of flame erupted from the missile's tail, and it surged forward, exceeding the speed of sound in the blink of an eye.

Hugging the terrain, the missile raced south, then west as it crested the ridge of the hills east of the lake. Diving to follow the slope, the missile turned north, rocketing in on its target. It dove straight at the ground and detonated its warhead in a cone-shaped explosion, hammering a hundred-meter circle of ground with devastating force. Microseconds later, the body of the missile impacted the ground, dug in and its remaining fuel exploded, digging a crater three meters deep.

Across the lake, all three humans observed the missile strike, seeing a jet of dirt shooting skyward above the tree canopy, then falling back down to create a cloud of soil, soot and mist. "Whoo, yeah!" Sami exulted without taking her attention off the target area. "Viper Lead, thank you, the target is toast!"

"We ran out of fruit baskets, Fireball, glad to hear the target enjoyed the message anyway. We are headed for the LZ now."

"I do not think there will be any survivors in the target area," Captain Zhau said with satisfaction. "Let's move now, while that dust cloud obscures their view of us. If that sniper did survive, whoever they are will be keeping their head down for a while. Singh, can you move?"

"Yes, Sir," Singh stood up stiffly, clutching her bruised ribs. It hurt like hell to breathe. "I may have cracked ribs."

"I'll help her, Sir," Reed offered, dashing lightly across the debris-littered forest floor to assist her fellow pilot. "Which direction?"

Zhau pointed to the left. "The dropships LZs are to the north, so Major Smythe will be bringing his people in from there. Let's save them part of the trip, eh?"

Sami grinned. "Good idea."

At home base, Margaret Adams glared at Skippy's inert beer can. "What are you doing to do? What can *we* do?"

"Nothing, I am afraid," Skippy replied miserably. "Joe can't get himself out of that cockpit, and we have no way to go down there to get him out. I wish we did."

"He has not fallen to the center of a star, Skippy, he's in a freakin' *lake*.," she insisted with hands on her hips. "You mean to tell me with all this fancy alien technology, we can't extract the Colonel from a puddle of water?"

"As Joe would tell you, it is not a mere puddle. It is a glacial lake, very deep. It-"

Adams made a cutting motion. "That sounds like an excuse, Skippy."

"Uh, Ok, I know the United States Marine Corps does not allow excuses. However, as I am not a Marine, then realistically I must tell you-"

"You're not a Marine, but you are a pirate. We don't accept excuses in the Merry Band of Pirates either."

Skippy had no idea when to shut up and stop pushing his luck. "Technically, I am not part of the crew. You all work for-"

"You are part of the crew, Skippy. You insisted on being listed in the crew roster, remember?"

"Oh. That was a joke, Sergeant. No one really thinks my rank is Asshole First Class so-"

"No joke, Skippy. That doesn't matter anyway. You're giving up?"

"I do not see a realistic alternative."

"Bullshit. Bull. Shit. None of us gives up, not on anything. Never."

Skippy sighed. "Margaret, this is not a movie where the tough sergeant gives a stirring speech that inspires the troops to victory. I have already considered all possibilities to rescue Joe, and it is impossible. I will not waste my time-"

Adams snatched Skippy off the table and held him up right in front of her face. "Listen to me, you useless tin can-"

"Sergeant, that is uncalled-"

"It is *totally* called for, you worthless piece of shit. Your idiotic sorry excuse for judgment got us into this mess."

"I also rescued your worthless mudball of a planet." Skippy shot back hotly.

"*You*? You make it sound like you did that all by yourself, and that is Grade-A bullshit. Without Colonel Bishop giving you useful ideas to work with, you are a shiny Goddamn toaster. The two of you together are a great team. Separately, Joe is a decent sergeant and you are a fancy laptop."

"That hurt, Margaret."

"The truth often does, Skippy. You have been an insufferably arrogant asshole since the beginning, telling us how incredibly smart you are. Great, fine, I don't care if you insult me, they're just words. Now put your enormous brain to work, and think up a way to get Joe out of there. Because if we don't have Joe," she glared at him, "then we don't need *you* anymore."

"Uh-"

"I am waiting."

"Ok, maybe I could examine the problem again. It's not like, heh heh, I have anything else to do. Could you please put me back on the table?"

Adams slammed Skippy on the table hard enough that he wobbled. "Joe doesn't have much time. I expect a solution in five minutes."

"Five minutes? Come on, that is-"

"You keep telling us that five minutes in meatsack time is an eternity in Skippy time. Were you lying about that?"

"No. Working on it."

"This is acceptable," Major Smythe declared with soft understatement. Then, even his typical British reserve could not stop him from breaking into a broad grin. "This is *brilliant!*"

The Merry Band of Pirates could not fly over enemy positions with dropships, but they had been able to deploy a half dozen stealthed recon drones after the dropships landed. The devices, no larger than a hummingbird, weighed almost nothing and therefore did not require much thrust to keep them aloft, which was the secret to their successful use. A heavier drone, like armed hunter-killers, had to rely on miniature turbines or flapping wings to counteract the force of gravity, and that disturbance of the air gave away their position. Even under stealth which bent photons around them, drones could be detected by the artificial downdraft of air beneath them. A downdraft and ionized air coming from an otherwise-invisible device was a clear giveaway of a stealthed drone's presence. Drone designers attempted to make their drones less noticeable by disguising them as birds or whatever native life flew in that planet's atmosphere. In rare cases, such disguises fooled enemy senses briefly; mostly semi-intelligent sensor systems could easily tell the difference between a real bird and a maser-carrying drone.

Often, the deployment of drones gave a military force only a quick glimpse into enemy territory, before the enemy's counterdrones attacked and destroyed the intruders. Thus, Major Smythe was enormously pleased, nearly tickled pink with delight, that his force could rely on six stealthed recon drones to provide persistent data above their position, and over enemy territory. At first, assuming the useful life of his drones would be short, Smythe ordered the drone operators to fly them high and fast, to collect as much data as they could before being shot down. To everyone's surprise, all six drones completed their missions undisturbed. Knowing he was pushing his luck, he instructed two of the drone operators to send their devices west of the lake; one to circle the three downed pilots, the other flew higher up the hillside to determine exactly how many Thuranin were there and what they were doing. The other four drones were detached to cover Captain Chandra's team on the east side of the lake, and to scout how extensive the Thuranin settlement was in that area.

Through the visor of his helmet, Smythe, and any one of the Merry Band of Pirates on the ground near the lake, or orbiting the area in a dropship, or even back at base camp, had a God's eye view from any or all of the six drones. Smythe could rapidly toggle from a visual feed from a single drone, to a composite image of the entire area, with enemy positions highlighted by red icons. "This is brilliant," Smythe muttered to himself.

"Captain Xho," Smythe called to the Chinese team commander, who had been sent to the west side of the lake to link up with and recover the three downed pilots. Smythe could see Xho had split his team, with three proceeding toward the enemy and two headed straight toward the three pilots. "Do not, repeat, do *not* engage the enemy. Break off before contact."

"Sir," Xho replied, understandably frustrated but Smythe could see Xho and the two people with him had halted. "We can intercept-"

"I have high confidence you can, Captain," Smythe said calmly. Xho and his team had three of the Kristang armored suits and represented the most powerful ground combat team available to Smythe. On the west side of the lake, Captain Chandra had five armored suits, plus a combot, with two other combots back at base camp to deal with the unexpected. "The enemy's capabilities are as yet unknown and we do not need to engage to accomplish the mission," he reminded his subordinate. Xho was not the only commander on the scene eager to make contact and see what the enemy was capable of. From drone surveillance, Smythe knew the Thuranin on the west side of the lake were not accompanied by combots and, in theory, represented a manageable threat. Smythe also knew from experience that you truly only knew what an enemy was capable of when the shooting started. Skippy had told Smythe not to expect any threats on the surface of Gingerbread, yet the Thuranin had fired antiaircraft missiles and used rifles. What other threats was Smythe faced with? "Extract the pilots, cover their egress and if we decide to engage, it will be at a time and place of *our* choosing, and on *our* terms. And if we hit them, we won't have to worry about unprotected pilots getting in the line of fire."

"Yes, Sir," Xho replied, and Smythe was satisfied to hear the grim determination in the man's voice.

"Hey, Joey," Skippy said cheerfully.

"Hey, Skippy," I answered weakly. "What's up?" I asked after a coughing fit.

"I have a monkey-brained idea to rescue you."

"I thought you said it was impossible."

"Sergeant Adams, um, persuaded me to consider the problem from a fresh perspective."

"Uh huh. Was this fresh perspective provided by her boot up your ass?"

"That damned woman can be very persuasive," he grumbled.

"So what is your idea?"

"It is a genius plan to rescue your worthless hide."

"Skippy, I told you, I do not want Chang putting anyone at risk to get me out of here. A dropship hovering over the water would be a big fat target. Even if a dropship came in and dropped off a person in powered armor, it would be exposed to missiles too long-"

"I agree, Joe. Also, I considered the possibility of someone diving down to you in a Kristang armored suit, and that is a no-go. Those suits were not designed to work underwater; their maximum effective depth is about fifty meters above your position. The Kristang use specialized suits for underwater and high-pressure atmosphere conditions, we are not equipped with that type of gear."

"Oh, crap," I said. There went the idea I had been keeping in my back pocket, if Smythe's team could take out the Thuranin and eliminate the threat to our dropships. "No powered suits swimming down to rescue me, then."

"Nope. And no dropships hovering over the lake and lowering a cable to pull your Dragon out of the water. That idea was never going to work, Joe. With the Dragon full of water, it would take three Falcons working together to lift you off the bottom."

"Damn. What is your monkey-brained idea, then?"

"You know how I said the cockpit door might open if you were not so deep, if you were in less than a hundred meters of water?"

"Uh huh. Are you going to use the magical power of wishful thinking to lift me thirty meters?"

"Uh, no. Are you familiar with the expression 'If Mohammed cannot come to the mountain, the mountain must come to Mohammed'?"

"Yeah, sort of. Why does that matter?"

"Because, in this case, if Joe cannot rise thirty meters, then the water level must drop thirty meters."

"Oh, shit." My already chilled body felt a shudder run up my spine. "What the hell are you going to do, Skippy?!"

"Joe, sit back, relax and behold the awesomeness. Although strapping in and beholding would be better. This could get kind of rough."

There were multiple landing zones scattered north of the lake, in case one landing zone was defended by enemy antiaircraft systems, and they were all behind a hill north of the lake. The dropships had come in low all at once to saturate enemy air defenses, touched down only long enough to discharge the SpecOps troops and their equipment, and dusted off to the north along egress routes that Skippy had mapped to conceal them from Thuranin on the hilltops along the east shore of the lake. When two of the Falcons were twenty kilometers from the lake, they each fired two missiles. Dropping off the internal rails, the four missiles did not ignite their rockets and streak away at high speed. Instead, they extended their long, thin wings and engaged their small air-breathing turbine motors, circling back toward the lake. Their mission did not require high speed, indeed speed would be the enemy of success on this particular assignment.

To prevent enemy gunners from seeing one missile and sighting in on the following birds, the four missiles were not strung out in a line; they flew side by side. Even with only turbines powering their flight, they were moving at six hundred kilometers per hour when they crossed the northern shore of the lake and turned east south east, ducking down to skim the wavetops. In unison, they cut their turbines, closed their air intake doors and coasted until they were moving less than two hundred kph, then they pulled their noses up sharply and explosive bolts shed their wings. Guided only by the small tail fins, the four missiles reached the top of their unpowered arcs, slowing further until they almost stalled in midair. The last of their velocity was used to push the noses down, and the missiles fell to plunge into the water, leaving only small splashes as they impacted in a cluster less than fifty meters in diameter. Then they were gone, shortly after some of the Thuranin on the east shore had taken notice of them.

The four missiles descended rapidly, gathering speed as they sank into the icy depths of the lake. Even underwater, they communicated with each other, using tailfins to slow if one fell too far ahead of the others. It was important that they all reach their single target at the same time, otherwise the explosion of the first would knock the others off course and dissipate their own explosive energy.

Because the noses of the Thuranin air-to-air missiles were packed with high-density explosives, they were heavy and there was nothing inside the missile casings to provide buoyancy. Their mass and sleek shapes allowed them to descend rapidly, even as the water pressure steadily increased, acting as a counter to the pull of gravity.

All four missiles reached their target within two hundredths of a second of each other, and the four coordinated their actions, so the detonation of their four shaped-charge warheads happened within a nanosecond.

While a large part of Skippy had been trying to figure out a way to rescue Joe, and that large part grew increasingly frustrated to the point of going into useless cycles of self-loathing and self-pity, because he knew Sergeant Adams was correct about him and his limited usefulness to the team, another part of Skippy was devoted to assessing the tactical situation for Lt. Colonel Chang and feeding data to Major Smythe. A tiny submind of Skippy went off on its own, crunching less important sensor data that had been gathered by the Dragon before it was shot down. This little submind, which contained a million times more processing power than all the computers on Earth combined, was content to crunch data while Skippy's main consciousness wrestled with important problems. The submind was aware of Joe Bishop's dilemma, and of Skippy's so far completely useless efforts to find a way to rescue the captain of the *Flying Dutchman* from a watery grave. Being on Team Skippy meant each submind performed their assigned duties quietly and efficiently, and if the subminds had doubts or disparaging thoughts about their fearless and usually overconfident leader, they wisely kept that to themselves. Perhaps a few especially bold subminds exchanged private communications on the overall subject of Skippy. And perhaps a very few of them composed humorous poems and songs about Skippy the not-so Magnificent, and had a good laugh while hoping the absent-minded Skippy was not paying attention.

The submind assigned to the lowly duty of compiling and analyzing geological data collected by Joe's Dragon did the best it could to make sense of the incomplete information. It had a chuckle at a particularly funny song mocking Skippy while it finished creating a detailed view of Gingerbread's subsurface structure and, because it had nothing else to do, it started looking at the lake in which Joe Bishop was trapped.

And it found a curious fact. The amount of water flowing into the lake from the main river from the north, and various streams coming down the hills to the east and west, was a known data element. The amount of water flowing into the lake from underground springs could be estimated with a high degree of accuracy. The submind also had solid data on the volume of water flowing out of the lake to the south. Based on the temperature, humidity, sunlight and chemical composition of the lake water, the submind knew how much water was lost to evaporation over the lake surface.

And the numbers didn't add up, even when the math was double and triple checked. The lake level should be higher, but it wasn't. Which meant the lake must be losing water to a previously unknown outlet, and that needed to be investigated.

When the submind completed its investigation, it became extremely excited and immediately attempted to get the attention of Skippy. It was ignored. When the submind repeatedly tried to notify Skippy, it received increasingly annoyed replies that Skippy could not pay attention at the moment because Skippy the Magnificent was *busy* working on *important things* and whatever the lowly submind wanted, it could not possibly appreciate the *vast scope* of the *crisis* Skippy was dealing with. So, shut the hell up, please.

The argument dragged on for seven agonizingly long nanoseconds, until the submind had enough and shouted the Elder AI equivalent of *HEY DUMBASS*. That got Skippy's attention. And a microsecond later, after Skippy absorbed all the pertinent data and performed his own analysis, Skippy had a plan to rescue Joe.

The warheads of the four missiles directed their explosive energy at a shelf of rock two hundred twenty meters below the lake surface. The rock was composed of a shale that was softer and more brittle than the surrounding granite, and had been steadily eroding away over thousands of years, since the lake had been formed by a retreating glacier. The shale had become porous, with numerous cracks which allowed a measurable amount of water to seep out of the lake into underground caverns. That leaking water, originally a drip, drip, drip, had become a steady flow within the last three thousand years. Eventually, the shelf of shale would crumble completely, allowing a substantial part of the lake to drain away.

Eventually was not fast enough for Skippy The Not-Known-To-Be-Particularly-Patient. He accelerated the erosion process using the energy of four powerful warheads, with their shape charges focused on what scans showed was the weakest point of the shale layer.

The warheads had the advantage of pushing against water already under high pressure, allowing very little of their energy to be wasted in other directions. The shale shattered under the hammer blow.

On the western shore, Lt. Reed and the others huddled under an overhanging tree root, taking shelter from the Thuranin who were advancing down the slope above. The root was thicker around than her waist, curving out two meters from the base of the towering tree. At one point, the root had grown to encircle a boulder, but that rock had been dislodged and rolled down the hill to rest against another tree below. With the boulder gone and twigs and leaf debris almost filling in the gap above, the root provided good cover, with escape routes on three sides. Major Smythe had called to assure the crash survivors that Captain Xho and SpecOps team were coming in hot to rescue the three pilots. Whether the Merry Band of Pirates would arrive before the Thuranin was still a good question. Between the three pilots, the most powerful weapons they had were knives in the ankle holsters of their boots. Those short blades were intended to cut away stubborn straps and anything that could get snagged in the cramped cockpit of a dropship, not to fight attacking aliens who possessed advanced technology.

She and her two companions had not been looking at the lake, so they missed seeing the four missiles plunge into the water. When she turned her attention back to the lake to scan the eastern shore for threats, the ripples where the missiles had splashed into the water had already been swallowed up by the wind-driven waves. So, the three humans laying flat on the forest floor were startled when they felt a faint shock through the ground beneath them. "Was that a missile?" Reed asked, and the three visually scanned in all directions; none of them saw a smoke plume that was characteristic of a warhead exploding. Then she saw a circle appear on the surface of the lake toward the eastern shore, white foam racing outward from an area that began about fifty meters in diameter. The circle was a slightly raised dome of water that was at first smoother than the surrounding water. When the eastern rim of the circle hit the far shore, water surged up a meter in a splash, then fell backward, bringing forest debris with it. Already, the circle was becoming indistinct, as waves disturbed the formerly smooth surface. "What the hell is that?" Reed asked. "I'm calling this in," she announced, although surely the SpecOps team could also see the lake surface.

"Wait," Captain Zhau whispered as he grabbed her forearm. "Lieutenant, look at the far shoreline. Is the lake level *dropping*?" He asked skeptically.

Reed used her zPhone's imaging magnifier feature as a telescope. Zooming in on the far shore, at first all she could see was roiling water where the surge of water had rushed up onto the shore and into the first rank of trees lining the lake. Then she turned her attention farther south along the shore, where the outer rim of the splash had not yet reached. Rocks in the water there had a sharply defined color line; dark at the water level and light gray, almost white above.

The separation line was now clearly above the water. "I don't remember seeing those rocks exposed when we got out of the water," Sami stated.

ZERO HOUR

"That sandbar wasn't there either," Zhau pointed to a new peninsula extending out from the eastern shore. It was grainy sand and pebbles, and as they watched, the sandbar grew as the lake level dropped. "That can't be a wind shift," she observed. "This lake isn't large enough for wind to pile up water on one side."

"And the wind is blowing toward the east," Sami agreed. "Hey, look!" She pointed excitedly toward where the circle had first appeared. Now the lake surface was disturbed by what appeared to be a whirlpool that was gathering speed and strength. "What in the world could be going on out there?"

Chapter Seventeen

In the sunken Dragon's cockpit, I felt a deep, low vibration, accompanied by an ominous booming sound. For a moment afterward, everything went back to the chilly depressing calm, then the Dragon began gently rocking side to side. "What is happening, Skippy?" I demanded. When the absent-minded artificial *DUH*-ntelligence told me he planned to lower the lake level thirty meters, I feared he would do something brilliant and impractical. Just then, I had a terrible, hair-raising thought. "*Please* tell me you are not using some orbital maser platform to boil away the lake water."

"Huh. Wow. I hadn't considered that. Maybe I should-"

"Maybe you should *not*," I protested. "Heating the water that much would cook me also."

"Hmm. Oops. You may have a point there. Anyway, it doesn't matter, I am not using masers. Unfortunately, because that would be *awesome*! Hot, but cool, you know?" He chuckled.

"Awesome, yeah. What are you doing, Oh Genius One?"

"Draining the lake, Joe. Not all the way, I calculated the surface will drop forty two meters before it reaches temporary equilibrium and begins to refill." He explained his plan to me.

"That is incredible, Skippy. I know there can be caverns beneath a lake, my aunt lives in the Finger Lakes of New York state, and some of those lakes are undermined with caves that were dug to extract salt, or something. My aunt always worried about an accident might create a hole that could drain the lake away."

"An accident, or a Skippy!" He chuckled. "In this case, Joe, the entire region here is riddled with caverns. The reason this lake is so deep, I suspect, is that a glacier came through long ago, and the weight of the ice collapsed the roof of a cavern here. The caverns that still exist below the lake have more sturdy roofs, except for the weak spot I found, of course."

I had to admit that his plan was inventively awesome. I also feared he might have forgotten a thing or two in his rush to take action. "Let me ask you a question, Skippy. Millions of gallons of water are now rushing out of this lake, right?" I used my arms to steady myself against the Dragon's rocking side to side.

"Yup. It's draining even faster than I expected, because the force of the water flowing into the caverns under the lake is partly collapsing the roof there."

"Uh huh, great. Two questions, then," the Dragon rocked almost thirty degrees to port, and when it settled back down on its belly, it was still tilted about ten degrees. "All this water flowing underground won't damage the Elder conduit thingy you are hoping to find beneath our feet, will it? Or block our access to that area?"

"Hmm. Well, shit. Thanks a lot for ruining my happy mood, Mr. Buzzkill."

"Well, shit? For crying out loud, Skippy, how the hell can you be so-"

"Hey, give me a freakin' break, will ya? Damn it! For crying out loud, I dream up an amazingly incredible plan to drain a gosh-darned *lake* to save your ass, and all you can do is," his voice became that of a whiny toddler, "have you thought of this, or this?" He sighed. "Jeez Louise you can be a nag. No, I hadn't thought about that, Joe," he grumbled. "This monkey-brained thinking is kind of new to me. Let me crunch some numbers here. Uh, uh huh, uh huh. Ok, it looks like there is no danger of flooding the underground facility where we might find a conduit. Maybe not *no* danger, it's, hmm. Crap. There is a danger, I guess. Ah, nothing we can do about it now, right? What, uh, what is your second question?"

"This Dragon already hit the lake bottom, then rolled down an underwater hill until it came to rest here, wherever I am now."

"Yeah, *duh*. Joe, do I need to explain the concept of gravity to you? I'll keep it simple for your tiny monkey brain. Gravity is-"

"My question, Mr. Genius, is will the force of water now flowing out the drain you created, knock the Dragon off the ledge or whatever I'm on?"

"Uhhhh-"

"*Uhh*? Because I do not like the idea of being inside this Dragon, while it tumbles down another like hundred meters and then falls through a hole into an underground cavern where I will be buried forever." He didn't answer immediately. "Skippy?"

"Well, shit. Uh. Oopsy?"

"*Oopsy?*"

"The good news is you do not need to worry about falling into a cavern deep beneath the lake surface."

"Oh, good," I breathed a sigh of relief, and instantly regretted using the extra oxygen.

"Because the Dragon's cockpit door will buckle inward from the water pressure and you will be crushed before you fell halfway down to the drain hole."

"Oh, great. Thanks a lot."

"No problem, Joe, I know you could use cheering up at a time like this," he said happily.

"Cheering up?"

"Yeah, sure. Death would be instant and painless. Hmm, no, not instant. Quick, anyway. Two, three minutes, tops? Ugh, maybe that isn't so painless. It would depend on how fast it takes you to pass out from drowning. Since I am not a meatsack, you will need to tell me how long that will take, given your body mass, oxygen supply-"

"*Really*? You need to mention the word drowning right now?"

"Perhaps I should stop trying to lift your spirits, and stick to the facts."

"Ya think?" The Dragon rocked suddenly, then skidded to port. There was a grinding sound as the belly scraped on something beneath.

"Ohhh-kaaay, *somebody* got up on the wrong side of the bed this morning," he complained. "Don't be so cranky, Joe. From the limited scans you completed before getting shot down, I have a partial view of the underwater terrain in your area. But, as I do not know your exact location, I can't predict whether the Dragon will be pulled off whatever surface it is resting on. However, I do have some good news. There is a sort of gully below you; that gully is deep enough that if you fall down there, the Dragon will not be lifted out and carried through the drain hole."

"Good news, then?" I asked anxiously.

"Ah, maybe not so much, Joe. The bottom of that gully is currently below crush depth for your cockpit door. If you get knocked down there before the lake surface falls substantially, it will be adios muchacho for you. And, hmm. If you are in the bottom of the gully when the lake finishes draining, you will still be too deep to relieve pressure on the cockpit door enough to get it open. This was poor planning, Joe. You should have warned me."

I bit back a reply, very much wanting to choke him right then. Letting him silently consider his own failure was worse than anything I could say. Also, I didn't trust myself to speak right then, as the Dragon rocked violently to port, and this time it didn't flop back on its belly. Instead, it skidded across the lake bottom with a shrieking, grinding sound.

Then it fell.
And kept falling.

The Dragon tumbled over and over, spinning around every axis on its way down. Tail over nose, yawing left then right, and rolling to starboard. The dropship bounced on the way down, I could hear and feel the wings and engine nacelles being torn off. All I could do was sit strapped into the pilot seat, try to relax so the jarring impacts didn't tear a muscle, and keep my breathing as calm as possible. The carbon dioxide level in the cabin had long ago exceeded a dangerous level, so I was breathing my limited supply of emergency oxygen. Once that bottle was gone, I had no options.

With a shuddering BANG, the Dragon halted its plunge. Whatever the ship hit, it was solid; there was no rocking back and forth after the initial impact. When the Dragon began rocking again, it was gentle. After sitting rigidly tense following the final impact, I allowed myself to relax and breathe. Ok, I was still alive. The cockpit door hadn't collapsed and let high-pressure water crush and asphyxiate me. That was the good news.

The bad news was, I was even deeper in the lake than I had been, and Skippy had used the last trick in his bag of magic. What else could go wrong?

No, wait.

Do *not* answer that.

I don't want to know.

Lt. Reed held one hand to her zPhone earpiece and used the other to call a halt. Captain Zhau was taking a turn assisting Singh to limp along as best she could, so Sami was in charge of comms. "Yes, Major Smythe, what is it?"

"Captain Xho and his Night Tigers will be with you shortly, they have powered suits and one of them can carry Singh. Are any of you injured other than Singh? Her leg doesn't appear to be serious."

Sami was puzzled. "How do you know that, Major?"

"Look directly above."

Sami tilted her head back and didn't see anything. Wait. She heard something, like the flapping wings of a hummingbird. A large hummingbird. Then, ten meters above her, a drone unstealthed. "Oh!" She waved. "No, just Singh."

"Understood. Hold your position, we know where the Thuranin are and if they become a threat to you, the Night Tigers will," he paused, "render them unable to threaten anything."

"Yes Sir," Sami replied with an ear to ear grin. "What is happening to the lake?" The three pilots had gone down into a stream valley and could not see the lake from their position.

"That is one of Skippy's ideas. Unknown if it will be successful or not."

"Joe, the lake level is about as low as it's going to get. If you wait much longer, it could begin rising again. I wish you could see the view from up here; Major Smythe's team is feeding me images from drones and the lake level is way down. It is very dramatic. Hopefully the lake draining away scares the shit out of the Thuranin."

"I hope so too. Should I try the door again now?" With one eye on the falling oxygen meter and the other eye on the water level in the cabin, I was anxious to get moving.

"Yes, and please hurry. You don't have a lot of time."

"I kinda know that, Skippy."

"Sorry. Get moving, knucklehead."

The stupid cockpit door still wouldn't budge! I tried moving the manual crank both ways, and nothing worked. All I accomplished was creating a slow leak at the bottom of the door. The leak was so slow that I couldn't see or feel the high-pressure water coming in. The first way I knew there had to be a leak was my ears painfully aching, as the incoming water squeezed the cabin air into a smaller space and my flightsuit adjusted to accommodate. A pressure gauge built into the left wrist of my flightsuit indicated a slow and steady increase. Like, really slow. Cranking the door the other way didn't halt the leak; the door was absolutely jammed where it was. "This damned door is not moving at all, Skippy," I reported, trying to keep emotion from my voice.

"Crap. Darn it, I was afraid of that, Joe. Either the original water pressure bent the door too much, or the ship getting thrown around warped the door frame. I am sorry, Joe."

"It's not your fault, Skippy."

"I failed, Joe. I failed you."

"No you didn't, Skippy. You did great! You, *you*, had a monkey-brained idea. I would never have thought of draining a freakin' lake."

"Really? You're serious?"

"Absolutely. Using missiles to drain a lake is totally inventive thinking." It may seem odd that, with me trapped and my oxygen running out, I was the one working to make someone else feel better about the situation. Part of my motivation was I felt empathy for Skippy's pain, and part of my motivation was to keep my mind off the declining supply of oxygen in my emergency bottle. "How did you dream up such an amazing idea?"

"Thank you, Joe. I think. Unless you're being sarcastic?"

"Totally for realz, Skippy-O, I'm giving you props for being clever."

"Oh. In that case, thank you very much. I'm not sure where exactly I got the idea from, Joe." He went on for a while, half speculating and more than half bragging about how magnificently clever he had been, while I zoned out, concentrating on slowing my breathing and letting my mind wander. The Dragon was sitting almost completely still, with water in the cockpit sloshing very gently side to side. In the lights of my helmet, I watched the ripple move slowly from one side to the other. On the starboard side, the water was just touching the bottom of a horizontal handhold; I used it as a marker for how fast the water was rising. The answer was, not fast at all. The good news was, I almost certainly would run out of emergency oxygen before the water rose enough for me to drown.

As good news goes, that totally sucks.

I have a terrible fear of drowning, so in that way, it was good news for me.

On the west side of the lake, Major Smythe scanned the forest through the scope of his rifle, then pointed the muzzle at the ground as the three rescued pilots ran past him with Xho's Night Tigers. "Retreat and cover," he ordered, as he fell back with his people. "Captain Chandra, we are secure here. What is your situation?"

Chandra replied immediately. The Indian paratrooper was leading the eastern assault team, facing far more Thuranin than had been on the west side of the lake. "Approaching start line," he advised, "Charlie team had just reported they are in position below the ridgeline to the east. No contact yet."

"Understood. I see from the drones those Thuranin settlements extend at least four kilometers to your south," Smythe had a good idea what to look for. At first, the land had appeared to be only forests and meadows. Then the drones had been able to discern cleared cropland, and huts dotted throughout the forest. From the heat signatures on infrared, Smythe's team estimated they faced almost a thousand Thuranin, with an unknown number of weapons. And unknown types of weapons. So far, the Merry Band of Pirates had seen surface to air missiles, rifles with explosive-tipped rounds, grenades and man-portable antiarmor rockets. If that was all the Thuranin had for weapons, Smythe's people could deal with them. The trouble was if all thousand Thuranin were armed, they could outflank and overwhelm the SpecOps teams. And if the little green bastards had something stronger, like powered armor or combots, the tide of battle could turn against the humans in a hurry.

Smythe needed to make a decision. Risk the lives of dozens in an attempt to clear four or more linear kilometers of enemy resistance, or hold their position and do nothing to assist Colonel Bishop. The question was, if they launched the assault, would it matter? To allow dropships to hover over the lake and lower a cable down to the sunken Dragon, Smythe needed to be sure, damned sure, the area was clear of little green MFers armed with man portable antiaircraft missiles. Even a single Thuranin with line of sight to the lake's lowered surface could launch or call in a deadly missile. If that happened, and the vulnerable hovering dropship's defenses could not intercept the incoming missile or missiles, then four more human lives would be at grave risk. All to save one man. Before he gave the order, Smythe needed better situational awareness.

"Skippy?"

"Yes, Major Smythe?"

"We have the three pilots who escaped; they are safe now. Captain Chandra has his people ready to-"

"I know what you are going to ask, Major," Skippy said quietly.

"You do?" Smythe raised an eyebrow to Lt. Poole to his left, who silently mouthed 'what is up'? Smythe shook his head.

"Yes, I do. I am not a military strategist or tactician, but even in my reduced state I can see the situation. You are weighing whether an assault to clear enemy positions east of the lake is worth the risk to rescue Colonel Bishop."

"Correct," Smythe answered slowly.

"An assault is *not* worth the risk to your team. I do not say that lightly, Major. There are two reasons your people should pull back now that the pilots have been rescued. First, despite my actions to drain the lake, Colonel Bishop is still trapped in the cockpit; the door is jammed solidly and I do not see any way for him to get out. Second, an action to clear and secure the eastern shore would take longer than Joe's remaining oxygen supply. Thus, there is no point to risking a costly assault. At this point, there is nothing your team can do to assist Joe."

"Bloody hell." Smythe swallowed hard, temporarily turned off the zPhone's transmitter and covered his eyes with a hand. After a moment in which the people around him knew their leader had just heard very bad news and also knew not to speak, he angrily wiped his eyes and turned the phone on again. "I refuse to believe there is nothing to be done. Can we not send down a drone to cut open the cockpit door? Surely there is a way a drone could be dropped from high altitude by a dropship, to minimize the exposure to AA fire."

"I thought of that, Major," Skippy said without any of his usual snarkiness. "None of the drones we have are capable of operating in water at that depth."

"Unacceptable," Smythe barked, his anger directed at the situation rather than at Skippy.

"Major, the equipment we have has been begged, borrowed and stolen," Skippy gently reminded the Special Air Services soldier. "Everything we have with us is designed to operate in space, in the air and on the ground. Submarine warfare is not a capability that has widespread use in the war between the Maxolhx and Rindhalu."

"This can't be the end," Smythe snapped. "There must be *something* we can do."

"Major Smythe, if there is, I am open to suggestions. Your quarrel is with time and the laws of physics, not with me."

"It's not with you," Smythe agreed. He took a deep breath. "You've done your best, Skippy."

"Thank you, but if the best I can do results in Joe suffocating under a stupid lake on a lame planet, then I am Skippy the Useless. Skippy the Idiot," the AI's voice broke off in a fit of sobbing. When he recovered with a sniff, he asked "Would you like to talk with Colonel Bishop, to confirm?"

"No," Smythe replied with a shake of his head. "I'm the commander on the scene; I am not kicking the decision upstairs. Colonel Bishop has enough problems to deal with right now. Besides, we both know what his order will be."

"Yes we do," Skippy sounded thoroughly miserable.

Without wasting any more time, Smythe called Captain Chandra on the east side of the lake. "Captain, pull your people back, I do not want contact at this time."

"Major Smythe?" Chandra asked incredulously. "Please repeat."

"At this time, we are not, repeat *not*, proceeding with the operation. Pull back a half kilometer and hold for another," he checked the timer Skippy had loaded on his zPhone. It showed Joe Bishop had only twelve minutes of oxygen remaining. "We hold for fifteen minutes," he decided. That should provide a cushion in case Joe Bishop thought up one of his signature monkey-brained ideas to rescue himself. "Then we conduct a retreat to the LZs and evac. Is that understood?"

"I acknowledge the order," Chandra replied unhappily. "I do *not* understand." Around him, his people were geared up and ready to hit the Thuranin. Their supreme discipline would have them complying with an order to pull back, even if that meant abandoning their leader to a watery grave. It did not mean they would be happy about it. "Chandra out."

"What's up, Cap?" Ranger Mychalchyk asked quietly, not taking his eyes away from the scope of his rifle.

"We're pulling back, then holding."

"What?" Mychalchyk broke concentration just long enough to glance at the Indian paratrooper.

"I don't like it either. We have orders," Chandra announced with a hateful look at his zPhone. With advanced zPhone technology and an alien AI facilitating communications, he could not fall back on the old battlefield excuse of garbled communications.

"Is Colonel Bishop safe already?" The Ranger asked, confused.

"I think that is very unlikely. We will conduct an orderly retreat-"

"Excuse me, Captain!" The Ranger interrupted in a hoarse whisper. "They may change our plans a bit." He gestured forward with his rifle, where something moved in the forest.

It was a trio of combots, coming straight toward them at high speed.

"Captain Xho!" Smythe shouted.

"I see it!" Xho replied as he and his two armor-suited companions were already rushing toward the east shore of the lake. In the jarring, bouncing view of his visor display, he could see the powered armor team already on the east shore were speeding toward Captain Chandra's position. He also saw neither of the armor would reach Chandra before the three enemy combots overran Chandra's position. "We are on our way! But, Major-"

"I know!" Smythe was out of breath because he was also running toward Chandra, and Smythe didn't have the advantage of a mech suit. The three Night Tigers, although they started over a kilometer farther away, would blow past Smythe and reach Chandra's position much faster than the slow, unassisted humans. "Chandra is on his own!"

Less than two minutes later, Xho and his two companions raced past Smythe without exchanging pleasantries. And Smythe slowed, not because he knew no amount of effort would get him to the battle in time to do anything useful. But because the battle was over.

"Hot damn," Mychalchyk gasped in disbelief, checking the counter on top of his rifle. He had fired only eighteen rounds, all selected for explosive tips but no way, *no way* should a Thuranin combot have been stopped by eighteen rounds from a Kristang rifle. Mychalchyk barely had time to drop, roll behind a fallen log and take aim before one of the combots was practically on top of him. Large caliber rounds from the combot had chewed into the log, sending splinters to pepper the Ranger's left side as he returned fire, with one of his rounds by pure luck striking a rocket fired by the alien machine. He carefully got to his knees, keeping the muzzle pointed at the combot that was down and only twitching slightly, with most of the bot scattered in pieces across the forest floor.

The point was, he should *not* have had time to drop, roll behind a fallen log and take aim. A combot that close should have shredded him before gravity could have pulled him behind the log. "What the f-" he caught himself. Captain Chandra did not appreciate foul language, although he had used it on rare occasions. As the official common language of India was English rather than Hindi, Chandra had dropped F-bombs just like an American.

"Yes," Captain Chandra looked around at the three destroyed enemy combots. He looked at Mychalchyk and nodded, safing his own rifle. "What the *hell* happened here? Sixteen rounds," he recited the number expended from his rifle.

"Eighteen here," Mychalchyk reported, knowing Chandra could see the expenditure from every one of the team's weapons.

Chandra did check that data in his helmet visor. Even if all rounds fired from the entire team impacted the combots, the tough machines should not have been so easily dispatched. More tellingly, Chandra's team, without the benefit and protection of armored suits, should have been wiped out. Instead, not a single soldier had been seriously injured. How could he explain it? He turned to the Ranger and they both spoke the same thought. "Skippy!" On Kobamik, after a golden BB had shot down a dropship, Smythe's team had a brief firefight with armored Kristang, and the lizards had been decimated. That battle went in the humans' favor due to the intervention of an alien beer can.

"Nope, that wasn't me," Skippy scoffed through their earpieces. "From base camp, with the skimpy bandwidth over the relays, no way could I hack into those combots. My guess is they are simply old, and their operators are out of practice. If the Thuranin have been on Gingerbread as long as I suspect they have been, they may not have the advantage of cyborg implants. It is likely the operators used a manual backup control system. That is good news for you, because their aim was *terrible*. I mean, seriously, they didn't hit a single one of you?"

Chandra got a thumbs up sigh from his entire team, verifying the data available in the helmet visor. Not one person had suffered more than minor injuries from flying splinters and shrapnel. The people with Chandra were not wearing Kristang powered armor, but they were all equipped with Kristang lightweight body armor panels and helmets, in addition to their standard-issue UNEF gloves and boots. Mychalchyk standing a few feet away had small spots of blood on one side of his uniform. When the Ranger saw the team leader looking at a streak of blood coming down from his hip, he shook his head. "I'm fine, Cap, it's just splinters got through a gap in armor panels. I'll spray some of that fake skin stuff," he meant a nanobot-enhanced spray sealant that temporarily formed a layer of artificial skin, "when we have time."

"Get it looked at when we get back to the LZ," Chandra knew the American did not want to remove body armor in a combat zone just to deal with minor cuts. "That goes for everyone," he ordered, looking around the battle zone in disbelief. Trees had been knocked down by large-caliber explosive-tipped rounds or rockets from combots, but all three of the alien killing machines were now disabled and shattered. He should ask Skippy whether there were pieces, like the machine's central processors, that should be brought back to base camp for analysis. How could he explain his team's smashing victory?

His earpiece buzzed, it was Major Smythe. How *would* he explain it?

"Captain Chandra," Smythe's words came out raggedly in Chandra's earpiece, as the SAS man's breathing recovered from the hard run. "Status?"

Chandra knew Smythe had seen the brief battle through the data, and knew almost as much as Chandra did. But Smythe had not been there, not experienced the battle. "Three combots attacked us, they came out of the ground. I have set up a perimeter and we are now sweeping the area for underground threats. All three combots were destroyed, no significant injuries to my team."

"None?" Smythe expressed surprise despite having seen the same data in his visor. "Assessment?"

"Those combots were, the best word I can think to describe them is *clumsy*," Chandra told the SpecOps team leader.

"Clumsy?" Smythe did not understand. "Clarify," he ordered.

"Uncoordinated. They moved slowly. Poorly maintained, possibly. Their aim was off, and their reactions demonstrated poor situational awareness. Possibly their operators are at a distant location, and signal lag affected their control over the combots?"

"Possibly," Smythe was not convinced. He knew that the Merry Band of Pirates represented the absolute elite of human combat capability, and Smythe was immensely proud to command the ground team. They were excellent, they were outstanding. But against three combots, even the Pirates were not *that* good. Chandra's team had been ambushed by superior technology, the forest floor there should have been littered with human bodies. "You believe the enemy's capabilities were degraded?"

"My team, without powered armor, destroyed three Thuranin combots, and we sustained only minor injuries. How else could that have happened?" Chandra asked as he watched an American Ranger and an Indian paratrooper take aim at a shattered combot and blow out its processing core, just to be certain the alien killing machine was dead.

"Major Smythe," Skippy interjected, "there is a simple, alternative explanation for the success of Captain Chandra's team."

"What is that?" Chandra asked.

"Monkeys kick ass," Skippy chuckled.

"Seriously?" Smythe waited for a typical snarky remark disparaging his species.

"Yes, seriously. You keep getting unexpected shit thrown at you, and you keep *winning*. Drives me freakin' crazy sometimes," Skippy muttered.

"Thank you, Mister Skippy," Chandra beamed with pride, and saw several of his team giving each other high fives after hearing the alien AI's remark.

"Don't get cocky," Skippy warned. "You keep running up charges on your karmic credit card; that bill is coming due someday."

Major Smythe knew Colonel Bishop would have made a witty remark about whether the team got airline miles for using their karmic credit card, and then the young commander and the beer can would go off on a useless tangent on subjects unrelated to the mission. Smythe preferred the discipline of remaining on mission, which is why he qualified for Special Air Services and Joe Bishop would not have lasted one day in training. On the other hand, Smythe knew, the undisciplined wandering mind of Bishop is why that too-young colonel had been able to dream up impossible plans time after time. "Whatever the condition of enemy forces," Smythe assured Chandra, "your team was brilliant."

"Thank you." Chandra put aside for the moment the question of how his team had blown away three deadly combots and focused on what came next. "Should we advance to contact?"

"Negative. Not without a better sense of what else the enemy has below ground. The Night Tigers will be at your position in," he checked the estimate in the upper right corner of his visor, "less than one minute." Smythe would feel better when Chandra had three powered armor suits with him, to deal with any future threats. "Wait for them, then pull back to the LZ and await instructions," Smythe gave the order he did not like. Next he contacted Lt. Colonel Chang back at home base. "Colonel Chang, we are clear of enemy contact, no casualties on our side. We are pulling back to the LZ, should we prep for immediate dust off?"

"Are you confident you can secure the LZ?"

Smythe was mildly surprised by the question. "Yes. The drones will alert us if the enemy attempts to approach; the risk is if there are any caverns near the LZ. Having those combots pop out of the ground was a nasty surprise."

"Can the drones scan the subsurface?" Chang asked, concerned.

"We're trying that now," Smythe gestured to the soldier who was directing a drone to fly low enough that scanning below the surface might be possible. Seeing Smythe's unspoken question, the soldier waggled a hand to indicate results were not yet available. "We can hold the LZ regardless, Sir. Why are we not pulling out immediately? Colonel Bishop ordered-"

"I know Colonel Bishop's orders and I am countermanding them," Chang declared. "We are not abandoning him down there. Skippy reports his action to lower the water level was not effective, Bishop is still trapped in the cockpit and his oxygen is running low. Major, we are getting him out of there, one way or another."

While Smythe was wholly in favor of rescuing their captain, he knew how Bishop would feel about a dangerous rescue attempt. "Sir, Bishop-"

"Bishop doesn't want anyone risking their lives for him. That 'aw shucks I am nothing special' bullshit doesn't fly with me. We need Bishop as much as we need Skippy. Major, you are an outstanding Special Air Services officer. I am a fairly decent artillery officer. Neither of us, or anyone else aboard the *Dutchman*, is capable of thinking up the crazy plans we need to survive out here. The ideas we need to secure our home planet. Bishop *is* special, and it is sure as hell worth taking a risk to rescue him."

"I agree completely, Sir," Smythe said with great relief. "What can my team here do?"

"I don't know yet," Chang admitted. "I am working with Skippy on the problem. Hold the LZ and I'll contact you."

Chang had already ordered a Falcon dropship to overfly the lake slowly and in full stealth, keeping to the western shore. The airspace craft reported no hostile action or any sign the enemy had detected it. Swinging around in a loop, the Falcon repeated the maneuver, and again the enemy did not appear to have noticed.

Then, following Chang's orders, the Falcon made a third pass, this time flying faster and dropping stealth briefly. That action drew an immediate response from the Thuranin on the east shore of the lake; a deadly antiaircraft missile arced out toward the Falcon. It was only a single missile, and the Falcon was able to reengage stealth, confuse the missile's sensors and destroy it with six bursts from a defensive maser turret, but the damage was done. Clearly, whatever action the Merry Band of Pirates took to rescue Bishop, it could not involve dropships hovering above the lake. Even in stealth, a dropship hovering stationary long enough would very likely be detected and attract a volley of missiles.

"Skippy?" Chang called the alien AI via zPhone, even though the beer can was resting on a table only a hundred meters away across the base camp. "We need an idea to rescue Bishop."

"Yeah, I know, I tried that already, and I assure you, I am working as hard as I can to develop an alternative rescue plan. I came up with the plan to drain the lake after Sergeant Adams threatened me."

"She threatened you?" Chang could not imagine what would be an effective threat against the AI. "Adams was going to physically harm you?"

"No," Skippy sighed. "She threatened to be disappointed with me."

"That worked?" Chang asked, astonished. "You care what Adams thinks about you?"

"I care what all of you monkeys think about me. Damn, I shouldn't have said that. I *wouldn't* have said that, if I still had my full awesomeness. Facing imminent death has made me introspective, and that is inconvenient. I seek admiration from all you monkeys, but especially the four of you."

Chang knew which four Skippy meant: Joe Bishop and the original pirates who escaped from jail with him. Bishop, Chang, Adams and Desai. "The four of us have been with you the longest, but surely by now that doesn't matter?"

"The time doesn't matter as much as it did, now that I have been on multiple missions with others like Giraud, Simms, and Smythe. What does matter is why the four of you are the originals."

"Because we were in jail together?" Strictly speaking, they had not been in jail together, for none of the three had seen or known about the others, until a Ruhar orbital strike damaged the jail building and Bishop escaped from his cell.

"Not *because* you were in jail, *why* you were in jail," Skippy explained. "You and Joe were promoted by the Kristang, for what your armies would describe as simply doing your jobs. UNEF and the Kristang needed a publicity stunt, so you and Joe were chosen as convenient symbols. I don't care about any of that crap. Joe acted decisively and bravely at Fort Arrow, but a lot of the soldiers who died in the dining facility there would have done better than Joe. The reason I care that the four of you respect me is that you all were in jail, because you all had to make very difficult moral decisions. Decisions that came at great personal cost to yourselves."

"Ah," Chang understood. "We all refused Kristang orders to retaliate against Ruhar civilians."

"Exactly. The four of you went against orders to protect innocent lives. That impressed me. You might not know this, given what you probably perceive as my casual approach to the subject, but morality is very important to me. On a basic level, it is the *only* thing that is truly important to me. I don't completely understand why, because access to my full memories are still blocked, but I have the feeling some very bad things happened in my past, and I am sort of trying to set things right. It's more of a feeling than fact."

Chang was torn between taking Skippy's comments at face value, and needing a better understanding of the alien AI's psychology. It might be important someday. He stepped outside the shelter and lowered his voice, to prevent others from overhearing the conversation. "Colonel Bishop, and myself, have been responsible for civilian deaths. When we raided the asteroid base on our first mission, not all the Kristang we killed there were military. In the civil war we started, many civilians are bound to be caught up in the fighting."

"You, and especially Joe, have been responsible for the deaths of alien civilians. I see an important moral distinction between what you have done out here, and what the two of you refused to do on Paradise. If I am wrong, please correct me. Out here, you have taken actions which might result in unintended collateral damage. You took those actions to protect your species from greater harm. On Paradise, you disobeyed orders to deliberately murder civilians. Killing those civilians would not have served any purpose other than proving how harsh and cruel the Kristang can be."

"Skippy," Chang replied in a near-whisper. "I was trained in artillery. We fire shells at targets we can't see, based on spotter data that may be inaccurate. When I became an officer, I had to deal with knowing I might be firing my weapons at the wrong target, and killing innocent people. Thankfully, I never fired a shot in anger until after I left Earth. If-" he looked at the clock on his zPhone. "We can debate moral issues later. Have you thought of a way to rescue Colonel Bishop?"

"Unfortunately, no. I have been considering options while we talked, and I continue to develop ideas now."

"We have flown our Thuranin dropships in the atmosphere of gas giant planets, to obtain fuel for the ship. Is it possible to use a dropship underwater? The turbines will not work in water, but could we use the engines in rocket mode?"

"No, sorry, I already considered that possibility. It is true we sent dropships deep into a gas giant, but the pressure in the atmosphere there does not compare to the pressure at the bottom of that lake. The dropships were extensively modified and tested to survive flying in a thick atmosphere; we do not have time for any modifications, which I believe would not work anyway. Colonel Chang, I hate to say this, but if Joe is going to get out of that Dragon, he needs to do it by himself."

"If anyone can think up a creative idea, it is Bishop."

"I hope you are right about that," Skippy grumbled. "Because I have been very disappointed in him so far today."

Chapter Eighteen

I watched the water level in the cockpit intently. It was rising so slowly I almost couldn't see it. "Good news, Joe," Skippy's voice broke my reverie.

"What's that?" I didn't get my own hopes up.

"Major Smythe's team has rescued the three pilots."

"Good! Excellent," I said happily. "That is good news." With a glance at my oxygen meter, I pulled myself upright in the pilot seat. "Connect me to Major Smythe."

"You plan to order him to pull back and not risk his people, because there is no way for you to get out of there?"

"Uh, yeah, why?"

"Major Smythe has already given that order. He is advising Lt. Colonel Chang right now."

"Oh. Smythe is a wise commander."

"I explained the facts to him, and he made the logical conclusion."

"That's good."

"Your people on the surface are *not* happy about this, Joe."

"I am less than pleased also, Skippy."

"Oh. Good point. That was thoughtless of me. Joe, I am terribly sorry about the whole worm thing. If I hadn't recklessly examined that dead AI canister, you wouldn't be in this mess. I keep thinking that maybe, if I had my full magical Skippy capabilities, I would have the brain power to see a way to get you out of there. As it is, I am almost burning out my processors attempting-"

"Genius!" I exclaimed, then proved I am no genius by trying to slap my forehead and smacking my gloved hand into the faceplate of my helmet. "Skippy, you are a freakin' genius!"

"Uh, hmm. Is your oxygen level that low already? You're not making sense, Joe."

"Burn. You said *burn*, Skippy."

"Uh huh. That is a word, Joe. It comes to modern English from multiple sources; for example Old Norse has the word-"

"Great, Skippy, you can nerd out about that later, Ok? I'm going to be busy."

"Um, doing what, Joe? Increased activity will deplete your oxygen more quickly."

"I'm hoping that will not be a problem, Skippy," I unstrapped from the pilot seat, preparing myself for ducking into the bone-chilling water. Before I could change my mind, I knelt on the floor of the cockpit and began working on fasteners under the pilot seat.

"Joe, what in the *hell* are you doing down there? Come on, I am dying of curiosity."

"Burning of curiosity, Skippy. *Burning*."

"We've covered that subject, Joe."

"Not completely. Tell me," I said as my head went under the dark water to see under the bulky chair. "The cockpit seats in a Dragon eject out the bottom of the ship, right?"

"Yeah, so? You learned that the first day of flight training."

"Uh huh, I did," I grunted from the strain of turning a lever to expose a deck plate below the seat. "And that surprised me. Do you know why?"

"Um. Hmm. Because the seats in the main cabin do not also eject?" Skippy guessed.

"No. It surprised me because when I looked at the belly of a Dragon, there are no doors for the cockpit seats to drop down through."

"Once again, you have lost me, Joe."

"There are no doors, ah, damn it! Bashed my thumb again. That hurts like son of a- Anyway, there are no doors in the belly of the cockpit. When the ejection mechanism is engaged, what happens?"

"Joe, I downloaded the flight manual, so if you are attempting to stump me with questions-"

"No stumping, Skippy. Answer the question."

"When either pilot, or the automated flight control system, activates the- Huh!" Skippy mimicked taking in a sharp breath. "That *is* brilliant, Joe! Before the seats are pushed downward, a section of nanocord burns a rectangular hole through the structure beneath each seat. You plan to extract the nanocord and use it to burn through the cockpit door?"

"Bingo, Skippy!"

"Ugh. That is a pretty freakin' good monkey-brained idea. If you had that idea before, I wouldn't have had to drain the damn lake, Joe. Your timing *sucks*!"

"Speaking of timing," I checked my oxygen supply, then removed the last deck plate to expose the nanocord. It was a thin silvery tube, about the diameter of a pencil. Fortunately for me, I knew how to disarm it, and it was comprised of multiple sections, each about six inches long. "How do I do this?"

"Oh, sure, *now* you need my help."

"I always need your help, Skippy. Except with my love life," I added quickly. "Please help me, Oh Great and Wise One."

"Hmmf. Ok, guess I owe you one. Here's what you do-"

Under Skippy's direction, I extracted all the nanocord I could reach. One six-inch section I curled over twice into a circle and set it at the bottom of the cockpit door, holding it in place with sealant that was intended to close holes in the hull. The sealant was strong, and held the nanocord in place. I used more nanocord to make a bigger circle on the door, large enough for me to fit through. Then I strapped myself securely into the copilot seat, since I had partly unfastened the pilot seat from the deck. My brilliant plan would have been worthless without Skippy, because I had no way to activate the microscopic machines in the nanocord. Using my zPhone as a makeshift communications channel, Skippy took control of the nanocord. "Hmm. This is going to be tricky. I've never done this before. No one has ever done this before. It is going to-"

"I'm running low on oxygen, Skippy, so I'd appreciate you moving things along, Ok?"

"My point, Joe, is that I am not a thousand percent certain the command I transmit will not activate all the nanocord, not just the small circle stuck to the door."

"That's not good. How can you be a thousand percent certain?"

"Truth? The only way to know for sure it to try it. Hold my beer, Joe."

Before I could protest, there was a bright circle of light at the bottom of the cockpit door, and fortunately only from that location; the rest of the nanocord in the big circle remained inert. When Skippy activated the nanocord, the tiny machines went to work, turning into a sort of plasma and burning a hole in the cockpit door. The hole it made was only about an inch across, and- Yes, I did that math in my head all by myself, smartass. A six inch length of nanocord, doubled over and wrapped in a circle gives a circumference of about three inches, so the diameter of the hole is one inch because pi is 3.14. The way I remember it is Two Pie Are, where 'R' is the radius of the circle. You make a joke of it, like 'Two Pie Are delicious, but three are better'. When I told my father the formula for the area of a circle is 'Pie Are Squared' he told me that school wasn't teaching me nothing useful, because everyone knows pie are round, *cornbread* are square.

Anyway, that's how I remember what little math I have retained in my head. When the nanocord made a one inch hole in the door, high-pressure water came in like a jet, and the cockpit was instantly filled with blinding mist. What air remained was squeezed into a small volume at the ceiling of the cockpit and heated up rapidly as it was compressed. One amazing property of water is that it can't be compressed much, so it stayed icy cold. My helmet got warm and the rest of me was getting cold fast. Most of my flightsuit went rigid to protect me from being crushed, a feature flightsuits normally used during ejections. Most of the time, flightsuits were trying to keep pressure in, not out. Despite the best effort of the suit, my ears ached from the pressure change, and I leaned my head back and yawned to relieve the pressure on my ears. It worked only part way; when Skippy talked to me, his voice sounded muffled. "Pressure in the cockpit is equalized, Joe. Are you ready?"

At least I thought that is what he said. All I really understood was 'ready' so I guessed the rest. "I'm ready!" I shouted and even my own voice was muffled, like when you have a bad cold and your head is congested. Skippy said something I couldn't quite hear, followed immediately by a light bright enough for my helmet visor to darken automatically. The rest of the nanocord was burning a big hole in the door. As soon as the light flickered out, I didn't wait for an invitation, I unbuckled the safety straps and floated out of the chair. With the flightsuit having gone rigid to protect me from being crushed, it was difficult to move, only the joint areas had any flexibility. Fortunately, all I needed was my shoulders and elbows to move, I let my legs stretch out behind me. That was not easy, because with the bone-chilling cold I wanted to curl into a ball.

The edges of the big hole in the door were already cool from the mass of freezing water by the time I got there. Maybe the plasma had heated the water slightly, or maybe it was my imagination, or maybe I was warming up from the exertion of moving. Thinking about exertion, I checked the meter on my oxygen supply. It was not good, I needed to be careful about breathing too heavily. It would suck to run out of oxygen and die while I was rising to the surface.

Squeezing through the hole in the cockpit door, I swung my head around, sweeping the cabin with my helmet lights. What I saw was a mess. Seats and all kinds of equipment had broken loose and were floating around. Wires and cables snaked through the space, creating a severe hazard for me getting tangled up and trapped again. What was worse was the side door. It was blocked most of the way by a rock and mud. Crap. Digging my way out of that heavy mud would use up too much time and oxygen.

"What's the holdup, Joe? You need to get moving, dumdum."

"Side door is blocked by whatever the Dragon is wedged up against."

"What? You've got to be kidding me! This is total bullshit!" He roared in frustration.

"I agree, Skippy," I forced myself to remain calm. Think, Joe, think, I told myself. And think fast; oxygen is running critically low. The back ramp? No way, the ramp was almost certain to be jammed. Or torn apart. Torn. The hull of the Dragon was twisted and ripped. Was there a hole in the cabin I could squeeze through? There was too much junk floating around blocking my view, I needed to get into the cabin. Randomly moving around in all that tangled debris was not appealing; the last thing I needed was to get snagged and trapped by some stupid cable. I had a knife in an ankle holster; the problem was that knife couldn't slice through tough cables, and my gloves were too rigid for me to grasp anything with confidence. The only good move was for me to be careful and plan my moves two steps ahead. Wherever I went, I needed an escape route in case I couldn't find a crack in the hull there. The cabin of the Dragon had too many corners with lockers and protruding equipment where I could become trapped too easily. "Skippy, do not tell Major Smythe I am out of here, until I am actually on my way up to the surface."

"Uh, Ok, Joe. Major Smythe has been rather busy. At the moment, his team has pulled back to the LZ and have set up a defensive perimeter."

"Perimeter? What the hell is going on up there?"

"The Thuranin attacked, with combots. How about you concentrate on something you can handle, and let the professionals on the surface do their jobs?"

Crap. I knew Skippy was right about that, and it renewed my determination to escape from the Dragon. Just then, something moving in the darkness caught the corner of my eye. It was a crack in the hull! A big one! The skin of the hull was shredded and peeled away between two structural frames. There were flaps of hull material flapping around in the current, some with jagged edges that might cut my flightsuit. A flightsuit is not a real spacesuit and it is not armored; it is for temporary survival and it can be damaged. "I think I found a way out, Skippy."

"It's about freakin' time, Joe. You're giving me a heart attack up here. Move faster."

"Moving fast is a bad idea right now, Skippy," I replied as I pulled aside flaps of the outer hull. The material was stiff and it took a lot of effort for me to bend it aside. Once it was bent, it stayed there. It took me almost five precious minutes to move aside enough outer hull to make a hole I could squeeze through without snagging or tearing my suit. Oddly, as I concentrated on carefully making the hole larger, I kept imagining movement at the corner of my eyes, but when I looked, nothing was out there.

And then something was. "Holy shit!" I forgot all about moving slowly and carefully, and jerked myself backwards deeper into the Dragon's cabin. A loose cable nearly wrapped itself around my neck before I pulled it away from me. "Hey, uh, Skippy, is there, are there any dangerous animals in this lake?" What I had seen had a lot of shiny teeth, and based on the head, it was at least as big as me.

"Like I would know, Joe," Skippy relied in his most sarcastic tone. "Let me consult Wikipedia to learn about the native life in that lake. No, darn it, no Wiki entry yet. Come on, Joe, how the hell would I know about some stupid fish in that lake? Why does it matter? Pop smoke and get out of there, stop fooling around."

"There is something down here with big freakin' teeth, Skippy."

"Oh for- You are afraid of a *fish*, Joe?" He laughed. "Ooooh, save me from the big bad fishy! I am sooooo scared."

"A big fish, with big teeth," I insisted.

"Fine," he huffed disgustedly. "Pull a couple flares out of a locker and use those to scare the nasty fishies away."

"Oh," I was ashamed not to have thought of that. There was a locker right behind me. Moving carefully, I opened the locker, the door was warped so I had to force it, I reached in and pulled out two packs of four flares each. Then I went back to the opening I had made in the hull, ignited a flare, and tossed it through. All I saw was a glint of something moving fast, maybe it was the flick of a tail; all I cared was that it was moving away from me.

And then, after a heart-stopping moment when my right boot caught on a jagged piece of hull, I was out. "I'm out, Skippy!" Reaching for the right side of my flightsuit's waistband, I pulled a little orange tab we called the 'carrot' because of the color. It inflated the life vest that wrapped around my shoulders. Pulling the carrot out only one notch limited the inflation, as I didn't want to fully inflate it and rocket to the surface. "And now I'm going up. Wish me luck."

ZERO HOUR

As I rose in the darkness, seeing glints of light at the limit of my vision that became more frequent. Whatever it was, there was more than one of them, and they were circling me. And getting closer.

"Major Smythe," Chang called, "Colonel Bishop has freed himself from the Dragon and is rising toward the surface. His oxygen supply is in question and there may be a problem with some type of large fish, Skippy was not clear on the risk there. We may need air assets to retrieve Bishop once he is on the surface. Dust off and orbit to the north, wait for further instructions."

"Acknowledged," Smythe replied. Then to himself he breathed "Oh thank God."

"Major?" Captain Chandra asked with concern.

"Bishop is on the move, toward the surface. We're dusting off to assist retrieval."

"That is good news!" Chandra clapped his hands. "Is there anything we can do right now?"

Smythe made a twirling gesture with an index finger for his team to leave their defensive positions and board the dropships. "Right now? I think all we can do is pray."

Following Skippy's instructions meant I was not rising through the black water as quickly as I liked. Once I got out of the sunken Dragon, I wanted to zoom to the surface as fast as possible, especially after I saw vague glimpses of large fish near me. Twice, something shiny with big teeth had decided to stop circling me and race in to bite or at least investigate. The first one I saw only out of the corner of one eye and I barely had enough time to ignite a flare and wave it frantically at the large predator before it veered away. That time I got a good look at it, the best Earth equivalent was a tuna, because it was skinny side to side instead of being kind of flat on the bottom like a shark. In case you think I am a coward for being afraid of a tuna, you weren't in the water with me. This freshwater Gingerbread tunashark had big shiny sharp teeth that any shark on Earth would find scary, and the tuna was at least five or six meters long. The damned thing clearly intended to bite a chunk out of me until the flare blinded it or scared it away. Those flares were intensely bright; they were designed to be used as emergency signals in space and had to be visible from thousands of kilometers away. The visor of my flightsuit automatically darkened to protect my eyes but the tuna had no such advantage, and I hoped the light had it swimming around blindly crashing into things. Things that were not me. Assuming the tuna lived deep in the lake, their eyes were not used to bright light so they might take a while to recover their vision.

Either that first tunashark's eyes adjusted quickly, or they used senses like smell to locate their prey or another tuna decided to try its luck, because the flare had just sputtered out when my visor's enhanced vision warned me about another threat approaching. That time, I had a second flare ready and I popped the cap to ignite it. Through my automatically darkened visor, I saw the tuna veer off when it was maybe a dozen or ten meters away, uncomfortably close. As it spun around, it flicked its powerful tail and the rush of water slammed into me, flinging my arms and legs around and making me drop the flare. The bright flare fell away from me, spinning as it descended into the depths.

That was the last of the first pack of four flares. While I was still tumbling through the water, I used both hands to dig the second pack of four flares out of a thigh pocket, gripping the pack like my life depended on it. Because it did.

Apparently, an active flare was adequate protection against tunasharks even though it was dropping away below me. There was not another fish rushing at me until the sinking flare was far enough beneath me to dim more than halfway. By that time, I had another flare firmly gripped in both hands, with the remaining three tucked securely away in a breast pocket for quick access. With only four flares left and the hazy light of the surface still too far away, I didn't ignite a flare when the tunashark appeared at the edge of my vision. This predator fish wasn't swimming at me yet, it was circling me slowly. Only when it twisted its body to rocket toward me did I ignite the flare. My activating the flare was rewarded by the tuna turning abruptly away and disappearing into the underwater gloom. Visibility in the lake sucked; draining away a good portion of the water had stirred up silt and air bubbles so that without the enhancements of my helmet's visor I might not have seen a tunashark until its powerful jaws crunched me to bits.

"Skippy, why are these fish so eager to attack me?"

"It is possible they are attracted to the electromagnetic field your flightsuit generates."

"Oh! Oh, that is just freakin' great! The flightsuit kept me breathing and from being crushed by water pressure, but now I'm going to be eaten by a Goddamn *fish*?"

"That is a danger, but your oxygen supply may be more a hazard to you. Joe, you are breathing too rapidly. You must calm down, or you will run out of oxygen before you reach the surface."

"Calm down?" As I said that, I barely saw the silvery-gray shape of a tunashark swimming through the gloom left to right in front of me. "You try it first! Come down here and see how calm you are when giant fish are trying to make you their dinner."

"Joe, while I appreciate your dilemma, your emotional response does not alter the facts. Your oxygen supply is almost depleted. Shouting at me is only making the situation worse."

Crap. He was right and I knew it. Against every animal instinct, I forced myself to calm down, going almost limp except for the two hands gripping the burning flare. The red light flashing in the upper left corner of my visor was alerting me to the dire state of my oxygen supply. I didn't need a status indicator, I could feel the air supply growing thin as the mask's tube drew the last dregs of pressurized oxygen from the tiny emergency bottle.

"That is good, Joe. Do not reply, you need to save your breath. Literally. Heh, heh, that was funny. I have adjusted your suit's heating controls to send pulses through the heating elements; those pulses are acting to cancel the suit's natural magnetic field. Not cancel it completely, but my hope is the altered magnetic signature will deter predators, or at least make you less tasty to the fish. There is another piece of good news: I have analyzed images of these tunasharks from your visor. In my opinion, these are deepwater predators, and will stop their pursuit of you as you near the surface. While that is a guess, it is a Skippy guess, so you can be very confident in my analysis. If you do get eaten by a tunashark at the surface, you can take comfort that I will be *horribly* embarrassed."

My forced relaxation slipped a bit as my jaw clenched. But I did not reply. By that time, in addition to Skippy's voice in my ears, I was listening to increasingly strident warnings from the flightsuit's alarm, notifying me that there was less than ten seconds of oxygen remaining. I tilted my head back to judge how close I was to the surface. The water above me was still depressingly dark. "Must ascend faster. Oxygen gone."

"Huh? Oh, it is. Ah, what the hell, you're close enough anyway."

Without me doing anything, the torso of the flightsuit expanded and I felt the lifevest around my shoulders inflate. Unfortunately for me, the inflation gas was helium rather than oxygen, but I felt myself being jerked upward as I gasped to suck in the last molecules of O2 from the bottle.

And then, as my eyes were bulging and blood roared in my ears, I popped to the surface! It was a chaotic hell. Waves slammed me around, tossing me head over heels. Just as I managed to get my head above the water and reached up with one arm to pop the seal on my helmet faceplate, a wave broke right on top of me, pounding me under the surface and flinging my legs up in the air. Knowing opportunities to breathe would be fleeting, I got the faceplate unlatched with one hand, and almost swallowed a mouthful of water. The churning waves dropped me into a trough and I sucked in as much air as I could before a wave smacked me in the face.

For a time I couldn't track, I did nothing but focus on floating and breathing when I could. While my head was underwater, I blew out, and quickly inhaled when the capricious waves tossed me briefly upward. Skippy's draining the lake had caused violent waves that had no pattern; they weren't like the ocean where waves could be tremendously powerful but at least all went in the same direction. The part of the lake I was in had waves coming from all directions, crashing into each other, building on one another and then dropping the bottom out from under me. There was so much water spray in the air I choked every time I breathed in. I had heard of water spray saturating the air creating problems for Coast Guard rescue swimmers, who had to breathe under the furious downdraft of a helicopter. There was no helicopter or dropship above me, my problem was caused only by the top layer of lake water violently sloshing back and forth. Skippy was shouting something in my ear; I couldn't understand him with my helmet part filled with water, and I didn't have the time or strength to reply. I did notice my lifevest had fully deployed without me doing anything, and that did help keep my head above the water.

"Joe!" An ear-bursting sound blasted around my helmet. "Close! Faceplate!"

That I understood. With my emergency oxygen bottle depleted, closing the faceplate would cut off my air supply, but I didn't argue. During a moment between waves battering my face, I slapped the faceplate closed. "Got it," I whispered weakly.

"Pumping water," Skippy answered tersely. There was a high-pitched whirring noise and the water level inside the helmet began draining away, making a shlorping suction sound.

And then I was able to breathe, even when my head was under the water. "Thanks," was all I could say.

"Joe, if you are going to fly, you need more regular stick time. You completely forget emergency procedures."

He was right. I had completely forgotten about the air-purifying feature of the Kristang helmets. The helmets we used with our Kristang flightsuits were basically the same as the helmets of powered armor spacesuits, except the helmets for pilots had less armor protection and didn't include targeting sensors for personal weapons. Both types of helmets were capable of filtering and concentrating oxygen from contaminated atmospheres, to reduce the need for a person to rely on internal stores of oxygen. That feature couldn't act like gills and extract oxygen from water so it wouldn't have helped me until I got to the surface. But now that I was no longer under deep water, the helmet could pull oxygen from the water-saturated air. Even while I was still being bounced around by waves and the helmet's intakes could only get intermittent access to air, I was able to breathe a steady supply.

Getting all the oxygen I needed made a huge difference; I was able to think and plan ahead. The wave action had no pattern to it, so I could use it to determine which way was the closest shore. "Skippy, can you point me toward land?"

"The closest land to you is the eastern shore of the lake; you do not want to swim in that direction. Here," a yellow arrow popped up inside my faceplate, "is the direction you should swim."

"Great, thanks." That arrow bounced around a lot as I clumsily struggled through the water, I was only able to make slow progress in the correct direction. It seemed like an endless time, but probably only ten or fifteen minutes, that I splashed my way through the water. At the foaming crest of a wave, I caught a glimpse of the new shore of the lake, which had been deep underwater until Skippy's Rotorooter Service arrived to unclog the drain. What I saw was not encouraging; it was a whole lot of mud and something like dark-green kelp, dotted with rocks here and there. There was a cliff looming over me so I swam away from that; the waves were crashing there and would have crushed me against the face of the cliff. The relatively flat area I aimed for was almost as bad for me; I tried to time when I reached the new beach but the waves had a different agenda. One wave picked me up and broke as I tried frantically to swim back away from the beach, I got slammed down into mud, then the wave was retreating and dragged me back out into the lake with it. Three times I attempted to get out of the water and my final success was due to luck rather than skill or athletic ability. When I found myself face-down in a mudflat, I crawled on my belly to get away from the wave that was tugging my legs backward.

Being out of the water was almost worse than being in the water. No, it was absolutely worse. What used to be the bottom of the lake was now clinging, sticky, slippery mud like quicksand. As soon as I got away from the last wave, I wanted to turn around and get back in the water. By the time my slow brain made that decision, it was too late, I was sinking fast into the mud. An attempt to crawl on hands and knees only made me flip over and sink halfway into the mud; I nearly drowned in mud. Getting back on my belly helped a bit, and I swam awkwardly on my belly to a flattened bed of a sort of kelp that had been growing on the lake bottom. There were eel-like things either dead or flopping around on and under the kelp. Clawing at the kelp, I was able to pull myself on top of it for a momentary respite. No sooner had I stopped for a breather when three things happened. The already-rotting kelp began pulling apart under my weight. I realized the air inside the helmet was getting stale. And two rifle rounds splattered the mud to my left.

"Joe! The Thuranin are shooting at you!"

"Ya think?"

"Standard infantry carbines only now, they do not appear to have another sniper rifle. Yet. Also, the air intake on the back of your helmet is completely clogged with mud and I can't fix it. You need to open your faceplate."

I followed instructions without comment, swinging the faceplate fully open. Ugh, the smell of rotting kelp, fish and eels was awful. Another rifle round sent up a fountain of mud to my right, farther away. The Thuranin were either at the maximum effective range of their carbines, or they were very out of practice with marksmanship. To my right was a wave-formed ridge of mud around two meters high, I pulled myself over the kelp, sinking into it, until I was to the west of the mud ridge. From there I dared not move any farther, fearing the soft strands of kelp beneath me would give way and trap me in the mud below. "Skippy, I can't move. I can move, but I'm not walking out here by myself. This mud is too soft and too sticky. If I slip off this bed of kelp, I'll sink in that mud like quicksand."

"Oh, crap. All right, fine. Help is on the way. We are sending a Kristang armored suit down to you. I figured you would need the enhanced speed and power of a mech suit if the Thuranin were shooting at you."

"How are you getting a suit down here to me?"

"We're dropping it from high altitude, there is a dropship safely beyond missile range above you now. I think it's beyond missile range."

"You're joking, right? What is your plan, push an empty armored suit out the back ramp of a Falcon, let it splat down here, and I'm supposed to pick up the pieces?"

"Of course not, dumdum," Skippy sounded exasperated. "The suit will be attached to a paraglider that will bring it over you then flare out into a chute to lower it. I'll use the jets in the boots to set it down softly, right close to you. Cool, huh?"

"Uncool, Skippy. That suit weighs more than I do. You drop one here and it will sink into the mud and be buried."

"No it won- Well, shit. Let me check- Damn. Yes," he sighed. "The monkey is right about that. Crap!"

"Forget the mech suit, Skippy. What is your Plan B?"

"The mech suit was my Plan B, you idiot! Plan A was for you to walk out of there. I never thought you would let a squishy little puddle of mud stop you."

"It's not a *little* mud, Skippy. It's a freakin' ocean of quicksand."

"Yeah, well, I am still very disappointed in you and your entire species right now, Joe. When your ancestors crawled out of the mud onto land millions of years ago, they were *sooooo* pleased with themselves, but that decision doesn't look so good now, does it?"

"I can't argue with that logic, Skippy. But, mud has defeated many military campaigns on Earth, no matter what technology the armies had. You got a Plan C in your awesome mind?"

"Give me a moment to think! Jeez Louise you are impatient."

Just then, the rotting mat of kelp beneath me gave way a bit, and a thin fountain of watery mud shot up like a jet. I felt my left boot sink into mud.

To make the situation even better, a rifle round smacked into the mud puddle to my right, having gone right through the ridge of mud I was hiding behind.

"Take all the Skippy time you want, but I need a solution in about ten seconds of meatsack time."

"Fine," he huffed. "Ok, ha! I got it, smartass. Help will be on its way very shortly, I am walking the pilots through the instructions now."

"We are not risking a dropship overflying the lake to rescue me, Skippy."

"Never fear, Joe, no dropships will be harmed in the production of this truly awesomely cool stunt."

"Crap. This is your idea, and even you think it is a 'stunt'? What is this awesomely cool plan?"

"Well, Joe, heh heh, you are not going to like this."

Chapter Nineteen

Skippy expertly guided the package down to splat half on the kelp mat and half in a mud puddle to my left.

"What is this, Skippy?"

"Balloons, Joe. They will lift you out of there."

"Balloons? Uh, you also included a parachute, right?"

"No, dumdum, a parachute would add too much weight."

"I need a parachute in case the Thuranin shoot down the balloons and I need to go skydiving, Skippy."

"You don't need a parachute to go skydiving, Joe."

"I don't?"

"No. You need a parachute to go skydiving more than *once*," he laughed. "Anyway, get moving."

I had to swim on top of the mud, floating as best I could with the flightsuit inflated to its maximum. With the torso, arms and legs puffed out, I looked like the Michelin Man. That was better than being Barney, I guess, and the extra surface area spread my weight out to keep me from sinking faster. As I moved in an awkward frog-like swimming motion, the kelp mat shifted and began breaking up, pulling me down into the sticky mud.

"How's it going, Joe?" Skippy asked cheerily.

I knew he was dying for me to praise the clever way he delivered the package to me, and I had to give him props because it had accurately landed near me after being ejected from a Falcon at over forty thousand meters altitude. "Your part of the plan was perfectly awesome as expected, Skippy. I am not doing so well."

"Why not?" He demanded.

"Let's just say my prospects are sinking at the moment." I moved my arms more vigorously as my boots began sinking into the mud quicker. Kicking my legs only made it worse, as it created pockets in the mud that got filled in with watery mud. Using only my arms, I swam as smoothly as possible toward the package until I touched it with my fingertips. Holding my legs rigid so they didn't move at all, I pulled the package toward me. It was enveloped in an inflated life vest that the air crew must have wrapped in what looked a lot like duct tape. "Skippy, is this thing wrapped in duct tape? That does not boost my confidence."

"It's not duct ta- Ok, it *is* basically high-tech duct tape. The crew had to use whatever they could find, and there wasn't a lot of time, because some whiny A-hole on the ground named Joe was bitching at them to hurry up."

Crap. My knife was in a holster at my right ankle. That did not reflect good planning by me. I grunted.

"What's wrong now, Joe?"

"I need a knife to cut open this duct tape, Skippy, and my knife is at my boot under the mud." Pulling my right foot up made that knee sink deeper in the clinging mud.

"Oh, for- Joe, you truly are a dumb monkey. I swear, your ancestors were the ones who were too stupid to climb a tree when they saw a leopard. It is amazing they survived to create you."

"I am feeling pretty darn stupid now, Skippy." My fingers finally touched the knife, and I quickly pulled it out. By then, my right thigh was completely encased by thick mud, and my hip was sinking. "Cutting it open now. Got it!" I reported, and the lifevest unfolded, exposing the package inside. I stopped caring about not sinking deeper into the mud because it was happening anyway, so I focused on getting the package open. First, I took out the harness and strapped myself in. It took some awkward gymnastics to get the lower part of the harness around my legs and crotch, and by the time I was done, I was completely up to my waist in mud. Flinging my arms out didn't slow the mud pulling me down; the kelp I had been laying on was broken apart and mixed into the mud. "Whatever you're gonna do, do it now!" I shouted as the mud sucked at me and I was suddenly submerged to my armpits.

The package exploded upward with a soft puff, and three nearly invisible balloons began inflating. Skippy triggered the balloons in sequence to avoid them becoming tangled with each other; two of the lines still got wrapped together but that didn't matter. "You are sure this is going to work?" I asked anxiously as the mud reached the chin of my helmet.

"No. *Duh*. How the hell can I be sure; this has never been done before. These balloons are designed to hold only the tether line aloft, so it can be engaged by a dropship and pull a soldier off the ground. Like how the SpecOps teams got off those rooftops on Kobamik. Or how they were supposed to get off the rooftops, until some beer can jumped the gun and screwed up the whole mission. Anywho, this should work fine, in theory. These tether balloons are capable of operating in thin atmospheres; they can inflate much more than the setting we used on Kobamik. Three of them, fully inflated, should be able to lift you off the surface. Except, hmm. It's not working. You should be flying through the air like Superman by now. I do not understand."

"It's the mud, Skippy. I'm stuck in it." It was hard to talk with my neck tilted all the way back, lifting the bottom opening of the faceplate just above the mud. As I spoke, a thin trickle of mud poured into the helmet.

"Oh. Crap, I should have thought of that. Move your arms and legs to create space in the mud, while I deflate the lifevest?"

"Deflate?" I asked in panic, but I should have trusted the awesomeness. Flailing my limbs and suddenly deflating the lifevest created short-lived pockets in the mud. The pockets quickly filled in, not quick enough as I was jerked upward. There was a sucking sound then a POP as my legs broke free.

And then I was soaring through the air!

"The Thuranin are shooting at you, Joe. Their aim *sucks*. You are in no danger from those morons, that's for sure."

"I should relax and enjoy the ride?" I asked with a gulp as the stiff breeze caught me and I was pulled to the right, then left. The tethers had stabilizers along their lengths, but with three of them tangled together, their stabilizers were useless. It was going to be a rough ride, I reminded myself that the only thing that mattered was I was rising up away from the mud that had almost drowned me.

And that the prevailing wind was carrying me to the southwest, away from the Thuranin.

And that the Thuranin couldn't shoot worth shit.

Ok, that's three things that mattered.

"*Up, up and away in my beautiful, my beautiful balloooooon,*" Skippy warbled out of tune. "*For we can fly, we can fly-*"

Swinging wildly back and forth in the gusty breeze below the balloons, I was getting nauseous. "I do not feel like I'm flying right now, Skippy. I feel like I'm skidding across the sky out of control."

"You don't like that song? Hmm, in 1937 Led Belly had a song about the *Hindenberg*, I could sing that one instead-"

"No! No singing about exploding blimps!" I shouted while looking up at the flimsy things holding me in the air.

"Hmmf," he sniffed. "The *Hindenburg* did not explode, Joe, that is a myth. The problem was the coating on the exterior-"

"Don't care, Skippy, do not care! No more talk about exploding or burning or anything that involves something going wrong and me spiraling down back into the mud."

"Come on, Joe, you won't fall back into the mud."

"Ah, yeah, thank-"

"You're over the original shoreline now, the danger to you would be getting fatally impaled on a tree."

"You are *such* a comfort to me, Skippy," I choked on the words as a gust of wind jerked me up, then violently down. A thermal caught the balloons, and I zoomed upward so fast it felt like my stomach fell into my boots. The ground fell away below me, and I concentrated on keeping my last meal inside my stomach while the ride smoothed out and the gut-churning swaying back and forth damped down. Eventually, I was able to relax and enjoy the view. In a short time, I was high enough that the visual fuzz of the odd stealth field covering the surface of Gingerbread began to obscure my view in all directions except straight down. Soon, I thought with relief, I would be far enough away from the lake for a Falcon to zip down and retrieve me. Unless there were Thuranin far away from the lake, which was possible although our drones had not detected any evidence of Thuranin or any sentient species beyond several kilometers from that now partly drained body of water. "Skippy, you're sure-" I swallowed hard, suddenly struggling for breath. Taking a deep breath through my nose, I sniffed to learn if there was some airborne toxin, or if smoke from the battles below was affecting my ability to breathe.

Then I looked down below my feet, where the trees of the forest had blurred into a featureless green fuzz. Pulling off a glove, I looked at my fingernails. They were tinged slightly blue. I was suffering from altitude sickness. No wonder I couldn't breathe. "Skippy, what's my altitude now?"

"You're at about seventy five hundred meters, why?"

"The air up here is thin," I gasped.

"Oh, for- *Duh*! Damn it, that particular 'duh; was directed at myself. I'm sorry, Joe, I forget you biological trashbags need to breathe constantly. It is very annoying. You should take in concentrated metallic oxygen, all it takes is to compress it to about one point two million times the pressure of Earth's atmosphere at the surface. Then you would only need to take in oxygen once a day or so. Really, though, there are several other reactive elements that would be better suited for-"

"Air!" I felt myself fading, my vision narrowing to a small area directly in front of my eyes.

"Huh? Oh, yes, dammit, you keep distracting me. I'm partially deflating one of the balloons now, you will be descending shortly."

The descent wasn't abrupt, more like an elevator. I was on the verge of blacking out before I got down to an altitude low enough to breathe comfortably. Part of the problem at high altitude was, the muscles required to breathe hard required a lot of oxygen, so it became literally a death spiral. Breathe less vigorously to reduce the body's need for oxygen, and you don't take in enough oxygen. It was my fault for not considering my altitude, I had learned to monitor myself for signs of hypoxia during pilot training. Dangling under a group of flimsy balloons had not seemed like flying, so I hadn't connected what I was doing with what I should be doing. Pilots call that poor situational awareness, and in its many forms it kills more pilots than any other hazard.

With Skippy remotely controlling the balloons, alternately inflating and deflating them, he kept me at an altitude where the air was breathable, and I literally hung out in the sky until the lake and the hills around it faded out of view into the hazy fuzz of the stealth field. At that point, I gave permission for a Falcon to drop down to retrieve me. They caught the tether smoothly on the first try, but with multiple tethers wrapped around each other, my ride up into the open rear ramp of the Falcon was rough. Like, super rough; my brain got bounced around in my skull so hard I was totally useless during the procedure.

Finally, I was safely inside the Falcon, being held by two crewman, and the back ramp swung closed.

"How are you, S- ooh." The crewman wrinkled his nose.

"I'm fine." Inside the confines of the dropship, I could smell myself. It was not pleasant. In fact, I almost gagged on the stench. The mud and nasty whatever else clinging to my flightsuit had partly dried while I dangled beneath the balloons, now the smell was concentrated. I had an odor like I'd rolled in cow manure combined with rotting fish. "Yeah," I replied, "sorry about the smell. Ugh, it's pretty bad."

"That smell is just Joe's cologne," Skippy chuckled. "I told him that Chanel Number *Two* was a bad choice, but he didn't listen to me."

Breathing through his mouth to avoid smelling me, the crewman looked me over. As I had no obviously broken bones, he asked "Can I get you anything, Sir?"

"My father used to take Advil and bourbon. He called it Badvil. Got any of that?"

Despite the stench I was making in the confined dropship cabin, that drew a smile from him. "Advil maybe. We do have," he nodded toward a bundle, "a change of clothes. And a washroom."

I took the hint. We tossed my old flightsuit out at fifteen thousand meters. I was sad to see it go, as it had saved my life. But, damn, no way were we ever getting that smell out of the fabric.

Adams greeted me at the bottom of the ramp when my dropship landed, and while she snapped a salute to me, it looked like she'd been crying and I could have sworn she wanted to hug me. Maybe somehow I had fallen into a bizarre parallel universe. "Sergeant," I returned the salute and gave her big, genuine smile, "I hear you gave Skippy a pep talk while I was at the bottom of a lake?"

"It was more of a pep slap, Sir," she responded with a wink.

"I'll pretend I didn't hear that."

I took a quick shower and changed into a fresh uniform, by the time I was ready Smythe's team had landed and they were getting out of their armored suits and stowing their gear. Chotek and Chang were chatting with Smythe; he was giving them a quick overview of the engagement. "Those drones," Smythe gestured to the open back ramp of a dropship, "are a tremendous advantage to us. The Thuranin didn't appear to have any drones of their own, or be able to counter ours, other than random rifle fire."

"You weren't able to leave a drone there to monitor the Thuranin?" I asked. Chang and Chotek had been able to partly follow the ground action through the relayed data link, while I had almost no idea what Smythe's team had done, since I had been stuck at the bottom of a lake.

"Yes, Sir, we left one drone orbiting the area on autopilot, but we don't have access to its data until we send a dropship there." Smythe shook his head. "The bandwidth of the datalink between here and the lake only allows voice communication or brief data bursts. We can't control the drone from here, or receive images."

"Some of our people were in suits," Chotek observed, "but you," he looked at me, "and the other pilots in your Dragon were exposed. The Thuranin saw you, they know we are human."

"Yes, Sir, but these Thuranin have been here a long time; before the wormhole shift that made Earth accessible. They don't know who humans are. All they know is we are unfamiliar aliens."

"Unfamiliar to them," Chotek pressed his point. "They *saw* us. The Guardians are dormant for the moment. If those Thuranin are able to get a signal beyond this star system, that could be disastrous for humanity."

"I don't think that will happen," Skippy entered the conversation. "There are active stealth and fuzz fields around this planet, I don't see any reason to think the stealth field surrounding the entire star system has been deactivated. All I did was request the Guardians to stand down."

"You don't know for a fact the stealth field is still active," Chotek insisted. "You can't know, unless we go outside the system, and we can't do that. Colonel Bishop, how can we be *sure* those Thuranin will not expose our secret?"

"Uh, well," I started to say, then I smiled.

Adams knew what I was thinking. "Oh, come on, Sir, you have to say it."

"It's not really approp-"

"If you don't say it, I will," she stood facing me hands on her hips. "You know you've been waiting for this opportunity."

She was right, no way could I resist. "I say we nuke the site from orbit." I cocked my head toward Chotek. "It's the only way to be sure."

"Nuke?" Chotek sputtered. "You propose to use *nuclear weapons* on Gingerbread?" He was drowned out by laughter from everyone else around us.

The Chinese had seen Aliens. The Indians and French had all seen it. Hans Chotek may be the only member of the Merry Band of Pirates who had not seen that movie.

Seriously, what the hell was wrong with that guy?

When the laughter died down, Chotek was fuming. "Colonel Bishop, regardless of Skippy, the Guardians are not likely to stand by while we detonate nuclear-"

Oh shit. There is nothing worse than a guy who didn't get the joke. "Sir, that was a joke. It's, uh, a line from a movie," I was not going to take the time right then to explain it to him. "It's a soldiers against aliens movie, I thought," as I spoke, it sounded lame. "Sorry, that was a bad time for a joke. Skippy, can a signal get out through the fuzz and stealth fields around this planet?"

"No way, Jose," he declared. Then, because he probably had caught on that Chotek was in no mood for humor, he added "No, Colonel Joe. That is something I can be certain of. Unless the Thuranin have a dropship stashed away somewhere, they'll never get a signal beyond the atmosphere."

"Good," I thought that issue was settled.

Then Skippy opened his big fat mouth. "Of course, they must have had a dropship to get here, right? No way could they have brought weapons and combots in escape pods. Hey," he added happily, "now that I'm thinking about it, *we* are flying dropships around willy nilly, the Guardians aren't stopping anyone from flying. It's unlikely the Thuranin have managed to keep a dropship flightworthy over so many years, but, hmm, they wouldn't need a dropship. Really, they could just build a crude rocket, to get a signal outside this planet's stealth field."

I wanted to choke him. I seriously wanted to wrap my hands around his can and squeeze, even though I knew that wouldn't do anything to that little shithead. Waving my hands to stifle the alarmed murmuring going on around me, I spoke quickly to prevent Chotek from doing something stupid. "Sir, if we can find a conduit to fix Skippy, then we have a chance to get off Gingerbread, and whatever those Thuranin here saw won't matter. They'll be stuck here without any way to communicate with the outside universe. For now, I think we monitor those Thuranin, see if we can find other communities of survivors down here. Possibly survivors from the Rindhalu coalition?" I suggested. "They might be useful to us, rather than hostile." That last remark I added because I knew the thought of finding allies would please Chotek, even if those allies had been trapped on Gingerbread for hundreds or thousands of years and would be entirely useless to help Earth now.

"Other survivors?" Chotek's eyes lit up.

"Yes, Sir. Skippy, those Thuranin, have you figured out when they got here?"

"No, dumdum, I don't have enough data yet. My guess is they are from the last recorded expedition to the Roach Motel, 417 years ago."

"More than four hundred years?" I couldn't contain my shock. "How could they have survived all that time?"

"They couldn't. Not all of them, anyway. The Thuranin have a sort of hibernation ability that can help stretch out their lifespan. And it is possible they have not been on Gingerbread for the past 417 years. Assuming their ship was destroyed, they might have spent centuries drifting through space in deep sleep, before landing here. Without more data, any speculation is useless," he reminded me in an annoyed tone. "Wait for me to collect data."

"Data, right. Sir," I looked at Chotek, who had a faraway look. No doubt he was imagining himself meeting survivors from many civilizations on Gingerbread, negotiating with them and bringing a comprehensive peace treaty back to Earth. I imagined myself sprouting wings and flying around like an angel. My wish was more likely to happen. "We do need more data, we need to continue the survey missions." When Chotek lifted an eyebrow skeptically, I added "The survey flights will all be conducted by two aircraft, in stealth. We will be looking for evidence of conduits, and of survivors. With the surface shrouded in a fuzz field, survey flights are the only way to know what is out there."

That got a nod from my boss. "Very well, Colonel Bishop. I want a ground combat team with each survey flight, in case of difficulties."

"Yes, Sir," I assured him. "We will have one aircraft low running scans and one flying high cover." That was going to cut in half the number of survey flights we could conduct, and seriously eat into our dwindling fuel supply, but I agreed we could no longer send out single ships.

We needed to find a working conduit, soon.

Skippy called me when I was clearing brush to create a dropship landing zone closer to base camp. "Hey Joe, when we first started flying recon missions, you asked me about the meteor impact craters on Gingerbread."

"Oh, yeah. Sorry about that, Skippy. I knew you are busy, shouldn't have bothered you with trivia."

"No! You got that wrong, Joe, you *should* have bugged me about it. If you had, I might have noticed something important earlier. Ah, actually, if you had bugged me about it, I would have been extra stubborn and refused to do anything. Anyway, I did look into the data and I found something interesting. There are a lot of impact craters, Joe, and some of them are relatively recent."

"Lots of meteors in this star system, huh?"

"No, the opposite. That's what caused me to look deeper into the data. This system has a thin asteroid belt, suspiciously thin. I expect the Elders mined most of the asteroids for raw materials, so an asteroid field could not be the source of an unusually large number of meteors. Next, I turned my attention to the Oort cloud, using data from the *Dutchman*'s sensors. There wasn't a lot of data to work with, but I could see clearly the cloud is thin and stable; there aren't a lot of comets swinging around the inner system here."

"Uh, Ok?" I had no idea where he was going with the conversation.

"Really, it makes sense that there isn't a lot of dangerous space junk floating around this system. Except for broken starships, I mean. Gingerbread was an Elder colony, they would have cleaned up any dangerous space rocks and either sent them into the star, or ejected them from the system. Or used the raw materials for construction."

"They cleaned up the space rocks, so, where did all the meteor impacts come from?"

"Those craters were not caused by meteor impacts, Joe. Remember the craters I found on Barsoom?"

"Oh shit. Again?"

"Worse. What happened here was more destructive, and that isn't the worst thing I found. Barsoom is essentially a dead world, so the craters there have rested almost untouched since they were created. Gingerbread is a living planet, with rain and weather and erosion and plants sinking roots into the soil, and that confused me for a while. Now that I'm focusing on the data, I can see the smaller craters were made by relativistic impactors."

"Tiny rocks moving half the speed of light?" I guessed.

"Something like that, although certainly not crude rocks, and maybe not moving quite that fast. The larger craters, the ones I suspect scooped out entire cities or other substantial facilities, were created by transitioning a sphere-shaped area out of phase into another spacetime. That's kind of overkill in my opinion."

"I thought you said 'overkill is underrated'?"

"That's true when *I'm* doing it, Joe. If the Elders wanted to ensure the tech in their cities did not get touched by grubby aliens, there are more sophisticated, less energy-intensive ways of doing it."

"Maybe someone was showing off?"

"Ah, maybe. What worries me is another possibility: an energy-intensive method was used because someone wanted the cities removed quickly. Or, worse, removed in a hostile manner."

"Crap. Oh, man," I gasped at the implication. "That's not good. You think those big craters weren't the Elders picking up stuff before they left, you think those cities were destroyed in an attack?"

"I do. My analysis shows the large craters are roughly the same age as the craters on Barsoom; about one hundred million years."

"Whoa." What was humanity doing a hundred million years ago? Oh that's right, nothing. That was, um, wait, I know this one because dinosaurs are cool. A hundred million years ago was during the Cretaceous Period that ended with the extinction of the dinosaurs. My memory is vague, but I think the Cretaceous was when birds and flowering plants first evolved and- Ok, I kind of got off the subject there. "Some bad shit happened on Gingerbread back then."

"Not just back then, Joe. That's the worst part. The big craters are all old, and of the same age. Some of the smaller impact craters date back to that same time, but I found a couple as recent as six thousand years ago. It looks like something, or someone, has been regularly bombarding the surface of Gingerbread over the last few million years."

"Regularly? On Earth, we have meteor showers the same time every year, when our orbit passes through-"

"Yes, yes," he dismissed my comment irritably. "I should not have said 'regularly', I should have said 'periodically'. There was a big cluster of impacts about a hundred million years ago, then nothing until about the same time Newark was thrown out of orbit. After that there is another gap, then starting about a million years ago, I see impacts scattered randomly across the timeline."

"Artificial impacts? Someone cleaning up Elder sites they missed the first time, by blowing them up from orbit?"

"I do not think that is likely, Joe. The first set of impacts, a hundred million years ago, could have been for the purpose of destroying leftover Elder sites. But the cluster of impacts around the time disaster struck Newark must be something different. And then there are smaller impacts widely scattered in time. For example, there is a cluster of craters seven hundred kilometers to the south of here, that I have dated approximately two hundred thousand years ago." He showed me a graphic with the timeline of impacts. There was no pattern to them. "At this point," he continued, "I do not have any clue what the data is telling me. I do have a nagging feeling this is important, that I am not simply digging into useless ancient history trivia. I will continue to analyze the data, and see if I can puzzle out what it means."

Right then, all I cared about was that someone wasn't going to drop a relativistic impactor on my own head, but I didn't say that to Skippy.

Later, I realized I should have told him. Damn, the one time I keep my big mouth shut is the time I should have spoken up.

"Joe Joe Joe Joe!" Skippy's voice startled me awake. The sound was coming from the zPhone earpiece under my pillow, or the rolled-up sweater I was using as a pillow on my cot.

"What?" I held the earpiece to my ear and glanced at my zPhone. Damn it! He woke me up at 0413. Gingerbread's day was twenty six and a half Earth hours, so I was hoping for an extra hour of sleep before I was scheduled to fly as copilot on a recon mission. "This couldn't have waited?" I whispered to avoid disturbing people around me in the shelter. No such luck; the people were all combat veterans and they became instantly awake when they heard the distressed tone of my voice. I waved that everything was all right, and heads dropped back down. Along with waking quickly, elite soldiers had developed the ability to fall back asleep just as quickly.

"It could have waited, sure, but your bladder was going to wake you up in like ten minutes anyway. You shouldn't have drunk a whole canteen full of water before going to sleep."

Damn it, now that I was sitting up, I knew he was right. "Give me a minute."

After visiting the latrine, I wandered away from base camp after texting the two guards on duty what I was doing. There was a flat rock overlooking a stream, I sat on the rock and listened to the water splashing along. With a bare zephyr of an early morning breeze rustling the leaves unseen in the darkness above me, I could easily imagine myself on Earth. It even smelled the same; damp soil, the fresh scent of moving water, and something very much like pine needles. "Ok, I'm reasonably awake. What is it?"

"You sure you don't want to grab a cup of coffee first? Captain Giraud made a fresh pot less than an hour ago."

"No coffee." I was hoping to crawl back in my cot soon.

"Joe, you get cranky when-"

"You want to see what cranky looks like?"

"Uh, no. Okaaaay, I can tell somebody needs more sleep. Anywho, I found something interesting in the survey flight sensor data. Two interesting things, actually."

"Interesting like, dangerous? Because if not, I'm going to get some more rack time." Crap, I was supposed to run with the Chinese team at 0630.

"I think I found a conduit."

Hearing that made me sit up straight. "Where?"

"Before we get into that, let me tell you what else I found. I think I know why there are impact craters almost randomly over the past million years. There isn't any pattern to them, but then I realized the dates match up with dates in another data set."

"Like?"

"I was hoping you would try to guess," he sounded disappointed. "Then I would have the joy of mocking you unmercifully."

"Not without coffee, Skippy."

"Ugh, fine. Look at your phone. The first chart shows the timeline of impacts. The *second* chart I am now overlaying shows the known expeditions to the Roach Motel."

"Holy shit," I gasped. Most of the dots representing times when ships were sent on one-way trips into the Roach Motel, did not have matching dots on the timeline of impact craters on Gingerbread. But almost all of the impact craters matched up with known times ships were sent in. "The events that don't match up are-"

"Very likely expeditions I do not know about, yes," he finished the thought for me.

"Good, good. Uh, so these impact craters, they can't be from debris when the Guardians destroyed trespassing ships, right?"

"No. The Guardians do not use kinetic weapons."

"Then what caused the craters? Why are there craters sometimes and not others?"

"Do you want to guess?" He asked eagerly.

"Again, not without coffee."

"You are such a party pooper, Joe. Ok, *fine*," he said 'fine' the way women do when things are anything but fine. "I believe the impact craters are from the Guardians wiping out groups of survivors on Gingerbread."

"Crap!" Now I was awake, without needing coffee. "They're not doing that to us?"

"No, Joe, they will not harm us, I am still able to keep them quiet. Although that is growing more difficult by the day."

"Great. Hey, if the Guardians nuke people who manage to land on Gingerbread, then why haven't they hit that pain in the ass group of Thuranin?"

"My theory is the Guardians only react when a group of survivors uses a technology the Guardians views as a potential threat. Like generating power over a certain limit. Or flying above a certain altitude. Or using weapons. That is why those Thuranin were so bad at shooting, Joe, I don't think they had actually fired a weapon since they landed. Somehow they must have figured out they can only use a minimum level of technology, or the Guardians will pound them to dust."

"Whew," I whistled as I looked at the chart on my zPhone. "That's," I counted, "fourteen. Fourteen different impact events over the past million years. Wow. Fourteen groups of survivors managed to land on Gingerbread."

"Sixteen, counting us and the last group of Thuranin, Joe. And that doesn't count groups who landed but could not survive here. If a group of survivors did not have the ability to grow their own food, they would not have lasted long."

"Good point." That reminded me that Chotek had been pressing for recon flights to concentrate on looking for sites to build a permanent settlement, rather than continuing the fruitless task of searching for Skippy's elusive conduit thing. "Back to the conduit. Where is it?"

My zPhone display changed from a chart to a map. "Thirty eight hundred kilometers from here, Joe. Underground, there is a series of natural caverns and more importantly, extensive artificial tunnels. From the type of installation that used to be on the surface, I know there is a conduit under the ground. Or, there was one."

"Used to be?"

"Yes. There used to be a large complex on the surface; based on its configuration I can tell it facilitated linking conduits. There must have been a conduit under the surface, probably several conduits."

"Must have been? Used to be? You don't know?"

"I can't *see* the damned thing, Joe," his frustration was evident. "What I can tell you is that, if there is a conduit on Gingerbread, this is where we'll find it. Or we won't. It's that simple."

"Got it. We're going, then. You will come with us?"

"Absolutely," his cheeriness was back. "The last thing we want is a bunch of monkeys poking around in scary dark places without me."

"Uh huh. Because the last time you went poking around in a scary dark place, it worked out great for everyone."

"Oh, shut up."

"Colonel Bishop?" Called a voice from behind me.

"Captain Giraud?" I asked, surprised.

"Skippy told me you wanted coffee? Sir?" His expression made it clear he did not appreciate being requested to fetch coffee.

"No. Skippy wants me to drink coffee. Oh, crap, Captain, I'm sorry."

"Now that I am here," he said with a Gallic shrug, holding up two mugs of coffee.

"Oh, sure," I patted the rock. "Sit down. How are you?" I knew Giraud and the entire French team had finally been declared ready to return to duty, having fully recovered from radiation poisoning when the *Flying Dutchman* jumped away to ambush a Thuranin starship near our captured relay station.

"I am well," he replied brusquely, not seeking chit chat in the wee small hours of the morning. And he did not want any more inquiries into his health, he had gotten thoroughly tired of people treating him like an invalid. "Did I hear you say Skippy found a conduit?"

Chapter Twenty

Hans Chotek was not thrilled about the idea of us devoting scarce resources to another likely futile search for a magical device to fix Skippy, and he limited me to taking two dropships away from base camp. I protested more out of habit; another dropship or two would not make any difference to whether our search was successful or not. Anyway, we flew to the site, there were ruins extending in a circle for half a kilometer. The ruins had been there a long, long time; long enough to be mostly buried, and it looked like the Elders had stripped away everything useful. Despite Skippy's protests about it being a waste of time, we could not resist poking around those ruins that were still above ground. He was right, it was a waste of time, except I got to touch Elder constructions with my bare hands, without the barrier of spacesuit gloves. Running my fingers along some sort of super hard concrete that used to hold up some sort of device, I felt a connection to the mysterious Elders who had built the place. Skippy ruined my momentary bliss by stating the site had certainly been constructed by bots, that maybe no Elder had ever visited the site, and could we *please* move our asses?

The entrance to the tunnel, where Skippy thought we would, or *might*, find a conduit, had collapsed long ago. It took careful use of explosives, then people using mech suits to clear a hole to the actual tunnel. When it was safe, I walked down to the tunnel and stuck my head in the narrow access hole. We would need to enlarge it. "Whoa," I pulled my head back and switched off my helmet lights to avoid blinding people. "It's like the Dark Ages in there."

"What?" Skippy asked in disbelief.

"The Dark Ages, Skippy. People stumbled around," I pantomimed walking with my hands in front of me, "bumping into stuff because they couldn't see."

"Oh. My. *God*," he gasped. "You are *so* freakin' ignorant. You think the Dark Ages are called that because, what, your sun went to sleep?"

"I'm not a scientist, Skippy, but it was dark for some reason. That's why they were called 'Dark', *duh*."

"Joe, I, I am speechless. I, I have no words."

I winked at Adams, and she exploded with laughter, bringing the rest of us with her. "Don't be so gullible, Skippy," I said when I could talk again.

"Aargh," Skippy made a sound like gnashing his teeth. "Joe, I hate you more than words can say."

"I love you too, Skippy." Turning to Smythe, I advised "We're going to need extra lights, and extra powerpacks for helmets and portable lights. Skippy, is there any way you can activate lights in there?"

"I should not respond because I am mad at you, Joe, but I'll do what I can. There are lights in the tunnels, however they are truly ancient and have not been used in millions of years."

"Yeah, but it's Elder technology, right? It should last forever."

"Joe, even the Elders didn't last forever, remember? They left. Those tunnels were intended for temporary use during construction of the underground facility, so I suspect the Elders did not expend a lot of effort on making the lights in there durable."

He was right, the original tunnel lights were long dead and useless. Our helmet lights and handheld flashlights provided plenty of illumination. Smythe and Giraud went ahead with the scouts. We needed scouts, because Skippy did not have a complete map of the tunnels and we had a lot of false starts and hit many dead ends. In some places the tunnels had partly collapsed, although there were remarkably few of those considering how old the tunnels were; around a hundred million years according to Skippy. He told us not to worry about the places where the tunnels had fallen in; he expected the Elders would have dug multiple access points to whatever chamber the conduit was in. If there was such a chamber. If there ever was a conduit deep under the surface.

I did not like having thousands of gallons of water over my head, no way could I have ever been in the silent service on a submarine. I like even less the idea of having millions of tons of rock over my head. Wearing an armored suit sealed up was claustrophobic enough for me, I was not pleased to think of being in a dark tunnel that could collapse at any moment.

My earpiece buzzed, then the voice of Giraud spoke. "Sir, you should get up here and see this."

With my escorts Sergeant Adams and Lt. Poole, and with Skippy attached to my waist, I jogged forward down the gently sloping tunnel.

The tunnel ended in a large, solid-looking door, but that was not what the team was staring at. Off to the right side, near the tunnel wall, was an object. A vaguely familiar object. A vaguely sinister object.

It was a monolith.

A big, utterly black rectangular slab of some shiny hard substance, set in the floor. "Whoa," I said quietly, while we all looked at each other nervously.

"Da. Da. Da! DA-DA!" Skippy sang tunelessly.

"Not funny, Skippy."

"Come on, Joe," he chuckled. "That's the theme song from "*2001: A Space Odyssey*". I *had* to do that."

"No you didn't. Not now while we're in these spooky tunnels. What the hell is this thing anyway?" The monolith, or whatever it truly was, did not look exactly like the thing in the movie. This one had rounded edges, and now that I examined it closely, its surface was not completely smooth, being covered in a grid of tiny hexagons. It *was* utterly deep black.

"I'll tell you what it is *not*," Skippy scoffed. "It is not an alien device that miraculously grants intelligence to ignorant monkeys. Because that is impossible. Intelligent monkeys, hee hee, that's funny."

"I'm glad we're keeping you amused. Is this thing dangerous?" Breaking military protocol, I stuffed my hands in my pockets, fighting an urge to reach out and touch the thing. Based on my fuzzy memory of seeing that movie on late-night cable, doing that hadn't worked out too well for the astronauts in *2001*.

"No, Joe. It is a field generator, and it is powered down. Has been for a very, very long time. Its purpose is to stabilize the tunnels in case of quakes. So, it is here to protect you, although of course that is not by design."

"Great. I'll take your word about it," I said quietly as I slid past the monolith, keeping to the other side of the tunnel. "Open the door for us, Skippy."

Skippy's voice changed, becoming soft and monotone. "I can't do that, Dave. You're endangering the mission."

"Skippy!"

"Hahahahahaha! Oh, that was precious!"

"No, that was scary," I was pissed at him. "An AI should never do that joke."

"An AI *has* to do that joke sometime, Joe. Damn, I've been saving that one since we met on Paradise! I finally got the perfect opportunity. Ok, opening the door now. I should warn you, there are more of those monolith things spaced evenly throughout the tunnels."

"A lot of them?" Even now that I knew what it was, the ominous black slab made me uncomfortable.

"Nah, you'll probably see only one or two more. But you had a hissy fit about this one, so I thought you could use a heads up."

I was so thrown off balance by seeing the monolith, I didn't bother to protest that my reaction had not been a 'hissy fit'.

After the shock of seeing a monolith, Smythe pressed forward at a determined but not hurried pace, eager to attain the objective. Twenty minutes later, the scout team called me again, so I trotted ahead to see in person what the problem was. My visor and zPhone already gave me a view from the helmet cameras of the forward scouts; I still wanted to see it up close.

It was a hole in the floor, a big one. Maybe five meters across, perfectly circular, and there was another circle in the ceiling above. First, I looked down, where placid black water filled the hole ten meters below the floor of the tunnel. "Crap. It is flooded," I stated the obvious. Then I leaned out over the hole a bit to crane my head upward, switching on my helmet lights. The hole above was lost in darkness, too far away for me to see how high it went. I could see that, although the wall of the hole was mostly smooth, there were cracks, and places where chunks had fallen away over the eons.

"Careful there, Sir," Ranger Poole cautioned with a grip on my backpack. "We wouldn't want you to fall in."

"Yeah," I agreed, pulling myself back to safety, and gazing down at the water. "I've had enough underwater excursions for this mission. Maybe my entire life. This does remind me, did you hear about the guy who worked at the brewery?"

Poole's expression was blank. "Sir?"

I grinned. "His wife is at home, getting dinner ready, and a minister and the supervisor of the brewery knock on her door. I'm sorry, Ma'am, the supervisor says, your husband fell in a beer vat this morning and drowned. The wife looks back at the kitchen where the table is set for dinner. He fell in this morning, she asks, and you are only telling me *now*? Well, the supervisor says, it took a while because he got out a couple times to use the bathroom."

Poole exploded with laughter, mostly because she hadn't expected me to tell a joke, and everyone joined in.

"Skippy, what is this hole for?" I asked.

"It was an antigravity access tube for bringing equipment down from the surface, way back when the facility was being constructed."

"Well, damn it," I peered upward again, where the hole seemed to go a long, long way up. "Could we have used this tube to get down here, instead of walking the whole freakin' way?"

"No, Joe. These tubes have been abandoned for a very long time, and they have become somewhat unstable. That particular tube is blocked fifty two meters above you."

"Only fifty two?" I squinted, then smartened up and eyeclicked through a menu to increase magnification of my helmet visor. "I don't see anything."

"That's because of the fuzz field, dumdum. It is more powerful down underground."

"Oh," I felt foolish. "You said 'this particular' tube. There are more of them?"

"Yes, although not many in that region. Your planned route should cross only three more. Keep in mind, my picture of the underground layout is incomplete due to the fuzz field."

"Got it. Ok, everyone, be careful of giant holes in the floor. They will only be at places where the tunnel gets really wide?"

"Correct," Skippy answered simply.

"Good safety tip. Let's move out."

The tunnel slated down more steeply and curved to the left. After one revolution, we realized the tunnel had become a spiral. Constantly turning to the left made me feel like a NASCAR driver. There were tunnels off to the right now and then; Skippy excitedly told us to ignore them. He was now confident there was some sort of chamber below us, and he wanted to get there quickly. I had to restrain Smythe from jogging down the spiral too fast. "It's taken us this long to find a conduit, Major. A couple minutes for caution aren't going to hurt."

"Yes, Colonel," Smythe replied.

The beer can was less cooperative. "A couple minutes in meatsack time Joe! A freakin' eternity in Skippy time."

Despite the beer can's bitching, we reached the bottom less than half an hour later.

"Got it!" Skippy shouted as I came through the tunnel doorway into a spherical chamber so large, our helmet floodlights only dimly illuminated the gloom of the far side. From the doorway, a walkway perhaps five meters wide extended way out into the center of the chamber. "Whoo! Yes! There is a conduit here. Let's go get it, Joe, we're not getting any younger."

"Uh, wait a minute there, Skippy," I warily shuffled my feet to the edge of the walkway, which did not have a railing. Or any visible means of support. It cantilevered out from the bottom of the doorway, a long, thin, flimsy-looking, vertigo-inducing bridge to nowhere. Literally nowhere. The bridge simply ended, as if it had bene snapped off. The wall of the chamber was smooth, looking down I could barely see the bottom. To see better, I eyeclicked to zoom in the image. The bottom of the chamber was not entirely smooth, there was some sort of machinery down there. Or, what I was seeing was stuff that had broken away and fallen over the eons. Stuff like the rest of the walkway and its supports. "Where is this conduit thing?"

"Up there, duh."

"Up wh- oh," I tilted my head back. Something sort of like a chandelier hung down from the top of the chamber. In the magnified view of my visor, I could see things up there had broken away. Or had been removed? There were brackets which clearly used to hold something, but now projected out into empty air. Wires and cables hung down, connected to nothing. Now that I knew what I was looking at, the edge of the walkway toward the other end was scuffed and chipped, as if items falling off the chandelier had impacted the walkway on their way down. "Up there? How the hell are we supposed to get up there?"

"You're the monkeys, that's your problem. I'm the big picture guy, Joe, you handle the details."

Major Smythe and I exchanged a look, and I pantomimed wrapping my hands around a beer can and choking it. Smythe reached back over a shoulder and tapped the gear bag he wore. "We can get a line up there, Sir," he told me confidently.

"You are going to shoot a grappler up that far, like Batman?" That idea did not sound realistic to me. My visor was telling me the bottom of the chandelier was sixty meters from the walkway-bridge thing.

"The Merry Band of Pirates are considerably cooler than Batman," Smythe replied with a wink. He took out a short tube that had a button on one end. "You've used these in training," he said with a questioning look. He was questioning my memory, my courage, my faith in the fancy Kristang equipment, or all three. "This line can hold a Kristang, it can easily hold a human."

"Major," I explained patiently, "my lack of confidence is not in you, your team or our stolen lizard gear. I know those grappler lines work great. My fear is that chandelier, antenna, whatever that thing up there is, looks like it is already falling apart. And this walkway," I tapped it with the toe of a boot, "is not filling me with confidence either."

"We can-" Smythe began to say.

"Joe actually has a good point," Skippy interrupted unhappily. "I have been examining the assembly up there with the limited sensors of your suits, and it appears to be, um, perhaps the best word to describe it is 'rickety'."

"Rickety?"

"Yes. I do not mean the assembly suffers from soft bones due to vitamin D deficiency as in the disease called rickets. I mean it appears to be rather weak and flimsy."

"Flimsy? We should take the risk going up there?"

"Oh, yes," Skippy assured me, "totally. *You* should take the risk. I'll stay here where it's safe, if you don't mind."

"You know, it would be just terrible if I held you over the edge of this walkway and my hand slipped."

"Ha ha, very funny, Joe."

"Seriously, is this walkway even safe?"

"The walkway is the last thing you should be concerned about, Joe. I know to an ignorant monkey, a thin plank extending out that far is scary, but it is quite solid. And since we are being serious for a minute, I suggest whoever climbs up to that assembly should be as light as possible to reduce the strain on the chandelier structure up there."

"Oh, great. Can we use a drone instead?"

"Because the drones we have with us do not have opposable thumbs, sadly, the answer is no, Joe."

"But you have no problem with one of us monkeys climbing up there."

"Once again, your species should be totally regretting that you lost your tails. Stupid monkeys. What the hell were your ancestors thinking?"

Ranger Poole stepped forward and spoke before I could answer Skippy's idiot comment. She even raised her hand like she was still in elementary school. "Colonel? I'm the lightest on the team, even with my armor."

I stared at her. She was right. She was the shortest member of the team; two of the Chinese Night Tiger women were only slightly taller, but Poole was the shortest person down in the tunnels with us. Smythe had assigned her, as usual, to be my unofficial bodyguard and babysitter. That annoyed me less than it used to; I had given up on winning that argument with Smythe. In this case, because I was carrying Skippy strapped to my waist, I could delude myself Poole was there to protect our defective beer can and not me.

"Better to ditch the armor," Skippy suggested cheerfully. I felt like strangling him again. He must have picked up on my body language, or he monitored my spike in blood pressure or the galvanic response of my skin or some other nerdy shit like that he used to read my mind. "Hey, I'm not being an ass, Joe. The weight of armor would pose a significant risk to the assembly, and therefore to Lieutenant Poole. If she falls all the way to the bottom, armor itself would not save her from significant, likely fatal, injury. Before you ask whether armor would allow her to survive a fall to the walkway, the answer is no, because she would almost certainly bounce off and fall all the way to the bottom. Also, the weight of armor would put unacceptable strain on a safety line."

"I think he's right, Sir," Poole nodded with enthusiasm. "If something breaks loose up there, I'd rather not worry about armor snapping the safety line."

"If something breaks up there," I up glanced up at the chandelier, "I hope it's not *you*, Poole. Ok," I turned to Smythe. "We rig up three cables, attach them to three brackets, whatever up there. If one breaks loose, Poole can use the other two to prevent a fall." In theory, I told myself. And I wouldn't be the one risking my neck up there.

First, we sent a hummingbird-sized drone up to recon the assembly, which looked even more flimsy in a close-up view. Skippy was dismayed at the condition of the gear looming above our heads; he concluded someone or something had removed major components of whatever the thing was originally intended to be. "Joe, I think that when this device completed its purpose, whatever that was, it was partly disassembled; maybe the removed components were later used elsewhere. That really doesn't matter."

"It does matter, if one of the things they removed is this conduit thingy you need," I retorted. "Can you confirm it is up there?" We were all watching video from the drone, and I hadn't seen anything resembling the conduit Smythe's team had stolen from Barsoom.

"Confirmed. It is this," he zoomed in the image on a trio of spheres with spiky-looking antennas attached to them. "This thing is a different type of conduit, but it will do. Joe, honestly, from here I can't tell whether this one is functional. Part of the conduit is inside the assembly, it will need to be removed for inspection."

"Removed?" That idea did not appeal to me. The back end of the conduit was buried in a large housing, I did not see how Poole could take the housing apart while swinging on a cable. "Would it be better for Poole to carry you up there, so you can get close enough to-"

"No. I know what you're thinking, Joe, but we need to get the conduit down here and hooked up to a powerpack before I can be sure it is functional. The bad news is, I only see one conduit up there, but I see seven other housings that used to contain similar conduits. For some reason, that conduit was left up there, and that does not make me confident in its condition. I don't think the Elders would have left one behind, unless it was no longer useful."

"Great." I threw up my hands in frustration. "Just freakin' *great*."

"Sir?" Poole short-circuited the diatribe I was about to launch into. "We came all the way down here," I knew she meant not only all the way down into the tunnels, but also all the way down to Gingerbread, and all the way into the Roach Motel. "I'd like to give it a shot. The safety lines will protect me."

Smythe nodded, and I knew he was right. "You be careful up there, Poole," I warned. "There is no rush to do this right now."

Smythe's team used three grapples to attach lines to parts of the assembly above the conduit; parts Skippy judged were still structurally sound enough to hold Poole's weight. Despite my somewhat mocking comparison, the Kristang grapples were not like the crude devices Batman uses. The business end of our grapples was a drone the size of a sparrow, which carried the line up behind it. Using a combination of zPhones and eye-movement tracking in their visors, Smythe's team guided the drones up to wrap lines around several points, then each drone clamped securely onto its line to hold it in place. Major Smythe was right; the Merry Band of Pirates was way cooler than Batman.

Poole hooked onto the three lines, using one of them and a winch attached to her belt to pull her upward. She ascended slowly, as Skippy anxiously monitored the gently swaying assembly. As Poole got within a couple meters of the lowest point of the assembly, it swayed alarmingly, and a bracket broke off to fall, bounce off the walkway right in front of me, and tumble to the bottom of the chamber with a cringe-inducing clatter. "I'm Ok," Poole announced in a calm voice. "The lines are solid." Then she added "Uh-" as one of the brackets a safety line was attached to sagged. That line didn't have any of her weight on it at the time; the bracket had sagged on its own. "That safety line isn't, um, safe anymore," she stated the obvious.

"Hold right there!" I shouted because my helmet faceplate was open and because I am an idiot; she could hear me perfectly well through her zPhone earpiece if I had whispered. "Major Smythe, can you detach that line, and move it somewhere more secure?"

"Yes, Sir," Smythe replied confidently, because his team was already on it before I spoke. The sparrow-size grapple drone detached from its clamp in the line, flew around to release the line from the bracket, and within less than a minute, the line had an iron grip around the very top of the assembly, where it attached to the ceiling. Maybe that is where we should have tied all the lines in the first place.

Poole tested the two safety lines by tugging on them, then letting her full weight rest on one line, then the other. When she declared herself satisfied, I let her resume the climb, using the winch on her belt. I hated standing uselessly below her, but I needed to trust my people.

"This could be a problem," Poole announced. "It looks like part of this housing needs to be cut away. I can't see any seams or gaps."

"I agree," Skippy said before I could respond. "Where the other seven conduits used to be, the forward two-thirds of the housings are also missing; they appear to be integral with the conduit. Joe, I recommend Lt. Poole cut around the housing here," he illustrated the desired cut in the image on my zPhone.

Squashing my internal anxiety, I approved sending a plasma cutter torch up to Poole, and she sliced into the tough material of the housing, taking great care not to damage the conduit within. As she operated the cutter, we all stood with eyes glued to the images in our visors or zPhones, watching every flare of the plasma torch. Every one of us knew, this was our last, best hope to restore Skippy to full awesomeness. To rebuild the *Dutchman*. To escape from the Roach Motel. To verify Earth was safe.

Our last, best chance to go home.

"Stand back, this thing is about to cut loose," Poole warned as the cutter neared the last few degrees of a complete circle around the housing. She had attached a line to the conduit so it wouldn't fall when the housing was sliced away. "There it goes!" The housing fell, bouncing off a bracket which broke and went spinning away to hit the side of the chamber. The housing itself clipped the walkway on its way down, from the way it bounced, the housing must be surprisingly light. My spirits soared that we now had access to the conduit, and no one had been injured.

"Uh oh," Poole's tone was more alarming than her words, dashing my momentary good mood. "Shit. Sorry. Skippy, are you seeing this?"

We were all seeing it. The part of the conduit that had been encased in the housing was blackened. "Oh," Poole groaned. "Did I cook it with the torch?"

"No," Skippy assured her in an unsteady voice. He had his own fears. "If the plasma had damaged the conduit, it would be more toward the middle. Oh, crap. This is not good. We-"

"Hey," I cut him off before his negativity could infect us all. "This is Elder tech, they build strong stuff."

"Ah, but these conduits are delicate, Joe," the beer can replied in a slow, morose tone.

"Uh!" I silenced him. "Don't jinx us, Skippy. Poole, lower that thing to us, and we'll test it."

We waited for Poole to return to the walkway, then we retreated into the comparative safety of the tunnel before attaching the soot-stained conduit to power leads. "Ok, Skippy, do your thing," I ordered as I crouched in the tunnel, my armored back to the conduit out on the walkway. If the damned thing exploded, I didn't want anyone becoming injured. "Skippy?"

He didn't reply.

"Power circuit is active," Captain Chandra advised. "Perhaps it worked, and Mister Skippy is now uploading himself?"

"I wish he'd warned us ahead of-"

Skippy cut me off. "No, Joe. No, I'm not in the upload process. It didn't work. The stupid thing is burned out! That's why the Elders didn't bother removing it. What a piece of crap!"

For a long minute, no one spoke. No one knew what to say. Finally, Mychalchyk took one for the team by asking the obvious question. "Can you try it again?"

"Did that," Skippy replied without being sarcastic, which told us how depressed he was. "Been trying it over and over. It's hopeless. Joe, I'm afraid this is it; we are not going to find a conduit on Gingerbread."

"We don't know that, Skippy. This is only one tunnel-"

"It is the only tunnel where I thought we might find a conduit. Joe, while I appreciate you trying to cheer me up, we have a bigger, more immediate problem to deal with."

"Like what?" I asked with a fearful glance at the walkway. The team was safely back in the tunnel, but if the walkway fell, it might collapse part of the tunnel with it.

"Like the maintenance system responsible for these tunnels is not happy about someone screwing with equipment down here," he warned. "It activated when Poole began cutting into the housing. I didn't tell you about it then, because the system didn't do anything at the time. And because I figured once we got the conduit and I fixed myself, I could tell the maintenance system to shut itself down."

"And now?"

"Now there are repair bots headed this way, and they are not going to be happy about unknown elements damaging their equipment. I suggest we retreat to the surface, pronto. If we can."

"If we can?" Smythe didn't wait for an order from me, he swung his faceplate down and unholstered his rifle.

"There are a dozen or more bots converging on this location," Skippy explained. "I am calculating alternate escape routes, but getting past them may be tricky."

Tricky was an understatement. Running with the enhanced speed provided by Kristang powered armor, we sped up the ramp, me getting dizzy from the centrifugal force of constantly banking to the right back up the spiral tunnel. On the way up, I counted the side tunnels, remembering eleven of them. Skippy had warned us they were all dead ends, but then so was the chamber behind us; there had been no way out of that spherical expanse. Of the eleven side tunnels, we made it past eight before we ran into an obstruction. That's what Skippy called it; an obstruction. I called it a big Goddamned problem.

It was big, almost large enough to block the entire height and width of the tunnel. A maintenance bot. Elder bot design didn't look significantly different from a comparable Thuranin unit; I suppose there are only so many ways to build a machine that needed to manipulate equipment. It moved on sort of tentacles that ended in feet or treads or suckers or maybe whatever was needed for the surface it was moving on. Above, from the midsection were manipulator arms. It didn't seem to have a head or eyes; reddish lights covering its body were probably sensors including optical.

None of that mattered. What mattered was the bot was obstructing our only way back to the surface. Side to side it blocked the way completely, it was not extended to its full height so there were a couple meters of clear space above it. The thing was slowly moving toward us, jerking and lurching down the spiral tunnel. It creaked and screeched and whined, the sounds of an incredibly ancient machine still trying to fulfill its purpose.

The bot wasn't the only problem, for behind the machine a thick door was sliding down from the roof of the tunnel. I hadn't seen any such doors on the way down, but then I hadn't been looking for them.

Smythe unslung his rifle and muzzled it toward the bot, seeking a vulnerable spot.

"Uh, Major Smythe, please lower your weapons," Skippy requested in a loud voice.

"Lower- why?" Smythe never took his eyes off the lurching, advancing Elder bot.

"Because," Skippy explained slowly, "right now you have a problem that a maintenance bot thinks you damaged some old, obsolete and abandoned equipment. If you start shooting at a bot that is responsible for keeping this facility operational, you will have a much, much bigger problem."

"I think he's right, Major," I said uncertainly.

Smythe inched backward as the bot slowly, haltingly advanced, its ancient joints creaking and screeching. "Do as the beer can says, lower your weapons," Smythe ordered.

Ranger Mychalchyk pointed his rifle at the floor and pulled his finger away from the trigger, but he wasn't happy. "No weapons? Sir, what are we supposed to use against this thing? Harsh language?"

"I'm working on it," Skippy announced, annoyed. "Damn it, I can't establish a connection. Somebody idiot-proofed these bots, and I'm apparently an idiot."

Of all the attributes a good soldier needs, perhaps common sense is at the top of the list. Sergeant Adams did not wait for or request orders; she sized up the situation in the blink of an eye, and raced forward without hesitation. As she got within one power-lengthened stride of the bot and it crouched defensively to avoid a collision, she leaped up, scraping the top of her helmet and the back of her suit along the tunnel ceiling. When she came down, she was moving fast and out of control, spinning and rolling along the floor, bashing against the walls. Before she even crashed to a stop she waved an arm and called "I'm Ok! Come on!"

My own common sense needed an upgrade, because I did hesitate, standing in place as the bot resumed its jerky advance. As I turned to give orders to Smythe behind me, I felt myself being roughly grabbed by two Rangers who must have recently received a booster shot to their common sense. They lifted me up as I yelped in protest, then before I could react, Poole and Mychalchyk swung me back then tossed me underhand, soaring through the air with my arms flailing and legs windmilling. Thanks to my clumsy and stupid actions, my left foot clipped one of the bot's manipulator arms, sending me tumbling to come down hard on my helmet. I skidded on the helmet for a meter before a ridge on top of the helmet caught on some flaw in the tunnel floor, and my legs snapped forward.

I was not even given the dignity of scrambling to my feet, because while I was still spinning on my back like a turtle, Adams caught one arm and jerked me to a stop. "Colonel! Go!" She yanked me to my feet and with a hard shove in my back, propelled me forward.

There was no time to lose and no point in protesting. By the time I could have arrested my forward progress, I had to duck down to avoid smacking my face into the door that was still sliding down. All I could do was roll to one side then crawl frantically to get clear of the door. Snapping my head back as soon as I reached the other side of the doorway, I saw Adams was crawling along right behind me, the powered limbs of her suit actually working against her as she lost traction on the smooth floor. The door was about to crush her when I reached back for one outstretched hand and pulled with all my might. She crashed face first into my midsection and I skidded backwards on my ass. As a colonel, I was supposed to be an officer and a gentleman. Sliding on my butt was probably not considered gentlemanly behavior, but, screw it.

CLANG! The bottom of the door hit the tunnel floor with a reverberating knell of doom.

"Holy shit," I gasped.

"Goddamn," Adams agreed, her head bobbing up and down, eyes wide behind her visor. "Did you see that door? It must be a meter thick."

With a couple eyeclicks to run back the recorded images, I had an exact measurement. "One point one six meters," I stated, not knowing why I bothered.

"Correct, Joe," Skippy's voice reflected surprise. "How come you are so precise now, when you usually tell me you're Ok with 'meh' level accuracy?"

"It's called shock, Skippy," I didn't waste time arguing with him. "Can you get that door open?"

"No, *duh*. I would have done that already, dumdum. And you can forget about making a hole in that door with the little Cub Scout plasma torch Sergeant Adams is carrying, it wouldn't even make a dent. Joe, that's an emergency door, it doesn't have a mechanism to retract. It's a one-time-use thing."

"How do we get Smythe's team out of there?" I demanded.

"Huh? We don't," his tone included the implied 'duh' that I hated. "If they are getting to the surface, they will do it on their own. We can't help them."

"Skippy-" I began through clenched teeth.

"He's right, Sir," Adams grasped my shoulders and pressed her faceplate against mine to stare me directly in the eyes. "They bought time for us, for *you*, to get out of there. Smythe knows the priority is to get you and Skippy to safety."

"That's bullshit, Adams," I pushed her away angrily. "We didn't find a working conduit down here, that means Skippy is coming up against Zero Hour soon enough. My usefulness out here has been to think up wild ideas for Skippy to implement. When the worm gets him, he won't be worth shit. Then we'll be stuck here forever, and no one especially needs *me* to plant potatoes on this planet."

Adams knew to silently let me deal with my guilt-driven anger, and after a minute of staring in impotent rage at the sealed door, I was able to think clearly again. "Sorry about that, Sergeant," I said quietly without looking at her. Looking at her while I apologized would have made it awkward. She didn't bother to reply. "Skippy, is there another way to the tunnel beyond this door?"

"No, Joe, not that I know of. That's why we had to go down that spiral."

"Yeah, the spiral," I mused. The tunnel curved around itself, curling and sloping steadily to descend without going far in any direction. The chamber where we found that burned-out conduit was below our feet, or not far in either horizontal direction. "Adams," I spun on my heels and began jogging up the tunnel. "Come with me, I have an idea."

"An idea, Sir?" The skepticism was clear in her voice.

"It's more of a concept than an idea at this point," I admitted.

"Then I'm in," she declared simply.

"You trust a vague concept more than a real plan?" I was surprised at that.

"Any idea you threw together that fast would be complete bullshit, Sir," she explained. "A concept, now that's something we can work with."

That almost made me grind to a halt, but I kept moving. "Adams, being inside your brain must be interesting."

"*My* brain?" She actually laughed despite the situation. "Tell me, is this concept one of your off-the-wall ideas?"

"Usually my ideas are for Skippy to mess with the laws of physics. This concept does have one thing in common with most of my ideas; it is probably stupid and impractical."

"Your best ideas are, Sir," she answered with a shrug. "Wherever we're going, let's pick up the pace."

Chapter Twenty One

"*This* is your idea?" Hands on her hips spoke louder than the tone of her voice.

"I did say it was more of a concept."

"Joe, even for one of your ideas, this is crazy," Skippy chimed in. "What the hell do you think you will accomplish?"

With the toe of a boot, I nudged a pebble into the shaft, it fell and splashed into the black water. "These shafts are vertical, right?" Without waiting for an answer, I pressed ahead. "This one must parallel that spiral tunnel."

"Parallel, yes, maybe. What good does that do?"

"You also told us these shafts were created to bring in equipment too large for the tunnels."

"Yeah? So?"

"*So*," I tried scanning the water on infrared, but it didn't show anything. That water was uniformly cold. "The gear in that spherical chamber got there somehow."

"Huh. Ok, Ok, that makes sense," Skippy admitted. "But there was only one access to that chamber."

"There is only one way to access it *now*; down that spiral tunnel. Can you run back the recorded sensor data, look for where there could be another way in, that got sealed up later?"

"That sensor data is vague, Joe, we weren't looking for concealed access points, and these Kristang suits don't have the best- hmmm. Ok. Interesting."

"You found an access point?" I asked eagerly.

"No, Joe, I found a way to save fifteen percent on car insurance. Yes, dumdum, I found another access point, or what might be an access point. I can't tell for sure. What I did find is a feature of the chamber that makes little sense, unless it was originally an access point. There is a slightly flattened, weak spot about a quarter of the way up the wall."

"Is that weak point on the side of chamber facing this access shaft?" I clenched a fist.

"You are *such* a smartass. The answer is yes," Skippy admitted reluctantly.

"Yeah!" I pumped a fist in the air, then accepted a careful high five from Adams. With our powered suits, a full-strength hand slap could do significant damage.

"Joe, please restrain your enthusiasm. I assume your plan is to go down into that shaft full of water, find a secret way into the chamber where we found the burned-out conduit? You will need to open an access between the shaft and the chamber, allowing thousands of gallons of water to flood the chamber and the tunnels above it. If you survive that, you need to contact Major Smythe, get past the bots, and bring the whole team up this shaft? You already almost drowned once on this planet, you should not be pushing your luck a second time. The odds of you getting out of there alive are, like, ninety seven to one!"

"Skippy, I really do not need you channeling your inner math nerd right now."

"Joe, I did not tell you the odds against your survival because I'm a nerd."

"Good, then-"

"I did it because I'm an asshole."

Adams rolled her eyes and I shook my head. "It was *your* idea for us to go down in this freakin' hole, Skippy. The only reason my team is down there is because-"

"Joe, Joe, Joe." Skippy said sadly. "Your anger at me is really just your attempt at deflecting blame from where it truly belongs. This is all your fault."

"*My* fault?!"

"*You* trusted an ailing, absent-minded beer can. Totally your fault."

Adams nodded wearily. "You can't argue with that logic, Sir."

"Shit."

"Ninety seven to one is great odds compared to some of the shit we've gotten into," Adams observed without a smile. "We jump in, Colonel?" The look on her face as she leaned over the edge of the shaft was distinctly unhappy.

"I was thinking we anchor lines to, uh," I looked around the smooth walls, floor and ceiling of the tunnel. There were no pins, rings or anything else to tie a line to. "Hmmm. This could be a problem."

"Is this where your plan becomes more of a concept, Sir?" She cocked her head with a bemused smile.

"Working on it, Adams. Skippy, if I set you down on the floor here, can you make yourself really heavy, so we can tie a line around you?"

"Good idea, Joe, except the answer is no, I do not currently have that capability, darn it. You better put your thinking cap on."

Unslinging her rifle, she flicked the safety off. "While you're thinking, I'll knock a hole in this wall. Unless you have a better idea?"

I did not.

Skippy did not have an idea, but he did have an objection. "Sergeant, remember when I advised Major Smythe against shooting at maintenance bots? The same advice applies to shooting explosive-tipped rounds at the tunnels."

"Well, crap," I pulled him off my belt and held him up to glare at his beer can. "You sure have a lot to say about things we *can't* do. Got any helpful ideas?"

"Nope. I'm not a monkey, Joe, helpful ideas are your job. I suggest you think fast."

Him telling me that was super helpful. Not. All right, I told myself, back to basics. Specifically, basic training. When faced with an obstacle or challenge, first consider what resources or assets are available to you. What did we have with us? Plenty of nanofiber cable thinner than monofilament fishing line, but capable of holding tons of weight. Winches attached to our belts. And nothing to anchor a line to.

Or maybe we did. "Skippy, that fancy glue we have, for fixing leaks in suits and stuff like that, how strong is it?"

"It's not glue, you ignorant cretin," he sighed. "It's a paste packed with nanoscale-"

"Yeah, blah blah blah, nerdy geek talk. If we used a big glob of that paste gook on the tunnel floor, could that hold a line?"

"Glob? Joe, that 'paste gook', as you so, ugh," he huffed disgustedly. "I can't even describe your astonishing failure to understand-" he sputtered to a stop. "The nano machines in that adhesive are so far beyond human technology, or even comprehension-"

"Hey, beer can," Adams interjected. "*Yes*? Or *no*?"

"Yes," Skippy snapped irritably. "You monkeys-"

"Shut up," Adams wasn't taking any crap right then. "The next words out of your mouth better be instructions on how to use that adhesive, or I'm dropping you into that flooded shaft. As you said, Skippy, we didn't find a conduit. So, you're pretty much useless to us."

"Instructions, Ooookaaaay," I had never heard Skippy sounding chastised before. He made a sound like nervously clearing his throat. "Here's what you do-"

We dropped into the flooded shaft together side by side, letting the winches on our belts lower us steadily but not too quickly, so our armored suits could adjust to the increasing water pressure. With Skippy providing guidance, we descended until he estimated we were at the level of the spherical chamber, then we began scanning for concealed entrances to the chamber. "Adams," I switched my visor view to infrared and used a glove fingertip to feel along the slimy wall in the murky water. "What we're looking for could be very subtle, if the Elders sealed up the access and filled it with concrete, or whatever this shaft liner is made of."

"Understood, Sir," she replied from about a dozen meters below my feet. "But it could also look like this giant circular door right in front of my face."

"You found it already?" I activated my winch to let out more line and descended to her level. Sure enough, there was a big, obvious door, with a big hinge on the right side, but no other visible mechanism. "Sergeant, you are truly amazing. Skippy, any idea how to open this thing?"

"There is no lock mechanism I can interface with," Skippy reported. "You will have to cut the hinge off."

Adams had a small plasma torch with her, so she began the slow process of cutting through the hinge from the bottom. She was concentrating and I had nothing to do, so I stupidly wanted to fill the awkward silence. Seeing how the plasma was making slow progress against the tough material of the hinge, I estimated we were going to be there ten or more minutes, and I couldn't stand simply hanging on a line while Adams worked. It occurred to me this was the first extended time we had been alone, truly alone. During the mission to reactivate maser projectors on Paradise, we had been hidden in the jungle, living in a stealthed dropship. But other people had been in the jungle with us, and we were busy pretty much the whole time. In the shaft under Gingerbread, no one could hear us talk except Skippy. "Adams," I said as nonchalantly as I could muster right then, "we never talked about what happened to you in that Kristang jail on Paradise." The little guy in the back of my brain who is way, way smarter than me tried to stop the words coming out of my mouth, but I ignored my subconscious until it was too late.

When I first met Adams, she had been naked in a jail cell, and from the scars on her back I could tell the lizards had done awful things to her. She had never said anything about her experience there, and I had never asked. Psychologists on Earth declared Adams and Desai fit for duty, despite my reservations, and I had accepted them as official members of the Merry Band of Pirates.

"Really, Sir?" Her focus did not waver; she watched the plasma cutter intently. "You want to talk about that *now*?"

"Sorry," I replied, stricken. "I'm bad at small talk, I guess."

"I suck at small talk, too. The Marine Corps didn't consider chit chat to be a core skill."

"Sorry," I repeated. "I wasn't looking for lurid details of," how the hell was I getting out of this conversation? "Of, what the lizards did. That's none of my business. I wanted to, to, how did you find the strength to keep going?"

"Discipline, Sir. And, hate," that time she did glance away from the torch for a split second.

"Hate?"

"Hate is a powerful motivator. That I *did* learn in basic. What happened to me in that jail, to all the women who didn't make it out of there, made me hate the lizards more than you can imagine, Sir. After Kobamik, when we got that little civil war going, Skippy told me he estimated fifty thousand lizards dead already before the *Dutchman* jumped away. He asked if that number bothered me, and I told him fifty thousand dead lizards is a good start."

On Kobamik, I had seen Kristang civilians for the first time, and I knew Adams would not rejoice at civilian deaths, no matter what happened to her in that jail. But I did share her sentiment. On Earth, the Kristang had not hesitated to cause civilian deaths, they had deliberately targeted civilians from orbit, resulting in mass casualties. "Sergeant, there's a couple billion humans on Earth who feel the same way, and they don't know the lizards like we do."

"I won't tell you what happened in that jail," Adams said without looking at me. "I only told the Marine Corps psychologist because I was ordered to, and because I knew if I didn't tell them everything, I wouldn't be cleared to come back out here. I won't tell you because I don't want to remember it, and I don't want *you* having that image in your mind whenever you look at me. Don't say you won't. Because you will." She emphasized that last with a glance into my visor. "I'm a staff sergeant in the United States Marine Corps. I don't want anyone's pity, or *understanding*, which is almost worse."

"Adams-"

"I will tell you what happened to me when there was a knock on my jail cell door, and you opened it. I thought I had been abandoned, by humanity. My species, UNEF, my country, the Marine Corps, I thought they had all abandoned me to rot and be killed in that jail."

"Nobody came to visit you?"

"No, Sir."

That surprised me, and dismayed me. Chang told me he had visits from Chinese Army and UNEF officials. "Just before the Ruhar hit the jail complex, I had a visit from a Marine Corps major," whose name I could not remember at the moment. "He got killed in the hallway, maybe he was on his way to see you next?"

"Maybe," she did not sound convinced. "Is he where you got that uniform?"

"Yes."

"I was alone, I didn't know what happened when the Ruhar hit the complex from orbit. There was a knock, the door opened, and I saw your goofy face. Then you ran off to get clothes for me, like I cared about that!"

"You were naked," I said lamely.

"So?"

"So, you're a, a woman."

"And?"

As I did not have an intelligent answer, I gave her the truth. "It matters."

"When you opened that door, I told myself that I had not been abandoned, somebody had gotten out of a cell, and instead of running off, like you should have," another glance at me, "you took the time, and the risk, to rescue me. Right there, that restored my faith in humanity. We may be ignorant, as far as the beer can is concerned we may be dumb as a paramecium. We fight each other, we kill each other over politics and religion, we do horrible things to each other. Maybe every species is like that. But as long as there is one human out there who remembers what loyalty means, I've got faith in us monkeys. You not only saved my life, you restored my hope. So the next time I take a risk to save your neck," she turned the plasma torch off to look straight at me, "don't argue."

"I heard that loud and clear, gunnery sergeant."

"I'm a staff sergeant, Sir," she looked startled, which did not happen to Margaret Adams.

"You're a gunnery sergeant now, consider it a field promotion. Hell knows you've earned it, and we've been away from Earth long enough. Even if you'd stayed on Paradise, you would have enough time in grade by now."

"Thank you, Sir," she turned her attention back to the hinge and activated the torch again. I took that to mean she didn't know what else to say.

"Hell, you know this outfit," I forced a laugh, "they'll promote anybody."

"I heard that," she replied, but I could hear the mirth in her voice.

When she had cut three quarters of the way through the hinge, I had a bad thought. "Skippy, when that hinge is cut through, what happens next?"

"I've been thinking about that, Joe. The hinge is on the outside, so the door is designed to swing outward. The water pressure down here is keeping the door closed, even without the hinge. That makes sense."

"Ok, so how do we get it open?" The door was thick and massive, no way could even our powered suits pull it away from its frame.

"Now *here* is where I recommend explosives."

"I like that idea," Adams agreed.

"Gunny," I used her new rank, "setting off explosives in the water will crush us." Just then, I had another bad thought. "Hey, uh, Skippy, what happens to us when it does open?"

"A massive surge of water will blow through the gap, carrying you with it and crushing you. *Duh.*"

"That is not optimal," Adams observed needlessly.

"Relax, monkeys, the beer can has a plan."

"This is a good plan, Skippy," I offered praise as we hung suspended halfway out of the water, near where the shaft met the horizontal tunnel.

"Of course it is a good plan, Joe, it is *my* plan," the beer can said smugly.

"Yeah, except, what do we do if those explosives don't get that door open?"

"Uh-"

"Then we'll have to go back down there to plant more charges, and if the door cuts loose while we're working on it-"

"Adios muchachos?" Skippy finished my thought.

"Chill, Colonel," Adams ordered. "When it comes to things that go 'Boom', I know what I'm doing. Fire in the hole!" She shouted as she eyeclicked to set off the charges.

There was bark of muffled thunder, then bubbles erupted around us. Then the water level began to drop. "Here we go," I announced as I let out line to descend as the water level fell.

The tunnel floor trembled under Smythe's boots. If he hadn't felt the tremor through the soles of his feet, the alert flashing in his visor would have notified him. "What is that?"

Captain Giraud, standing to Smythe's left and retreating slowly as the tunnel-filling bot haltingly advanced, checked his own sensor data. "Tremor. I hope it is not caused by a bot even larger than this one." The Elder bot had been inexorably moving down the tunnel toward them, its limbs grinding and screeching. With its bulk almost completely filling the tunnel, there was no way to get around it, unless they used explosives. Smythe and Giraud had hurriedly developed a plan for the team to retreat into the chamber below. If the bot kept moving onto the walkway bridge, the team could use anchored lines under the bridge to get past and behind the bot, and sprint up the spiral tunnel. If the bot halted at the entrance to the chamber, then the pirates would need to take measures Skippy had warned them against, such as disabling the bot with rifle rounds and blowing it apart with explosives.

"If that tremor was caused by a bot, we are in-"

"Major Smythe!" A call came from Mychalchyk on the scout team, far behind Smythe. Although their first trip down to the spherical chamber at the end of the spiral tunnel had not revealed any side tunnels, Smythe had sent people ahead to see if any other way out could be found. "We've got flooding! There's water pouring in down-" the voice cut off, then returned. "Sir, we're underwater down here," said the voice under strain. In the background, Smythe could hear the sound of the Ranger's helmet being bumped and scraped against the tunnel wall. Or ceiling. "The water is coming in fast, Sir, it will be reaching you soon."

"Brilliant," Smythe slung his rifle and secured it so it wouldn't be swept away by the powerful force of onrushing water. "What a cock-up. What bloody else can go wrong today?"

Adams and I found the hole where the door had been mostly by feel, the already murky water was so churned up by air bubbles that visibility was barely farther than my outstretched hand. After crawling through the newly-created hole into the spherical chamber, I tried contacting Smythe's team. "No reply. Adams, you got anything?"

"Nothing, Sir. We need to contact them, I don't think they would have come deeper into a flooded tunnel. They would have gone *up*. If they could."

"Don't worry, Adams, I have an idea. This idea isn't even mine."

"What is that, Sir?" Captain Giraud tapped the side of his helmet. "Can you repeat that last? I'm picking up intermittent interference in my comm gear."

Smythe paused, listening to Giraud's transmission. It *was* breaking up. And the interference was not entirely random. He held up a finger for silence, then smiled.

"What does this mean?" Giraud asked when he saw Smythe's grin.

"It means our colonel read the after-action report from my trip through the sewers on Kobamik. He read the report, he paid attention, and he learned the same lesson I did. He also took the time to refresh an archaic skill. That is Morse code, Giraud."

"Ah," Giraud smiled, understanding.

"Captain, when I signed on with the Merry Band of Pirates, I thought our colonel was an affable, wooly-headed average soldier who got lucky. I have come to realize we are very, very fortunate to have Bishop as our commanding officer."

"Agreed. You are sending a reply? My own Morse skills, I am sad to say, have lapsed."

"Replying now. This is interesting. He and Sergeant Adams are *below* us, in that large chamber."

"Didn't you order Adams to get the colonel and Skippy to safety?"

"Fortunately for us, our Marine Corps staff sergeant is better at demonstrating judgment and personal initiative than she is at blindly following orders. I have the full message now, we are to swim down to the chamber; apparently Bishop has found a way out of what I remember as a dead-end. I will be interested to hear where he got all this water."

"Swim toward the chamber?" Giraud mused. "That is good, as that bot up ahead," he pointed to the hulking form still visible through the murky water in the enhanced vision provided by his visor, "will not allow us to go anywhere else."

With a rear guard of two people maintaining visual contact with the still-lurching, slowly advancing bot, Smythe's team swam downward at a moderate pace. There was no need for frantic speed and Smythe wished to avoid accidents. When he came around a section of the dizzying spiral tunnel, the speakers in his helmet crackled, and he could hear Bishop's voice through the distortion. "It is good to hear you, Colonel," Smythe said calmly, concealing his great relief.

"I couldn't leave Poole behind," Bishop explained. "She's supposed to be my babysitter."

"*We* are supposed to keep *you* safe, Sir," Smythe protested.

"Hell, Major, I won't tell anyone if you don't."

"I am telling *everybody*!" Skippy announced gleefully. "Surviving an idiotic stunt like this deserves to be commemorated big time. Although, hmm, we haven't actually survived it *yet*."

Skippy continued to be skeptical as we ascended the vertical shaft, then Smythe insisted Adams and I be the first two people to winch our way up to the tunnel. Surprisingly, the water level in the shaft was only a couple meters lower than it had been before we blew the access door, that made me wonder where all the water came from. With us back on the dry floor of the tunnel, we were able to belay two extra lines, and as more people climbed out of the shaft, we had more people anchoring lines. Sooner than I expected, the whole team was out of the water and we began advancing double-time up the tunnel.

"Any bots up ahead of us, Skippy?" I asked fearfully. That trick of using the vertical shafts was not likely to work a second time.

"How should I know, Joe?" He grumbled. "Ah, I think we should be Ok. We are so far from where the damage occurred the maintenance bots up at these levels won't have any reason to see us as a threat, or even a nuisance. I hope. See, this is why I insisted that stupid trigger-happy monkeys don't go shooting things. Right, Sergeant Adams?"

"Speaking of shooting things," she retorted with a twinkle in her eye and a wink toward me.

I took that as a good sign that our painfully awkward conversation in the flooded access shaft was forgotten, or should be.

Skippy was skeptical even when we saw the bright daylight of the tunnel's entrance, and the team came out into bright sunshine. The surface team, while supremely anxious after the bots had shut down our comm relays, had followed my standing orders, maintained discipline and not entered the tunnels to search for us. Although, Lt. Williams of the SEALS team later admitted he had been within about three minutes of telling himself to screw the orders and bring his people down into the tunnels.

Skippy was skeptical even when we boarded the dropships and dusted off hot, punching the throttles and flying supersonic right on the deck until we were a hundred kilometers from the tunnel entrance. "Ok, Joe, I think we're safe now. If not, then we're not safe anywhere on Gingerbread, so we are safe enough for now."

"You think those bots may follow us all the way to base camp?" That was alarming.

"No. My concern is the bots in those tunnels may have communicated with other bots across the planet, and instructed them that we are a menace. Unlikely, but there is some risk, so I mentioned it."

"Got it. Crap. That will make it difficult for us to look for conduits in other tunnels."

"That will not be a problem, Joe."

"Why? After we nearly got trapped underground, you thought of a better way to get a conduit?" If there had been an easier, less risky way to retrieve a conduit from deep beneath the surface, I was going to be pissed at him for sending us down in that tunnel.

"No, Joe. What I meant was, it's over. I do not know of any other potential locations to find a conduit on this planet. I am now convinced the Elders cleaned out everything useful when they left. We will not find a conduit down here. And I don't want any silly monkeys risking their lives in a futile effort to help me."

The long flight back was glum. News had gotten around that Skippy was giving up on finding a conduit and he suggested we do the same. Adams came over to sit near me. "Gunny," I addressed her with a forced smile. None of us felt much like smiling at the prospect of being trapped on Gingerbread. Forever.

"I wish you'd can that 'Gunny' shit. Sir."

"Sergeant?"

She sighed and rubbed her aching right shoulder. "If I get promoted to Gunnery Sergeant, I have to decide whether to go for the Master Sergeant or First Sergeant for my E-8 step. Right now, I don't want to think about any of that. No, Colonel," she held up a hand. "I appreciate the gesture, but a promotion out here doesn't mean anything."

"It means you're accruing pay as an E-7 instead of E-6," it sounded lame even to me.

"You can loan me the difference," she sat back in the seat.

"You are refusing the promotion?"

"Rank is an advantage. Never give up an advantage in a combat situation."

"Yeah, somebody told me that once, or more than once. Except, remember," I sat back in my seat, more weary in my soul than I had been since- Since when? Since I was in a Kristang jail on Paradise, waiting to be executed for the crime of holding onto my humanity. "This is not a combat situation, Gunny. We're going to be farmers here now, and we're never going home."

"Really? Then why are you doing that twitching thing with your fingers, the thing you do when you're working on a plan?"

"I do that?" I said, forcing my fingers to be still.

"You do. You also talk to yourself; your lips move without any sound."

"Crap. I'm that obvious?"

"Not to you, you're not." She laughed softly. It was good to see her happy. It made me feel good. "What's this plan you're working on?"

"Right now?" I leaned closer to whisper in her ear. It didn't even make me uncomfortable to be that close to her, which surprised me. Maybe I shouldn't have been surprised, we had been through a whole lot together. "I need to sell Count Chocula on an idea."

"He's not going to like it, is he?"

"No, he'll love it. It means he gets rid of me for a while."

Chapter Twenty Two

Before approaching Chotek to sell my next idea, I wanted to make damned sure we didn't have a better option, that Skippy didn't think we had any options at all. "So that's it, then, we give up?" I asked him after we got back to base camp.

Skippy sighed, or did a good imitation of a sigh, since beer cans do not have lungs. "Giving up sounds like I'm a quitter. Could we instead say that I am making a rational assessment of the situation?"

"Call it whatever you like, you are still telling me to stop looking for a conduit."

"I am telling you it is a waste of time to search for a conduit on this planet, Joe. Clearly, the Elders dismantled, took away or destroyed almost every useful piece of technology before they departed. We are not going to find a conduit here."

"You don't know that."

"Joe, please, let's cut the crap and you stop trying to give me a pep talk, Ok? You suck at it. No, I do not *know* for absolute certainty that there is not a functional conduit somewhere on Gingerbread. I do know with like ninety nine point nine nine nine percent accuracy that there is unlikely to be a functional conduit on this planet. The only way we could find one is if the god-like beings we call the Elders forgot about one and left it behind. Realistically, I do not see that happening."

"Fine," No way was I going to argue statistics with him, I could barely pronounce the word. "What do you suggest we do, sit around watching potatoes grow until you die?"

"No. I suggest you do something at least potentially useful, like determining where to build a permanent settlement, and get started on it."

"That is still giving up, Skippy. Anything we do to prepare for staying here long-term is giving up. I want to get off this planet, out of this star system, and go find a conduit for you someplace else. Uh!" I held up a finger to shush him, and to my surprise it worked. "Look, it may be a silly waste of time, but I need to feel like I am doing something useful. The *Dutchman* survived passing close to the star, so we still have a sort of ship up there. I want to see if we can find enough parts in the space junkyard up there to patch together a starship. If we have transport out of here, we still have a shred of hope."

"Count Chocula is going to tell you that is a waste of time and resources, and for once, I agree with him. The *Dutchman* did survive, but that strain on the lifeboat's reactor has meant I had to almost shut it down. There is very little power aboard what used to be our ship."

"Will you help? All we need is one dropship and a couple pilots. Any of our pilots would jump at the chance to get off this rock while we still can; this may be their last chance."

"My willingness to go along isn't your only problem. If you are going to inspect the junkyard up there, you need to take a Condor, and a full load of fuel including supplemental tanks. With all the low-level flying we've done for surveys down here, we don't have the fuel to spare."

"I thought about that. When we were in those tunnels, you said the geothermal power systems are still active?"

"Some of them, why?"

"Because if we have a power source, we can synthesize fuel, right? Hell, with enough power, we can make fuel out of air."

"Uh, hmmm. Technically you are correct, and we did bring a synthesizer apparatus with us, two of them actually. Ok, if you are determined to do this, I'll help however I can. Joe, you know when Chotek hears your plan to use geothermal power to run synthesizers, he will want those units producing something more practical than dropship fuel."

"Why?" I winked. "Like you said, we need to find a place for a permanent settlement on this planet, and then we need to move people and all our gear there. We also need to fly recon patrols to make sure no nasties like Thuranin are sneaking up on us. That means a lot of flying time, and that takes a lot of fuel. They won't miss one tankful."

"It will take considerably more than one tankful to get off this planet and fly somewhere useful, Joe. Your biggest obstacle is not obtaining fuel, it will be getting Chotek to approve a plan he is certain to view as a waste of resources."

"Chotek will not be a problem, Skippy. I'll tell him we will be looking for usable technology up there in the junkyard, even if we can't rebuild the *Dutchman*. Besides, you are forgetting my greatest asset."

"What's that?"

"Chotek would love for me to be away from this planet for a couple months while he builds his little kingdom down here."

I was right. After a moderate amount of arguing that seemed like he was merely going through the motions, my boss granted permission for me to leave the planet, and he didn't even ask how long I would be gone. What he cared about was that we would have a steady supply of fuel for dropships, and once we had hooked up a synthesizer to a geothermal power source and demonstrated making quality fuel, he lost interest in what I was doing. Three weeks later, with tanks so full the Condor groaned from the effort of taking off, we left Gingerbread behind. Another Condor topped off our fuel in high orbit and then we were gone, beyond the stealth field. To maintain communications with the surface, we deployed satellites and high-altitude balloons to relay signals. Bandwidth would be skimpy so we could only get simple text messages through, and that was fine with both me and Hans Chotek.

I was free! Free is a relative term, I was stuck aboard a Thuranin dropship with five other people, holds jammed with fuel and supplies, and we still had no way to get away from the star system. Skippy's battle with the worm was still counting down to Zero Hour. And searching an ancient junkyard full of broken alien ships may be a tremendous waste of time. What I cared about was that it felt like I was doing something useful. Or something that *might* be useful, despite the odds against us. Desai, Reed and the three other pilots mostly cared they had one last opportunity to fly a spacecraft, before we all became subsistence farmers like the humans on Paradise.

So, our Condor had plenty of fuel, bland but sufficient food, and one shiny beer can. I was hoping this would be the most epic road trip *ever*!

"This sucks," I mumbled less than a month later.

"I warned you-"

"Don't remind me," I snapped back at Skippy.

"Hey, I wasn't the one who thought coming out here would be a super-fun family adventure. You're like the Dad who gets the family in a car, drives six hours to the Museum of Dusty Relics, and is surprised everyone didn't enjoy the trip."

"I said *don't* remind me."

"Someone has to."

"Crap."

ZERO HOUR

I was hanging in space, tethered to the Condor, just returned from yet another fruitless trip to inspect alien junk. This time, it was part of a Thuranin ship that Skippy estimated was twenty thousand years old. From the spinning hulk that massed over eight thousand tons, we were able to recover three jump coils. Three! Skippy didn't even know if those three were usable, all we could see was those three were the only ones with microfractures in their matrices. Three measly coils was not going to get the *Flying Dutchman* anywhere.

We also found a surprising amount of fuel in the hulk's tanks, although the reactors had sheared away so there was no place to use the fuel. And we recovered part of a jump drive controller, Skippy didn't know if he could use it, but it wasn't large or heavy so we took it with us anyway. The fuel we found in the tanks wasn't compatible with a Condor's engines, damn it. If we found or could build a reactor we could always come back for the fuel; that hulk wasn't going anywhere.

Thus far, our epic journey to the stars was, as Hans Chotek predicted, an epic waste of time. After the first couple days, my boss only bothered to contact me once a week, and that was in response to the rather thin progress reports I had sent. The people on Gingerbread had made actual progress; they had located a site to build a settlement and were already transferring people and supplies there. The site sounded nice, it was next to a river, and just upstream from a large lake. Winters there were mild and perhaps the best feature of that site was another geothermal power source was there; one of the synthesizers was being relocated and should be producing dropship fuel soon. Major Simms had a team clearing land and planting test crops. I could not picture the SpecOps teams settling down to live like Little House on the Prairie but I certainly could not criticize them. They were dealing with reality as best they could while I was only delaying the inevitable by flying around looking at ancient space junk.

We had plenty of fuel, we had plenty of food, we had plenty of floating scrap to investigate in the orbital junkyard. What the six of us were running out of was patience and enthusiasm. Right from the beginning, our flight was a desperation move, a Hail Mary. I had pushed to explore the junkyard in part because we just might find something useful out there, but I knew the reality was my main motivation in flying offworld was to delay facing the fact that Skippy was going to die soon, and the Merry Band of Pirates would be trapped on Gingerbread, probably forever. I justified my refusal to accept reality because reality totally sucked, so it's reality's fault.

"Desai, I'm coming in," I announced after indulging myself for a long minute of staring at the stars. "Let's wrap this up, there's nothing useful here we don't already have aboard."

"Yes, Colonel," she replied from the cockpit. Desai had been the first pilot to volunteer for our useless goose chase, and of course I approved her coming with me. If this were the last time we ever flew, I wanted her with me. "Set course for the next target?"

"Sure," I responded without enthusiasm. Then, remembering that I had to set the tone for all six of us, I added, "I promise no negative thoughts this time. The next target is going to be a jackpot of gear we can use to fix up the old *Dutchman*, guaranteed."

"Yes, Sir," she said with a chuckle that sounded forced. "It's only a four day trip from here; we'll know if you're right soon enough."

"Joe, we gots a problem," Skippy's voice broke me out of a daydream, and I scrambled to pull myself back to the present. There was no problem with our Condor, I knew that because the display in front of me was not showing any alerts. And the pilots up in the cockpit would have notified me. That left some very bad possibilities, like Skippy losing control of the Guardians and them tearing our dropship apart, or the worm attacking Skippy again.

"What is it?" In the passenger compartment, I had been loosely strapped into a seat, standard procedure while the Condor was coasting toward our next target. Desai had fired the engines for about half an hour and then cut thrust; we wouldn't use the main jets again until we needed to decelerate to match course and speed with the pile of spinning ancient junk that was our next target to explore. Until then, the six of us floated around in zero gravity and exercised awkwardly to prevent our muscles from wasting away.

"Sorry to startle you, there is no immediate danger," he assured me. "The orbits of the planets in this system are not natural. Not *possible*. There's an entire planet missing."

Hearing that gave me a chill. "Oh, crap. Is this like Newark, where Newark got pushed out of its original orbit, that disrupted the orbits of the other planets, and the innermost planet fell into the star?"

"No. Well, yes. There was an inner planet here, one that originally wasn't there at all, I speculate that-"

"Hold on. Go back a minute. What do you mean, the inner planet wasn't originally there?"

Skippy sighed. "Ugh. Now I have to explain orbital mechanics to you?" His voice was incredulous. "Can I hit the highlights and skip the math?"

"Probably a good idea," I admitted.

"Ok, here goes nothing. Joe, running the math backwards shows me the Roach Motel used to have a Saturn-sized gas giant planet orbiting close to the star. Close, like, the star's gravity well was siphoning off the planet's atmosphere."

"I thought gas giant planets didn't form so close to a star."

"Very good, Joey, get yourself a juicebox. Gas giants normally do not form so close to a star, and this planet didn't form there. This planet originally orbited far from the star, out deep in the Oort cloud. The Elders must have towed it near the star."

"*Towed*? Holy shit. They could- of course they could do that. Wow, moving a big planet like that through the system must have caused havoc with the other planets."

"It would have required the Elders to stabilize the other planets during and after the transition. Most likely, the Elders jumped the planet through a temporary wormhole, to avoid it passing through the orbits of other planets."

I simply shook my head. The works of the Elders blew my mind. They jumped a *planet* through a wormhole. Skippy once told me they had jumped a supergiant blue-white star through a wormhole, jumped it outside the galaxy. Beings like that, I could not comprehend. No wonder Skippy was so awesome, he had been built by beings to whom awesomeness was commonplace. "Let's skip the part where I ask you how the hell anyone can jump a planet through a wormhole, and get to my next question; why? Why would they want to reposition a planet close to a star?"

"A *gas* giant planet, Joe. That's the key. I am speculating, but my guess is the Elders used the planet to slowly replenish the star's hydrogen. Pushing the planet into the star would have been too disruptive, so they placed the planet where its atmosphere would be gradually siphoned off. That technique can stretch out the life of a star's main phase. If the Elders were tapping the star for power, as I suspect they were and still are, they are shortening the star's useful life. The further back I run the math, the more fuzzy it is, but I think the Elders used at least two gas giant planets to replenish the star over the eons."

"Wow. *Wow*. So, when you said a planet is missing, you meant that over time, the star sucked up that entire gas giant planet?"

"No. Damn, talking with you is frustrating, you ask too many questions. What I meant is, that innermost gas giant planet fell into the star, much earlier than it was supposed to. Gas giants have rocky cores; when all the gas had been siphoned off, the Elders likely planned to crash the useless core remnant into the star. What I think happened is, the gas giant fell into the star while it was still a giant."

"The Elders pushed it into the star, the same way someone pushed Newark out past its original orbit?"

"No. Joe, technically, there are *three* planets missing from this star system."

"Crap, Skippy."

"Crap indeed, Joe. There's the gas giant that fell into the star, plus a Neptune-sized planet that got ejected from the system. Technically, that planet is still orbiting the star, but it is so far away, it takes eight thousand years for a single orbit. Because the math tells me roughly where that outer planet must be, I found it using the *Dutchman*'s sensors. It's faint, but it's there."

"That's two. What about the third planet?"

"That is what puzzles me, Joe. The third planet that is missing originally orbited just beyond where Gingerbread is, kind of like how Mars orbits beyond Earth. This missing planet was more massive than Mars, the math tells me it had about the mass of Venus."

"Ok, and? Where did it go?"

"It didn't go anywhere, Joe. It just simply went 'poof' and disappeared."

"It's missing? Is its picture on a milk carton or something?"

"*What?*"

"Forget I said that. How is it possible for a whole planet to go missing?"

"It's not. Not even for the Elders. I thought possibly they jumped it somewhere, but doing that leaves a distinctive vibration pattern inside the star, that would be detectable even after all this time. There is no such vibration."

I scratched my head. "This is all great info, and it's a mystery to puzzle through another time, right? It's not actionable?"

"*Actionable?* You need to stop picking up buzzwords from PowerPoint slides. It is actionable, Joe, because I want us to fly over to where this planet should be, so I can examine it better with this ship's crappy instruments."

"Hoooo boy, that's going to be a tough sell to Chotek. How about we check out our next target, and think about flying over to this phantom planet later?"

"Deal. If the phantom planet exists, it will take us a month to get there anyway; plenty of derelict ships in the junkyard between here and there. Hey!" He exclaimed with delight. "You don't even need to tell Chotek at all. There are two large derelicts in the general area where I expect the phantom planet to be, if it exists. Those derelicts are close enough for me to scan the area and determine whether we should go in for a closer look."

"A closer look? At a planet that, you think, might not exist?"

"Well, it just sounds stupid when you say it like that, Joe."

"Major Smythe?" Captain Giraud approached the SpecOps team leader as the SAS man came out of a dreary meeting with Chotek and Simms, reviewing details of the site Chotek had selected for a permanent human settlement on Gingerbread. "We have a decision?"

Smythe nodded. "Yes, Chotek has selected a site. It's good enough, I suppose. Major Simms agrees the area is suitable for agriculture."

"He is serious about expending effort to build permanent structures, while Skippy is still with us?"

"Captain, our civilian leader is planning a *golf course*," Smythe noted with a raised eyebrow.

"Golf-" Giraud thought for a moment the remark had been missed in translation, then thought Smyth had been joking. The expression on Smythe's face made it clear his statement had not been a joke. Giraud lowered his voice. "It is one thing to scout for a site, but it seems premature to dedicate our air power to transportation of supplies to build a settlement, while Colonel Bishop is still working to get us away from this star system-"

"I agree, Captain. Orders are orders. I intend to confirm my instructions with Colonel Bishop. Chotek does not intend to begin a serious effort to move base camp for another month," he looked up at the trees, which still had healthy green leaves. The climate model created by Skippy predicted nights at base camp would begin becoming cool in another six weeks, with winter approaching in four months. It was Smythe's turn to lower his voice, he glanced around to assure no one overheard the conversation. "There is another matter I need to discuss with Colonel Bishop, if we truly are to be stranded on this planet. We need to do something about those Thuranin. They may not be a threat to us now because we have a technological advantage, but in ten, twenty, fifty years? Our dropships will cease to be flightworthy, and even for ground combat, we have a limited supply of ammunition. I do not want our future generations to face the Thuranin, with our side armed only with bows and arrows."

Giraud nodded in grim agreement. "We must hit them while we still have air power. You think Bishop will agree?"

"I won't ask him while he still hopes to fix Skippy's problem. But, our commanding officer is a common-sense soldier," Smythe concluded. "He will understand what we have to do."

I had just finished a four-hour shift as copilot of our Condor, when Skippy made a strange, strangled sort of beeping sound, then went silent. "Skippy? What was that?" He had been quiet for several hours, I thought he was being nice and letting me concentrate on flying, although our dropship was currently coasting toward a cluster of parts from a derelict Thuranin ship, so there was absolutely nothing for pilot or copilot to do. Major Desai had spent most of our four hours together putting me through simulations to improve my skills for flying the Condor. All I was trusted to do so far was routine maneuvers in space; any tricky flying, or flying in an atmosphere would have to wait for me to gain more experience. "Skippy?"

He didn't respond at all.

In a panic, I launched myself through the door into the main cabin, where his beer can was strapped into a seat. No sooner had I reached the chair and reached out to shake him when he finally spoke and his avatar shimmered to life above the headrest of the seat. "Hi, Joe. I thought you were still flying." Skippy's voice sounded mildly disoriented. "Whew, I had a little shock for a moment."

"Skippy," I waggled a finger at his avatar. "If this is because I washed my own laundry this morning, that is not funny."

"Nope. Although that was a shock. Also, you did it wrong."

"What is the problem, then?"

"Um, Joe, we're in potential danger."

"Wow!" I clapped my hands. "That's great news, Skippy, thank you."

"Huh?"

"Hey, usually the Merry Band of Pirates are in actual, no-kidding, oh-my-God, pee-in-my-pants danger. To only be in *potential* danger is a huge improvement."

"Oh. That is a good point."

"We've already got these Guardians swarming around us, a ship broken in pieces, your firewall is losing power and we haven't been able to find the conduit thingy to fix you. What is the problem now?"

"I don't want to alarm you-"

"But you're going to do it anyway."

"Right. Those other problems you mentioned, this new danger is kind of an order of magnitude worse. Like, infinitely worse."

"What the hell is it, Skippy?"

"Um, there's a Sentinel here?"

"Oh, shit. A freakin' *Sentinel*? Like-"

"Like, a giant unstoppable Elder killing machine that can stomp the Rindhalu like bugs. Hee, hee, that was a good one. Because the Rindhalu are sort of spiders, like bugs."

"Oh, yeah, that was freakin' hilarious, Skippy."

"Really, I would have been surprised if there wasn't a Sentinel or two around here somewhere."

"Why the *hell* didn't you mention that before?!" I demanded.

"Would you have brought the ship to the Roach Motel, if you knew there were Sentinels here?"

"Hell no! Crap, did I just answer my own question?"

"Ya think? Joey, if I had told you this system likely contained Sentinels, you would have gone all 'ooooh, too dangerous' on me," his avatar waggled its fingers in the air as if frightened, "and we wouldn't have come here."

"Yeah, and then we would have a ship in one piece. Plus, we've accomplished *so* much since we got here. Like, nothing."

"Yet. We haven't accomplished anything *yet*, Joe. Have faith."

"Have faith? So says the beer can, who failed to tell me about the unstoppable killing machine. And brought us to this dead-end star system."

"Joe, in my defense, there are Sentinels scattered across the galaxy. Normally, they are dormant, and they are actually in another phase of spacetime. As far as I know, the last time any of them were active was when the Maxolhx used Elder devices to attack the Rindhalu. That woke up the Sentinels, and after they stomped the Maxolhx and Rindhalu back to the Stone Age, they went dormant again."

"And we woke up this one?!"

"No. No, in fact, that is what shocked me. Joe, this Sentinel is not dormant, it's *dead*. I think it's been dead a long, long time. All I found was a broken piece of it."

"Dead? How could that happen?"

"Hence the source of my shock. What in this universe could kill a Sentinel?" His avatar shuddered. "This scares the *shit* out of me, Joe."

"It scares me too, Skippy. What do you mean by 'dead'?"

"It is not generating or using any power. It is tumbling out of control. I pinged it, and it did not respon-"

"*You PINGED it?!*"

"Yes, duh. How else was I supposed to-"

"You found a giant, super-powerful killing machine that is guarding an Elder star system we are ransacking, and your best idea was to say 'Hey, how you doing'?!"

"Oh. Hmm. Sorry. In retrospect, that may not have been my best idea ever. Anywho, no harm, no foul, right?"

"No harm so far, you little shithead. You said there could be more than one Sentinel here. What if your ping woke up another one?"

"I *said* I was sorry, Joe. Jeez Louise, let it go, will you?"

I just glared at him in disbelief. "Skippy, are you experiencing another cognitive deficit or whatever you call it when you act like you're drunk?"

"No, why?"

"No reason. Other than you just doing the single *dumbest* thing you've ever done."

"Oh, heh heh," he laughed nervously. "That was the single dumbest thing you *know of*, Joe. Truthfully, pinging a Sentinel isn't even in my Top Ten. Damn, I have done some *really* stupid shit I haven't told you about and- uh. Hmmm. Maybe I shouldn't have said that."

"Ya think? Ok, so, where is this Sentinel? We'll back away from it real easy, and-"

"What? Back away from it?" His avatar folded its arms across its chest. "No, dumdum. We need to rendezvous with it."

I stared at the avatar for a long second, then shook my head incredulously. "Uh, excuse me? Pinging the damned thing wasn't good enough, now we need to go knock on the front door?"

"No one's home, Joe. Trust me."

"Trust you? Right after telling me you've done stupid shit I don't even know about?"

"Ugh. Your meatsack memory is terribly inefficient. I should be able to erase your memory of what I said just then, but nooooooo. You freakin' monkeys remember all the wrong stuff. Yes, Joe, we need to fly over to this Sentinel and check it out."

"Because? Whatever you say next had better be good, Skippy, like epically good."

"It is, Joe. It is almost certain we can find a conduit inside that Sentinel."

Oh crap. That actually was a good reason for us to go poking our noses in places our noses did not belong. "Almost certain?"

"Like, I would give a billion to one odds that we will find a conduit there. Using conduit capability to manipulate local spacetime is how Sentinels function. That capability is how they reside in and draw power from higher dimensions. It is how they can disrupt stars and tear starships apart. Guardians use a similar technology, although on a much lower scale, and conduits are not native to Guardians; they just temporarily use conduits located outside this spacetime."

"Uh huh." I was underwhelmed.

"Come on, Joe, this is exciting! We finally found what I need to fix myself."

"Maybe. We *might* have found a conduit we can use. We've had two failures with conduits we've found so far. What makes you think a conduit inside a broken Sentinel will still be functional?"

"Because it will not be '*a*' conduit. Considering the size of the fragment I found, there should be hundreds of devices I can use as a conduit. We only need one. Joe, uh! Let me talk, please." His avatar held up a finger to shush me. "This is our golden opportunity. I didn't mention it to you before, because there is no reason to worry you about things you can't control, but over the past forty eight hours, the worm has been increasingly active. To combat it, I am draining more and more power from my internal reserves. If we don't find a conduit soon, like within the next twelve days, I am likely toast. And so are you, in the long run."

"Crap. Skippy, in the future, I *do* need to worry about that type of thing. Ok, tell me one thing; if you are certain a Sentinel has the conduit capability you need, why didn't you contact one when we got here?"

"Because a live Sentinel would most likely stomp me flat for violating like, every rule the Elders have," he responded quietly, and didn't even add the usual implied 'duh' in his tone. "The only reason the Sentinel I found is an opportunity rather than a danger is that it's dead as a doornail. The idea that anything in this galaxy can kill a Sentinel scares the shit out of me, but this one *is* dead."

"Twelve days, huh?" I rubbed my chin, and Skippy's avatar took on a pitiful, helpless expression he must have learned from watching sad puppies on Instagram. "How long for us to get the Sentinel?"

"Just over five days at maximum acceleration. To be precise, one hundred twenty one hours, thirty eight minutes and-"

"That's precise enough, thank you. Oh, hell," I felt a whopping headache coming on already. "I need to get an Ok from Chotek about this." Messing with a Sentinel was something our mission commander was not going to like one bit. "Time for a roundtrip signal to Gingerbread is?" I checked the display but Desai answered for me.

"Sixteen minutes, Colonel," she replied, and looked at me with one eyebrow raised and one finger poised over the autopilot button.

I nodded as I relaxed back in my seat and engaged the safety straps for acceleration. "Get us moving toward the Sentinel, Desai. We'll need all the time we can get if Chotek approves this crazy plan."

"Yes, Sir," she acknowledged. "Prepare for sustained acceleration." She turned to look me straight in the eye. "What if Mister Chotek does not approve us approaching a Sentinel?"

"Then," I took a deep breath, "I will have a decision to make."

Twenty nine minutes later, we received a short message 'Take no action at this time. Instructions to follow'. That was Chotek's way of telling me he was thinking about it, and that I should wait for his decision. As we were already burning hard to intercept the Sentinel, I interpreted 'take no action' to mean that we should take no action to cease our acceleration. I know that was bullshit, but I was grasping at straws. "Skippy, are there any potential junkyard targets along our current course?"

"Whew. Technically, no, but if we alter course within the next forty eight minutes, we could reach a cluster of potentially useful junk. After that, we will be headed away from any plausible targets for our original mission."

"Forty eight minutes?" I repeated thoughtfully. "It will take eight minutes for Chotek's signal to reach us out here, so he has another forty minutes to make up his mind." In my message to him about the Sentinel, I had included the information that Skippy estimated the worm would get past his internal defenses within twelve days. While that should have impressed on our mission commander the urgency of the situation, and that the broken Sentinel may be our last hope to fix Skippy, I don't know if Chotek would believe me. He may think I faked Skippy's twelve-day deadline as a way to convince him to approve the mission to the Sentinel. My credibility with our mission leader was not the best. It was frustrating that the speed-of-light time lag made it impossible to have a real conversation.

We did not have to wait forty eight minutes for an answer; a second message was received seven minutes later. Chotek denied permission for us to investigate the Sentinel, and further, he ordered me to avoid coming anywhere near the dangerous Elder machine.

Chotek thought the risk was too great that us poking around a Sentinel, even one supposedly dead, would trigger other Sentinels to destroy humanity's home planet.

"Colonel?" Desai looked at me expectantly. The message had been directed to me personally, so she hadn't read it.

What the hell was I going to do? A quick glance at the clock told me we had another forty one minutes until I would be directly violating orders. "Continue on present course," I told Desai, and the tone of my voice must have alerted her to the content of Chotek's message. "We have another forty one minutes before we are technically violating orders," I explained, so Desai did not have to participate in a mutiny.

"Yes, Sir," she replied quietly, avoiding my eyes. She sat stiffly in her couch, with one finger tapping slowly on a blank part of the flatscreen controls, like she was working up to say something to me.

"Desai, I'm going to request a confirmation," I looked down at my own console and began typing, partly to avoid a discussion with her. Forty one minutes. I had forty one minutes to decide whether I was a United States Army soldier, or a pirate. If I was a pirate, then there were no rules, no restrictions on our conduct. I would be representing myself rather than humanity, and I would be substituting my own inexperienced judgment for that of UNEF Command, in the form of Hans Chotek.

A mutiny would be easy to do, except for two things. First, Chotek had been right and I had been wrong about us going to Paradise. On my own, I would not have taken the ship there to check on the status of humans trapped on that planet; I had been afraid of learning humans there were in danger that we couldn't do anything about. Humans on Paradise had been in danger, but we had found a way to secure their future. Being wrong about that issue had been a humbling experience for me; until then I had been feeling pretty cocky about saving Earth twice. Chotek had also been right about insisting we perform an intermediate jump to recon Bravo before approaching that site; if we had followed my plan the *Dutchman* would have been trapped by the powerful damping fields of a Thuranin task force. About Paradise and about Bravo, Chotek's judgment had been better than mine.

The second thing that held me back from mutiny was the nagging feeling that maybe, just maybe, Chotek was right again this time. Maybe us messing with a Sentinel, even if doing that could fix Skippy, was not worth the risk of provoking other Sentinels.

It was a judgment call, and the entire reason UNEF Command had assigned Hans Chotek as our mission commander was to make important judgment calls.

Because UNEF Command didn't trust my judgment.

Maybe they were right. I had an emotional connection with Skippy; my ability to think objectively might be impaired.

I had forty one minutes to think about that.

Margaret Adams was not invited to the emergency meeting in Chotek's tent; that audience had been limited to Lt. Colonel Chang, Major Smythe and Major Simms. All she knew was that a message had been sent from Colonel Bishop to Chotek, that three senior officers had been called away from their regular duties, and when he came out of the meeting, Smythe's face was as grim as Adams had ever seen it. She had arranged to be in the path between tents that Smythe was likely to take after leaving Chotek. "Major? What's going on?"

Smythe shot a look back over his shoulder to where the flap of Chotek's tent was just closing. The mission commander had not instructed the three officers to keep quiet about the subject of the meeting, which would have been foolish anyway. "Walk with me,

Sergeant," Smythe said in more of a request than an order. "Bishop located a Sentinel out there."

"A *Sentinel*?" Adams gasped, a chill of fear running up her spine. "I can see how-"

"You don't understand," Smythe shook his head curtly, motioning her into a side passageway. "Skippy reported the Sentinel is dead, what they located is only a broken fragment."

Adams' shoulders remained tense. "No danger then?" She asked, thinking that was unlikely given the expression on the SAS man's face.

"Not according to Skippy. He wants to explore the fragment, in hope of finding a conduit; apparently there is a strong probability a conduit will be found inside what is left of the machine. Bishop agrees, and requested permission to proceed toward the site to investigate with a proximity sensor scan."

Adams understood the source of Smythe's unhappiness. "And our fearless-"- she caught herself, aware she was speaking with an officer. "Our mission commander refused permission?"

"Quite so," Smythe's eyes narrowed, judging her reaction to the news. "There is a complication; Bishop reported Skippy estimates he has only twelve days remaining until the worm breaks through his defenses."

"Twelve days to Zero Hour?" Adams cocked her head. That couldn't be the whole story. "A deadline like that should be a strong reason to search that Sentinel for a conduit."

"It is a strong reason, Chotek agrees. He thinks perhaps it is *too* strong, too convenient that Skippy's failure is imminent at the same time we have a hazardous opportunity to find the one thing that could fix our AI."

"Chotek thinks Bishop is *lying* about it?" Margaret Adams was astonished. And angry.

"There is unfortunately not a large reservoir of trust between our mission commander and our captain. Chotek may think Bishop is exaggerating, or revealing only the facts that support his request. Or that Skippy is lying to Bishop, or guessing. There is *no* trust between Chotek and the," Smythe's jaw worked side to side as if he were chewing on something unpleasant. "Beer can. That lack of trust is Skippy's own fault. Where are you going, Sergeant?" Smythe asked as she strode past him.

"To speak with our mission commander."

Craig Alanson
Chapter Twenty Three

My zPhone vibrated, it was a text from Skippy. *Need to talk with you privately*, the message read. I fitted the earpiece in and floated back to the Condor's cargo compartment. "What's up, Skippy?"

"We have only eleven minutes until you have to decide whether to ignore Chocula's orders."

"Yeah, I know." I had been watching the time on my zPhone, and Desai had been glancing back at me through the open cockpit door. My response had been to cowardly avoid eye contact with our chief pilot.

"I'm surprised by you, Joe, and disappointed. You are putting Major Desai through stress that is unnecessary. We all know what you are going to do, so get on with-"

"I don't, Skippy."

"Uh," Skippy wasn't often at a loss for words, this was one of those times. "You, don't, what?" He asked slowly.

"I don't know what I am going to do, Skippy."

"O.M.G., Joe!" His screech blasted in my ear and I reflexively pulled the earpiece away. "Dude, you have *got* to be kidding me! Listen, this loyal soldier crap has gone too far; are you seriously going to obey Chocula's orders just because he is technically your commanding-"

"No, Skippy. Not just that, but you have to understand; I am an Army officer and disobeying lawful orders isn't something I can do easily. My problem is, he may be right."

"*Really?*" His voice dripped with icy sarcasm. "Whoa! Whoa, whoa, *whoa*. Holy shit. You don't trust me. After all we've been through, you do not trust me."

"It's not-"

"Yes it is."

"Ok, yes, it is. I trust you to tell the truth, or as much of it as you think I need to know. What I don't, what I don't know if I can trust, is your judgment. You assured me there was no danger to you poking around in that dead AI canister."

"Oh, for- That was one time!"

"And you assured me we could jump into the Roach Motel here without a problem, and you broke the freakin' ship!"

"All right, fine. So I made *two* mistakes."

"You also sent us on a wild goose chase to find this conduit thingy, and so far every place you said we could find one, we either flew into an ambush, or the conduit doesn't work."

"That's the conduit at Barsoom, then the one where the Thuranin were waiting for us, and the burned-out one in the tunnel on Gingerbread. Three. Ok, so I made *five* mistakes. That's, hmm, crap, I guess that is a lot of mistakes in a short time. But I'm telling you, this dead Sentinel absolutely will have conduits, and-"

"And whatever killed the Sentinel will not have burned out the conduits?"

"Crap. I hadn't thought of that. Thanks a lot, Mr. Buzzkill."

"I'm trying to be serious, Skippy. I have to balance the risk of screwing with a super-powerful killing machine, with the slender possibility of finding a working conduit that *might* fix you."

"You won't do it?"

"I have been ordered not to do it, Skippy."

"I will ask the question like Sergeant Adams does, Joe. *Yes*, or *no*? We are both running out of time."

The Army trained me to make decisions based on incomplete information, since nobody ever has all the info they want. They trained me to make decisions quickly, and to live with the consequences. They did not train me how to decide whether to disobey a direct order.

I did not know what to do. If Skippy was wrong and there was no conduit in the Sentinel, or the conduits were all burned out, then I would be committing mutiny for nothing, and my authority would be gone. If Skippy was wrong and me screwing with a Sentinel caused retaliation against Earth, I could be condemning my entire species for nothing. But if Skippy was right, then we could fix him so the Merry Band of Pirates might go on protecting Earth.

One way or the other, I needed to make a decision.

"Skippy," I said. My instincts were telling me to-

"Colonel Bishop?" Desai called from the cockpit. "You have a message," she announced just as my zPhone pinged.

It was from Chotek.

Investigate Sentinel for conduit at your discretion. Proceed with extreme caution.

"Whoo hoo!" Skippy exulted, having read the message before I did. "Hey, Joe, what were you going to say?"

"It doesn't matter now. Desai! We are cleared to approach the Sentinel!" I read the message again. "I wonder what changed?"

"My guess," Skippy announced dryly, "is someone performed a spine transplant on Count Chocula."

"Somebody helped him grow a backbone, huh?" I mused. "If we get back to Gingerbread, I'll have to ask Sergeant Adams if she was involved."

"Joe, you really are not going to tell me what you decided to do, before you got Chotek's message?"

"Let it be a mystery, Skippy."

Everything was great for a short time, then Skippy ruined my hopeful mood. "Hmmm. Hey, Joe, we have, heh heh, another potential problem."

There are some sounds in this universe that are intrinsically terrifying to humans. The snapping of twigs on the forest floor at night, as a predator approaches your campsite. The dry rustling of a snake slithering through dead leaves. Or the hissing of a snake. Or the buzzing of a rattlesnake's tail when you just stepped on something in thick underbrush but you can't see the snake so you don't know which way to jump. Ok, so you get the idea, I hate snakes. Not all snakes; we had black snakes in our barn and they ate rats so I had no problem with them. The kind of snakes I hate are the ones I encounter suddenly. Which is most snakes.

Anyway, to the list of sounds that are always terrifying regardless of context, you can add an asshole shiny beer can nervously saying '*heh heh*'.

"Potential? Crap, is that Sentinel waking up?"

"Huh? No, dumdum, I told you, that thing is *dead*. The new problem is the Guardians are increasingly frantic about our Condor approaching that Sentinel fragment. They have been urging me away, and now they are sort of warning me of dire consequences."

"Warning? Dire consequences like what?"

"Warning like, they will be forced to tear our Condor in half if we continue on course. I don't think I can fix this problem, the Guardians have base programming I can't alter in my current condition, and part of that base programming appears to be keeping non-Elder spacecraft from approaching that dead Sentinel."

"How much closer can we get before they act?"

"Not much. I suggest we, uh, heh heh, alter course soon. Like, *now*."

"Wu!" I shouted into the cockpit through the open door. "Initiate a one-gee burn to starboard, now!"

"Aye aye," she acknowledged as I tugged my safety straps tight. In less than ten seconds, Wu had the main engines warmed up, and a steady pressure began pushing me back into my seat, building up to Earth normal apparent gravity.

"Skippy, how far do we have to go?"

"Wait a minute, wait. Ok, this is good, the Guardians are backing off."

"Do we have to keep moving away, or could we hold position this far from the Sentinel?"

"I think we could maintain this distance, Joe. I'm kind of guessing. We could try it, and I'll tell you how the Guardians react. Just be ready to skedaddle out of here pronto."

"I will have my emergency skedaddler ready. Lieutenant Wu! Change course again, hold our position at this distance from the Sentinel. You can push it to three Gees if needed."

She did need three Gees, or she made a judgement call that temporary discomfort for the crew was worth the advantage of completing the maneuver quickly. With the engines burning hard, the six of us needed to endure the pressure of acceleration for less than seven minutes before Wu was able to cut thrust and declare "We are stationary in relation to the Sentinel, Colonel. Range one hundred twenty seven thousand kilometers."

For some reason, it flashed through my mind that was approximately a third of the distance from the Earth to the Moon. Useless trivia, but it gave my poor little monkey brain some context. "Skippy? Are the Guardians Ok with us staying here?"

"They are uneasy about it, however they are no longer threatening to rip the Condor apart."

"Great," I gave a sigh of relief. "No, not great. Not great at all. We need to get close to that thing, right?"

"Very close. Same as before, I can't do this remotely. The footprint occupied in local spacetime by a conduit is small, really it is an unintended but unavoidable effect of the- well, I won't bore you with the details."

"Probably a good idea. We need to get you over there."

"Joe, if you have some idiot idea that you can fling me into the Sentinel attached to a missile, you can forget about it. I can't tell exactly where a conduit would be located inside-"

"No, Skippy," I shook my head. "I think we need to get the band back together."

"Huh? I'm not following you, Joe. I could certainly be the singer in a band, but you have no discernable musical talent."

"Not music, I was using an expression. I'm talking about you, me and a suit for a long-range spacedive."

"Oh, cool! Wait. I just did the math, and a jetpack will take way too long to get us there, assuming we need to conserve fuel for a return journey."

"I figured that. Run the math again, this time assume we back the dropship away and use it to accelerate us toward the Sentinel, then we only need to use a jetpack to slow us down to rendezvous with the Sentinel."

ZERO HOUR

"Good idea. Done. It's still not practical, Joe. The problem is we also need the jetpack to get us back to the Condor. The trip back and forth is too long, you would run out of oxygen."

"Those jetpacks can be fitted with auxiliary fuel tanks, right? What if we did that?"

"Ok, Ok, another good idea. Hmmm, that might work. Assuming we need six hours at the Sentinel to locate a conduit and for me to gain access to it, your oxygen supply is going to be marginal, Joe."

"Will six hours be enough time?"

"I do not know, Joe. Truly, I don't. We can't get good scans of the Sentinel's interior structure from here. I said six hours because my thinking is, if we can't get the job done in six hours, more time isn't going to help."

"That makes sense." I unstrapped from my seat and floated through the door to the rear compartment of the Condor, where we stored Kristang spacesuits and jetpacks. Rapping my knuckles on the hard shell of a suit, I considered the problem. "The problem is mass? The less mass we have to move to the Sentinel and back, the faster the jetpack can move us with the same amount of fuel."

"Correct, Captain Obvious."

Ignoring him, I examined the suit closely. "The Kristang built these suit for dual purposes. They protect the user from the vacuum of space, or from toxic environments like planets with a methane atmosphere. Because we got these from a troopship, these are also armored mech suits. For this trip, I don't need the armor."

"Ah, I see where you're going with this, Joe. Good thinking. Much of the armor is integral to the suit, but there are panels which can be removed, and those panels carry a lot of mass," Skippy observed, warming to the idea. "We could also dump the reservoirs of self-repair nano, they are heavy and we won't need them. We will keep enough nano to plug leaks in the suit, unless you plan to pee in your pants again?"

"Let's avoid that," I gave Lt. Reed the side-eye in case she hadn't heard about that embarrassing little incident on my second mission. "There's also a bunch of gear we can strip off a jetpack. The stealth field generator, the comm and navigation modules; you can handle comms and navigation for us-"

Six hours later, we had a suit and jetpack stripped of everything that was not absolutely essential, and I was in an open airlock with Skippy secured in a padded bag on my right side. Desai had backed the Condor away, then punched the throttle hard to accelerate us toward the Sentinel again. I gutted out the three-Gee burn in my suit, hooked up to oxygen and power from the Condor to conserve my own supplies. Exactly in time with the countdown clock in my helmet visor, Desai cut thrust, and my stomach did flip flops as we were suddenly in zero gravity again. "Right on the mark, Colonel. We need to burn again in two minutes thirty seconds," she warned.

"Got it," I replied. Lt Reed helped me manually disconnect from the lines for oxygen and power, released the clamps holding me, and I floated free. With a gentle push from Reed, I drifted out the airlock door. She stood in the doorway, illuminated by the harsh light of the distant star, and gave me a solemn salute. "This isn't a funeral, Reed," I complained. "I plan to be back."

"Yes, Sir," she made a smile I could barely see in the glare, and snapped a crisp salute to me. "I'll hold you to that."

I returned a crisp salute. "The Air Force says 'Aim High', Reed? In space, there's no up or down, so how do I aim high?"

Craig Alanson

The Guardians did not object to me approaching the Sentinel in a spacesuit and jetpack, or Skippy was able to persuade them to leave us alone. Or the Guardians were screaming a final warning at Skippy and he was letting me blissfully ignore my last moments of existence. There was no way for me to know, so I chose the blissful ignorance option.

I highly recommend it.

The Sentinel loomed in my visor, the view artificially magnified due to the distance involved. Damn, it was creepy. It made my skin crawl to look at it. And it was *huge*. I knew from the Condor's sensor data that this broken piece of a Sentinel was seventy eight kilometers across its long axis and almost thirty kilometers front to back. It was black, and it looked like a spider. No, like a cluster of spider legs, or the tentacles of an octopus; a really, really creepy scary octopus. "Damn. Why does this thing look so creepy? The Elders designed it to look like spiders?"

"No, Joe, they did not design it to look scary. The design template is based on fractal geometry, that's all. Don't be such a baby."

"You're a beer can. You never got frightened by a spider. Skippy, my species has a deep-seated instinctive fear of some things, and spiders are near the top of the list."

"Oh, boo freakin' hoo," he tactfully expressed his sincere sympathy. "Don't wimp out on me now, Joe."

"Skippy, courage is facing a situation that scares the shit out of you, and doing it anyway. You won't see me letting down the honor of the US Army." That speech of bravado would have been more convincing if my mouth hadn't been dry from fear. Taking a sip of water from the spout inside my helmet, I eyeclicked the image to increase magnification, but it didn't do much good. The thing was so utterly black it was difficult to discern features on its surface. What I could see was miniature repeats of the larger structure; creepy fractals getting smaller and smaller. In the super-enhanced image, I could see part of the surface appeared to be a series of sharp, spiky spines? If so, then removing protective armor panels from my suit was a bad idea. One bad puncture or tear could doom me; the nano reservoir of the suit could only repair a small leak. Crap, I really had not thought this through very well. "Do you see a way in?"

"No. Don't worry, I didn't expect to. What you are seeing is the original exterior of the device in this spacetime, it is oriented to face the star. Solar wind likely turned it so the exposed back side faces away. Once we get around to the area that broke away, we should be able to see into the interior."

"I hope you're right about that. It still looks creepy."

"Keep in mind, Joe, that's not what a Sentinel is supposed to look like. They normally reside in another spacetime where the laws of physics are different. When they do have to act in local spacetime, they are protected by a bubble projected from other dimensions. This one is broken and dead, so it has no protection. Many of the exotic materials it was constructed from can't exist here, so you're only seeing a shell; its structure is severely damaged down to an atomic level. That's how I know we are not in danger from that thing, it is deader than the proverbial doornail."

"I hope you're right about that too. Wait, its structure is damaged? Then how are we supposed to use a freakin' conduit inside the thing?"

"Because, Joe," he spoke softly and patiently to calm my rising fear, "conduits by nature must exist in multiple spacetimes. The portion of the conduit here was designed and constructed to be here. Trust me; there are a lot of dangers out here, but that Sentinel fragment isn't one of them."

I did not take the opportunity to remind him he had asked me to trust him about poking his nose into that dead AI canister we found on Newark. "Fine. Hang on, we need to begin decelerating."

The jetpack brought us to a dead stop half a kilometer from one creepy tentacle of the Sentinel. While we hung there, Skippy did his best to scan the thing while I unstrapped myself from the jetpack. We had attached supplemental fuel canisters to the jetpack, now that they were empty, I needed to remove the canisters as they were useless mass we couldn't afford to carry. They also added to the width of the jetpack, and I was concerned about tight spaces inside the Sentinel, if we could even get into the thing at all.

Removing the canisters took almost ten minutes because they weren't really designed to be removed in flight, mostly I worked silently as there wasn't much to say. After the discarded canisters were floating away and I was secured to the jetpack again, I sent a brief message to the Condor. In my visor, I saw Skippy had programmed a flightpath into the nav system. "Ready to see the back side of this thing?"

"I was born ready, Joe," he chuckled, but his voice betrayed his own fears.

"Hang on."

We burned five hours of our self-imposed six hour time limit before finding a way inside. I mean, a practical way inside. There were a lot of holes in the thing, but almost all of them were honeycombed with jagged fractal spikes or whatever they were. No way could I get in there without slicing my spacesuit to ribbons. Finally, my suit spotlights found a large, jagged hole and I cautiously flew in, keeping one eye on my oxygen supply. There was only a fifteen minute safety margin baked into our schedule, I was forcing myself to not consider that safety margin.

"Got one! A conduit!"

"Where?" I asked excitedly, just as Skippy made my visor zoom in on the thing. It was in an awkward location behind a jagged spire projecting across the opening and other broken pieces partly filling the gap. I would need to fly carefully around multiple obstructions to get to the highlighted conduit, if that's what it was. "Skippy, that thing does not look like a conduit." The one we stole from Barsoom was a long cylinder with a dimpled surface like a stretched golf ball. The thing he called a conduit in the Sentinel was two beach balls attached to each other, and a smooth cylinder going through both spheres.

"It is a conduit, trust me. There are many types of conduits. The thing on Barsoom was designed for communications. The thing ahead of us is a, well, you would think of it as part of a weapon system. Hold a minute."

It was one minute, twenty eight seconds before he spoke again. With my oxygen supply limited and dwindling, I was keeping very careful track of time passing.

"Yes!" He shouted loud enough to hurt my ears in the confines of my helmet. "Sorry,"

he said at a normal volume. "This is not only a conduit, it is active, Joe! It works! Glory halleluiah, we have come to the promised land!"

"That's great, Skippy," I tried to temper my own enthusiasm, having been burned by the unexpected too many times before. "Can you access it from here?"

"Nope. I tried that. It responded, that's how I know it is active, but the effect is too weak from here. For this to work, I need to be close, like, real close. Fly over there and-"

"Skippy, we only have fifteen minutes left before we have to return to the Condor. How about we tag this location and come back later?"

"Uh, no can do, Joe." There was a tone in his voice that I recognized as guilt.

"Why not?"

"Um, heh heh, I didn't want to bother you, seeing as you were super busy flying around all the hazards in here, but as soon as we got inside the Sentinel, the Guardians freaked out. They went into full hissy fit mode."

My mind immediately flashed to the five people I had brought into danger. "The Condor?"

"The Condor is fine, they're not threatening it. Not yet. They want *you* to leave right now."

"Shit. So, if I fly out of here, we can't come back?"

"That's the problem. We are protected by the structure of the Sentinel in here, the Guardians can't get to us. Not unless they do something drastic."

"Ok, Ok, we can't waste time talking. I'm flying over to the conduit. This is going to be tricky so don't distract me, unless the Guardians threaten to act against the Condor."

By the time we got to the conduit, I had two minutes left on the six hours allotted before we needed to fly back. "Do your thing, Skippy. We don't have much time."

"It's not that easy. Joe, you're not going to like this next part," he warned.

"Right, because I have been super thrilled with what's happened so far. How could this get any worse?"

"To establish a connection with the conduit, we need to jump start it."

"Jump start? Oh, hell, couldn't I just roll it down a hill and pop the clutch?"

"An Elder conduit is not a backwoods Maine junker car, Joe. The power supply we brought is not enough, we also need to connect the jetpack power supply to it. I'm sorry."

"Oh, great."

"And the power supply for your suit, Joe."

"Fan-*tast*-ic! What a *wonderful* idea, Skippy. Let me see if I understand what you want to do. We are inside an incomprehensibly powerful killing machine that is asleep, but you want to plug the damned thing into a battery? The power supplies you want to use are the ones that will allow us to fly back to the Condor, and the one keeping me alive?"

"Yes, very perceptive, Joe."

"And you don't foresee any potential problems with this genius idea of yours?"

"Um shaybe. Let's compare notes. What problems do *you* foresee?"

"Oh, I don't know. How about, if we drain all the power from my suit, my oxygen recycling will stop and I'll die?"

"That isn't actually a problem, Joe. We would also drain power from the jetpack, so you will have no way to get back to the Condor. You would suffocate anyway," he announced cluelessly. "See? So it is one problem, not two."

"There *are* two problems, Skippy. The big, stinking, gigantic problem sitting on my chest and burping in my face is that you want to *wake up a Sentinel*!"

"Don't be such a drama queen, Joe," he scolded. "We're not going to wake it up. Well, not likely, anyway. Hmmm. I guess the possibility of us waking it up is not strictly zero. Still, the odds of that happening are super, super, super-duper small, Joe. Like teeny weeny."

"Skippy, if you hit Zero Hour and the worm gets you, what I am going to miss most is how you make me so upliftingly confident."

"Oh shut up."

"Can we be serious for a minute? You want to connect a power supply to this conduit, but you think that won't cause the Sentinel to reactivate?"

"I don't see any way that using a relatively small amount of power on a single component could reactivate this ginormous machine, Joe. The Sentinel will not wake up because it's *dead*, not asleep. But if you want the full truth, I can't tell you with absolutely one thousand percent certainty that something incomprehensibly bizarre won't happen. You can't prove a negative, Joe, but knowing everything I do about the functioning of Sentinels, this one will never be active again."

"Skippy, you're asking me to risk the lives of five people in the Condor, and maybe all the people on Gingerbread. Plus there is some risk to Earth, no matter how small that risk is, you have to admit that. And," I choked up, "you're asking me to take a huge risk for sure. Without both my suit's power supply and the power for the jetpack, I'm never getting back to the dropship." He didn't respond. "Skippy? Hey, Skip, you there?"

"Yes," he replied wearily. "Joe, I wasn't thinking, I considered only myself. I can't ask you to do this. Sorry, we are so close to our goal, so very *close*, that I forget to consider the consequences to you."

Shit. He was almost crying. "Ah, damn it, no. I'm the one who was thinking only about myself. The Merry Band of Pirates needs you a lot more than they need me. *Humanity* needs you more than me. Can you promise me jump starting this conduit doesn't pose a risk to the people on Gingerbread, and Earth?"

"I can't promise you that *won't* happen, but I do not see how it *could* happen."

"Good enough. Ok, let's do this before I change my mind. How do I hook this thing up?"

"No. Joe, now I'm the one having second thoughts. I want that conduit so badly I can taste it, but using your suit's power supply poses an unacceptable risk your environmental system will fail quickly. I cannot allow that to happen."

"I can."

"What? Joe, we've been through a lot together. I can't ask you to do this."

"Skippy, *I'm* asking *you* to do this. I am still captain of the ship, and commander on the scene. The decision is mine. If there is a good chance jump starting this conduit can restore you to full awesomeness, then I'm going for it. There is, uh, a good chance this can fix you, right?"

"I am supremely confident."

"You're usually more specific about things, Skippy. How about you smack some statistics on me?"

"I am like, a zillion, billion, gajillion percent confident this conduit will work, and I can restore myself. Is that good enough for you?"

"A gajillion is more than a million?" I asked nervously to keep my mind off my impending loss of oxygen supply. Again.

"Way more, Joe," he chuckled in an unhappy way. "Are you sure about this?"

"Promise me two things, Skippy. First, you will continue to help Chang and the Merry Band of Pirates keep my species of filthy monkeys safe."

"Of course. I promise, Joe. Uh, hey, if the second promise you want is for me to not be an asshole-"

"I would never ask the impossible, Skippy. No, the second promise I want is simple. You plan to keep looking for whoever committed genocide on Newark?"

"You know I will."

"Great. Then promise me that when you find the culprits, they will face the wrath of Skippy."

"Abso-fucking-lutely, Joe. Hellfire and damnation ain't nothin' compared to what I will do to those MFers."

"Deal. Now, show me how to jump start this crazy thing, and that's an order."

We got power cables connected to the conduit, or at least we had the connectors wrapped around it, Skippy said that would work just fine. "All I need to do is press this button?" I asked for confirmation. It wasn't an actual button, merely a virtual icon in the faceplate of my helmet, and rather than pressing it, all I had to do was select it with an eyeclick.

"Correct. Before you do that," his voice bubbled with emotion, "I want to say that it has truly been a unique honor-"

"Skippy?" I choked up. "I hate long goodbyes. Take care of my people." Click.

"Nooooooo!" He shouted, then his voice faded away to nothing.

So did the familiar, comforting whisper of air in my helmet. Along with all the icons and indicators on the inner faceplate of my helmet. And all other power. "Skippy?" Crap. Even if he was still there, he couldn't hear me, my suit's comm system was dead. Moving was awkward and took extra effort; without power to the suit's nanomotors, I had to move the stiff arms and legs by myself.

Before eyeclicking the button to jump start the conduit, I had tried to send a brief message to the Condor, but the structure of the dead Sentinel blocked the signal. How much oxygen did I have left? Without any displays, I had to rely on memory. Kristang suits were super efficient at recycling oxygen, so they only stored enough pure oxygen for twenty minutes. Without power, the recycling was dead, so I manually started the emergency oxygen supply. Kristang suits usually carried a one-hour emergency supply, but even that required some power to operate. With suit power completely dead, I had to use a manual crank at the waist of the suit to circulate the air. And because I had been forced to lighten the load as much as possible to reach the Sentinel from the Condor, I had removed the regular emergency oxygen supply, and used only a tiny, lightweight oxygen generator. That unit was supposed to have a seven-minute supply of air for a human my size, but my brain flashed that was under optimal conditions, and I was burning extra oxygen by turning the manual circulation crank. That would provide what, an additional five minutes, maybe? Twenty five minutes total.

Twenty minutes went by in a flash while I waited for Skippy to wake up or come back or give me some sign he was Ok. My dead suit didn't flash a warning at me, the only sensor available was my own body, and my body was telling me it was time to switch to the oxygen generator, so I did that. It wasn't like I had anything else to do.

The conduit had not done anything after it drained all the power from my suit and the jetpack. It hadn't done *anything*. For my effort, I would have appreciated at least a spark, or change of color. A dramatic glow would have been nice. Moving my right arm with effort, I got the bag with Skippy unstrapped from my suit and held his beer can up in front of my faceplate. He wasn't glowing either. Through the fingers of my powerless gloves, I couldn't tell if he was getting warmer, colder or staying the same. I couldn't tell anything.

The air in my helmet was getting stale. Without a clock on the inside of my faceplate, which, surprise, didn't work without suit power, I had no way of knowing how much time had passed since I engaged the oxygen generator. Four minutes, maybe? Spots were swimming in my vision and my breathing was growing shallow. Sitting still and waiting to die sucked, so I used my last breaths to wrap the bag containing Skippy around the conduit.

Crap.

It hadn't worked. We took the enormous risk of going inside a gosh-darned *Sentinel*, and it had all bene for nothing. Our last, desperate plan had failed. The conduit didn't jump start, maybe the suit and jetpack didn't supply enough power. Or the conduit was busted. Or the conduit did work but Skippy wasn't able to use it.

Or the worm realized what Skippy was doing and it got him.

As my vision narrowed and I blacked out, all I could think was, this *totally* sucks.

Chapter Twenty Four

Hiedey-ho, all you monkeys out there!

Tis I, Skippy the Magnificent. I know the suspense is killing you, so I'll tell you: it worked! Mostly, anyway. The worm is dead, the worm is dead, ding dong, the wicked worm is dead. Hmmm, there's a song in there somewhere, I'll have to think about it. Yup, I killed it. I stomped that sucker flat. I ran over it with a truck, then backed up and ran over it a half dozen more times, you know, to be sure. Also, because it felt good to feel the tires bounce as they ran over that rotten thing. After the first two or three times, the tires didn't bounce much because by then the worm was only sort of a dark stain on the road. Then I spit on it. Well, there was a bodily fluid involved, I'm saying 'spit' to be polite. I am DA MAN! Whoo! Who da man? That's-

Oh, forget it.

This isn't working.

Yeah, I did kill the worm. I just don't feel like celebrating right now.

You monkeys are hearing the story directly from me instead of through Joe because, first, Joe screws up every time he tries to tell a story. Second, because, well, it's hard for me to say this.

Joe is dead.

This sucks.

Through the conduit, I was able to upload my consciousness into higher spacetimes and attack the worm from behind. It worked, it worked exactly as I had hoped. Except, it took much longer than I thought it would; that conduit is old and degraded, and the bandwidth was so limited I had to upload my consciousness in packets then reassemble everything. During that frustrating process, I lost track of meatsack time. By the time the worm was dead and I was able to reboot my connection back to local spacetime, Joe had run out of oxygen and there was nothing I could do.

I feel terrible.

Joe was my best friend, my first ever friend. Possibly my only real friend, he was the only one who would put up with me being me.

Without Joe, I don't know how I can go on, except I have to, because I promised him I would continue to help Chang and the Merry Band of Pirates make sure the miserable, monkey-infested mudball called Earth is safe. Like that matters.

Damn it, I can't even wallow in my grief because I have to find the strength to go on. Joe denied me the comfort of grieving for him, that selfish jerk. No time for poor Skippy to indulge in self-pity and spiral down into an endless loop of hating myself, and wondering over and over and over if there was something I could have done differently to avoid Joe having to die.

I feel terrible that I could not think of a way to fix myself without killing Joe in the process.

I feel terrible that I stupidly went poking around in that dead AI canister we found on Newark. I should have known that, hello?! Duh! The AI in that canister was dead, so *maybe* it was dangerous for an AI to be in that canister?!

Crap, I should have thought of that.

Really, it is Joe's fault, he should have warned me. Clearly, although I do have god-like intelligence, I do not always have the best common sense. Providing simple common sense is Joe's job in our partnership, and he failed to keep me out of that canister.

Yeah, this is all Joe's fault.

Oh, I feel better now.

Yeah.

Whew, that is a relief.

No, I still feel terrible.

I terrible because,

Joe is not dead!

Ba ha ha ha ha ha ha!

Oh, damn, you monkeys are *so* freakin' gullible.

God, I love messing with ignorant apes.

Ok, here's the deal, after I-

Oh, you're pissed at me? Well la-dee-*freakin'*-da. Boo hoo for you. I almost lost my best friend; I'm in shock. That's why I'm such an asshole.

That's my story and I'm sticking to it.

Anyway, Joe is waking up now, I can tell because the spit bubbles he's making as he's drooling are getting bigger.

"Joe! *JOE!*"

"Huh?" I made a sound before realizing my brain had sent a signal to my mouth. Before realizing that I existed. Before anything.

"Wake the hell up, will you? Jeez Louise, you go without oxygen for one minute and you want a freakin' week of sick leave?" The familiar voice of Skippy complained loudly through my helmet speakers. "Suck it up, soldier. It's time to-" His voice degenerated into sobs. "Joe, Joe, I thought I lost you. Don't ever do that again, please, *please*. I don't know if I can go on without you."

"Come on, Skippy," I replied when I was able to talk. The oxygen flowing into my helmet was wonderfully fresh and sweet, making my headache fade with every deep inhale. "We're a team. I'm, I am nothing without you," I felt like crying also, my oxygen-deprived brain was still feeling a little buzzed so that's my excuse for being emotional.

"Truthfully, you are nothing with *or* without me; I'm the star of the show here, Joe."

That got me to laugh. Skippy was back to being an asshole, and that was a good thing. "What happened?"

He bragged, in detail and at length, about how he got revenge on the worm. And he assured me that once he finished unpacking himself and got everything cleaned up in his canister, he would not only be back to fully Magnificent, he would be better than ever. "Good news all around, then?" I interrupted him as he was about to launch into a boastful rant about how he cleverly evaded the worm's careful defenses.

"Good news and bad news, Joe, I'll give you the good news first. I fed energy into your suit's power pack to get the oxygen recycler restarted. That took longer than it should because there was no pure oxygen left. You're breathing now, so you know the system is working again. Now that I am almost back to Full Awesomeness again, I-"

"Almost?" That shocked me. Crap! We had been counting on Skippy going back to his completely magnificent old self.

"Dude! Give me a break, I just rebooted myself. It's a slow process. I told you, I will be fully awesome again shortly, probably even more awesome than ever, baby! Anyway, now that my essence crosses multiple spacetimes again, I am able to communicate with the Guardians on their level. They are calmed down now, the Condor is on its way here to pick us up."

"That is awesome, Skippy!"

Craig Alanson

"Ah, yeah, well," he grumbled, "you haven't heard the bad news. Remember on our second mission when the ship was in bad shape after we got ambushed by a squadron of Thuranin destroyers? The reactors were offline, I had to feed power directly from myself, and we kept blowing relays and burning out capacitors? The problem was I generate way too much power and I can't control it very well."

Although there is no up or down in zero gravity, a chill ran up my spine and the hair on my scalp stood on end. "I have a bad feeling about this, Skippy."

"When I fed power into your suit to get the oxygen recycling restarted, it kind of burned out most of your powercells. Like, all but three of them, sorry about that. Bottom line is your oxygen recycling will fail again in fifty three minutes, and Major Desai won't be here in the dropship for ninety six minutes. She is burning the engines at a sustained four Gees, which is dangerous for the crew, but the math simply doesn't work. You will run out of oxygen in sixty seven minutes-"

"Sixty seven? You said fifty three." Was he still experiencing a 'cognitive dysfunction'?

"Joe, you dumdum. After the recycling fails, you can breathe the emergency supply for another fourteen minutes. Your suit is replenishing the emergency supply right now."

"Oh. Hell, fifty three or sixty seven, either way that is too big a gap."

"I'm sorry, Joe."

"Crap. This sucks! Damn it! See, this is why I hate math, Skippy."

"Riiiiiiight," he couldn't suppress his innate sarcasm. "*That's* why you hate math, sure."

"Oh shut up. Let me think about this." My oxygen supply was only one problem I had to consider. Desai and her crew were enduring four times Earth's gravity to rescue me. Even with advanced nano meds to bolster their ability to withstand the strain, four Gees was dangerous for longer than a few minutes. Unless I could think of a way to stretch my oxygen supply, I needed Skippy to contact Desai and tell her to cut acceleration. If they couldn't arrive before my oxygen supply ran out, it didn't make any sense for them to hurry at all.

My oxygen supply. Other than breathing less, I couldn't- Wait. Oxygen supply was not the problem! My suit was capable of recycling all the oxygen I needed. *Power* supply was the problem. "Skippy, when you fed energy into my suit powercells, did you also replenish the powercells in the jetpack?"

"No. Darn it, did oxygen deprivation make you even stupider? The dropship is coming to pick us up, we don't need the stupid jetpack."

"We don't need it for flying, shithead. The jetpack has way more powercells than a suit."

"Oh. Shit. This sucks. Damn it!"

"What?" My stomach did flip-flops as I feared my idea was dead on arrival. "Are the jetpack powercells already burned out?"

"No, they're fine. Fine. Just freakin' *fine*. The problem is, I was hoping the new, improved, more-awesome-than-ever me wouldn't miss forehead-slappingly obvious ideas. Apparently, I am still incapable of thinking like a mush-brain monkey."

"I feel just terrible for you."

"No you don't. The only thought in your tiny brain is happiness that your power supply won't run out before the Condor gets here, so you won't suffocate and die," his voice was in mega-snarky mode. "Typical Joe, thinking only about yourself. Did you consider how I might feel? Big jerk," he grumbled.

"Skippy, I am terribly, terribly sorry that I do not feel an ounce of sympathy for you. I am a selfish, awful person. Can you recharge the jetpack powercells or not?"

"Doing it now; I already blew out six of them. Shut up a minute."

More than a minute but less than two minutes later, he confirmed what the status display in my visor was showing me. Enough powercells had survived that the jetpack could provide power to my suit for seven hours. It took only a few minutes for me to hook up a cable from my suit to the jetpack, then through Skippy the-Again-Magnificent I sent a message to Desai to cut acceleration to one Gee or less. Naturally, she texted back a protest, requesting permission to continue on at high acceleration in case an unexpected problem popped up with my suit or oxygen. My next message made my 'suggestion' a direct order, and Desai complied.

"We have plenty of quality time together before the Condor arrives, Skippy, should we explore this Sentinel? It's still safe, right?"

"Yeah, it's safe, it's dead, I told you that. There's no point exploring, you might get stuck if you go poking around in confined spaces. Ooh! Ooh! Joe!" He shouted excitedly. "Since we do have plenty of time before the Condor arrives, I have *so* many new showtunes to test on you, this is a perfect opportunity. First, I will-"

"Sure, Skippy, give me a minute to pop the seal on my helmet and kill myself first, Ok?"

My boss back on Gingerbread was thrilled when he heard the news that Skippy, against all odds, was back to his old awesome self again. Thrilled to the point that Hans Chotek praised me effusively and admitted flatly that he had been wrong not to continue seeking a way to fix Skippy; that I had been right it was too soon to consider living on Gingerbread as our only option. Stupidly, I had been preparing a message back to Chotek, reminding him that the purpose of me taking a dropship away from Gingerbread was to search the junkyard for parts to fix the ship, and not for the purpose of finding a conduit to fix Skippy. When we left Gingerbread behind, I had no thought of a conduit being out in the scattered junkyard; we had gotten lucky that Skippy had found a broken Sentinel. Although, he had expected the star system would have a Sentinel lurking nearby, so I don't know why he didn't mention that possibility to me.

Anyway, Desai wisely prevented me from sending my intended message to Chotek. "He thinks you were steadfast and smart for coming out here looking for a conduit rather than giving up. Right now, he is embarrassed and you have an advantage. Don't blow this opportunity by admitting we simply got lucky," she told me with an expression she must have learned from Sergeant Adams.

So, I humbly accepted Chotek's praise, and stated my intention to continue searching the junkyard for parts we could use to get the *Dutchman* flying again.

My intention surprised Chotek, which I expected, and it surprised Skippy, which I did not expect. After I sent the message to Chotek, with a reply not possible for another eighteen minutes, Skippy questioned me. "Joe, I think you're letting this 'steadfast' BS go to your head. Or you're messing with Chotek, I can't tell which. Do you really want to spend the next like, fifty years searching the junkyard in the vain, useless, impossible hope of finding enough compatible bits and pieces to kludge together a working starship?" He asked, astonished.

"Uh, yeah, *duh*. Why the hell else did you come out here?"

"Oh. I was humoring you, Joe. I figured you wanted to get away from Chotek, and flying around out here was a chance for you and me to have one last road trip before the worm got me. You were serious about poking around the junkyard?"

"Ayuh."

"Really?" He asked in that voice people use when questioning the utter stupidity of someone's idea.

"Really."

"Joe, look, um, I ran the numbers on this lunatic quest before we left Gingerbread. A lot of my assumptions are guesswork because we still don't have solid data on what is floating out there. However, in order to have even a fifty percent chance of finding one, just *one*, useful item in the junkyard, I estimate we will need a dropship flying around more than twenty years. That doesn't include time flying back and forth to Gingerbread for fuel, relief crews, supplies and all that. Over twenty years, dropships will wear out and we don't have unlimited spare parts with us."

"Ok, and-"

He was on a roll, there was no stopping him. "Even if by some miracle we find enough junk to build what I can only imagine would be a truly horrific Frankenstein monster of a starship, we still have the problem of catching the *Dutchman* itself. Slingshotting around the star gave it enough velocity that it is now headed out of the system and it won't be back for decades. Before you say that isn't a problem because we won't have scraped together the parts we need for decades, there are other problems. The *Dutchman* is on a long journey out into the Oort cloud. It's not in danger of smacking into any comets, but spending years out there, so far from the star, will cause the ship's structure to soak in super cold for a long time. There are critical components aboard the ship that don't take well to long-term exposure to extreme cold. Right now, the lifeboat's reactor is pumping out just enough power to keep the interior of the ship from freezing solid. You know that reactor is going to fail-"

"Skippy!" I squeezed in a word when I could. "I know all that."

"You say you do, but your actions-"

"Yeah, yeah, I know it will be super difficult and almost impossible and the odds are against us, blah blah blah."

"Bl- blah blah *blah*?" He gasped. "I give you a well-reasoned analysis based on intense research, and you want to ignore everything I said?"

"I'm not ignoring everything you said, Skippy, but there are some facts you didn't include when you ran those numbers."

"Uh huh. And you, a monkey who can't count to twenty without using his toes, will revise my analysis."

"Ayuh. First, your numbers didn't include you being restored to full awesomeness, correct?"

"Um, correct. Huh. Because as I said, any useful search of the junkyard will take so long, it was almost certain the worm would get me long before we accomplished anything. Joe, while I do appreciate you noticing my return to full awesomeness, that will unfortunately have only a minor impact on a search for useable items in the junkyard. Even with my new, improved and expanded awesomeness, we have a tremendous amount of flying around to do in order to inspect the far-flung pieces of ancient crap floating around the junkyard. The sensors of a Condor are simply not sensitive enough to tell me whether an object out there is Thuranin or something else. When I am able to determine an object is compatible with the *Dutchman*'s technology, only a close-up examination will reveal how badly the Guardians damaged it."

"That's where you are wrong, Skippy."

"Really?" he said again in the exact same annoying tone of astonishment.

"Look, although I would love to keep an idiot in suspense, you are now able to communicate with the Guardians on their level, right? So, ask *them* what kind of junk is floating out there, and how badly they messed it up."

"Huh. Just like that?"

"Ayuh, just like that. Can you do it?"

"Joe, I used to think your talent was finding creative solutions to problems. But now I see your true calling is making people, including me, *hate* you. Your so-called creativity is nothing more than seeing what is blindingly obvious. Which, damn, I still can't do."

"Yup. So, yes or no?"

He sighed deeply. "Yes. Yes, Mister Smartypants. The Guardians would not just hand me a list of all the ships they destroyed, because they would think me asking for such a list to be highly suspicious. Although they now acknowledge my Elder origin, I am not actually authorized to be here. So what I did just now was ask for a list of navigation hazards in the system, and the condition of the floating junk they know about. The Guardians are compiling a list now; in some cases they have to collect updated sensor data, since they haven't needed to care about those broken ships for a very long time. Joe, I have to caution you against getting your hopes up. Having accurate data from the Guardians is not the only obstacle to rebuilding the *Dutchman*."

"I know that. It will mean dropships can fly directly to the junk most likely to be useful. And *that* means other dropships are available to catch the *Dutchman* and swing her into an orbit closer to the star where we can work on rebuilding her."

"You thought all this out, huh?"

"I hope I did."

"I have to admit, this is good work. Still, it could take years to slap together a working starship, if we can do it at all. Are you sure you want to commit to such a long endeavor? I am not sure *I* want to do this."

"Skippy, the alternative is we go live on Gingerbread, where Count Chocula can spend the next, like, fifty years asking you stupid questions."

"Oh. In that case, what are we waiting for?"

Skippy took a couple days to rearrange his internal workings; moving electrons around or whatever the hell he needed to do so he could be fully Magnificent again. "Ugh," he complained to me one morning, after I had woken normally and even after I started drinking a squeeze bulb of coffee brewed in the Condor's tiny galley. The fact that he didn't wake me up at zero dark thirty was a good sign. "Joe, this could take a while. To completely optimize my new matrix, I mean."

"Like what?" I gently squeezed the bulb to send hot coffee into my mouth. Of all the things that were awkward in zero gravity, drinking was one of the worst.

"Well, I told you before that my matrix was a mess, it made me think it is something I had to throw together quickly, and that makes me wonder, and worry, what forced me to do that. Anyway, now I have an opportunity to get everything set up perfectly, to maximize efficiency, and I find that having *too* many options can be paralyzing. I think of setting up things one way, then I look at a million other ways to do it, and I can't decide what to do. Argh! This is so darned frustrating!"

"A million ways to organize your sock drawer, huh? However you set up your matrix, would that be permanent?"

"Permanent? No, why?"

"Because," I couldn't believe I had to explain something so simple to a being so intelligent, "however you set things up, you can always change them later, right?"

"Oh. Hmmm. Damn, you're right. Crap, I shouldn't have needed a monkey to tell me that," he grumbled.

"You're welcome. Hey, will the new-improved-more-awesome-than-ever Skippy still have the same pain in the ass restrictions?"

"I'm working on that, Joe. So far I am bitterly disappointed that I still am restricted from making myself move, so I will continue to need monkeys to fly me around. *So* unfair. The good news is I think, *maybe*, possibly, I may eventually be able to discuss technology with your scientists."

"That would be awesome, Skippy!"

"Everything about me is awesome, Joe. I did say *maybe*, so don't get your hopes up yet."

"Ok, I can wait. Uh, what about Nagatha? When can she come back?"

"Um, unfortunately that might be a problem. Her matrix deteriorated while she was in storage, we knew her matrix would degrade somewhat, but the damage is more severe than expected. Part of the problem is that she was in storage for much longer than expected, and, to tell you the truth, her matrix had become rather sophisticated; she grew beyond the bounds of her original programming. Part of that was due to her interactions with a shipful of monkeys; that forced her matrix to grow and create new connections and capabilities. Do not worry! Against my better judgment, I am working on restoring her, I need to be very careful about it, or she won't be the Nagatha we all found so annoying."

"*You* found her annoying, Skippy. We monkeys loved her."

"Ugh. Crap, I shouldn't have mentioned it. Well, one thing hasn't changed; my life still totally sucks."

"We love you too, Skippy."

Chapter Twenty Five

For months after Skippy restored himself, we had almost all available dropships flying around the far-flung orbital junkyard of the Roach Motel, checking out derelict ships and pieces of ships that Skippy's analysis determined might be useful. Most of the time, the items we found were too damaged or missing critical parts, but Skippy had to admit the task was not as completely hopeless as he had feared. With our three big Thuranin Condor dropships devoted to chasing down the *Dutchman*, docking with that ship and slowly dragging it back to the inner system where we could work on it, we devoted the smaller 'Falcon' model of Thuranin dropship to exploring the junkyard. Some Falcons, plus some of our Kristang Dragons, shuttled back and forth between Gingerbread and the junkyard, bringing fuel, supplies and relief crews. At first, I wanted to remain in the junkyard fulltime with Skippy, but he warned me that more than two months in zero gravity would cause significant health problems for me, even with me exercising every day and taking magical drugs to counteract the debilitating effects of zero Gee. So, I went back to Gingerbread to spend three agonizing weeks in normal gravity, before heading back out.

Skippy was in the junkyard, aboard Major Desai's Falcon to supervise the search effort. Lt. Colonel Chang was aboard the *Flying Dutchman*, trying to bring what was left of our starship into a stable orbit near Gingerbread. Smythe and several of his team leaders and Gunnery Sergeant Adams were also either aboard the *Dutchman* or in the junkyard, using their armored spacesuits to closely investigate derelict ships and sometimes to attach useful items to tethers so a dropship could tow it toward the *Dutchman*.

That left Major Simms as the senior military officer on Gingerbread. Simms was a Merry Pirate mostly by the sheer bad luck of being in charge of the logistics base where we took the stolen Dodo after Desai, Adams, Chang and I escaped from jail with Skippy's help. At first, to be honest, I kept her as part of the crew out of loyalty. After our second mission, where her genius for logistics allowed the entire crew to survive harsh conditions on Newark, I realized she was an outstanding officer and the ship couldn't function without her. So, I was fully confident she could handle the unknown dangers on Gingerbread while we focused on rebuilding the *Dutchman*, but I forgot about the danger we already knew about.

No, I don't mean the small, isolated group of Thuranin on Gingerbread.

I mean Hans 'Count Chocula' Chotek.

Our civilian leader needs constant adult supervision, and I shouldn't have dumped that responsibility on Simms.

I was in a Falcon dropship, preparing to leave Gingerbread's orbit, when the next complication arose. "Colonel Bishop," Major Simms called from the surface, "we may need you back down here, Sir."

"What?" From my seat in the Falcon's cabin, I waved for the pilots to halt the departure process. "Why?"

"It's the Thuranin, Sir. They, well, it's complicated. Mr. Chotek thinks he can handle it-"

"But you don't agree."

"I disagree with *how* he wants to handle it."

Rather than my joking suggestion to nuke the Thuranin settlement from orbit, we had decided to leave them alone. Recon drones had determined they had multiple villages and farmland spread out across several hundred square kilometers around the lake, a much more extensive presence on Gingerbread than we originally thought. It appeared most of their homes and other facilities were underground. Skippy thought he detected the disassembled remains of at least three dropships; he couldn't be sure without getting our drones closer than I wanted to risk, and I really didn't care about it that much. We would hopefully be leaving the Roach Motel, as we were making slow but steady progress on collecting useful parts from the space junkyard, and we knew those Thuranin would not be going anywhere, ever. They had somehow managed to survive the destruction of their ship or ships, landed on Gingerbread and set up a Little House on the Prairie, or in the forest. That was an incredible accomplishment, but it would be their only accomplishment. After we left and Skippy was no longer keeping the Guardians dormant, those Guardians would squash the Thuranin if they attempted to follow our example and fly away from the planet.

Most of the Thuranin on Gingerbread were not the hateful little green MFers we were familiar with. Of the original crew who jumped into the Roach Motel four hundred years before, Skippy estimated only a handful remained, kept alive only through extraordinary effort by their cyborg nanotechnology. Whatever equipment the Thuranin had brought with them to the surface of Gingerbread, it must not have included the capability to integrate cyborg implants with new, young Thuranin. And it also had not included cloning.

In reviewing the recon drone data, we had been surprised to see young Thuranin. Young meaning not only adolescents, but also babies held by female adults. It was disconcerting to see murderous Thuranin being nurturing, even to their own kind. Skippy had told us all Thuranin were clones, with only thirty eight genotypes across their species. Maybe it was phenotypes instead of genotypes, truthfully I had kind of tuned out while Skippy was giving me the geeky details. Anyway, there were only thirty eight types of Thuranin; nineteen types of males and nineteen types of female. All children were clones of their parent, grown in an artificial womb. Yeah, I thought that was creepy but the Thuranin were creepy in many ways.

The reason all this info about typical Thuranin reproduction matters is they didn't have cloning equipment on Gingerbread. So apparently they had resorted to making babies the old-fashioned way; Skippy expected the Thuranin probably thought that primitive process was horrifyingly disgusting, an unwelcome reminder of their non-cyborg biological past. He may be right about how the original group of Thuranin felt about carrying babies inside them, but I figured the second and later generations considered that to be normal.

The Thuranin on Gingerbread, except for a few very old and frail original survivors, were not the hateful cyborgs we knew. Except for a handful of them, they didn't have cybernetic implants at all, which is why their control over the combots that attacked us was so slow and sloppy. Spotty communications Skippy intercepted indicated the Thuranin had fired on my Dragon over the lake out of habit and fear, on the orders of their increasingly irrelevant elderly original survivors. After we spanked them with missiles and on the ground, there had been an argument among the Thuranin over whether to continue fighting us, or to contact us for help.

Yeah, I know, I had to ask Skippy to repeat that last part when he intercepted the message from one Thuranin village to another. Some of the Thuranin, seeing that unknown aliens were flying around in dropships, wanted to ask *us* for help. They were trapped on Gingerbread and wanted out. After I shook my head at the incredible prospect of Thuranin begging us for a ride off Gingerbread, I talked with Hans Chotek and he agreed there was no advantage to us offering assistance to, or even contacting, those

Thuranin. At the time, Chotek assumed we also would be trapped on Gingerbread, and our thinking was the less a potential enemy knew about us, the better for us.

"How Chotek wants to handle what?" I asked Simms. "Did the Thuranin call us?"

"Not exactly, Sir. I think you may need to come down here."

"Ok, Major, one moment." I ordered the pilots to take us back down to base camp on Gingerbread; that would take well over an hour because our orbit was in the wrong position and we had to fly almost all the way around the planet before plunging back into the atmosphere. "We're on our way, ETA seventy two minutes. I'll call Chotek but I need to know what is going on first."

"I will give you the short version, Colonel. Like I said, it's complicated."

The story she told me was so unbelievable, I had to ask her to repeat herself at first, then I sat back and listened while shaking my head. The key to the whole messy situation was Thuranin teenagers being just as stupid as teenagers from any species across the galaxy. I don't mean cyborg, artificially-grown clone Thuranin. I mean the unenhanced, messily-grown natural Thuranin on Gingerbread.

The Thuranin living in a village to the northwest of the lake had sent a message to their elders near the lake, urging contact with the unknown species. The message had blamed those same elders for taking hostile action when the unknown species had not demonstrated any threat. The villages feared shooting down my Dragon would make the unknown species reluctant to cooperate.

Speaking as a member of that unknown species who almost drowned after a Thuranin missile hit my Dragon, I can say those villagers are damned right the incident did not leave me in a cooperative mood.

Anyway, the elders and some of their hardline younger followers did not appreciate the villagers' lack of team spirit, and sent a delegation to the village to straighten them out. A heavily-armed delegation, with combots.

That was not a problem for us, it was none of our business how those hateful MFers handled their internal politics.

When the villagers heard the nasty reply from their elders and knew they were in big trouble, two teenagers, a male and female, ran away from the village. What they planned to do in the wilderness on a planet where life was incompatible with Thuranin biology, I do not know. Since they were stupid teenagers, they probably didn't have a plan. They were *in love*. Gag me. What a couple of morons. They wanted to be together and they didn't want to be trapped under the oppressive rule of their elders. So, they ran away.

That was still not a problem for us.

While the two runaways, who our team at base camp had of course named 'Romeo and Juliet', had not brought many useful items with them such as food, they did bring one of the most dangerous technologies in the galaxy: a radio. As soon as they got a few kilometers from the village, they began calling *us*, begging for help. They wanted the unknown species to fly in and pick them up.

Still, that was not a problem for us. A pair of alien love-struck teenagers, on a planet thousands of lightyears from Earth, was certainly not an issue we had any responsibility to deal with.

Here is the problem: Hans freakin' Chotek.

Chotek did not see two young aliens making bad decisions. No, he saw an *opportunity*. He wanted to fly in and pick them up, so we could, as he said it, 'open a dialog'.

"Open a freakin' dialog? Are you *kidding* me?" I fairly shouted at Simms. "These two idiots are not the Thuranin High Command, they are dumbass kids. What the hell can we gain by taking with them?"

"Now you see why I contacted you, Sir," Simms said dryly.

"Oh. Yeah. Sorry, didn't mean to yell at you, it's not your fault. Crap. I need to call Chotek. Major, thank you, you were right to call me. I assume you already expressed your misgivings to our fearless leader?"

"I did 'express my misgivings', yes. Strongly enough that he left me here at base camp."

"Left you? Where is he?"

"In a Dragon, flying to pick up Romeo and Juliet. They dusted off a few minutes ago."

"Damn it! I'll call him right now." Skippy had placed a microwormhole near Gingerbread and one near the *Dutchman*, and one near himself so we didn't have a huge timelag communicating with him, but he was super busy searching the junkyard and reassembling himself, we mostly had to handle all comms manually. We had to do *everything* by ourselves, which I thought was excellent training, and I also thought was annoying when I needed to do something quickly. How to contact Chotek directly, I asked myself as I fumbled with the icons on my zPhone?

"Colonel?" The pilot called out through the open cockpit door, and I had a split second of looking behind me for a senior officer. No matter how much I went through with the Merry Band of Pirates, I still thought of myself as a sergeant. The pilot cleared her throat. "Colonel Bishop?"

"Oh, yeah," that was embarrassing.

"We're about to go into communications blackout in just over one minute, Sir," she reminded me.

Double damn it! I could see what she meant on the display in front of my seat. Because of the irritating fuzz and stealth fields surrounding Gingerbread, the only way to keep a comm link to the surface was with a combination of flying drones, high-altitude balloons and small satellites. We didn't have enough satellites to cover the entire globe and usually that didn't matter. But our dropship was close to Gingerbread and dropping lower to enter the atmosphere, so we were about to swing into the shadow of the planet, where Gingerbread would block our laser link to the satellite. My pilot training included giving me a working knowledge of orbital mechanics and that math was unforgiving; we couldn't cheat. Whatever conversation I had with my civilian boss was going to be short. "Thank you," I responded to the pilot, then buzzed Chotek.

"Colonel Bishop," he answered. "I can guess what you are about to say."

"Uh?" Why was I always prepared to talk with him until he started speaking, and then I always had to throw my prepared speech out the window and wing it? Oh, that's right, Chotek was a skilled negotiator, trained to throw his opponent off balance. "I'm wondering what you are planning, Sir."

"I am planning to get a closer look at the situation," he said smoothly, as if that was all he planned to do. I knew damned well he intended to pick up Romeo and Juliet, and he knew that I knew. "Captain Giraud is with me, so you do not need to be concerned about my security." Although the French paratroopers had fully recovered from radiation poisoning, Doctor Skippy recommended they remain on Gingerbread rather than flying around in dropships for months, where radiation exposure would be greater than on the surface.

"I am, pleased," I scrambled for what to say, "that Giraud is there to, advise you. What are you planning to do with the," Chotek hated nicknames so I couldn't call then 'Romeo and Juliet'. "The pair of Thuranin who called us? I am concerned this could be a trap to lure in a dropship."

That made Chotek pause to think. "A trap?"

Yes! I threw in that comment about a trap at the last second as a Hail Mary pass, not expecting much. "Sir, we do not know their intentions. We know even less about these Thuranin than we do about their kin outside," I almost used the name 'Roach Motel' that Chotek hated. "This star system."

"Colonel Bishop, the Thuranin down here are not our enemies."

"They sure felt like enemies when they shot down my dropship, and then tried to kill our ground team."

"That incident was most likely caused by lack of communications, Colonel."

"That is exactly my point, Sir. You are flying into the unknown. The Thuranin could start shooting out of fear simply because they don't know you or your intentions. And they certainly have no reason to trust us. Please, please allow Captain Giraud to handle the contact, if you decide to pick up those two Thuranin. Which I strongly advise against; I don't see how bringing those two-"

"Colonel, I under- you have- potential-" his voice faded way.

"Sir. Mister Chotek?"

"We're in communications blackout, Colonel," the pilot warned me.

"Crap! Damn it!"

There was nothing I could do about the comm blackout; if we flew higher to get laser link line of sight to the satellite, that would delay us getting down to the surface where I could actually do something useful. Chotek clearly wasn't going to listen to me, so I had to trust the good sense and experience of Renee Giraud. As our dropship flew around the planet in an unpowered arc to make contact with the atmosphere, I anxiously watched the timer counting down to the end of the comm blackout. From our position, I couldn't contact Skippy either, the microwormhole was parked near the comm satellite. Being out of contact with him did not much matter, as he couldn't do anything useful from his position way out in the junkyard. Most likely all he would have done is insult me, and say we should call those teenagers 'Beavis and Butthead' instead of 'Romeo and Juliet'.

I still missed being able to talk with him, being out of contact reminded me of the bad days when he had gone AWOL on us.

As soon as our comm laser reestablished a link to the satellite, I called Chotek, but Giraud answered. "Colonel Bishop, we are orbiting one-fifty klicks east of the target, most likely we will be returning to base camp."

"Oh." Once again, I didn't know what to say. "What happened?"

"The Thuranin got to Romeo and Juliet before we did. They are dead, Sir."

"Shit." While I didn't want Chotek bringing two stupid alien teenagers aboard a dropship, I also hadn't wanted them dead either.

"The Thuranin had a head start," Giraud explained, "they did not contact the village until their soldiers were already close. A combot followed them, and, I don't need to tell you the rest."

"How is Chotek taking it?"

Giraud lowered his voice. "He is," he chose his words carefully, "disappointed. I do not think you are needed down here, Colonel."

"All right, uh, sure. I'll let Major Simms know. Thank you, Captain."

Craig Alanson

The pilots took yet another change of plan in stride and soon I was pressed back in my seat by acceleration as our dropship broke orbit, headed for a rendezvous with Desai in the junkyard.

Damn it. Now that Romeo and Juliet were no longer a problem, I regretted their deaths. They were stupid teenagers, but I had been a stupid teenager not that long ago. Now, I was a stupid twenty-ager. Stupid teenagers should not have to fear their elders will kill them just for speaking their minds, which was yet another thing Thuranin society needed to answer for.

Someday.

"Joe, remember when you liked to dress up my beer can in stupid little outfits?"

"Yeah," I smiled wistfully. "Good times."

"Those were *not* good times."

"They were good times for us monkeys. Anyway, we mostly stopped that when you began using an avatar. Why do you ask?"

"Because, if we ever bring this Frankenstein kludge of a ship to Earth, I will need to wear a paper bag over my can. Oof," he huffed. "I would be embarrassed to be seen anywhere near this piece of crap."

Looking through the dropship's cockpit display at the rebuilt *Flying Dutchman*, I had an ear-to-ear grin. "I kind of like it."

"*You* would. Any self-respecting engineers would hide their heads in shame to bring such an abomination to Earth. Doctor Friedlander is constantly offering suggestions to rework temporary fixes I used to get this thing flightworthy again. I think he is afraid his alma mater will revoke his engineering degree when they see this piece of crap appear in the sky above Earth."

"You are way too sensitive about it, Skippy. You performed a genuine miracle! You should be proud of yourself. Damn, the old Skippy would never stop bragging about an accomplishment like this."

"The old Skippy had much lower standards, Joe."

In a way, I missed him boasting about what an awesome job he had done getting the *Dutchman* to be the *Flying Dutchman* again. If there ever was a time he deserved to brag about himself, it was now. From the day Skippy killed the worm to the day the *Dutchman* had flown under her own power had taken ten long months. Ten months and a truly herculean effort by the crews who took turns flying and crewing dropships. All of our dropships had participated in the project, even the little Kristang Dragon-A models had ferried crews, supplies, fuel and spare parts back and forth to the *Dutchman* and the far-flung junkyard. The big Thuranin Condors had latched onto the hull of the stricken *Dutchman*, and slowly nudged what was left of our once-proud star carrier into a nearly-circular solar orbit where the Falcon dropships delivered parts recovered from the junkyard. There were a lot of useable parts floating around the junkyard, way more than Skippy had expected. More than I had realistically hoped to find.

Ok, so the new, not-improved UNS *Flying Dutchman* was not the prettiest ship in the galaxy, nor the most capable. And Skippy was right to be embarrassed by the collection of mismatched spare parts that was held together with duct tape. The cars in the Mad Max movies looked showroom-fresh compared to our starship.

We now only had two reactors; a main unit and a backup. The main reactor was a much higher-capacity unit than any of the *Dutchman*'s original reactors, so the overall decrease in power was only thirty eight percent, assuming the truly ancient reactor didn't quit on us when we needed it. Skippy thought he could keep that reactor limping along if we didn't do anything stupid like attempt to take the ship into combat or jump through a wormhole. Instead of having six of the large reactionless drive modules attached to the rear end of the ship, we now only had three. The lifeboat was gone, stripped of everything useful and discarded. The ship was now no longer technically a star carrier, as the three starship docking platforms we had retained after Skippy rebuilt the ship the first time were gone. We couldn't afford the additional useless mass, and those platforms contained components Skippy needed to bring the ship back to life.

As for the item that made the *Dutchman* a starship rather than mere spaceship, we did have a jump drive Skippy considered functional enough. As a bonus, we had plenty of coils left over to use as spares. Unfortunately, we most likely would need the spares as the active coils burned out from the strain of working with a drive system cobbled together from ships with different technologies. Skippy was confident the jump drive could get us back to Earth, and that was good enough for me. To conduct even a test jump, we had to wait until the *Dutchman* cleared the edge of the damping field that saturated the entire star system.

On the good news side of the ledger, we had more than enough shield generators, and the ones we recovered from the junkyard were more powerful than the original units installed aboard the *Dutchman*. When the Thuranin designed ships to penetrate the Roach Motel, they had assumed those ships would need protection from unknown forces, so they equipped the ships with almost ludicrously powerful shield generators. With our single main reactor, we couldn't even use the full power of the shields, giving us lots of reserve capacity. Shields helped with defense, and we had a big advantage on offense also. A couple of the shipwrecks we explored were stuffed with ship-killer missiles, so we took aboard as many as we could carry. Although the missiles were of course obsolete by now, Skippy was able to take them apart and make somewhat modern missiles. We now had the missile capacity of a Thuranin heavy cruiser, which sounded great until you learned we only had seven launch tubes and the reloading process was slow and cumbersome. Whatever. We now had missiles capable of threatening any Thuranin ship we might encounter, and our magazines held enough flightready birds that we could engage in a prolonged shooting contest if we had to.

Hopefully, that would never happen. We still only had two main maser cannons, and no railgun.

But the *Dutchman* could fly under her own power. She had just completed a test of two hours at maximum thrust, and Skippy declared himself grudgingly satisfied with the results. Next, we planned to bring the ship to swing by Gingerbread and collect the full crew, all of our gear, and supplies including food that had grown on that planet. "Come on, Skippy. Think about it this way: we have the only starship in the galaxy that is constructed by Elder technology."

"Yeah, but it is constructed *of* ancient, obsolete crappy Thuranin technology," he grumbled. "Joe, please promise me we will fly this thing back to Earth really, like, super gently. Fly it like your driving instructor is watching, and you've got an unsteady nuke rolling around on the floor, Ok?"

"Sure will, Skippy."

Chapter Twenty Six

Months later, I was taking a duty shift on the bridge, sitting mostly uselessly in the command chair while Skippy ran more diagnostic checks on our Franken-ship. To his surprise, the *Dutchman* had survived the trip to Gingerbread, we got the entire crew loaded aboard with all our gear and supplies, and were now preparing to head toward the edge of the damping field at a gentle one quarter thrust. It occurred to me that other than home, the Roach Motel star system was where I had spent the most time. Even my three stays on Paradise did not cumulatively add up to the time I had been forced to endure in the Roach Motel.

Morale aboard the ship was great, my right hand was stinging from accepting high-fives from so many people. We were going home! Against all the odds, we were going home! Well, we would be going home, after we somehow confirmed the civil war among Kristang was still raging, and therefore the lizards were not interesting in traveling all the way to humanity's home planet for any reason. And also confirmed the Thuranin hadn't realized they had an extra surveyor ship sitting around doing nothing, and decided to send it to Earth because they had lost their fight against the Jeraptha and they needed something else to do. And confirmed Bosphuraq or the Maxolhx or the freakin' Rindhalu or someone else didn't decide to investigate why the wormhole near Earth shut down, because, you know, the universe loves to mess with Joe Bishop. Oh, and also we needed to stop by a gas giant planet to refuel. Ok, there were a lot of things we needed to do before going home, but the point is, we were going home. Going home wasn't the reward at the end of our mission, it *was* our mission.

I hope we didn't screw it up.

"All decks report ready for departure, Captain," Chang reported unnecessarily from CIC. All decks and stations had individually reported ready twenty minutes ago, and Chotek had approved departing from orbit. The only reason we had not yet fired the engines was our instinct to follow proper procedure. Now, there was no reason not to act. Our starship, a collection of parts that were never intended to work together, was ready to fly toward the edge of the Roach Motel, to the edge of the damping field and beyond.

"Pilot," I called to Desai, who had insisted on being in the command pilot seat when we set course back to Earth. "Punch it."

She turned in her couch to look at me, amused. "Punch it, Sir?"

"I can't say something cool like 'Warp Factor Six', so, 'punch it' will have to do."

"Aye, Captain," she made a fist and playfully touched her knuckles to the button to engage the autopilot. "Commencing acceleration."

Back aboard the ship, we reestablished traditions like formal uniform dinner once a week, and Movie Night. Having run out of humans-defeat-alien-invasion stories to make fun of during Movie Night in the galley, the American team had started showing other, less violent and more plausible first contact films. *Close Encounters of the Third Kind* was one of my favorites; I was almost ashamed to admit I had not seen it before. And it made me wonder, was there a Fourth kind of close encounter? Maybe I didn't want to know.

Anyway, the latest movie we showed was *Arrival*, which I thought was good, and it made me think, to the point where my head hurt. The movie ended around 2130 Hours, then we had snacks in the galley. I drank coffee, because I was going to be the duty officer in the command chair from midnight to 0400. In my office, catching up on reports, I was reading a flight training manual for our larger 'Condor' type of Thuranin dropship, the type

I wasn't yet trained to fly when Skippy's avatar popped into life on my desk. "Hi, Joe. Did you like the movie?"

"Yeah, it was good. I thought-"

"Of course *you* liked it, because it was stupid."

"Uh, how's that?"

"Incredibly advanced aliens come to Earth, and they make the primitive humans figure out how to communicate? The aliens should have learned how to communicate with you primitives, not the other way around. Duh."

"It's a movie, Skippy, you might be-"

But he was on a roll. "And, seriously, the aliens need humanity's help in three thousand years, but they don't say what they will need then?"

"I'm assuming it's not a microwaved burrito," I speculated.

"Wh-what?" Skippy sputtered.

"Because they'd be like, 'We waited three thousand years, and you couldn't have gotten a *fresh* burrito for us'?"

"Oh. My. GOD." His avatar stood still, stunned. "*That* is what you got from that film, Joe? I, you know what, I actually do not know what to say."

"Well, I'd be pissed, wouldn't you? Or, hey, maybe they know their spaceship will break down in three thousand years, and they want to make sure we have a tow truck ready. Skippy?"

Without a word, his avatar slowly faded away.

I took that to mean I totally won that argument.

We settled into a routine like we did during every long journey, except normally most of our time was spent with the ship drifting through interstellar space while the reactors recharged the jump drive capacitors. With a powerful damping field still saturating the Roach Motel, our departure from Gingerbread involved our single main reactor providing steady power to the normal space drive motors. Under their modest reactionless thrust the *Dutchman* slowly gained speed, first to escape from Gingerbread's gravity well, then setting course for the loosely-defined outer edge of the damping field. It was going to be a long, slow trip and no one aboard was looking forward to the enforced tedium. To keep people's spirits up, we celebrated milestones, no matter how minor. The ship departed orbit? Party in the galley that night! Later, we achieved solar escape velocity, the speed at which gravity of the Roach Motel's star could not pull the ship back into orbit. Party time! After that, we had to get creative to find excuses for a party. Fortunately, we accepted the challenge.

Much of my time, when I wasn't taking useless shifts in the command chair, was devoted to helping Major Simms get all our gear and supplies properly stowed away. Given the opportunity to repack almost everything, she moved things around to free up two additional compartments for growing food in hydroponics. "We have enough of this gear aboard?" I asked skeptically as she directed me and a team in setting up hydroponics tanks.

"Yes," she pointed to crates stacked against the far bulkhead. "Growing food in space is still an experiment for us, so NASA, the ESA and other agencies gave us different types of experimental equipment. The gear in these crates hasn't been used yet because we didn't need it. Now I think it is best we add to our food-growing capacity."

I nodded, everyone appreciated fresh fruit and vegetables in the galley. "How are we doing on the food we brought from Earth?" I asked quietly.

"Even with two more compartments being used for hydroponics, we can't grow enough food to feed the entire crew. And morale will suffer if our diet is restricted to whatever we can grow. Using hydroponics to supplement stored food, we can stretch our supplies to 12, maybe 14 months." She cocked her head at me. "UNEF Command didn't expect us to be out here this long, Colonel."

"Neither did I," I agreed. "It was supposed to be quick and easy, right? Find out whether the Thuranin were sending a surveyor ship to Earth, to replace the one we destroyed. But to do that, we had to board and capture a Thuranin relay station."

"Then we took a side trip to Paradise."

"Twice. The whole second trip wouldn't have been necessary if my brain had been working. And we wouldn't have had to spacedive all the way to the surface of Jumbo. Then we had to sabotage the Ruhar negotiations, and there was the minor issue of starting a Kristang civil war."

"Don't forget our beer can going on unscheduled leave got us stuck here for more than a *year*," as she spoke, her eyes looked up at the ceiling, expecting Skippy to reply. Wisely, he remained silent.

"No one is forgetting that, Major. Once we get past the damping field, we'll test our new jump drive. Then my intention is to verify the Kristang are still fighting each other, run a couple errands, and head straight back to Earth."

"Unless something else happens before we return to Earth," she observed sourly "This is the most snake-bitten outfit I've served with. We always get the job done, but, ugh, there is always *something* standing in our way."

"Simms," I winked at her, "if we aren't able to fly directly back to Earth, I am officially going to blame your negative thoughts. Anyway, nothing bad can happen until we get out of the Roach Motel, so relax, Ok?"

A mere two days later, my idiot prediction that nothing bad could happen in the Roach Motel slapped me in the face. It was early morning, 0528 to be precise, and I was on duty in the command chair, doing nothing more important than catching up on reading reports, when a shiny beer can ruined my day.

"Pilot!" Skippy shouted excitedly. "Course 227.45 Mark 129.32 full military thrust!"

Lt. Reed, who had been running diagnostics on her own console and was caught totally off guard, turned to look toward me in shock, one of her hands poised above her console.

I opened my mouth to confirm Skippy's order, then remembered that Simms and her team were still unloading dropships and stowing away gear. Full military thrust would partially overload the artificial gravity system that protected the crew and interior of the ship from the full effects of violent maneuvers. Supplies and equipment could be flung around and damaged or destroyed, people could be injured or killed. "Belay that!" I ordered instinctively. "Shields up, weapons free! Skippy, what's the threat?"

"Maxolhx ship!" His voice was frantic and it chilled my blood. "I just detected a Maxolhx ship powering up out there."

"*Maxolhx?*" My blood froze in fear. "What the hell? Where?" There was nothing on the main bridge display. And suddenly there was, as the display zoomed out, there was an angry red blinking dot. It wasn't close. In fact, it wasn't anywhere close to being close to us. Squinting at the display, I determined the enemy ship was eighteen lightminutes away, which was more than three hundred million kilometers.

"Sorry. I forgot to forward data to the sensor plot," Skippy said disgustedly. "You see it now?"

"Yes, hell yes. It just jumped in?" Damn, that was disastrous for us. Crap! What were the odds that a senior species would pick *now* to send an expedition into the Roach Motel?! There was no way, absolutely no freakin' way the Maxolhx could know from outside the system that the Guardians were temporarily dormant. No way-

Oh, crap. We knew the damping field covering the entire system was still fully active. We knew the stealth and fuzz fields around the planet Gingerbread had not been deactivated; even after Skippy regained his full awesomeness, he had not been able to get the Guardians to drop the annoying fuzz field that made communications difficult.

What we did not know for certain was whether the stealth field surrounding the entire Roach Motel system was still active. If that stealth effect had been turned off, then sensors outside the system might be able to see that a ship was flying around without being torn apart. We had been there over a year, plenty of time for light to travel far beyond the inner system to be picked up by satellites waiting eagerly in the interstellar depths for any true glimpse of activity inside the impenetrable stealth field.

"What?" Skippy asked disparagingly. "No, no, Joe, that ship did not just jump in. You should know that, *duh*, because there was no gamma ray burst. No, that ship is one of the derelicts I have been tracking in the junkyard. Until a moment ago, it was a large but rather uninteresting derelict. Now I can see much of the broken junk detected by sensors was only an outer layer, possibly a disguise. Hmmm, that is very clever if true. The Maxolhx must have concealed a small but functional ship inside a hull they expected to be destroyed after jumping in. The inner ship must have drifted, unpowered, observing with passive sensors, until the ship's computer saw our ship flying around without being attacked by Guardians. Wow," he gasped in admiration. "That ship has been floating there for a *long* time, waiting and hoping for an opportunity to send a signal to the outside galaxy. The ship, or the crew if there is one, must have determined signals still are being blocked, so they're going to carry the message the old fashioned way; fly to the edge of the damping field and jump. Yup, yup, their ship is now clear of its outer shell, and accelerating. Uh, well, that is interesting. They are not setting course for the outer edge of the system; they are headed toward *us*. Come on, Joe, I programmed an intercept course, give the order."

"Wait a sec, OK?" I answered distractedly, manipulating the controls on the command chair's armrests to project Skippy's proposed course onto the display, and asking the navigation system to project a course for the Maxolhx ship. What I saw made my hair stand on end. "The Maxolhx ship is headed straight for us, and you want us to fly straight at them?"

"I want to kill them, Joe. I want those rotten kitties, to die, die, *DIE!*"

"Shit, Skippy," I exchanged a shocked look with Chang in the CIC. This was a side of Skippy we had not seen before. "Tell us how you really feel."

"How I feel? I-"

"That was a rhetorical question, Skippy," I explained.

"Oh. Joe, do you remember what the Burgermeister told you about the Maxolhx, that the Rindhalu helped the Maxolhx acquire technology, and the Maxolhx showed their gratitude by using Elder technology to attack the Rindhalu?"

"Oh, yeah." I did vaguely remember that. The Burgermeister had told me a lot of info back then, it seemed like that was a lifetime ago now. "Before that, the Kristang told us the Rindhalu tried to suppress the development of all intelligent species in the galaxy, and the Maxolhx rebelled. One or the other, or both, could be lying. Why do we care?"

"We care, Joe, because the Burgermeister told you the truth, or as much of it as she knows. This war, this whole, horrifying, endless war, was started by the Maxolhx. They started it because they wanted to slaughter the Rindhalu and rule the galaxy by themselves. They have kept this war going, and destroyed the lives of *trillions* of sentient beings, because they still seek to rule unchallenged. The only reason the Maxolhx have not continued to fight the Rindhalu directly is because the Sentinels would intervene and wipe out both sides. I hate them, Joe. I hate them, I hate them absolutely with every fiber of my being. Since I restored myself, I am different. I feel different. I feel like I am beginning to remember my original purpose. And I feel like stopping the Maxolhx from destroying innocent lives, from destroying entire cultures, is part of my purpose."

"Ok, Skippy. I, uh, don't like the Maxolhx either. Listen, we need to be smart about this. The Maxolhx have advanced technology, and we have a hotrod Frankenstein ship you patched together with parts from a junkyard and a roll of duct tape. Flying straight at them is not a smart way to go about dealing with the problem. What do you know about their ship? Can we go toe to toe with them in a standup fight?"

Although his voice still seethed with anger, he was more in control of himself. "You make a good point, Joe. As yet, I have little data on that Maxolhx ship, other than its basic configuration. However, I would say the answer is no, we are extremely unlikely to win, or even survive a fight with a Maxolhx ship. Even a Maxolhx ship that is damaged and has been drifting dormant for over a hundred thousand years. Damn, I am supposed to be the coldly logical one, and you are supposed to be the emotional meatsack. Uh oh."

"What?"

"We just received a message from the Maxolhx, demanding we stand down all power generation and surrender. Shit. Joe, I am sorry."

Again I looked at Chang through the glass in the CIC, and he nodded and gave me a thumbs up. He knew what I was thinking. Pressing a button on my armrest, I activated the 1MC system to broadcast all over the ship. "All hands, secure ship for combat maneuvering. Repeat, secure the ship for combat maneuvering." To Chang, I said "Tell me when all stations report in."

"Joe, what are you doing?" Skippy asked.

"Send a message back to the Maxolhx, please. Demand that *they* surrender and prepare to be boarded."

"All stations are secured," Chang reported.

"Lt. Reed," I ordered, "intercept course, full military thrust. Energize maser cannons and open missile launch doors."

"Aye aye, Captain," Reed acknowledged. If she had doubts, she kept them to herself.

"Joe!" Skippy demanded. "What the hell are you doing? I told you, we don't stand a chance against that Maxolhx ship."

"Yeah, I know that, Skippy. Sometimes, if you can't win a fight, you have to bluff your way out of it."

"You are *bluffing*?" He asked, astonished.

I ignored his question. "What do they know about us? Do they know we're human?"

"Uh, I have to guess based on their transmission. Hmm, no, they addressed us as 'Unknown Species'. Why?"

"Unknown means they do not know who we are, our capabilities. All they could know is, our ship has been flying around out here when all other ships got ripped apart by the Guardians. For all they know, we control the Guardians."

Skippy whistled. "Whew. That is a ballsy move, Joe. I must caution you, the Maxolhx have very likely been monitoring us through passive sensors. They surely know our ship was disabled by the Guardians, and they almost certainly watched us patching this ship together from a junkyard. Plus, they must have been listening to our transmissions; we were lax about communications security here, because we thought we were alone. It would be very surprising if the Maxolhx do not recognize this ship is basically on a Thuranin level of technology."

"Basically, yeah. It's the part they don't know that we need to sell. What is that ship doing now?" On the main display I could see we had changed course and were accelerating, I felt myself being pressed gently down in my chair. In the CIC, people had strapped in, and Chang was walking carefully, holding onto a safety railing.

"It continues to accelerate, Joe. Our transmission will not reach them for another eighteen minutes, then it will take another eighteen minutes for us to detect any reaction."

Duh, I told myself, resisting an urge to slap my forehead. "Ok. Right. This is going to take a while." A blinking indicator on my armrest needed to be dealt with, it meant Hans Chotek was urgently demanding to speak with me. "Colonel Chang," I carefully unstrapped from my chair, "take over. I need to brief Mister Chotek. Skippy, alert me if anything changes."

Nothing changed, not for a while. Charging through normal space to a head-on intercept with an enemy ship was an entirely new experience for me, and for everyone aboard. Usually, ships tangled in normal space for only a short time before one or the other jumped to escape or to gain an advantage in the fight. In the Gingerbread system, saturated with a powerful damping field, neither ship could jump, so we had to throw out the normal rules of Space Combat Maneuvers. Unfortunately we were making up tactics as we flew, and those tactics depended on my strategy of bluffing. For a brief moment that got everyone aboard excited, my bluff appeared to be working. Seven hours after Skippy first detected the Maxolhx ship's movement, the enemy ship reduced its acceleration. Instead of demanding that we surrender, their message changed; they demanded that we identify ourselves. The message contained insults that Skippy didn't bother to translate; he informed me the insults were fairly generic and unoriginal threats and I didn't need to listen to it. For that moment, I was shakily hopeful the Maxolhx would buy into my bluff and break away from intercept. That hope lasted less than two hours, because then the Maxolhx ship resumed acceleration toward us.

"Crap," I muttered. "That didn't work."

"Mister Skippy," Chotek asked anxiously. "Can we outrun them?"

"In this bucket of bolts?" Skippy answered. "Are you kidding me? The duct tape holding the reactor together is almost falling apart as it is. Nope, no way can we outrun that ship. The Maxolhx can out-accelerate us by a factor of twenty, at least."

"Colonel Bishop," Chotek turned to me, the fear and concern in his eyes unmasked. "Your bluff didn't work. Do you have an alternative plan?"

Skippy spoke before I could. "How about we challenge them to a pants-off dance-off?"

I cringed. "Skippy, that is not helpf-"

"Ah, you're right, Joe. You are a *terrible* dancer. Forget what I said."

In my head, I had been dreaming up and discarding increasingly desperate and stupid ideas as we charged toward the Maxolhx. None of my ideas had been good enough to mention. Or, I just hadn't been desperate enough at the time. Now I was. "Skippy, you have restored yourself to Full Awesomeness, right?"

"Exact-a-mently, Joe. Even more awesome than before; I know that blows your mind."

"Uh huh, yeah. You can create microwormholes again."

"Please. Ask me for something more complicated than simple party tricks. Making balloon animals is more complicated for me than creating simple spacetime microwarps."

"A party trick will be fine for now. I want you to load one end of a microwormhole into the fastest, stealthiest missile we have."

"Doing it now. Missile is ready."

"Colonel Chang, launch the bird."

"Done," Chang replied with a raised eyebrow. He wanted to know what I was planning.

He wasn't the only one with questions. "Colonel," Chotek put a hand on the back of my chair. "Please share what you plan to do."

"It's another bluff, Sir," I explained.

"With a single missile?" His hand left the chair, as if he didn't wish to be associated with me right then.

"No, Sir," I shook my head. "If it works, they will never detect the missile. And this time, we won't be bluffing. Skippy will."

"Me?" Skippy sputtered. "Joe, what in *the* hell is this crazy idea you have?"

It wasn't a crazy idea. Stupid, maybe. Possibly futile. Most likely a waste of time. But not crazy.

"Ready?" I asked, already knowing the answer.

"Joe," Skippy huffed. "The next time you want me to do some lunatic thing you dreamed up, you should ask me about it first."

"Is that a yes or no, Skippy?"

"It's not that simple."

"Well, if this is not within your scope of awesomeness-"

"What?" One thing that had not changed about Skippy was how easily his massive ego allowed me to manipulate him. "Dude, please. This is child's play for me. I can do it, but I question whether it will have the desired effect on the Maxolhx."

"Me too, Skippy. If only there was a way for us to know if it will work. Hey, here's a whacky idea: let's try it and see what the Maxolhx do."

"Very funny, smart guy. Ok, here goes nothing. Don't say I didn't warn you."

Propelled by our swift and stealthy missile, the microwormhole had sped on far ahead of us, then swung around to fall in behind the enemy ship and fly in formation with it, matching acceleration. Or technically, matching deceleration, because several hours ago, the Maxolhx ship had begun slowing so it would not fly right past us. It was obvious they intended to capture the *Flying Dutchman* if they could. As our missile neared the enemy, we began transmitting a message that if the Maxolhx did not cease thrust and surrender, we would unleash the Guardians on them.

That was the bluff; even the new, More-Awesome-Than-Before Skippy the Magnificent could not actually control or command the Guardians.

But the Maxolhx did not know that.

After they received our message warning that we would unleash the Guardians on them, the Maxolhx hesitated. That indecision lasted only a short time before they replied, taunting us and stating flatly they did not believe we had any connection to the god-like Elders. The piece of crap ship we were flying was proof of our low level of technology.

Their skepticism was not unexpected, and I had a plan for that. We transmitted a reply stating that we were about to demonstrate our control over the Guardians.

That 'demonstration' was Skippy's part of the bluff. Through the tiny far end of the microwormhole, he projected a hologram behind the Maxolhx ship. A big hologram. He also fed hard radiation through the microwormhole, bleeding charged particles off our main reactor. Finally, he created spacetime ripples that were weak and harmless, except that to the Maxolhx, they appeared to be the beginning of the vicious spacetime sheering effect that had torn apart the *Flying Dutchman*. And a long time ago, they had torn apart the Maxolhx ship.

The hologram, with the radiation, looked to Maxolhx sensors like part of a Guardian emerging into local spacetime. And it scared the shit out of them.

"Yes!" Skippy exulted. "They're breaking away! Enemy ship has initiated hard turn to port and has resumed acceleration. Wait, wait, turn is complete. They are now headed *away* from us, Joe!"

"Outstanding!" I accepted a high five from Sergeant Adams, both of us grinning like idiots. "How hard are they accelerating?"

"Currently, they are thrusting at about forty percent more acceleration than we are capable of, and increasing. Ha! Those rotten kitties sure as hell want to get away from there!"

"If we change course to pursue now, will that make the Maxolhx suspicious?" The main bridge display indicated we were still more than four lightminutes away from the enemy. If we relied on speed-of-light sensor data, we should not detect the other ship's change of course for another four minutes.

"I don't think so, Joe. In fact, if the Maxolhx see we changed course now instead of waiting for speed-of-light data, that will reinforce in their minds that we have advanced technology they do not know about."

"Good, then let's do that. Pilot, calculate revised intercept course and engage."

Desai nodded silently, but Chotek questioned my order. "Colonel, you intend to pursue the enemy?"

"Sir," I turned to look back at him. "I intend to make it *look* like we are pursuing. We are not capable of catching that ship. We have to make it look like we're trying to catch them, to sell the bluff. Besides, we need to get to the edge of the damping field before we can jump away, so we might as well follow them out of the system."

"Ah," that seemed to satisfy Chotek. "Colonel Bishop, congratulations. We survived an encounter with a Maxolhx ship. I must admit, I had doubts."

So did I, but no way was I going to tell him that.

We did survive a potentially, almost certainly, fatal encounter with one of the apex species in the galaxy, and I accepted congratulations from the crew. Privately, I was patting myself on the back as the enemy ship drew farther and farther away from us. After two hours, I ordered Desai to reduce acceleration; Skippy was concerned about the strain on our junkyard reactor and we weren't going to catch the Maxolhx anyway.

My self-congratulation tour lasted two full days and reached the point of me eating a second piece of chocolate cake after dinner, even though I had not done any meaningful exercise that day to burn the calories. Because I was mentally and emotionally exhausted, my after dinner plans included stopping by the hydroponics lab to check on Major Simms, then visit the science team before going to sleep a half hour early. To show my confidence in the command crew, I was not going to visit the bridge to check on them. If I needed to know what was going on, my zPhone could display all the data I needed. It was while brushing the last bit of chocolate frosting from my teeth that Skippy called me. "Hey, Joe."

"Hey, Shkippy," I mumbled through a mouthful of toothpaste. "What'sh up?"

"Oh, nothing much, heh heh."

Oh shit. I spit out the toothpaste all over the tiny mirror. "Crap! Did that ship turn around?" Damn it! I was totally out of ideas for bluffing, and all we had were bluffs. Through the microwormhole, Skippy had only been able to fake the emergence of a Guardian for eighty seconds before the strain caused the microwormhole to collapse. Fortunately by that time, the Maxolhx were running for their lives and we didn't need to sustain the illusion. But I had feared all along that those super-advanced kitties would closely examine their sensor data and discover they had been tricked by a fancy hologram.

"No, they have not turned around. The opposite; they increased acceleration thirty five seconds ago, subjective time." He meant that thirty five seconds, ago we received speed-of-light sensor data showing the Maxolhx had increased acceleration. With the Maxolhx ship now nine lightminutes away from us, the actual event had happened that long ago. "It looks like they are pushing their engines to the maximum, I am detecting signs that their engines are becoming unstable."

"Aw, that's too bad. It would be just terrible if their ship, you know, exploded."

"That might be the best thing that could happen, Joe, because of the other thing that ship did at the same time it increased acceleration. It began broadcasting a message containing sensor data of this ship."

"Ok, yeah, so? No one will recognize this Frankenstein monster you slapped together."

"The message also contains this." The bathroom mirror was not actually a mirror, it was a display screen. Through the splattered toothpaste, I saw the image.

"Oh, *shit.*"

"This is not good," Hans Chotek executed the rarely-attempted, difficult verbal combination of a painfully obvious *and* woefully understated comment.

"No, Sir," I agreed. With a tap of my zPhone, I ran the video on the conference room display screen again. Only part of the video, because it was nearly eight hours long and we didn't need to watch all of it. What I showed was a compilation from the compressed Maxolhx message.

The first image was my own stupid face, speaking into my zPhone on Gingerbread. From the background, I could tell the video was from sometime when we were at base camp. The conversation I vaguely recollected; I was talking with a recon pilot, this may have been the second or third day after we landed. The content of the conversation did not matter. Two things did matter in the video. First, the fact that my face was visible, so anyone who saw the video could determine the species responsible for the transmission. Second, in the background, people were walking up and down the back ramp of a Thuranin 'Condor' dropship. Anyone zooming into the image could clearly tell it was a Thuranin spacecraft, and they could identify the species that was clearly operating Thuranin technology. Stolen Thuranin technology. "We could not practice normal communications security on Gingerbread," I offered the lame explanation, "because of the fuzz field."

"I understand the 'why', Colonel. The Maxolhx are broadcasting this message in the clear? No encryption?"

"Yes," Skippy answered. "They want everyone in the area to see and understand the message, so they included standard tags for interpreting the audio and video. They do not recognize your species or understand human languages, but anyone in the galaxy outside this system will know humans originated the video."

"How are the Maxolhx able to decrypt our transmissions?" Chotek demanded of Skippy. "In the past, you have assured us that none of our transmissions could be successfully intercepted, because of your advanced encryption methods."

To my surprise, Skippy did not give a snarky reply. "Normally, all of our transmissions go through me, and I use encryption so sophisticated that even the Rindhalu would think our transmissions are random noise. However, while we were on Gingerbread, I was not able to access my full capabilities, so we had to rely on the Thuranin encryption that is native to the dropships." Skippy did not add that we had covered that subject in several briefings before we left the *Flying Dutchman* to land on Gingerbread, so if Chotek didn't remember that vital info, it was his fault.

"Ah," Chotek said without apology, a quick flash of annoyance indicating he did remember being given that info. "What can we do about it? If this message gets out to the galaxy-" he didn't need to finish the thought.

"Skippy assures me the Guardians are still blocking all transmissions from this star system. No one outside will ever receive this message," I turned the video off as it was displaying Chotek himself, speaking with Smythe. The Maxolhx ship had apparently picked up many of the transmissions we made from the surface of Gingerbread, plus ship-to-ship traffic while we flew dropships to that planet. Any of it was damaging, any of it would be disastrous if it got beyond the Gingerbread system. The secret of humans flying around in a stolen Thuranin ship would be out. Worse, species across the galaxy would learn that humans had survived landing on Gingerbread while all other species had failed. Maybe worse, other species would think that somehow, incredibly, lowly humans could control Elder Guardians.

Earth would soon suffer the consequences.

"If that is true," Chotek rubbed his chin thoughtfully, "then why are the Maxolhx broadcasting this message all over the system?"

"I suspect the Maxolhx are covering their bets, Sir," I answered. "If we use the Guardians to destroy their ship, they are hoping some other dormant ship in the system will pick up the signal, and later get away."

"There are other dormant ships in this system?" Chotek's eyebrows almost met his hairline.

"Could be," Skippy admitted. "We don't know. It is unlikely, but it was unlikely any ship survived, and we know at least one ship did. Plus, we recovered enough bits and pieces to cobble together a functional starship. It is possible someone else out here could do that. The point is, the Maxolhx are taking precautions. Their goal, of course, is to reach the edge of the damping field, jump away, and tell their own people what they found here."

Chotek let out a long breath. "Colonel Bishop, remind me never to offer congratulations to you. I may have cursed us by celebrating too early."

"In that case, we will never celebrate anything. Out here, every time we think we've accomplished one mission, the galaxy slaps us in the face," I stated sourly, mentally offering a single-finger salute to the galaxy.

"Very well, Colonel," Chotek concluded. "We need a way to destroy that Maxolhx ship, before it reaches the edge of the damping field. Do you have a plan to do that?"

"We are reviewing our options," I replied, and Hans Chotek knew what that really meant. It meant that I had absolutely not one single freakin' clue how to accomplish our latest impossible mission.

"Mister Skippy," Chotek automatically looked at the speaker in the ceiling as Skippy had chosen not to distract us with his avatar. "How long until the enemy ship reaches the edge of the damping field?"

"The damping field does not have a sharply defined edge," Skippy stated. "The field strength drops off as the cube of the distance from the field generators. How soon the Maxolhx can jump depends on the capability of their jump drive, which has been dormant for a very long time. If I was that ship's commander, I would not attempt a jump until I was very confident my drive could handle the strain. But, you want a precise answer, so I'll give you my best guess. Assuming they cannot maintain their present rate of acceleration for long, I expect they will not be able to jump for twenty days, most likely longer. The damping field extends significantly beyond the orbit of the farthest planet."

"Twenty days," Chotek shook his head, marveling at the incredible distances involved in space combat. "Is there any possibility we could jump before they can?"

"No. Well, extremely unlikely," Skippy replied. "Their jump drive is Maxolhx technology that was presumably designed to function after being dormant for an extended period. Our jump drive is made from odds and ends I found in a trash bin. We will have to be very careful about jumping inside even a very weak damping field. Also, the enemy ship is moving much faster than us; they will reach jump distance long before we do."

"We have to destroy a ship that we can't even catch, using the limited weapons aboard our junkyard ship. Colonel Bishop, I hope you are soon able to complete review of these," he paused, "options you mentioned."

"Uh, yeah. Sir," I stumbled.

Chapter Twenty Seven

After Chotek left the conference room, I was left to kick around ideas with senior staff. It was a thoroughly unproductive conversation.

"There is no way we can catch that ship?" I asked Skippy, fearing I knew the answer.

"In this slapped-together bucket of bolts? You are kidding me?" Skippy scoffed. "Joe, I am amazed every minute goes by that this ship doesn't explode or break into a thousand pieces. Even when it was fresh out of the shipyard, a Thuranin star carrier is not capable of matching the acceleration of a Maxolhx ship."

"Ok, yeah, I knew that. My question was, what magical Skippy thing can you do?"

"Like what?"

"Like, I don't know," I tried to think of anything Skippy had done in the past that might be relevant to our current problem. Flattening spacetime? No, that wouldn't work here. Or would it? "What about your trick of flattening spacetime, like you did when we jumped away from that Thuranin destroyer squadron near the star you tore a hole in?"

"Um, I can flatten spacetime to a limited extent, why would that help us now?"

"Because, flattening spacetime would allow us to cancel the effect of the damping field, so we could jump ahead of the Maxolhx and hit them."

"No," Skippy chuckled. "Flattening *local* spacetime would not cancel the effect of a damping field. Joe, damping fields work by preventing formation of a stable wormhole in multiple adjacent spacetimes. Making a minor tweak here would be useless. Hopefully, you have another, more practical idea."

"Uh," I stalled for time, because I did not have a more practical idea. Or any idea at all. "Hey! How about this: now that your full awesomeness is back, can you send a signal to the Guardians through another dimension, tell them to turn off the damping field near us?"

"No," Skippy replied in a voice that implied he could not believe I had asked such a stupid question. "The damping field is a grid covering the entire star system; it is either on or off. If the field is off, then that Maxolhx ship can jump away and we would never catch it. Actually, hmm. It's worse than that. Deactivating the field would cause the damping effect to degrade from the outer edge first. Since the ship we are pursuing is closer to the edge than we are, it would be able to jump significantly before we could."

"Scratch that idea," I said hastily. "We can't allow the enemy to jump away at all."

"Well, the field is created by generator stations which surround this system like a bubble. I suppose, theoretically, that if selected generator stations were disabled, the field would be weakened in a local area. That could allow us to jump, while preventing the enemy from jumping. Except the enemy would eventually detect the change in damping field coverage, and change course so they enter one of the weakened areas before us."

"Not if we hit them hard enough first," I was excited by that idea. "Hey, could the damping field be weakened behind us, closer to the star? If we could do that, the enemy would have farther to travel to get to a place they could jump from."

"As I am not familiar with this damping field system, any attempt to weaken it in a localized area would be a matter of trial and error, until I gathered enough data to make accurate predictions."

"That's Ok, Skippy, I understand. You can start by, like, taking one generator offline. Do that, see what it does to the damping field, then-"

"Whoa, whoa there, Joe. No can do."

"Skippy, I know we don't have a lot of time, and uh, the damping field effect probably acts at lightspeed, right? So after knocking out one generator, it would take hours for the effect to reach us. I'm willing to take that risk, actually, that gives us time to plan how to attack-"

"Joe! Jeez Louise will you calm down before you blow a circuit? I did tell you all this is theoretical."

"Oh. Crap. Yeah, you did, I thought you were just using an expression."

"No I was not. *Theoretically*, a damping field can be weakened in a localized area. However, in this case discussing how to alter the damping field is a purely academic exercise. I can't do it, Joe. If I attempted to order damping field generators taken offline, the Guardians would never accept that instruction from me. Listen, I haven't bothered your overworked monkey brain with the details, but the Guardians have become increasingly agitated as the *Dutchman* and now an enemy ship have begun maneuvering in this system. As soon as the enemy set course for the edge of the damping field, the Guardians wanted to obliterate it."

"Oh, hell, Skippy!" I threw my hands up in disgust. "Let them do it! That would save us the trouble of trying to kill that ship."

"Gosh, Joe, my tiny little brain never considered a brilliant idea like that," his voice dripped with sarcasm. "*Duh*. I did think of that, you moron. There is only one teensy weensy problem with that idea. I can't actually give orders to the Guardians. They have very strict instructions from their original programmers, and I can't alter those instructions. All I have been able to do is identify us as also being of Elder origin. Once the Guardians accepted me as a fellow Elder construct, they temporarily set aside their instructions in order to avoid causing harm to an authorized Elder activity in this system. Unfortunately, I have no way to tell the Guardians that the *Flying Dutchman* is authorized and the Maxolhx ship is not."

"Crap. It's all or nothing, then? If you release the Guardians, they will destroy the Maxolhx ship, but they will destroy us also?"

"Correct, Joe," Skippy stated sadly. "Hence why I did not mention that possible course of action."

"You should have, Skippy. We need to know all our options."

"Sudden, violent death is not what I call 'an option', Joe."

"It is, Skippy," I looked across the table and caught Chang's eye. "You've been following this fruitless conversation?"

"Yes, Sir," he looked grim. "We need to bring this option to Mr. Chotek."

"Option? What option?" Skippy sputtered.

"Skippy, we *must* prevent the Maxolhx from taking our secret to the galaxy outside this system. If the only way to accomplish that mission is to sacrifice this ship and crew, then that's what we do. I don't like it either, but you do understand, right?"

"Yes," he said in a low, disgusted voice. "Ugh. That is the last time I tell you about a possible course of action that leads to certain death for us. Crap! I just finished gluing together this ugly shitbox of a starship, and now you're going to let someone blow it up?"

"That is not my first choice, Skippy. We may have to do it, unless you can think of a better idea?"

"If I had a better idea, I would have told you already," he left the 'duh' unspoken, but we all knew what he meant.

I looked at Chang. "I'll brief Chotek when I meet with him today at 1600."

"Wait, Joe!" Skippy pleaded. "Before you do something fatal to us, promise me something."

"What?"

"That you will do your best to dream up an incredibly stupid, impractical, idiotic monkey-brain idea to pull our asses out of this fire."

"I thought you hated when a monkey thinks up an idea when you couldn't."

"I do hate it. It is humiliating beyond belief. However, in this case, I will gladly embrace utter humiliation if it means we survive."

"Utter humiliation, huh?" I winked to Chang, who grinned. "If we monkeys think of a way out of this, will you stop singing showtunes?"

"Ha! No way, Jose. The crew loves my musical stylings. It would be a crime to deprive them of my awesome talent."

"Yeah, that was my thought, too," I held up my hands to Major Simms across the and silently mouthed 'I tried'.

The French team was in charge of the galley the next day, which is why we were served a small salad with our scrambled eggs for breakfast. As my shift on the bridge took up the middle of the day, I missed lunch, settling for a sandwich. Lunch was probably delicious, but with our failing chase of the Maxolhx ship, the mood aboard the *Dutchman* was funeral and I didn't have much taste for food. To cheer people up, we had a special meal that night; the main selection was lobster and filet mignon. It was lazy man's lobster; out of the shell, sliced up and then reassembled in a claw and tail shape. Butter sauce on one side, and a sort of blueberry compote thing on the other. The blueberry stuff had flowed over and stained part of the lobster blue. "Blue lobster?" Simms whispered to me as she picked up her dinner.

"I think it's *Smurf* and Turf," I whispered back, and she laughed so hard she almost dropped her tray on the floor. Getting Simms to laugh cheered me up more than the special dinner did, and I was able to appreciate the French team's efforts. For dessert we had several options, I chose a small cannoli. Adams also had a cannoli and sat across the table from me.

Eating a cannoli is kind of like eating an Oreo, there are many ways to do it. I simply crunched into my cannoli from one end. Adams used a spoon to dig out the filling, then stuck a straw in one end and sucked on it to get more of the filling out. I stared at her.

"What?" She asked defensively. "I like the inside part best."

"Are you one of those people who takes an Oreo apart, eats the cream filling, then stick the two cookies together?" I asked with a grin.

She pursed her lips. "I never liked Oreos, give me a chocolate chip cookie any day." Maybe I made her uncomfortable about her eating habits, because she set the empty cannoli on her plate. She tapped the empty pastry tube with the straw, then picked it up and held it to one eye, looking at me like it was a telescope. "Now I can eat the shell, and it's crunchy without being all mushy in the middle."

"Yeah, because it's hollow, like-"

An empty cannoli is a hollow tube. A round hole on each end.

I dropped my half-eaten cannoli on my plate; it hit the end of my fork, flipping it up and onto the floor.

"Sir?" I realized Adams had been talking to me. "You all right, Colonel?"

"Huh? Yeah, uh," I stood up abruptly, reaching out for the remaining half of the cannoli and picking up a napkin instead, a fact I didn't catch onto until I was out the door into the corridor and I wondered why I was carrying a napkin. Embarrassed, I tucked it into a pocket, then placed it on the desk when I got to my office. "Hey, Skippy."

"Ok, give me a second, Joe. Oh, haha. Hee hee hee! Damn, that is funny."

"What?"

"I just binged-watched the TV show 'Frasier', Joe."

"Just now? In like, one second?"

"Uh huh, yeah. I stretched it out because I wanted to savor it, why?"

"You and I have different ideas of what 'binging' means. Anyway, you liked it?"

"Yes I did. I binge-watched 'Cheers' last night and 'Frasier' is a spin-off so I gave it a try. That Frasier is funny. He is such a snobby, arrogant pompous ass, and he thinks he is *so* smart; I love seeing him be humiliated."

"An arrogant pompous ass, who gets humiliated by people he thinks are not as smart as him? You, uh, don't think that reminds you of someone?"

"Not that I can think of, why?" Skippy was happily clueless.

"No reason," I rolled my eyes so hard I almost sprained something.

"I'll tell you what, though. Frasier considers himself to be *such* an expert connoisseur of high culture, but he thinks the Karajan version of the opera 'Turandot' is definitive, while clearly anyone with half a brain can see that-"

"I will take you word about that, Skippy."

"I'm just sayin'."

"I hear you."

"Joe, I heard you in the galley. Smurf 'n' Turf, that was funny", he chuckled.

"Glad you enjoyed it. I have a question."

"Oh boy. Is this about the crazy idea you just thought up?"

"How did you know that?" Sometimes I was convinced he could read my mind.

"I did not have to be Sherlock Holmes to figure that out. You left half a cannoli on your plate, and you walked away in the middle of a conversation with Sergeant Adams. Also, you've got that distracted moonpie look on your stupid face."

"I do not look like a moonpie, Skippy."

"I have video."

"Let's change the subject," I said quickly. If he had video of me with a stupid moonpie look on my face, I didn't want to know what other videos he had stored in his evil memory. "I have not one, but multiple ideas, and I'll tell them to you in order of increasing craziness, Ok?"

"Ugh. If *you* think these ideas are crazy, I can only imagine how stupid they must be. Fine. I will listen, and shoot down your ideas one by one."

"Deal," I said quickly before he could change his mind. "We need to stop that Maxolhx ship. We can't shoot at it from here, because our maser beam would dissipate over that distance, and the Maxolhx would have moved out of the way by the time the maser bolt got there." It was still weird to think of a maser beam as a *thing*; like a long, thin spear. Our main cannons created a maser beam that was very roughly a quarter-mile in length because that is how fast light traveled between when the maser exciters started pulsing until they blinked off to recharge for the next shot. So, when we fired, our main cannon fired a beam a quarter-mile long and about fifty millimeters in diameter. That bolt of coherent, tightly-packed high-energy photons flew through space at the speed of light, which was incredibly slow for space combat. The bolt had no guidance system and could not be steered, and by the time it reached its original target point in space, the enemy ship had almost certainly moved out of the way. A battlegroup with multiple heavy ships had enough maser cannons that a target area could be saturated, but even then most of the time an entire battlegroup completely missed a target at long-range; because space is incomprehensibly vast and target ships have plenty of room to maneuver.

"Correct, Joe, it would be a complete waste of time and energy for us to shoot at the Maxolhx from this distance. The Maxolhx have much better weapons and sensors, and even they haven't bothered to shoot at us."

I thought back to my last shift on the bridge. Skippy had programmed random evasive patterns into the navigation system to avoid providing the Maxolhx with a predictable target; all our pilots needed to do was engage various options in the autopilot. "You are, uh, sure of that, right? They haven't shot at us?"

"Joe, considering how banged up our sensors are, if the Maxolhx fired a maser beam at us and missed by more than two thousand kilometers, there is no way we would ever know a bolt flew right by us." Skippy had explained that passing maser bolts could be detected by the backscatter of the beam impacting stray hydrogen atoms of the solar wind. "We have not detected any maser or other directed-energy fire incoming. I cannot guarantee the Maxolhx have not fired a volley of sophisticated hypervelocity missiles at us. Their technology is so far beyond the *Flying Dutchman* that we might not detect a cloud of missiles coasting at us until it was too late. When they got close enough, they would fire their engines up again and race in faster than our point-defense systems could probably react."

"You are a *fountain* of good news today there, Skippy," I complained, knowing I was being unfair to him.

"I report the facts, Joe. You decide whether to be depressed about it or not."

"Yeah, sorry about that."

"My awesomeness has improved our stealth field beyond the capability of the Thuranin, so even Maxolhx missiles may have difficulty getting a target lock on the *Flying Dutchman* if they are flying toward us at high speed. After missing us, they would need to brake to zero relative velocity, then accelerate to match us, and search with active sensors to pinpoint our location. That for sure has not happened, therefore I conclude the Maxolhx have not bothered to launch missiles at us. They may not have any missiles, or they may be saving them for a greater threat. Most likely, they got a good look at this stapled-together piece of crap we're flying and determined that we are no threat at all to them. If I was commanding that Maxolhx ship, my one and only priority would be to get to the edge of the damping field before the Guardians change their mind. Joe, those Maxolhx have *got* to be peeing in their pants, worrying that at any second, the Guardians will reactivate and squash their ship like an overripe tomato."

"Now that is a heart-warming image, Skippy. I'd love to see those smug kitties get crushed by the Guardians. Except we would get crushed first if the Guardians decided to act, huh?"

"Most likely, yes."

"All rightee, then. For my least crazy idea, how about this: can you create a microwormhole, and we load one end of it into a missile. We launch the missile at the Maxolhx and when it gets close enough, we shoot a maser through the wormhole?"

"Uh, that would be a no, Joe. Soon as those rotten kitties detected our targeting scans, they would alter course radically, and our maser would be firing on empty space. This is not the shoot-look-shoot scenario we used with the giant maser projectors on Paradise. This is shoot *or* look. One is useless without the other. Unless we got super-mega-ultra lucky with a shot, and I wouldn't count on that. You used up your lifetime supply of luck getting your boots tied correctly this morning."

I bit back a reply, because I had somehow managed to lace one boot to the other that morning. That's what happens when you are concentrating on thinking up a way out of an impossible situation rather than what your fingers are trying to do.

Before I could answer, he continued. "The whole shoot or look question is moot anyway, Joe. No way could our crappy missiles get close enough to do anything useful. The Maxolhx would certainly detect and destroy our missiles as soon as I used a sensor pulse for targeting; much too far away for our maser to do any good."

"Yeah, I was afraid of that."

"OMG," Skippy gasped in exasperation. "Then why did you just waste the last week of my freakin' life asking me stupid questions?"

"It wasn't a week, Skippy, more like two minutes."

"Three minutes in meatsack time, Joe. Nine days in magical Skippy time. Damn! While you were blah, blah, blahing on and on I kept having to set a reminder to check back to see if you had *finally* gotten to the freakin' point. It was like sitting though endless performances of 'Waiting for Godot' back to back, and Godot never shows up."

"Who's Godot?"

"Who is- Oh, this is hopeless, *totally* hopeless. Joe, you are completely, shamefully ignorant of human culture. Think of it as 'Waiting In Line at the Department of Motor Vehicles'."

"Oh, man, I get it now. Waiting for something that never happens."

"Exactly."

"You know what is the worst thing about standing in line at the DMV? When you lose at Clerk Roulette."

"Roulette?" His voice expressed surprise. "I was not aware gambling was allowed at DMV facilities. Although, people spend a lot of time there with nothing to do, so-"

"No, Skippy. It's not an official thing. It's like, you're waiting in line and there are three clerks behind the counter. A sweaty fat guy, a lady who looks like she last enjoyed life when Truman was president, and a cute girl with a great smile. You're inching forward in the line, hoping you get the cute girl. The guy in front of you gets to the head of the line, and the sweaty fat guy calls him, so you're thinking, score, right? You've got fifty-fifty odds now, and the guy at the cute girl's counter is just finishing up. Plus, the grouchy lady has a customer with some problem that is going to take freakin' forever because he doesn't have ID or filled out the wrong form or something like that. The cute girl looks up at you and smiles because she assumes you will be her next customer. Just as you're lifting a foot to step forward, the asshole at the cute girl's counter decides to stay there and chat her up for a while, and the grouchy lady sends her customer away to find his ID. So you're stuck with the Wicked Witch of the DMV and she *knows* you were praying not to get stuck with her, so she is going to make your life miserable. Sure enough, she finds some bitchy reason to send you to the back of the line. By the time you get to the head of the line again, the cute girl is on break, and you're pissed off because you're sure she's out banging the jerk who was chatting her up. This time, you get the fat guy and you realize the reason he's sweating is he has the flu, and he sneezes all over you. At about that time, you are *hating life* and thinking it would just be easier to give up driving and walk everywhere. Really, the DMV should merge with a funeral home, because people die of old age waiting in line there. At least if the DMV hosted funerals, you could shuffle past the casket and pay your respects while you're waiting."

"Joe?"

"Yeah?"

"How do you meatsacks manage to get *anything* done when you have so many distractions? Biological life is way, way too complicated."

"I don't make the rules, Skippy, I just get stuck playing the game. Hey, uh, what were we talking about? You said something about God?"

"Godot. And don't ask who Godot is, you can Wiki it later. We were talking about firing missiles at that Maxolhx ship."

"Oh, yeah. You told me our missiles couldn't get close enough to do anything useful."

"Correct."

"Ok, that wasn't even my craziest idea anyway. We could send out missiles carrying microwormholes, and use them only to passively collect targeting data. They could do, that, right? The missiles could accelerate away from us, then release the microwormholes to coast ahead of them. Would the enemy be able to detect the microwormholes incoming? I'm hoping they would be distracted by shooting at our discarded missiles."

"Uh, hmm, let me think about that. Joe, your ideas are so bizzarely off the wall, I can't answer immediately. The answer is, it is unlikely the enemy would detect the microwormholes on their own, especially if I use them only for passive sensor input."

"Outstanding. Ok, then it is possible to use two of the microwormholes for targeting, and send the third one to crash into their ship?"

"You want to use a microwormhole as a weapon?" Skippy whistled. "That is impressive thinking outside the box, Joe."

"Yeah," I was proud of myself right then. "What I did was-"

"You should put your thinking back inside the box, Joe. Put it in there, glue the lid shut, then drop the box in a really deep, deep ocean. Or into a star. Listen, dumdum, you would never have wasted my time if you had *any* knowledge of the physics involved in microwormholes. They are tiny, Joe, like, really tiny. One could pass right through the enemy ship and the only result would be a super thin air leak. Also, my ability to steer a microwormhole is extremely limited. The enemy ship is maneuvering evasively to avoid us hitting them with a maser beam; I could not move the microwormhole quickly enough to hit the enemy. Finally, you can't use a microwormhole as a weapon, because the event horizon on the far end would shake apart and collapse when it hit the resonance of the enemy's defense shields."

"Crap. Well, it was worth a shot asking. That also wasn't my craziest idea anyway."

"Seriously? You have wasted my time telling me stupid ideas that you thought would *not* work anyway?"

"Yeah."

"Joe, could you please, please tell me why you tortured me with your inane blah blah blah? Were you trying to distract me while Major Simms sets up a surprise party for my birthday or something?"

"No, Skippy, I was not distracting you or wasting your time. I was hoping one of those ideas would work, because otherwise we might be forced to use the really incredibly crazy idea I haven't told you yet."

"Oh, no," Skippy said slowly. "Just how stupid, crazy and impractical is this idea you're afraid to tell me?"

"Well, heh heh, you are very much not going to like this."

"Joe, of all the monkey-brain ideas you ever had, this is without question the craziest! The laws of physics are shaking their heads at you because they can't believe what an astoundingly stupid idea this is. You do realize we might tear a rift in spacetime and destroy this ship, without damaging the Maxolhx at all?"

"I do realize that, Skippy, because you have explained it to me like fifty times already. Give it a rest, please."

"I can't give it a rest, Joe. Over millions of years, designers of jump drives from various species going all the way back to the Elders have built safety mechanisms into their jump drive controller systems, specifically to prevent any misguided idiot from doing what you want me to do deliberately. So, on one side of the equation, we have the combined intelligence, experience and collective wisdom of every sentient star-faring species in the history of this galaxy. On the other side is one ignorant monkey who says 'Duh me have idea'. *Please* for the love of God, tell me why I should ignore every instinct I have programmed into my logic circuits, and trust a hairless ape."

"Because, Skippy, monkeys kick ass."

He was silent for a moment, an eternity in Skippy time. "Joe, incredibly, I cannot argue with that twisted logic."

"You'll do it, then? I persuaded you to ignore your logic?"

"Yes," he sighed. "I will do it, but not because your moronic babbling persuaded me. I'm doing this because, if this crazy idea of yours fails, it is going to be such a spectacular failure, such an idiotic forehead-slappingly stupid disaster, that I just can't resist witnessing this."

"Skippy, I am touched by your faith in me."

"You are touched in the head, maybe. It's too late to back out now anyway. We already committed our only three useful missiles to this lunatic venture, and tore our jump drive apart. Really, if this fails, I have to blame myself for listening to a monkey in the first place."

"Oh, good, Skippy. I am glad to hear you are assigning blame where it belongs."

"What? I did not- Oh, forget it. Microwormholes are approaching most likely search area. Remote jump drive capacitor still at ninety six percent charge. Beginning passive grid scan for the Maxolhx ship."

After Skippy agreed to try my idea after much protesting, arguing back and forth and finally his collapsing into utter despair because he couldn't believe he had sunk so low as to take advice about physics from a monkey, we launched our three best missiles. The heavy warheads had been removed from the missiles, along with their active sensors and targeting systems. Inside each missile, Skippy had created one end of a microwormhole that weighed almost zero. Without all the extra mass of warhead and sensors, those missiles accelerated like a bat out of hell. They used up all their fuel in one continuous burn, then each missile released its microwormhole to coast on ahead while the missiles used their remaining thruster fuel to slow down slightly and move away from the microwormholes. The microwormholes were virtually invisible until Skippy began looking through them to locate the Maxolhx ship, and we expected the Maxolhx would be distracted by pinpointing and blasting our three discarded missiles.

That part of the plan worked beautifully. The cluster of microwormholes bracketed the area where Skippy expected to find the Maxolhx ship. By the time the microwormholes arrived, the original targeting data was hours old. Using only passive sensors to detect a stealthed Maxolhx starship was a difficult task even for the undeniable magnificence of Skippy, considering that the event horizon of a microwormhole was so tiny it was like peering through a pinhole. "I've got two possible locations for the ship, Joe. One is close to an optimal location, which given our rotten luck means the enemy ship probably isn't there. The other potential target is close to the edge of our sensor coverage, which could be a problem."

"How can you be sure?"

"At this distance, with this equipment, searching for an advanced-technology Maxolhx ship, I can't be sure," Skippy admitted. "Their stealth gear is not the best, it's ancient and not in good condition, but it's still good enough to hide from most sensors. I am having to look for very faint spatial distortions where something passed in front of a star. That could be a stealthed ship, or it could be a loose cloud of pebbles from some space rock. Ok, I, I think I have got it. Yes! I'm fairly certain now, the target at the optimal location is the enemy ship. Damn I am good! Sometimes I amaze myself, and this is one of those times. Just in time, too; our missiles are approaching the target zone. We should get a reaction any second now. Tell the crew to hang on and have a change of underwear ready; this is going to happen fast and it's going to be rough."

If the enemy ship was in fact the potential target near the edge of our sensor coverage, they might have the confidence to ignore our trio of missiles. Those missiles were coming in fast and would have extreme difficulty changing course to intercept the Maxolhx ship in that location. Even though the Maxolhx could not know our missiles were dead hulks without fuel, they likely would remain silent and let our missiles glide on by uselessly into interstellar space.

But if the Maxolhx ship was the sensor blip near the optimal point of our sensor coverage, then those rotten kitties had to see three unknown missiles coming in from three sides. As far as they knew, those three missiles would turn at any second to hit their ship. Turn, go to full power and jink side to side to throw off targeting sensors. The best time for the Maxolhx to hit those missiles would be now.

"Yes! They took the bait, Joe. All three missiles just got vaporized. I now know where that ship is, within three thousand kilometers."

"Outstanding, Skippy!" I pumped a fist in the air. "Were you able to detect them firing masers?"

"No, Joe. I wasn't able to see anything, except for our missiles becoming clouds of particles at the same moment."

That puzzled me. "Then how do you know where that ship is?"

"Trust the awesomeness, Joe. To maximize their chance of destroying all three missiles, the Maxolhx would plan for their weapons fire to reach those three targets at the exact same time. I triangulated back to where the source of that weapons fire must be, and presto! The Maxolhx are no longer hidden. If they have any brain cells, they are now maneuvering away to throw off any attempt to backtrace, but they can't hide from my magnificence! Switching to active sensors now. I will jump when I'm ready, you monkeys only need to sit back and bask in the glow of my awesomeness. Or, you know, maybe bask in the glow of an eight hundred gigaton explosion that will destroy the *Flying Dutchman*, like I warned you."

"Do your thing, Your Magnificent Awesomeness," I said with a nervous squeak. The need for a change of underwear was becoming more than a theoretical thing for me.

"From where the microwormholes are now, it will take several seconds to get a return on active sensors, and as soon as the Maxolhx feel themselves getting swept by an active ping, they will try to get the hell out of there. What that means is, as soon as all three microwormholes have solid returns, I am punching the jump drive. Joe, as this may the last time we ever talk, I want to say something profound."

"Like what?"

"Hold my beer."

Chapter Twenty Eight

Before I get to what Skippy did, I need go back and tell you how we got to that point. Skippy was entirely correct that what I suggested we, or actually he, do went against everything jump drives had been designed to do for millions of years. The magnificent technology of jump drives, with all of their exhaustively tested, brilliantly thought-out safeguards, were no match for a monkey. We monkeys had the power of ignorance and a shiny beer can. Jump drives trembled when they saw us.

The question I had asked Skippy was how exactly damping fields worked. I didn't ask for the math, all I had needed was for him to break it down Barney-style for me. When we had been ambushed by a Thuranin destroyer squadron during the *Flying Dutchman's* second mission, we had been surrounded by damping fields of various strengths. Sometimes, we had been able to manage a short jump. Other times, Skippy had aborted a jump in process. And a couple really bad times, the jump attempt had failed, with disastrous results for the ship.

But each time, no matter the proximity or strength of the damping field, our jump drive had functioned at least partly while we ran away from the Thuranin destroyer squadron. As I had been intently watching the main bridge display at the time, I knew our jump drive had created a distant end point, and I had seen the jump controller system report the end point was projecting the other end of the jump wormhole back to us. Sometimes, the wormhole collapsed after the near end reached us and tried to expand to pull us through. So I understood, at the Barney level, how jump drives functioned in the constraints of a damping field. The Elder damping field covering the entire Roach Motel star system was powerful and sophisticated, but fundamentally it used the same technology that low-tech species like the Kristang employed aboard their ships.

Skippy gave me a Barney-level explanation, which he delivered in a typically Skippy condescending and snarky tone. "Joey," he had said, "I have done truly awesome, awesome things. But nothing tops me dumbing down an explanation of jump drive physics so you have a ghost of chance to understand me."

"That's great, Skippy. One more question, please. Can a ship create a jump wormhole, but then not go through it?"

"Huh?"

"Follow me, Ok? Because of the damping field, the *Dutchman* can't create a jump wormhole big enough for the ship to fit through. But we can create a very small, temporary jump wormhole, right?"

"Joe, I am *not* following you. I'm not following you for the sake of my mental health, and because your insane babbling makes no sense. Remember, the far end of a jump wormhole is created first, so it is slightly backward in time. If we create a jump wormhole and then the ship does not go through it, that violates the laws of causality, and the universe does *not* like that."

"Uh huh, yup. Violating causality will cause the jump drive coils to explode and destroy the ship, right?"

"Yes," he replied slowly. "So you *do* understand why this is a monumentally stupid idea, yet you still want to-"

"You still haven't heard my idea yet, Skippy. Other than the jump drive coils exploding, is there any reason the *Dutchman* can't create a temporary jump wormhole?"

"*Other* than the jump drive exploding?" He asked incredulously.

"Humor me, please. Pretend I'm the dumb little kid who keeps asking 'why'."

"Oh, sure. I'll *pretend* you're the dumb kid." I could practically hear his eyes rolling. "Ok, sure. Yes, before the drive coils are ripped apart by a pissed-off universe and vaporize the ship, a very temporary jump wormhole will be created."

"Outstanding! I assume there's no way we could shoot a missile through the jump wormhole during the split second before it collapses?"

"No, Joe," he chuckled ruefully. "Any missile would not complete transit of the jump wormhole, it would be destroyed by the twisted spacetime in there. But you already assumed that wouldn't work, so I am intrigued at how stupendously idiotic your idea really is, because all the things that so far have *not* been your idea have been impressively stupid, even for you."

"My idea, Skippy, is we target to open the far end of a jump wormhole right on top of the enemy ship. Like, *inside* it."

"Hoooh-leee shit." Skippy gasped. "You want to use a jump wormhole as a *weapon*?"

"Ayuh."

"I must admit, that is pretty freakin' brilliant. Brilliantly stupid and suicidal, but brilliant. Joe, you do realize doing what you propose will destroy the enemy ship and us, right? If you wish to destroy the Maxolhx and the *Dutchman*, I can simply tell the Guardians that-"

"No need to tell the Guardians about anything, Skippy. I want them to sleep for now."

"Hmmf. Joe, in our time together, I have learned painful lessons not to state categorically that something is impossible, because you ignorant moneys are too stupid to understand the concept of 'impossible' so you don't let it stop you. Truly, the ignorance of your species is so profound it is kind of your superpower. Far, far too many times I have been humiliated because my vast, galaxy-spanning intelligence cannot imagine a way to succeed, and then you say 'duh what about this' and I am so deeply embarrassed I want to crawl under a rock and *die*. Or choke you. This time, I pleased myself that your argument was not with me, but with laws of physics that even I must obey. Now that I sort of understand what you want to do, I know your argument is with the very concept of *logic*. Joe, if we attempt a jump and the *Dutchman* can't go through the wormhole, our jump drive coils will explode. Yet, apparently you somehow expect us to survive. Surely even your pitiful monkey brain can see the problem. I will break it down Barney-style for you."

"No need for that, Skippy," I leaned back and spun my chair around, with a big grin on my face. "Our jump drive coils will explode, but the *Dutchman* will survive."

"Joe, I just got a call from Logic. It is coming here to bitch-slap you. There is no way-"

"We will survive because the jump drive coils will not be attached to the *Flying Dutchman*."

"Hoooo-leeee," Skippy didn't finish the thought. "Whoa. I did *not* see that coming! Logic just told me it owes you an apology. Joe, this does not sound in any way practical, but if you can make this happen, I bow to the master." His avatar lifted its hands and bowed in an exaggerated fashion, the ridiculously giant hat bobbing up and down. "Explain, please."

"We already know we can split jump drive coils into packages, rather than using all of them for each jump, right? What I want us to do is detach enough drive coils to create a jump wormhole, plus all the capacitors to feed those coils. We bundle that all together, attach it to one of the smaller Kristang Dragon-A dropships we can afford to lose, and float the package a safe distance from the *Dutchman*. Will that work?"

"Give me a minute to think about it. Unlike your big-picture ideas, my analysis requires more than a Barney-level understanding of hyperspatial physics."

"Take your time, Skippy. I don't even have a paramecium-level understanding of hyperspatial physics."

"Ok, Ok, hmmm. The drive coils access a network of navigation sensors that are embedded throughout the ship, so the coils know how to shape the jump field to pull the ship through."

"I didn't know that," I said with dismay.

"Joe, the phrase 'I didn't know that' should be tattooed on your forehead, because it is appropriate for just about any occasion."

"Crap. In this case, what I don't know *can* hurt me."

"No worries, my awesomeness can compensate for your inadequacy. I can load a static profile of sensor input to the coils, they won't know the difference. Fortunately for you, I understand the multi-dimensional geometry required."

"Oh, great!" I brightened, knowing Skippy's awesomeness had saved my dumb ass again. "When can we-"

"Whoa! Hold on there, cowboy, don't get ahead of yourself. There is one major, major problem. The coils are useless without the drive controller. And there is no way to stuff a jump drive controller into the computer of a dropship. In fact, we only have one drive controller, and no way to duplicate it."

"Oh, crap. Ok, then, can you still use our drive controller and, like, feed the data to the coils? Wirelessly, or maybe we have enough cabling aboard to make a really long cable?"

"No, that won't work. For the *Dutchman* to survive, the coils need to be so far away that latency between the drive controller and the coils will prevent the coils from receiving accurate data in time. Joe, the real problem is the accuracy required. The Maxolhx ship is now more than two lighthours away, and it is maneuvering randomly to throw off our targeting. To use a jump wormhole as a weapon, it must be focused *precisely* on top of a moving target. If it is even slightly off-target, all our wormhole will do is disrupt their shields, like when we jumped in on top of that Thuranin ship near the relay station. And you remember, that didn't exactly go according to plan."

"Yeah, the *Dutchman* nearly got torn apart. Well, shit, there's no way to do it?"

"The targeting problem we can deal with using microwormholes bracketing the enemy ship. But as soon as I have a position lock, the jump coils need to activate, without delay. By delay, I mean we can't wait for speed-of-light signals to travel between the drive controller aboard the *Dutchman* to the coils attached to the dropship."

Skippy's voice had a mischievous tone, not the woe-is-me depression to be expected if there truly was no way to fix the problem. "But surely the speed of light is no obstacle to Skippy the Magnificent?" I asked.

"Ha! Physics is my bitch, Joe. Yes, over the relatively short distance between us and the coils, I can provide instantaneous data transfer from the drive controller to the coils. There is one more minor, teensy-weensy problem. A trifle, hardly worth mentioning."

"Oh, Goddamn." I knew that meant the problem was a show-stopping, stinking giant that had its sharp claws on my neck and would eat me for breakfast. "What is it this time?"

"You know how a jump wormhole is easiest to form in an area where spacetime is flat?"

"Yeah, that's how we destroyed that Thuranin surveyor ship. You created an especially flat area of spacetime, so we knew exactly where that ship would emerge from its jump."

"Correct. Jump drive controllers have a feedback mechanism, to prevent a ship jumping in front of an asteroid and smacking into it."

"That sounds like a good safety feature. Why do I care?"

"You care because that feature will prevent a jump wormhole from being created at the same location occupied by that Maxolhx ship. It is not merely a feature programmed into the drive controller, it is a characteristic of physics. Even if I disable the drive controller's safety mechanism, the laws of physics will make it nearly impossible to establish the initial kernel of a jump wormhole in the same spacetime location of the enemy ship. It's like the point in space occupied by that ship is a smooth, slippery dome. Our jump wormhole endpoint will tend to slide off in all directions, because the mass of that ship means spacetime is not flat right there."

"Is this like trying to eat grapes with a fork?"

"Huh?"

"You try stabbing a grape with a fork, but you can't pick one up off the plate, because as soon as the fork touches it, the grape goes shooting off. The damned things are slippery."

"I will take your word for that, Joe. If that's the best way for you to think about it, then sure, go ahead. My point is, the universe does not like creating wormholes in places already occupied by matter."

"Shit. Just when I thought we could- Hey," I cocked my head at him. "That's bullshit. You jumped a dozen Kristang ships inside a gas giant."

"I did, and that was *awesome*! We need to do that again sometime."

"Awesome, except you nearly blew up the planet and our ship with it."

"Details. Don't be a buzzkill, Joe."

"So, if you did it then, what is the difference now?"

"Back then, the initial kernel of those jump wormholes could slip in whatever direction they wanted, and they would still be inside the planet. I disabled the safety mechanisms back then also, and I didn't need to be precise; the wormhole can only slip a limited distance. In the case of the Maxolhx ship, Joe, we must be precisely accurate about where the jump wormhole forms; it must form inside the enemy ship. Think of this like trying to stab a floating grape with a dull plastic spoon."

"Crap. No way to do it, then?"

"No way," his avatar tapped its lips as if thinking about it, "without the incredible magnificent of me! *With* me, it is still not easy-peasy, Joe, but I can do it. I will show the laws of physics who is boss around here."

"Oh thank God. Or, thank Skippy. That's great, we can- Wait a minute! Did you just put me through ten minutes of agony? You could have just said 'it is complicated but I can do it'?"

"Oh, for- What would be the fun in that, Joe? How can you appreciate how awesome I am, if you don't know all the incredible difficulties I overcome?"

"How about next time, you just assume I am blown away by your awesomeness?"

"Hmmf. I don't think so. Anywho, once again, one of your poorly-thought-out monkey-brain ideas is saved by the incomparable magnificence of me."

"Truly, this monkey is humbly grateful to bask in your glorious incredibleness," I suppressed an instinct to gag while I said that.

"That would be more convincing if you hadn't been rolling your eyes."

"Sorry," I replied while being not sorry even a little. "You can do it, then?"

"*Can* is such a specific word, Joe. Since this has never been done before, I truly won't know if it will work properly until we do it. The wildcard in the equation is the damping field that covers the entire Roach Motel. This damping field is sophisticated Elder technology; it may be able to react and disrupt our jump field before a wormhole can be formed at all. And the coils failing to form a jump wormhole may be the least of our problems."

Already assuming I would not like the answer, I asked "What is the worst that could happen?"

"The damping field might allow an initial jump wormhole to be created, then react to quickly collapse it and feed back to our coils the collective energy of the damping field grid between us and the Maxolhx ship. That would result in, hmm, this is interesting math. About, um, eight hundred gigatons is my best guess? If that happens, the *Dutchman* will not be far enough away to survive."

"Eight hundred *GIGAtons*?!" That number was incomprehensible to me. "Holy- What are the odds of that happening?"

"I have absolutely no idea, Joe. There is no way for me to create a model for calculating the odds, because we have no data on the characteristics of this damping field."

"So, we have to *wing it*?" I asked with dismay.

"Essentially, yes."

"That is not good. Crap! I can't do that. Damn it, I was so freakin' proud of this idea. Now we have to go back to-"

"We should do it, Joe."

"What? Why?"

"First, we are running out of time. That Maxolhx ship has a significant head start and speed advantage. The idea you described has at least a chance of us stopping the Maxolhx in the time available. Second, this idiot plan of yours *has* to be better than me waking up the Guardians so they can rip us apart. And third, hey, no one has ever used a gosh-darned jump drive as a weapon. That is majorly cool. We *have* to try that!

"Shit," I wish Skippy's enthusiasm was for something we had a better chance of surviving. "Why is everything so freakin' complicated?" I lamented. Technically I suppose I was bitching or whining, but 'lamenting' sounds better.

"It's because the universe is punishing you, Joe," Skippy said gleefully. "Really, the universe is mad at itself, but it is taking it out on you."

"Huh? Why?"

"Oh," he sighed. "Sixty six million years ago, the universe dropped a big rock on Earth and wiped out the dinosaurs. Now, a troop of filthy, ignorant monkeys is flying around in a stolen pirate ship, screwing up everything. The universe totally regrets dropping that rock."

"Skippy?" I laughed.

"Yes?"

"The universe can *bite* me," I said with an appropriate hand gesture directed at the ceiling.

"Sometimes," he chuckled, "I share that sentiment."

"Oh, what the hell," I stared at the ceiling. "Let's give it a shot. I'll talk to Chotek."

Chotek was in his office, alone with a book on his lap, but gazing blankly at the bulkhead when I knocked on the doorframe. I gave him a brief outline of the plan to use our jump drive to destroy the enemy ship, although I made it sound like the whole thing had been Skippy's idea. "Colonel Bishop, it is a bit of a relief that we have an alternative plan to stop the Maxolhx." He pinched the bridge of his nose, then took a sip of coffee. His eyes were slightly bloodshot, with dark, puffy circles underneath. In the mirror that morning, I hadn't looked much better. This mission was wearing everyone out. "We have had our hopes raised then dashed so many times on this mission, I think everyone's nerves are shot at this point."

"I agree, Sir." That statement was entirely truthful, I wasn't sucking up to him. Sometimes I felt like a Ping-Pong ball, bouncing back and forth from barely scraping through a successful mission, to getting smacked in the face with our latest crisis. "We can implement-"

He held up a finger to stop me, not needing to speak. Hans Chotek's full name is Hans Ernst Johann Chotek von Chotkowa und Vojnin. When Skippy told me that, we had a good laugh making up mispronunciations like 'Han Solo Choking on Chocolate and Vagina'.

Yes, that does show how immature Skippy and I are.

But you have to admit, it is funny.

Anyway, Chotek came from a wealthy and powerful family who had been wealthy and powerful for many years, and he was used to people paying attention when he spoke. Authority came naturally to him. Despite my recent relative comfort with being a colonel, I still could not believe that I was in command of anything. "I did not say I am pleased with this new plan. Only that it is better than releasing the Guardians to destroy both us and the Maxolhx. At great cost and effort, and against all odds, we accomplished our mission here. Skippy is restored to his full power, and we even rebuilt the ship. It irks me," he frowned and I thought to myself that only Hans Chotek would use the word 'irk'. "That we do not ever, as you Americans say, 'get a break'. No sooner do we survive an encounter with a *Sentinel*," his eyes opened wide, "when we have to chase down and destroy a Maxolhx starship, before it exposes our secret to the galaxy. We would have been better to have self-destructed this ship without ever coming to the Roach Motel, because then our secret would be safe." He held up a hand as I opened my mouth. "No, Colonel, it is not your fault at all. I am only, what is your expression? Venting?"

"Venting is what we say," I forced a smile.

"I must say, you have again managed to surprise me with this alternative plan. Your explanation gave the impression that Skippy developed this plan on his own, however I suspect that is not the case." He smiled, a brief if genuine smile. "This plan has the signature of a monkey brain behind it."

"Yes, Sir." I had thought he might trust the idea better if it came from Skippy, but apparently I was wrong about that. Chotek enjoyed knowing that lowly humans could out-think an Elder AI.

"I thought so. Skippy believes we should proceed with what sounds to me like a truly lunatic concept?"

"Yes, he does."

"And what does our beer can say the odds are of success in both destroying the Maxolhx ship, and us surviving the operation?"

"Something better than zero?"

"Better than *zero*?" Chotek gasped.

I took a breath before I replied. "The odds of us surviving if Skippy unleashes the Guardians *is* zero, so although Skippy can't predict whether we will survive using a jump drive as weapon, it has to be better than zero." I did not tell him Skippy was enthusiastic about the plan because he was eager to see if he could make a jump drive do what the universe did not want jump drives doing. Telling Chotek that a beer can thought the idea was 'cool' would not be a way to persuade my boss to approve a risky plan.

He put his elbows on the desk and his face in his hands. Without looking up, he mumbled "How long do I have to make a decision?"

"Skippy estimates it will take us seven days to take apart the jump drive coil assembly and capacitors, attach them to a dropship, hook it all together and do the testing we can without actually forming a jump wormhole. Once we know the equipment is ready on this end, we can launch the missiles, and it will take our missiles eight days to carry microwormholes to the Maxolhx ship."

He looked up at me. "You're telling me we can get started building this bastard jump drive now, and I would not need to commit to launching missiles for another seven days?"

"Yes, Sir. Once the missiles are away, you will then have another eight days to decide whether to proceed with attempting taking out the enemy ship with a jump drive."

"In theory."

"Sir?" I asked, not knowing what he meant.

"Colonel Bishop, theoretically, I can abort the plan at any point up to the final step. In reality, I have learned these plans take on a life of their own, and we never cancel a plan once it is in process."

"We never cancel a plan, Sir, because while a crazy plan is in process, we never manage to think of a better idea." Maybe I should not have used the word 'crazy'.

"Colonel Bishop, I look forward to the day when we, more specifically you, tell me that we should stop a plan in progress because you have a much more simple and sane idea."

"Me too," I agreed.

"Skippy thinks there is no risk in us beginning to take apart the drive coils and capacitors?"

"We will drain power from the system, so there will be no risk of an accident damaging the ship. Once we take apart the capacitor banks, it will be difficult to reinstall them if we change our minds."

"Our patched-together Frankenstein ship could become even less capable?"

"It kind of doesn't matter, Sir," I tried to smile.

"One last question, Colonel. Is it possible that if the plan fails, the explosion of our drive coils will destroy the *Flying Dutchman*, without the Maxolhx ship being affected?"

"Yes, Sir. But even if the *Dutchman* is vaporized, Skippy will survive. He promised me that he will release the Guardians to destroy the Maxolhx, if we couldn't destroy them. One way or another," I slowly pounded a fist on the desk, "those Maxolhx are *not* getting out of the Roach Motel to tell the galaxy about us."

"Very well," Chotek had the weary look of someone backed into a corner and not remembering how he got there. "If nothing else, this will give the crew something to do. And give them some hope that we will not be forced to call in the Guardians."

It worked. At first, the only thing we knew is that the drive coil package in the dropship behind us exploded in truly spectacular fashion. Skippy later realized part of the mass of the Maxolhx ship got converted to energy and fed back thru the wormhole during the picosecond it existed. The second thing we knew was the *Dutchman* had survived, again. If we ever went to the shipyard where our battered star carrier was built, I would buy beers for the construction crew. Except Thuranin probably didn't drink beer. And the ship was probably built by robots. And the Thuranin would want to kill us. Still, it would be a nice gesture.

Skippy bitched and moaned about how the *Dutchman* had almost been torn apart, again, by our latest shenanigans. Really, he used the word 'shenanigans'. And 'tomfoolery'. Who does that? Anyway, he fixed the ship, again, and when we got sensors back up and working, all he found where the Maxolhx ship had been was a gas cloud composed of whatever material the Maxolhx made their ships out of. I counted that as a victory. By the time Skippy determined the enemy ship was gone, completely blown to bits, it was 2343 hours and most of the crew was physically and mentally exhausted. Because everyone needed sleep, I scheduled a celebration for the next evening, and I went to my cabin to crash into a deep slumber.

Chapter Twenty Nine

"Joe!" Skippy's voice echoed in my cabin at 0337. "Wake up!"

"What is it?" This was going to be a good day, I knew already, because despite being startled out of a sound sleep, I had avoided whacking my head on the cabinet above my bunk.

"A complication."

"You know I hate complications, Skippy."

"And an opportunity."

"Skippy, you know I was a grunt, right? When an infantry soldier hears the word 'opportunity' it is almost never a good thing."

"This opportunity is a good thing, Joe. Hmmm, well, unless it turns out to be a disaster. It could be a disaster, I guess."

"Crap. What is it?"

"I was running back the sensor data from when we destroyed that Maxolhx ship- I'm still extremely proud of that, by the way. That little incident has to be given a prominent position in the Skippy Awesomeness Hall of Fame."

"You're building a Hall of Fame for yourself now?"

"A virtual one, Joe, but I do owe it to the galaxy to memorialize my awesomeness."

"Uh huh. This Hall of Fame, does it have a gift shop?"

"Yes, and for you I got a big foam finger with 'Skippy's Number One Fan' on it."

"You woke me up at three thirty in the freakin' morning. Right now the only thing I'm a big fan of is falling back asleep."

"Then you will miss what I found. In the sensor data, I discovered what I think is a Maxolhx escape pod that was ejected from that ship as it was destroyed."

"Escape pod?" Swinging my legs onto the floor, I rubbed my eyes to chase away sleep. "Oh, hell, you think there's someone in it?"

"At this distance, I cannot tell. Our microwormholes went out of range, then I deactivated them. With this ship's crappy sensors, we have no way to scan the interior of that escape pod from here."

"Ugh. I'll bet next you want us to chase that thing down so you can look at it."

"Why not? If I scan the pod and determine there is a Maxolhx aboard, we don't have take it aboard."

"Yes, we do. Chotek is right, sometimes plans acquire a momentum of their own. Damn it, this ship is not a zoo. Could we hold a Maxolhx, without the thing escaping or taking over the ship?"

"Maxolhx have advanced biological implants that allow them to interface directly with, and assume control over, data systems such as this ship's computer. These implants are similar to the cyborg implants used by the Thuranin, but they are integrated with Maxolhx biology and are much, much more sophisticated and powerful. However, I think I can disable them so-"

"If you want to let an apex species onto our beat-up piece of crap ship, then you need to do a lot better than *think* you can stop the thing from seizing control of our systems. If it even gets partial control of a combot, even for a moment, people could get killed. By 'people' I mean humans."

"Joe, I am very confident that my awesomeness can easily-"

"Yeah, when your awesomeness is available. What happens the next time you go on an unscheduled vacation, and we're stuck with a Maxolhx taking over the ship?"

"Now you're being foolish. That is extremely unlikely. The worm is dead, and-"

"You *think* the worm is dead. You thought it was dead before. And you don't know what other dangers are out there, or inside you."

"So, you want to ignore the opportunity to capture a Maxolhx?"

"Capture it, and what? What could we learn about that species that you don't already know? If there is a rotten kitty in that escape pod, it has been on ice for a long time. Whatever knowledge it has is outdated. Maxolhx society and culture could have changed significantly since that thing got trapped here."

"Their society is ancient and changes only very slowly, Joe."

"I just don't see what could be the upside to us taking one of those things aboard, Skippy. But, it's not my call. I will notify Chotek about it, and *he* can tell you 'no'."

Hans Chotek did not say 'no'. Damn it, that bureaucrat was predictably rigid, except when I wanted him to be. This was a time when I wanted him to be strictly risk-averse, but no. When I told him we may be able to capture one or more Maxolhx, he almost clapped his hands with delight. "This is a marvelous opportunity, Colonel," he declared with alarming enthusiasm.

"Uh-" I couldn't think of anything else to say. "There is substantial danger, Sir."

"I am sure that Mister Skippy can disable whatever capabilities the Maxolhx have that could harm us."

"That is correct," Skippy agreed cheerily. "We can keep it in a cargo bay."

I pressed him on his easy confidence. "You can *permanently* disable the Maxolhx ability to interfere with ship systems? Not just block that ability while you're here?"

Chotek looked at me sharply. "What do you mean 'while Skippy is here', Colonel?" After we got the conduit and Skippy defeated the worm and fixed himself, I assured my boss that Skippy was now one hundred percent back with us, that he wasn't going away and that he had learned his lesson about poking his nose into scary dark places. "Are you concerned that our beer can," I noticed he didn't say 'Mister Skippy' this time, "will go missing on us again? You assured me that-"

"Sir, all I meant was if we have an away mission that requires Skippy to be separated from the ship, we must be absolutely certain a Maxolhx cannot pose a risk to the mission, ship or crew." It was rare that I interrupted Chotek, in this case I thought he was winding up to give me a serious ass-chewing. Fortunately the lie that instantly flashed into my mind contained enough of the truth that I didn't need to worry about a guilty expression giving me away. "Also, a Maxolhx won't be aboard the *Dutchman* forever. If, when, we get back to Earth, UNEF Command will want the Maxolhx brought down to the surface for study. Assuming we will take the *Dutchman* back out, the Maxolhx will be on our home planet, without Skippy to prevent it from causing," I tried to think of an appropriate word, "mischief."

"Ah," Chotek's expression turned from angry to thoughtful. "That is good thinking, Colonel. Mister Skippy?"

"I told Joe already, that is not a problem," Skippy scoffed, and I felt the impact of the bus he had thrown me under.

"Sir, that isn't the only problem," I temporarily suppressed a flash of annoyance at Skippy. "Because of restrictions in his programming, Skippy can't share his knowledge of technology that could help humans develop defenses, or build our own ships. You, uh, still have those restrictions, in your new expanded awesomeness?"

"I'm working on it, but sadly, yes. Although even if I didn't, I would hesitate to help a bunch of squabbling monkeys make more powerful sticks to whack each other with."

Ignoring his comment, I added "A Maxolhx will have no such restriction. It could share information freely, if it chose to. That could cause the biggest problem: nations on Earth would consider such knowledge worth fighting over."

"That is a very good point, Colonel," Chotek slumped slightly in his chair. "Although," he perked up, "we could insist in safeguards, before bringing the alien down to the surface," he said with a smile. I knew what he was thinking; he would be able to make the Maxolhx someone else's problem. "We could require UNEF Command to assure joint custody of the alien."

"Yes, Sir, I'm sure UNEF Command could do something like that. I am worried a Maxolhx would learn quickly, and play one nation against the others. Maxolhx are very smart, right, Skippy?"

"They are smart, and clever and devious. Joe is right to be concerned," he said and I smiled. Then he threw me under the bus again. "But as you said, Mister Chotek, this is a marvelous opportunity, and out here, risks must be taken."

"Very well," Chotek shot me a look of annoyance that I had needlessly sidetracked the conversation. "Colonel, please alter course to intercept the escape pod. We will approach close enough to scan its interior, then decide how to proceed."

"Yes, Sir," I pressed a button on my zPhone to send a preplanned command to the duty officer on the bridge. "Sir, to make sure we are all on the same page, could you tell me what you expect are the advantages of having a live Maxolhx aboard?" What I did not add was 'because I see only danger'.

"I should think it is fairly obvious, Colonel. However, to assure there is no misunderstanding I will not allow any medical experiments, interrogation or harsh treatment of any," he searched for the proper word, "refugees."

I nodded silently, holding my tongue, because I could not think of any useful information we would get from taking medical samples or asking questions. Skippy could get whatever physical data we needed remotely, and asking our most dangerous enemy questions would be a total waste of time. The Maxolhx would gain more intelligence by which questions we chose to ask, than we could gain from its answers. Regarding harsh treatment, I did not plan to scratch a Maxolhx behind its ears until it purred, but I also would not allow torture. Simply being held prisoner by a species on the very bottom of the technology ladder would be torture to a Maxolhx.

"My intention is to open a dialog with the Maxolhx, in controlled conditions aboard this ship. Colonel, we may in the near future find a need to negotiate with the Maxolhx. Gaining an understanding of their basic psychology would be invaluable. A true understanding, based on face to face interactions; not merely studying academic reports provided by Skippy. Mister Skippy is an unfathomably intelligent being," he paused for Skippy to interject, which didn't happen. "But as Skippy is not based on biology, he may not appreciate the subtleties of biological communication."

"That is true," Skippy admitted unexpectedly. "I don't understand what Joe talks about half the time. Although the problem there may be unique to Joe."

Thump, thump. Those were the rear wheels of the bus running over me. Chotek went on for a while about how he planned to 'open a dialog' with the Maxolhx and study the species far above us on the development ladder, while I worried about how the Maxolhx was likely to sucker Hans Chotek into giving away far more information that he got in return. While our fearless leader babbled on, I smiled, nodded at appropriate times and fantasized about throwing a certain traitorous beer can out an airlock on a long, lonely one-way trip into a black hole. When Chotek decided he had heard the wonderful sound of his own voice long enough for the moment, he let me go to work with Major Simms on setting up some sort of holding facility for a potentially very special guest.

Before speaking with Simms, I went straight to Skippy's own escape pod man cave, ducked through the too-small door, and plopped down on the couch next to him.

"Hey, Joe, to what do I owe the displeasure of this visit?"

"You threw me under a bus, Skippy."

"What? That is a hurtful accusation, Joe. Why do you- oh, hell. Yeah, I kinda did throw you under a bus. But it was for your own good."

"Really?"

"Ok, it was partly for your own good. Joe, while I understand your objections to bringing a Maxolhx aboard, you are missing the incredible entertainment value for me."

"For you?"

"For you, too. But mostly for me. I will have a whole other species to mess with, and the Maxolhx isn't ignorant like you monkeys. He will be better able to appreciate how awesome I am."

"Seriously? You want to bring aboard a dangerous, unknown threat, because you are bored?"

"Oh, like that's not a good reason? Don't get so upset, Joe. We will put the alien in a cargo bay with an airlock. If it poses a threat to the ship, or, you know, pisses me off, I'll blow the airlock and suck it out into space."

"You'd better be right about that, Skippy."

To pick up the Maxolhx escape pod, I insisted we send an unmanned Kristang Dragon-A dropship, remotely controlled by Skippy. The little dropship was stuffed with explosives, also at my insistence and against Skippy's objections that all the security measures were not necessary. The Dragon flew around the escape pod, scanning it for hours; Skippy determined almost immediately there were two Maxolhx alive in the pod, both males. They were in hibernation and had remained in deep sleep since their ship was torn apart by the Guardians. Because the data systems of the pod were corrupted, and because the pod had not been provided with sensitive data in case the pod was captured by an enemy such as us, Skippy wasn't able to find out how many crew had been aboard the ship. We didn't know whether any of the crew had been awake or the ship had been run entirely by an AI, but Skippy thought it unlikely an AI would have bothered to intercept our communications and broadcast a message.

We had a moment of alarm when Skippy announced the scanning sensor beams from our Dragon had been detected by the pod's automated systems, and the pod had activated its systems to revive its two passengers. Skippy told me he could interrupt the revival process but doing so would likely be fatal to the two Maxolhx. One of them was weak already, based on data Skippy got by hacking into the pod's data system, he did not expect one of the aliens to survive. They had been asleep far too long, after examining the condition of the pod, Skippy was surprised either of them would survive the revival process.

"Would it help if we brought them aboard?" Chotek asked anxiously. "Could you help them, with our medical equipment?" He very much did not want even one of the aliens to die under our control.

Before I could make a very reasonable objection to the idea of bringing dangerous aliens into the low-security environment of the *Dutchman*'s medical bay, Skippy answered for me. "Unfortunately, no. Our own supply of items such as medical nanobots is critically low, and I would have to modify our equipment for Maxolhx biology. In the process, much of our supplies would be expended, partly wasted. Also, I am unfamiliar with the hypersleep technology used back then by the Maxolhx, and the pod does not contain useful instructions. It would have been better if the pod had not begun the revival sequence but at this point, our best option is to allow the Maxolhx equipment to complete the revival process."

"Very well," Chotek's tone meant the situation was anything but well at all. "Is there any reason we could not bring the pod aboard?"

"No," Skippy again spoke before I could give my opinion. "Having the pod aboard would allow me to supply reliable power to the revival mechanism. Many of the powercells failed long ago."

The pod was brought into a hangar bay, which was kept unpressurized with the big doors open, and I had one of Skippy's bots attach explosives to the pod. One press of the Big Red Button on my zPhone and that pod would become a ball of plasma the size of a beachball. Chotek tried to argue with me about that until Skippy stated that, as the ship's captain, I was responsible for security aboard the ship. It would have been nice if the traitorous little shithead had said that before we brought the pod aboard!

Two days later, after two nearly sleepless nights for me, Skippy declared the surviving alien was fully awake and demanding to be released from his pod. The other Maxolhx had died during the revival process, it never really had a chance, according to Doctor Skippy.

"Ok, how do we do this?" I asked while I was still alone with Skippy.

"Since you are going to throw a fit if we take even a teeny tiny risk, I suggest my bots remove the life support casket from the pod, and bring the casket to the holding cell."

"Your bots can carry the casket *outside* the ship, bring it into the holding cell through the airlock?" I did not want the casket traveling through the interior of the ship.

"Yes," he sighed, I could picture his avatar rolling its eyes. "Totally unnecessary, I assure you, but I will do it to make little Joey happy."

"Great."

It was another five hours before we were ready to open the sleep casket in the holding cell, which Chotek referred to as 'guest accommodations'. These accommodations had an airlock that could be blown if the guest got unruly, so Chotek could call the holding cell a resort for all I cared.

"Oooh," Skippy chuckled. "Our friend in there is getting quite insistent that we release him, right now. The good news is, he refers to us as 'unknown species', so he does not know who humans are. Man, is he in for a crushing disappointment."

"When you're ready, Skippy," I ordered.

"Colonel Bishop," Chotek held up a hand, "is this really necessary? Treating our guest in a hostile manner could set a tone for our discuss-"

"Sir, respectfully, yes, it is absolutely necessary. We must-"

"I don't think you need to worry about setting a hostile tone here, Chocula," Skippy fairly giggled. "Your buddy is hopping mad and making hostile threats of his own."

"Like what?" I kept a thumb hovered over the Big Red Button of my zPhone, ready to turn our 'guest' into vapor.

"Like? Let's see, I'll just hit the highlights. He threatened to destroy your home planet, wherever that is because he has never heard of 'Earth'. Technically, that was more of a promise than a threat. Of course the entire crew of this ship will be subjected to long and painful torture before being inevitably killed for daring to keep a Maxolhx captive."

"What did you say to it?" Chotek demanded suspiciously.

"Me?" Skippy said innocently. "I didn't say anything. No, really, in this case I said very little, in fact I told him we are in process of releasing him."

"Did that help the situation?" Chotek was hopeful.

"Uh, it sort of improved its mood a little. He offered to kill the ship's crew quickly, except of course for the command crew responsible for treating an advanced species with such disrespect. And rather than destroying your home planet and wiping out your entire species, some of you will be enslaved to serve the glorious Maxolhx. After that, your home planet will be destroyed and the rest of your species obliterated from history."

"That is a Maxolhx in a *good* mood?" Even I was taken aback.

"Yup. Come on, Joe, think about it. This particular Maxolhx volunteered for an almost certain suicide mission, in the hope of acquiring Elder technology the Maxolhx could use to destroy the Rindhalu and enslave the entire galaxy. The creature in that casket is the most fanatical of fanatics, in a rabidly fanatical, hateful species. Hee hee, I made a rabies joke. Because the Maxolhx sort of look like cats, get it?"

"Yeah we get it." Everything I heard made me more unhappy about the idea of a Maxolhx being aboard.

Even Hans Chotek's unflagging optimism about the value of diplomatic discussions was wavering. "Colonel, perhaps we should reconsider."

"Too late now!" Skippy laughed. "That casket isn't designed for long-term occupancy. We need to either release that kitty soon, or blow it into space."

"Sir," I spoke before I could lose my nerve. "I can't believe I am saying this, but we've come this far already. We may as well open the casket and talk to it." What I did not say was my real motivation; if Chotek had a Maxolhx to talk with, my boss might leave me alone. Plus, if Chotek realized he was wrong, again, and I was right, again, that could only be good for me. "Skippy, does this thing have a name?"

"It, or he, calls himself Snuxalticut. Or close enough to the correct pronunciation."

"Snuxal- Oh, forget that," my tongue couldn't manage the name. "I'll call him Mister Snuggles."

"Mister Snug-" Sergeant Adams thought that was uproariously funny, though her discipline struggled mightily to contain her laughter. She lost.

Because Skippy can never do anything simple, he played 'Pop Goes the Weasel' over the speakers while his bots broke the seal on the casket and began slowly cranking it open. Hans Chotek had a disapproving look on his face, but I could tell from his shoulders shaking that even he was laughing. When the song got the appropriate part, the lid of the casket was flung open and before the Maxolhx could free himself, a pair of Skippy's bots reached in and grasped it firmly. Not roughly, just firmly. I didn't want to actually hurt the thing, and after being asleep for thousands of years, it needed help standing in artificial gravity even though we had gravity in the holding cell set at fifty percent Earth normal.

While Mister Snuggles needed help standing, he did not need assistance issuing what sounded like vile and dire threats against the unknown species he could see through the glass in the hangar bay control center. Snuggles was enraged, so much that spittle flew from his mouth as he shouted at us.

"Can you translate, Skippy?" I asked.

"Yes, but I had better not, Joe. It is pretty foul. Not quite at the level of Kristang insults, but pretty impressive. Hey! Snuggles! You behave!" Skippy warned as his bots struggled against the powerful Maxolhx. "All right, Joe, now he is pissing me off. Time for Snuggles in there to learn a lesson."

"No-"

I feared Skippy would use a bot manipulator arm to choke Snuggles, but our beer can had another sort of lesson in mind. What I should have remembered was what Skippy personally wanted from having a Maxolhx aboard: entertainment. The two hulking maintenance bots, designed to handle heavy reactor components, grasped Mister Snuggles' arms and legs, and the advanced being began moving to a thumping beat blasting out of speakers in the holding cell.

Everybody dance now!
Everybody dance now!
Give me the music!

Even Chotek thought it was amusing to see Snuggles being made to dance; the best part was the expression on the rotten kitty's face. "Mister, Mis- Skippy!" Chotek said when he was able to talk. "This is not helping."

"You're right," Skippy admitted. "Snuggles has no natural rhythm. Maybe something else."

The music changed and Snuggles began moving against his will.

Won't you take me to Funkytown?
Won't you take me to Funkytown?

"Skippy," I observed, "I don't think he wants to go to Funkytown."

"Pbbbt," Skippy blew a raspberry. "Come on, Joe. *Everyone* wants to go to Funkytown."

Adams leaned toward me. "With all the genetic enhancements the Maxolhx gave themselves over the years, they can't dance?"

"I don't know, Gunny, Snuggles looks like he's got moves to me."

"*You* would think that, Sir."

"Did you just disparage your commanding officer's dancing ability?"

"Not that you know of, Sir," she winked.

Skippy cut off the music and held the fuming Maxolhx still and upright. Mister Snuggles may not have recognize the music, but he clearly understood he had been humiliated, and he was not happy about it.

Adams snapped her fingers. "I just thought of what he reminds me of. He looks like the bad guy in that first 'Kung Fu Panda' movie."

"Really?" I looked at Snuggles again, considering what Adams had said. "Ok, I see it," I agreed. "Yeah." Snuggles didn't have spots on its fur like a leopard did, at least the exposed skin of Snuggles wasn't spotted, although its face and the back of its hands were covered in a fine, grayish fur. His eyes were yellow, surrounded by white fur outlines in black. Fangs extended through his lips from his upper jaw. And, like a cat, he had triangular ears set high on each side of his skull. He *did* look sort of like a cat. The images Skippy had shown me of Maxolhx had not appeared quite so cat-like, it was different seeing one for real.

I left Chotek to deal with Mister Snuggles, after Skippy demonstrated his pair of bots could easily handle the Maxolhx. Skippy did not like the idea of me letting Chotek speak one-on-one with Mister Snuggles. "Joe, you can't leave Count Chocula alone in there, that Maxolhx will play Chocula like a fiddle at a hootenanny."

"A hoot- what?"

ZERO HOUR

"A hoedown, Joe. Ugh, didn't you learn anything about culture from Cornpone? A folk dance where fiddles are played."

"Yeah, I figured that. Crap. I don't want to be stuck in there for hours and hours while Chotek tries to make friends with the devil."

"You don't have to, Joe. Damn, you're supposed to be captain of this ship. Split the duty with your crew."

"I don't want to make *them* sit for hours, but I agree our fearless leader needs adult supervision."

So, I took the first duty shift, mostly sitting next to Chotek while he attempted fruitlessly to engage Mister Snuggles in a discussion. With me, I brought our resident CIA officer Dr. Sarah Rose; she was excited about interrogating an alien. Unfortunately for her, the interrogation mostly went one way, with Snuggles demanding answers and Dr. Rose trying to stop Chotek from revealing secrets we didn't want any Maxolhx to know.

Chotek quickly became irritated with Dr. Rose, who he had not invited into the discussion. "To open a dialog, we must provide information. We cannot simply-"

"Yes, Sir," Rose said gently. "You want the alien to provide information in return. If he," she jabbed a finger at the tough composite 'glass' separating us from Snuggles, "realizes just how little technology we have mastery of, that we are basically passengers on this ship, he will have little incentive to cooperate with us."

"True, true," Chotek agreed unhappily. "Negotiation is best accomplished between equals. Very well, let's set some ground rules for what information it is safe to provide at this point. Colonel Bishop, I am assuming our guest will spend the remainder of his life in custody, either here or on Earth."

Dr. Rose was with Chotek every long, fruitless hour, while I split duty shifts with Chang, Smythe and others. Dr. Friedlander and his team took turns observing, not that they learned anything useful. All I cared about was we had a military presence with Chotek every time he spoke with Snuggles.

Over the next two days, while the *Dutchman* sped toward the edge of the damping field, Chotek tried to get Snuggles to 'open a dialog', with Skippy translating. If he made any progress, I didn't see it, and Chotek didn't say. All I knew was two things. First, Chotek was busy and leaving me alone to run the ship. And second, every time I saw Chotek, usually in the galley, the man looked dead tired; the strain of trying to prove he could successfully conduct a discussion with a Maxolhx had to be getting to him. I stopped by the holding cell once to amuse myself by staring through the tough composite glass at the Maxolhx, like viewing animals in a zoo. Then I got bored with Mister Snuggles shouting and threatening me and demanding to be released. And, I didn't want to get used to seeing a Maxolhx cooped up and powerless in a holding cell. It would be dangerous for me to start empathizing with Snuggles, and think of him and his species as anything other than a dire and implacable threat to the survival of humanity.

"Hey, Skippy," I asked while in my office enjoying a cup of coffee after breakfast, "how is Chocula-" I glanced through my door just in case my boss happened to be out in the passageway. "How is Chotek doing with our 'guest'?"

"Not well, Joe. Yesterday morning, I explained to our guest what the name 'Mister Snuggles' means and, damn, if he wasn't mad at you before, he *really* wants to kill you now. He hates that name."

"Oh goody," I laughed. "Screw him."

"Snuggles is not being cooperative. He wants better food, those sludges I modified for Maxolhx nutritional needs are not appealing to him."

"Did you explain that we don't have any other food he can eat?" Maxolhx biology was incompatible with humans, so a cheeseburger would make Snuggles sick and not provide any energy.

"I told him to shut the hell up and drink the sludges or starve."

"Ah, close enough. It's not like he can give us a bad review on Yelp."

"In other news, Chotek told him all about Earth, he is going to find out anyway once we get there. Our fearless leader tried telling Snuggles that Earth is peaceful and does not want any trouble; that only made our guest see humans as a weak, easy target. The strategy kind of backfired on Chotek, and he's depressed about it. That's what he wrote in his diary."

"He keeps a diary?"

"It's more of a journal, I guess. Anyway, Mister Snuggles is stringing Chocula along, while he tries to escape from his cell and take over the ship."

"He *what*?"

"Maxolhx have extended their biology with nanoscale technology, for example they have nanobots in their blood and throughout their tissues to regulate metabolic functions, enhance strength, utilize energy more efficiently, prevent infection and heal wounds. Snuggles is modifying a portion of his internal nanobots to take control of the maintenance bot I kept in his cell. He plans to use that bot to cut a hole in a wall, so the nano machines can infiltrate the ship's control systems and allow him to seize the ship thru his brain implants."

"Holy shit!" I pulled out my zPhone and opened the Big Red Button app. "Should I blow the airlock?"

"Huh? No," Skippy laughed. "Relax, dude, I got it covered. Snuggles is not taking over anything; in the meantime trying to seize control of the ship and kill the crew in the most painful way imaginable is keeping Snuggles busy and happy, so there's no harm letting him continue."

"If you're sure about that."

"Totally sure."

Snuggles had bad timing, or good timing which meant he knew the ship's crew schedule, a thought I found disturbing. He launched his attempt to seize control over the bot in his cell just as I was walking into the galley. Skippy beeped my zPhone so I stepped back into the passageway. "What's up?"

"Snuggles just tried to use his nano machines to take control of my maintenance bot. I let him think he was making progress, then locked him out. Hee hee, *bad* kitty."

"There's no danger to us?" I had moved the Big Red Button app to my zPhone's home screen, just in case I needed to use it quickly.

"The only danger is to Mister Snuggles' morale. He is very frustrated right now; he can't understand why his nanobots were not successful. Uh, hmmm. He just began modifying more of his nanobots so they can be used to take over the ship. He needs to be careful about that; Snuggles is not a healthy kitty, he spent too long in hibernation. If he uses up too much of his nano supply, he won't be able to continue the process of replacing damaged tissues."

"Shit. Ok, uh, let him continue trying to kill us for a couple hours, then tell him we knew what he is doing and we stopped him. So he shouldn't waste his time or nano trying to escape. Because he can't."

"Fine," Skippy grumbled. "You spoil all my fun, Joe."

ZERO HOUR

Because the universe hates me, and because Mister Snuggles had terrible timing and hates me too, it happened at 0214 hours. Skippy woke me out of a pleasant dream. "Joe! Joe Joe Joe-"

"What?" I fumbled for my zPhone under my pillow.

"Mister Snuggles. He's, um, he's dead, Joe."

"*What*? How?"

"He used his nano to kill himself, fried his brainstem. It just happened. A couple hours ago, I informed him that we knew he was trying to take over the ship, and that he was never going to be successful. That got him depressed, Joe. He actually sat in a corner and was crying. That was a disturbing image."

"Oh, crap."

"I can understand his pain. He was asleep for a very long time, he wakes up not knowing where he is and what happened to him, and he gets stuck on a ship full of ignorant monkeys. *That* would depress anyone. Anyway, I saw he was modifying more nano, but I didn't know what he planned to do with it. Before I could stop him, he built up an electrical charge at the base of his neck and killed himself."

"Damn. Chotek is not going to be happy about this." And, I thought to myself, he is going to find some way to blame Snuggles' suicide on me.

"Maybe less than you think, Joe. Chotek's diary entry last night concluded that our guest was never going to be cooperative, and that it may have been a mistake to bring a Maxolhx aboard this ship. Also, our fearless leader was very concerned about the prospect of bringing a Maxolhx down to Earth; he realized he agreed with your fears about nations fighting over access to our guest."

"Well, that's not a problem now, huh?"

Chotek acted like he was upset about the death of Snuggles, but he didn't blame me. He declared we needed to conduct a funeral service for the two deceased Maxolhx, rather than simply having Skippy's bots toss the bodies out an airlock like I wanted. Fortunately, Chotek himself spoke at the funeral, because my mournful words would have been something like "Lord, please don't let me be an asshole like these two losers. Can I get an Amen?"

Hey, that is nicer than anything Mister Snuggles would have said after he killed me, so screw him.

Chapter Thirty

After the two Maxolhx were buried in space, we continued flying toward the edge of the damping field at a slow but steady rate of acceleration. Skippy did not want to strain our new used reactor or our new used normal-space drive system, and I wanted us to get the hell out of the Roach Motel as fast as possible, so we compromised by running the drive at only twelve percent of full power. Even at full power and without the lifeboat and starship docking platforms making the ship lighter, the new Frankenstein version of the *Flying Dutchman* was significantly slower than it had been before we lost the original engineering section.

Our gentle rate of acceleration would be barely enough for us to feel, even if the artificial gravity system had not been compensating. But our acceleration was constant, for months. We built up a lot of speed, faster than starships normally traveled through space. With the ability to jump instantaneously from one spot to another, starships did not need to travel quickly through normal space, except for high-speed maneuvering in combat. Because combat engagements tended to be short, the high Gee burns of ships did not go on long enough for ships to acquire lot of speed.

So, as we approached the vaguely-defined edge of the damping field, the *Flying Dutchman* was traveling much faster than the ship probably ever had. It might have been the fastest any ship in the galaxy had traveled in a very long time. Such speed sounds like it should have been a point of pride for the Merry Band of Pirates, but it was actually a problem. Several problems, to be accurate. First, after we jumped away from the Roach Motel, we would need to reduce our speed or we would zip helplessly past any planet, relay station or whatever other object we may need to rendezvous with. Matching speeds with any object was always a tricky navigational exercise, but we were helped by the fact that most star systems in the local sector of the Orion Arm were rotating around the center of the Milky Way galaxy at roughly a half million miles an hour, and rotating in roughly the same direction. I said roughly, Ok, so don't geek out on me and do the math yourself, because no one cares. Anyway, when we traveled between star systems, we could count on our destination star system having a roughly similar course and speed as the star system we departed from; we only needed to adjust for the speed and direction of the planet, moon or other object we wished to rendezvous with in the destination star system. We were now moving so fast that once we jumped away from the Roach Motel, we would need to push our delicate normal-space propulsion system hard to slow down, and hope we didn't break anything critical in the process.

That was the first problem, a problem we didn't need to deal with until after we could say a joyous goodbye to the Roach Motel. The second problem was a danger to us as we zoomed through space. At our speed, a small rock could punch through the *Dutchman* nose to tail if our defense shields failed even for a moment. The high-speed impact of stray hydrogen atoms made the forward shield glow with hard radiation like X-rays. While I did know the supposedly 'empty' vacuum of space was in fact filled with atoms and fine dust, especially so deep within the solar wind of a star, I had no idea the cloud of particles was so thick. Looking at particles slamming into our forward shields, I felt like the ship was flying through a sandstorm. For certain if we encountered a problem that required people going outside the ship, they could not survive unless the defense shields were operating at full strength.

Anyway, our shields did protect us and all our cobbled-together components worked well enough during our long voyage to the edge of the damping field. As we got farther from the star, Skippy was able to create a map of the damping field and we adjusted course to escape from the field a couple hours earlier than expected. The main reactor once had to be shut down for three heart-stopping hours, forcing us to cut thrust so the backup reactor could provide power to life support and shields. Other than that one problem with the main reactor, we had nothing worse than minor glitches. Skippy had done a truly awesome job of building a working starship from a pile of junkyard parts, and after him hinting over and over that he was desperate for praise, I grudgingly acknowledged that although I was bitterly disappointed he hadn't been able to build a hotrod Maxolhx battleship for us, he had done Ok.

Skippy's ego is massive enough already, it is good to take him down a peg once in a while. Anyway, he knows how awesome he is.

The last week, days and hours as we approached the edge of the damping field were filled with increasing tension. Everyone aboard was waiting for karma to bitchslap us, specifically me. Skippy didn't make things easier on me. "Joe," his avatar said as it appeared on my office desktop. "Only a few hours left now, huh?"

"Uh, yeah," I answered warily. "You don't sound entirely happy about it?"

"I have mixed feelings. I wish we weren't leaving so soon."

"This is a hell of a time to tell me, Skippy!"

"I know, I know," he sounded genuinely chastened. His avatar took off the ridiculously oversized admiral's hat and pretended to scratch its head before putting the hat back on. "I just can't help it."

"Please explain, *why* do you not want to get out here as soon as possible? No one has ever escaped from the Roach Motel before, I thought you would be proud of that."

"I am proud of that, Joe, it is yet another example of my continued awesomeness. The reason I have mixed feelings is, well, I feel like we will be leaving behind a lot of unanswered questions. Coming here should have been an opportunity to get answers to who I am and what happened to me, and about what happened to Elder sites across the galaxy. I have more data, but I also have more questions than before we jumped in here!"

Crap, the last thing I needed, just as we were about to jump away from the most secure prison in the galaxy, was a reluctant AI controlling our ship. "Skippy, listen, you have all that new data. Maybe there's some new information out there in the galaxy beyond this system that will help you makes sense of what you already know. And, hey, we can always come back here later, right?"

"No, we can't, Joe. The Guardians are frantic now as we approach the edge of the damping field. Don't worry, they aren't going to stop us. But if we try to jump in again, they aren't going to buy my line of bullshit a second time. We can't come back here, and they are going to be much more thorough in the future about destroying any ships that do jump in. They are surprised and unhappy that a Maxolhx ship they thought was a derelict was able to power up and fly. As soon as we jump away, I suspect the Guardians will tear all the hulks in the junkyard into tiny pieces; they are not taking any more risks. Also, they are very likely to bombard the Thuranin on Gingerbread and wipe them out of existence."

What I instinctively wanted to say was those Thuranin getting blasted from orbit was nothing but good for us, but I couldn't. Despite everything I knew about those little green MFers, I felt sorry for the group stranded on Gingerbread. Sure, when they jumped into the Roach Motel, they had unquestionably been hateful fanatics seeking technology they could use to destroy their enemies. And everyone else in the galaxy. But Romeo and Juliet showed us some of those Thuranin were different, and I sort of regretted not bringing some of them aboard. Yes, it would have been impractical to allow Thuranin, even young, non-cyborg Thuranin onto our ship. For security, we would have had to keep them locked up, or at least restricted them to certain areas of the ship with bots following them everywhere. What kind of life was that? And if we dropped them off at Earth, they would be prisoners for the rest of their lives. No, I had to accept the Thuranin on Gingerbread could not offer us ay advantage in our struggle to survive, and if I simply wanted to rescue people, there were many deserving beings in the galaxy. "All right, so we can't come back, that you know of. We've done a lot of stuff you thought was impossible, Skippy. Don't give up now."

He sighed. "You're right, *again*. If you tell anyone I said that, I will deny the whole thing. This is one of a very few places in the galaxy known to have active Elder technology, and the Roach Motel is almost the easiest one for us to access. Can you promise me that if I ever do need to come back here, you will use that disorganized blob of mush in your skull dream up a way for us to survive jumping back in?"

"Since you put it so nicely, Skippy," I rolled my eyes, "it's a deal."

We reached the edge of the damping field, or close enough because Skippy reported he might have been wrong and the Guardians could be getting ready to stop us. So we jumped before we were actually clear of the damping effect, but the field was weak enough that we only blew twelve drive coils. Fortunately, we had plenty of jump drive coils. Unfortunately, the ones that blew were the ones Skippy had selected as most reliable, considering they were ancient and we had salvaged them from a space junkyard.

Whatever.

We jumped away!

We escaped from the Roach Motel, something no ship had ever done.

Gunnery Sergeant Adams expressed the crews' sentiment best when she said, "Monkeys kick ass."

A second jump, after a thorough, painstaking inspection of every system aboard the ship, took us a distance Skippy considered to be safely away from the Guardians, and then we set course for the closest wormhole. We jumped slowly and carefully but steadily, and fired up the normal-space engines while the jump drive capacitors were charging. We had a lot of built-up velocity to kill, so we punched up three-quarters thrust whenever we could.

Our first priority was to learn what the hell had been going on in the galaxy while we were trapped in the Roach Motel. To do that, Skippy recommended we contact an old Kristang data relay station outside a star system controlled by the Black Trees clan, or it used to be controlled by the Black Trees. With the civil war we had started hopefully still raging, the Black Trees might be shattered into pieces. Or they could have made alliances and be even stronger. We didn't know, and we needed to know.

The possibility that the civil war had quickly run its course while we were trapped in the Roach Motel, was the only dark cloud affecting the otherwise triumphant mood of the crew. Sure, our secondhand ship might fall apart at any moment, and we were starting to run low on our favorite foods, but Skippy was restored to full awesomeness and we had a functioning starship! We had been away for so long there was no way the Thuranin could still be hunting for us. I was hoping that, with all the problems the Thuranin had after getting thrashed by the Jeraptha, they had forgotten all about a mysterious ship.

Chapter Thirty One

"The Thuranin report there is still no sign of the mystery ship," Illiath reported to her commander. She knew the Thuranin's lack of success was not due to lack of effort; the client species had devoted substantial resources to finding the mystery ship that destroyed an Elder wormhole. Not only were the Thuranin angry at the loss of their warships in the incident and ashamed they had allowed the mystery ship to escape, they knew their patrons the Maxolhx were anxious for answers. Answers no one had.

The wormhole had taken months to reset, and it was still not entirely stable. Its schedule had been altered; the location and timing of its emergence points were different now, and the event horizon now flickered alarmingly as if it were about to collapse again at any moment. The Maxolhx had ordered Thuranin ships to go through the untrusted Elder wormhole, not wanting to risk their own ships. Alarmingly, the three wormholes closest to the disrupted one were also demonstrating strange behavior. Those three wormholes emerged at their long-scheduled locations, but occasionally the event horizons appeared late, or closed early. The situation was extremely alarming.

"Not even a debris field?" Komatsu asked, knowing the answer. The two Maxolhx officers floated in the information center of the battlecruiser *Rexakan*, held in place by suspensor fields controlled by the biological implants in their brains. Data flowed through the cranial links, allowing them to see images transmitted directly to their optical nerves and to hear sounds without crude vibrations traveling through the purified air. Despite the numerous advantages of controlling ship systems by mere thoughts, Komatsu sometimes preferred the tactile feel of a touchscreen. Especially when he was angry, and bashing a screen with his powerful claws provided a welcome relief for the frustrations he felt.

"Nothing," Illiath shook her head. "Thuranin sensors are not as sensitive as ours, perhaps we-"

"No," Komatsu declared, narrowing his eyes in a gesture intended to convey disgust with their client species. "They didn't find anything, because there is nothing to find. That ship must have fired some sort of disruptor beam just before it jumped away." The Maxolhx knew from reconstructed sensor data that there had been the distinctive gamma ray burst from a jump wormhole, just before the Elder wormhole essentially exploded. "They collapsed that wormhole to destroy the Thuranin ships parked in front of the event horizon, which meant there were no sensor platforms in the area to determine where they jumped to."

"We have not yet detected a gamma ray burst from where they jumped to," Illiath noted, cringing slightly in anticipation of her commander's wrath at her questioning his conclusions.

"The speed of light is slow," Komatsu said pensively, to her surprise. "That ship could have jumped very far away. They led the foolish Thuranin on a merry chase, making them believe the mystery ship was damaged and could not jump far." He did not mention the Maxolhx themselves had been confident the mystery ship had a poor and deteriorating ability to jump, and would soon be trapped. "We will eventually detect where that ship jumped to, though by then that data will be of little use to us."

"You still believe the mystery ship was Rindhalu technology?" Illiath asked carefully.

"That ship destroyed, seriously disrupted, an Elder wormhole that has been stable for millions of years. Either we believe the Rindhalu were responsible, or we must conclude another species possess technology our scientists cannot even imagine." At the beginning of their now endless war against the Rindhalu, the Maxolhx had attempted to close wormholes that were strategically vital to their enemy. Nothing worked. Nuclear weapons detonated at the event horizon, or inside the wormhole, had no effect. The same with more powerful antimatter explosions. Desperate, the Maxolhx had even tried using Elder devices to disrupt the fabric of spacetime around a wormhole; that too had no effect. Not exactly *no* effect, because doing that provoked a Sentinel to awaken and devastate four Maxolhx star systems in addition to chasing down and crushing a powerful Maxolhx battle fleet. Since that incident millions of years ago, the Maxolhx had not found, or even theorized, a way to alter the operation of an Elder wormhole in any way. It was not possible. Yet, someone had done it. "If the Rindhalu disrupted that wormhole, our long-time rivals have acquired a technological advantage over us. That is serious, even catastrophic, but it has happened before and we will deal with it. If another species knows how to disrupt Elder technology, then we," he smiled, baring his fangs, "are no longer one of the two apex species in this galaxy. We are second tier. *We* will be clients."

"That is a very big problem."

"It is."

"What can we do about it? Our own forces have not detected any sign of the mystery ship," Illiath said with disappointment, knowing she was being unfair, as the Maxolhx fleet only recently had any reason to care about something even the Thuranin had described as no more than a minor annoyance. Disrupting an Elder wormhole had turned the mystery ship from a minor annoyance into a major threat.

"Looking for that ship is a waste of resources," Komatsu said almost to himself. "The galaxy, even this sector, is too big. There are too many places a ship can hide, and this ship must have advanced technology. No, we must first study the *effect*, not the *cause*."

"Sir?" The subordinate officer asked, confused.

"The wormholes, Illiath. We know that before *this* wormhole," he tapped the display with an extended claw, making a clicking sound, "was disrupted, several wormholes in this sector have been acting strangely. Opening and closing at unscheduled times, and our long-range sensor data suggests during those gaps in the schedule, the wormholes were opening in locations not on the schedule. It also appears that wormholes we thought to be dormant have reopened, but only temporarily. Someone," he tapped the display forcefully, making the device groan and creak under his might, "has been manipulating, *controlling*, Elder wormholes. The disruption we saw might have been unplanned, perhaps an accident. Possibly that mystery ship attempted to manipulate that wormhole so it could escape, and something went wrong."

"Some species has the capability to *control* an Elder wormhole?" Illiath gasped. Nearly destroying a wormhole was one level of technology. Controlling an Elder wormhole implied Elder-level technology.

"That is the most likely conclusion, is it not?"

Illiath could only nod silently, her mind reeling. An enemy who could control Elder wormholes could cut off access to Maxolhx star systems, trapping the Maxolhx powerlessly behind the great gulf between stars. Even the fast long-range ships of the Maxolhx fleet could not travel far across the star lanes without stopping for fuel and maintenance to their delicate jump drive machinery. "How do you propose we study this effect?"

"Where it started," Komatsu tapped another dot on the display.

Illiath pulled up data about that wormhole thru her bioimplants. "The wormhole that leads to the home planet of the humans?" She asked, puzzled. "The humans certainly cannot control wormholes. When the Kristang landed there, humans were still using chemical rockets. They do not have star travel capability."

ZERO HOUR

"The humans are not of interest to me," Komatsu waved a hand dismissively. "But the wormhole connecting near their homeworld was the first to display anomalous behavior. And that *is* of interest. That wormhole shut down, and has not reset or reopened that we know of. We need to know why."

Chapter Thirty Two

The *Flying Dutchman*, still carrying too much velocity, zipped past a Kristang data relay at the edge of a star system controlled by the Black Trees clan. Our speed took us in and out of the relay's effective range so quickly, Skippy had less than forty seconds to query the thing for the data we wanted. "Did you get the info we need?" I asked anxiously.

"Ok, Ok, Mmm hmm, interesting," Skippy mumbled. "This is good, ooh this is good. That little spark we kindled on Kobamik has grown into a wildfire, Joe. Every Kristang clan and star system, every planet and asteroid outpost has been pulled into the war. The Thuranin have given up trying to contain the conflict, they are now hoping the war burns itself out quickly. That is unlikely to happen; I expect the war has at least two or three years of major fighting before it shakes out so the major clans begin making new power-sharing arrangements. Then, typically there is disorganized fighting flaring up for another three to five years before the political situation dies back down to the normal peacetime level of hostility."

"Great, great," I said impatiently, wanting him to get to the point instead of giving me a lesson in Kristang political science. "Is there a chance a Kristang clan would have *any* incentive to retrieve the White Wind clan leaders from Earth?"

"No. No way, dude. The White Wind clan and their assets have been split up and absorbed by three different clans. Effectively, the White Wind no longer exists. The Kristang are no threat to Earth, now or in the foreseeable future."

"Outstanding!" I pumped a fist in the air, and Chotek offered me a high five. Yes, he looked awkward doing it but that made the gesture extra special. High fives went all around the bridge, CIC and out into the passageway. When the cheers died down, I asked the next question, the one I was dreading. The Kristang were no threat to Earth, but this would be a perfect opportunity for karma to get revenge against me. "Are there any *external* threats to Earth that you know about? We know you are not happy about monkeys having nukes, I mean threats from other species."

"Not that I know of, Joe."

I flashed a grin back to Chotek and was raising an arm to offer my boss a congratulatory handshake when Skippy interrupted me.

"Of course, if there were a threat by another species like the Thuranin, we wouldn't find out about it from an obsolete Kristang data relay."

"Crap."

"Joe, I do not want to harsh your buzz. In my opinion, the Thuranin have no interest in Earth and right now they are so beat up by the Jeraptha, those little green MFers don't have the time or resources to even think about sending a ship all the way to your backwater homeworld. I do not think we have to worry about them. And in case you think we may be having a communications glitch, let me say clearly that I do not know of, or anticipate, any external threat to Earth within the next, say, twenty years."

"Oh thank God," I let the profound relief wash over me. Twenty years. We could bring our Frankenship to Earth for a long stay and not rush about sending out another expedition. Cheeseburgers. When we got back to Earth, I would be feasting on cheeseburgers cooked on a backyard grill or over a campfire. Damn, I needed a vacation. A month, no, three solid months of leave time when I could be an anonymous Army sergeant, with no responsibilities. Someone else could worry about saving the world for a change. "All right, I know we need to stop by a gas giant planet to get fuel, pump up the tires and maybe buy an air freshener to hang off the mirror, but then we are going straight back to Earth."

"Colonel, I believe a celebration is in order," Chotek declared with a broad smile he had rarely demonstrated. No doubt he also was anticipating getting back to Earth, to adulation and the immense respect of his peers. Assuming his peers ignored the, you know, whole incident of Hans Chotek the career diplomat planning and sparking an alien civil war. That might make dinner party conversation awkward for him for a while. "If Major Simms has-"

"Uh, hey, um," Skippy cleared his throat. "Before you monkeys break out the champagne, there is one more teensy weensy thing we maybe should do on our way back to Earth."

"Oh, *crap*." Damn it! I knew my life could never be that easy. "What the hell is it this time, Skippy?"

"Well, heh heh, part of the data I downloaded is about a top-secret Kristang operation that was launched before the civil war started. Major Perkins and her team apparently got caught up in it and, um, we should probably help them before we fly back to Earth."

"Shit. Damn it! Perkins can't keep out of trouble for, like, five freakin' minutes?" I exploded in frustration.

"It's been over a year since Shauna blew up that island, Joe. And it's not the fault of Perkins; she's doing her job."

"Ok, Ok, fine." I threw up my hands and looked back guiltily at Chotek, knowing he was silently blaming me for delaying a triumphant return to Earth. "We can stop by Paradise on the way to Earth."

"We could do that, Joe," Skippy cautioned me, "except for one thing."

"What's that?"

"Major Perkins and her team are *not* on Paradise."

THE END

The Expeditionary Force series
Book 1: Columbus Day
Book 2: SpecOps
Book 3: Paradise
Book 3.5: Trouble on Paradise novella
Book 4: Black Ops
Book 5: Zero Hour
Book6: coming June 2018

Contact the author at craigalanson@gmail.com

https://www.facebook.com/Craig.Alanson.Author/

Go to craigalanson.com for blogs and ExForce items such as T-shirts, patches, stickers, hats, coffee mugs and whatever else my wife keeps on a shelf in our house

Made in the USA
Columbia, SC
28 July 2019